P9-DSV-754

WITHDRAWN
No longer the property of the
Boston Public Library.
Sale of this material benefits the Library

No longer the property of the
Boston Public Library.
Sale of this material benefits the Library.

ROBERT KIRKMAN'S
THE WALKING DEAD
TYPHOON

ROBERT KIRKMAN'S
THE WALKING DEAD
TYPHOON

A Novel

WESLEY CHU

Skybound Books / Gallery Books

New York   London   Toronto   Sydney   New Delhi

An Imprint of Simon & Schuster, Inc.
1230 Avenue of the Americas
New York, NY 10020

This book is a work of fiction. Any references to historical events, real people, or real places are used fictitiously. Other names, characters, places, and events are products of the author's imagination, and any resemblance to actual events or places or persons, living or dead, is entirely coincidental.

Copyright © 2019 by Simon & Schuster and Robert Kirkman, LLC

All rights reserved, including the right to reproduce this book or portions thereof in any form whatsoever. For information, address Gallery Books Subsidiary Rights Department, 1230 Avenue of the Americas, New York, NY 10020.

First Skybound Books/Gallery Books hardcover edition October 2019

Skybound is a registered trademark owned by Skybound, LLC. The Walking Dead is a registered trademark owned by Robert Kirkman, LLC. All rights reserved.

GALLERY BOOKS and colophon are trademarks of Simon & Schuster, Inc.

Robert Kirkman's The Walking Dead: Typhoon is based on the comic book series The Walking Dead by Robert Kirkman, Tony Moore, and Charlie Adlard.

For information about special discounts for bulk purchases, please contact Simon & Schuster Special Sales at 1-866-506-1949 or business@simonandschuster.com.

The Simon & Schuster Speakers Bureau can bring authors to your live event. For more information or to book an event, contact the Simon & Schuster Speakers Bureau at 1-866-248-3049 or visit our website at www.simonspeakers.com.

Interior design by Davina Mock-Maniscalco

Manufactured in the United States of America

10 9 8 7 6 5 4 3 2 1

Library of Congress Cataloging-in-Publication Data has been applied for.

ISBN 978-1-9821-1780-1
ISBN 978-1-9821-1782-5 (ebook)

To Russ,

For helping me navigate through the apocalypse

ROBERT KIRKMAN'S

THE WALKING

DEAD ™

TYPHOON

1

THE NEW WORLD

From a distance, Fongyuan village appeared to exist outside of time. Nestled in the lover's embrace of the Yuanjiang River in the heart of Hunan province, it was an ancient and beautiful place that held tightly to its storied past and fought bitterly against the ravages of change. Lush mountains rose above the morning mists, like spines on a dragon's back. A dance of stark white cranes stood on its bank, impassively scanning the water for small prey. The muddled algae-ridden river, wide and meandering, curved through the valley like a spotted mountain viper.

The village was a collection of densely stacked old structures dating back to the Song dynasty, along with the occasional multistory twentieth-century apartment building, all capped by traditional curved roofs and flying corners. Several buildings on both sides of the river jutted over the water on stilts, reminiscent of the cranes wading in the shallows. A waterfall cut through the mountains in the distance, feeding a narrow stream that meandered to join the Yuanjiang. Apart from the overgrown flora, burned-out car husks, and the occasional toppled structure, the village looked idyllic.

Over the centuries, Fongyuan had withstood famine, foreign invaders, and civil unrest. It had fought bitterly against the Japanese during the Second World War and served as a stronghold to revolutionaries during the ensuing Chinese Civil War. Every time destruction had come for Fongyuan, the village had persisted, rebuilding itself dozens of times over a thousand years.

What it could not survive, however, was the dead rising from their graves.

Out of the mist, two figures ambled onto a stone road at the edge of the village, their movements stilted and clipped. They bumped into one another as they walked, as if deep in a drunken conversation.

Chen Wenzhu leaned over the edge of the roof and studied the pair impatiently as they passed underneath his perch. They looked worn, skin flayed to the bones, probably victims from the first days. The lucky ones.

The first figure, gaunt and slightly stooped, swayed down the rough, steep cobbled path, shoulder deflecting off a wall before careening into the middle of the street. She was missing her arm from the elbow down. Half of her jaw was exposed under a thin layer of loose flesh that gently quivered in the wind. Her dress, once an ankle-length floral cascade of vibrant pink, was now tattered, faded, and stained dark with blood and viscera.

The pair were unusual in that the smaller one followed closely behind the taller one and was holding her hand. Shirtless and barefoot, it looked like a little boy who couldn't have been more than five or six. He had an untouched, angelic face and black hair in a bowl cut. He could have almost passed for living if it were not for the distant look in his eyes and the ugly gash across his neck.

The two *jiāngshī*, as they were now called, were doomed to walk the world forever in this undead existence until someone pitied them with a second death. A final death.

Jiāngshī.

Zhu clicked his tongue. That was what everyone called the dead-who-refused-to-stay-dead. It was an old name, one shrouded in folklore that dated back as far as the Qing dynasty. The jiāngshī of legend were corpses reanimated by magic or spirits. They were terrible creatures who fed on *qi*, or the life force of a person.

The dead that rose now, these things that plagued the land, were something else entirely, and their reality was much, much worse than their namesake.

Ming Haobo, crouching next to Zhu, wondered aloud. "What do you think, Elena? Mother and child? Teacher and student? Two strangers who found each other when the outbreak swept the village?"

The third person on their wind team, Elena Anderson, made a muffled sound suspiciously like a coo. "I think it's a grandma. She looks like an Agatha or a Maribelle. That little boy's name is Bobby. Little Bobby came to visit Grandma Maribelle out here in the countryside."

"Maribelle probably baked cookies and mooncakes for Bobby." Bo stumbled a bit on the English names, but Elena grinned at his effort. Who knows, one day his English could be better than her Mandarin.

"You always go straight to food, Bo."

Bo shrugged. "Every time I visited my *năinai*, all I did was eat well."

Elena nudged him in his generous midsection. "That explains so much." They watched as Maribelle led Bobby to a staircase jutting out of a house. She bumped up against its side and continued to walk in place. Elena sounded wistful. "Maribelle probably took Bobby on long strolls through the village."

Bo played along. "They flew kites and caught dragonflies at the playground a few blocks back."

"They went fishing down at the stream every morning."

Bo pointed at a third jiāngshī farther back that had just turned onto the street. "Maybe that one behind them is the grandfather. What do you think his name is?"

Elena pursed her lips. "He looks like a—"

"That's enough," interrupted Zhu. "We're losing light." Although he tolerated anything that would take their mind off reality, he didn't approve of this game. Giving names to the dead made their job much harder than it needed to be. Besides, all this mucking around was going to get someone killed.

Zhu pointed to the smaller jiāngshī. "Elena, shoot the one on the left. I'll take the one on the right." He looked over at the third jiāngshī. "Bo, take out the *yéye*, the grandfather."

Elena and Bo got to work. Bo crept down the length of the curved roof toward his assigned jiāngshī while Elena drew her bow. All three dropped down from the roofs at the same time. Elena took a moment to find her balance, favoring one leg as she rose to her feet. The street was slanted and the cobblestones uneven. Zhu didn't wait for her as he rushed the pair.

He was about to bury his machete in Maribelle's neck when an arrow streaked over his shoulder and punched into her skull. Maribelle dropped like a sack of bones as the undeath left her. Zhu changed targets quickly and brought his blade around to the smaller figure, lopping poor little Bobby's head off in one fluid motion.

He shot Elena an annoyed look and slapped his right arm. "This is right."

"Sorry," she muttered, lowering her bow. "I got them confused again."

Zhu nodded, but wondered if that were really true. More likely she didn't want to shoot the little boy; Elena was sensitive like that. Understandable, but developing empathy for things you had to kill was dangerous. It was a lesson he'd learned early in his childhood when he used to name the family chickens. The day his yéye grabbed two of his favorite hens and wrung their necks before taking them into the kitchen was one of the most traumatic of his life.

Zhu gave her the benefit of the doubt. "We'll review again later. How's your leg?"

"I rolled my ankle. I'll be fine."

He glanced back just in time to see Bo's sledgehammer explode the last jiāngshī's head like a melon, splattering flesh and bone against the back wall. The big man immediately pulled out a rag and carefully wiped his hammer clean.

Bo rejoined them a moment later and glanced down at their handiwork. He looked crestfallen. "I hope you're eating mooncakes in heaven, little Bobby."

The wind team hurried off the main road and sprinted down the winding side street. Zhu kept an eye on Elena as she tried to keep up with her injured leg. Stones cut from all different shapes and sizes, mashed together like a giant puzzle and worn down after centuries of use, made the path rough and uneven. The single-story buildings that lined both sides were built from a patchwork of wood, stone, and concrete blocks, each layer of materials a time stamp of its era. The roofs above each building hung low and stretched out over the street, covering the sky, save for a narrow strip down the center.

As they continued moving, weaving, and pushing past small clusters of jiāngshī, Zhu searched for another opportunity to get back to higher ground. It was never safe to stay on the ground in a village for more than a few seconds. Besides, they were a wind team; up above was where they belonged, moving silently and safely like the gusts whistling overhead. Fortunately, they were still at the outskirts, or else the jump down from the roofs would have been suicide. The shadows from the setting sun were growing longer. They had to find shelter soon.

The street itself was surprisingly clean and empty, considering it had not been swept or maintained in many months. This was likely due to the start of the rainy season that had drenched most of the province the past couple of weeks. A light breeze was blowing in from the north, kicking up swirls of mist and tickling the hairs on the back of Zhu's neck. The wind carried with it faint traces of rot but also the freshness of spring and the minute promise of new life.

Zhu signaled for his team to stay close. They sped halfway down the street before turning into a narrow alley barely two body-widths wide. A jiāngshī with its back to him turned and extended its arm. It just managed to growl before he kicked it in the chest, sending it toppling over a pile of refuse. Zhu's machete stabbed into its eye socket, and he continued down the alley without slowing. He made a left, then a right, and then stopped at yet another intersection to get his bearings and to check if his team was still behind him. Elena was only a step behind, and Bo pulled up a few seconds later, puffing heavily.

"It's nearly dark," she said, her eyes darting across each possible path. "Are you sure you know where we're going?"

One street had a barricade of crates and an overturned ox cart. Before it was a cluster of jiāngshī huddled around a pile of garbage. That left only one way to go, except it would lead them in the wrong direction. Unless . . .

Bo stared at that group uneasily. "Which way, *xiǎodì*?" Calling him little brother wasn't exactly an accurate term of endearment. Bo was actually almost old enough to be Zhu's father.

"We're almost there." That was a small lie. Zhu wasn't sure. Much had changed over the years and nothing looked familiar anymore, especially after the world had fallen apart. His chest clenched. He shouldn't have come here.

He hurried down the only way available, giving the rest of his team no other option but to follow. They were halfway down the street when Zhu found what he was looking for. He tossed his machete onto the tin awning of a chicken coop, and pulled himself up. Elena and Bo followed on his heels.

"Watch your step." He glanced around the edge of the coop where the roof supports sat. Who knew how many jiāngshī were inside the buildings beneath their feet. The three navigated the ancient maze of high and low roofs before finally dropping down to an enclosed courtyard where two jiāngshī were stuck in a muddy koi pond. They raised their arms at the sight of people, but were otherwise not a threat. The team scaled the opposite wall and tightrope walked gingerly along the perimeter until they reached the second-story balcony of the adjacent building. A short jump later, they entered what appeared to be an abandoned apartment building.

Zhu shed his duffel and sniffed. The air had no trace of rot, thankfully, but he paused at the doorway as a wave of familiar memories and nostalgia washed over him. "We should be able to rest here." They were fortunate to have a roof over their heads tonight. He wasn't sure they would make it by sundown. The village was only a half day's journey from the farthest yellow flag, but it had taken his wind team two days to navigate a safe route through this uncharted region.

The sparse living room had a couch on one end, a tube television in the corner, and a broken rocking chair. Even after all these months, the elements had not found a way to invade this building. The place looked neat, tidy even, save for the thick layer of dust. Just like he remembered. Old memories flooded Zhu's head: the familiar smell of his nǎinai's hotpot, the long nights the family spent together watching fireflies light up the sky, spending an evening with his sister in the living room taking apart the kite so they could make bows and arrows from the frame. Bo hit a little too close to home earlier when he was chatting with Elena: this used to be Zhu's grandparents' home. His parents actually lived in the apartment downstairs, but any place on the ground level was far too dangerous to investigate. The last time he was here, the apartment was overflowing with four generations of the family Chen. Now, as far as he knew, he was the only one left. Zhu had no idea what had happened to any of them. His grandmother must have perished early on. She was to be ninety-nine this year. As for his parents, grandfather, and sister, Zhu lost contact with them shortly after the power grid and phone lines went down. He had not heard from them since.

The place now looked peaceful and empty: empty of death, of jiāngshī, of violence. For that he was glad. He had steeled himself in preparing for the worst. Zhu turned away from his team and squeezed his eyes shut, murmuring a goodbye to his family and apologizing for not being here when they needed him. He should have been a better son and returned home as soon as he realized that the government was losing control of the outbreak. Should have taken the first bus back to the village when the infection spread. Should have walked when the buses and trains stopped running. But he didn't. Now the only thing he could do was finally put his past to rest and move on. He had no other choice.

The final days before the country fell were filled with confusion and chaos. The Ministry of Health's last report had warned that there could already be seven hundred million jiāngshī. That meant over half of China's population had perished within the first few weeks of the outbreak. That number would only be higher now, six months later.

At the time, the government had assured its people that everything was under control. Everything would be well again! The people would overcome, the dead would be cleared, and the survivors would rebuild! China would survive as it always had, on the strength and determination of her people!

They trumpeted that message all the way up to the final moments, when Beijing suddenly went quiet. Panic spread to the rest of the body once the head became silent. Many of the local governments collapsed. Outside of large cities, the roads were the most dangerous places to be in China. People from the cities tried to flee to the countryside to get away from the rivers of dead, and those from the villages tried to flee to the cities where they thought the government could protect them. The result was that travel ground to a halt in every direction. Anywhere people congregated and sought refuge, death soon took up residence. The outbreak found an abundance of carriers, spreading to every corner of the Land Under Heaven.

Elena, picking through the drawers and cabinets, put her hands to her hips. "How did you know about this place, Zhu?"

There were definitely places with easier access and better amenities in which to hole up for the night, but Zhu would rather not get into that right now. He did not want to spend the next few hours talking with his team about his past. The guilt was still fresh and the pain raw. Besides, they had a job to do. But as long as he was coming back to Fongyuan, Zhu knew he would regret it if he didn't at least stop by his family's home one last time. This could be his last chance. "It's just an abandoned apartment." He pointed at a stove tucked in the corner. "Get a fire started. Bo, check the kitchen. I'll search the rooms."

Zhu wandered down the hallway clutching his machete. If there were a jiāngshī in here, they should have heard it by now. They definitely would have smelled it by now. One couldn't be too certain, or careful, however.

His grandparents' bedroom was bare except for a large traditional stone bed and wooden dresser. All the drawers were opened and empty. The opposite wall with one window was decorated with several portraits of his nǎinai and yéye that spanned from their teenage years into when they were both gray, wrinkly, and stooped over. The largest picture on the wall displayed his extended family, which easily numbered into the fifties. If Zhu looked carefully, he could just see the upper half of his teenage head on the far right, right next to the blotted-out face of his cousin's ex-husband. Nǎinai was merciless when it came to family.

On a small table in the corner was a shrine to the Buddha with spent incense sticks still resting in cups. A *xiàngqí* board sat on a small bench next to the bed, its pieces set up and ready for a chess game that would never happen.

Zhu picked up one of the pieces—the elephant—and noted its worn edges and many scratches, no doubt from all the times he had hurled it angrily to the ground in frustration. He was a sore loser when he was young, and his yéye was merciless, even to an eight-year-old boy. Zhu tapped the piece on the board before placing it back exactly where he had found it. Maybe someone else would find it and put the game to good use. It just wouldn't be him. Games, while highly sought after at the Beacon, were given low points as scavenge. Besides, he couldn't bear thinking of someone else playing his grandfather's xiàngqí set.

The next room had two small beds with the headboards meeting in the corner. One was perfectly made. The other was a mess. On the near side were two desks lined up side-by-side. Zhu stood at the doorway for several seconds. This was where he and Ahui had lived. Their parents' place downstairs was only a one bedroom, and they worked all the time, so he and Ahui had spent most of their childhood here. He walked over to the messy bed and sat down, taking everything in.

This room looked much smaller and more cramped than he remembered. He glanced at where the two beds touched. He and Ahui would stay up late, whispering to each other for hours at night until their yéye would barge in and threaten to make them kneel in opposite corners until dawn.

When they were little, Ahui used to steal ramen packs from their mother's convenience store. During their afternoon naps, she would stay up and suck on the pepper packs. That went on for an entire summer until nǎinai discovered a mound of opened ramen packages with the noodles discarded under her bed. Of course, being the older brother, Zhu never gave her up and took the blame. To this day he couldn't recall a time when he was switched that badly.

That was when he noticed it.

Zhu got up and walked to the desk closest to the window. He pushed aside the dusty notebooks and manual pencil sharpener and pulled down a discolored photo taped to the wall. It was a picture of a scrawny twelve-year-old boy wearing a stupid grin flanked by two girls, both slightly younger. All three were in school uniforms. The boy and one of the girls could have passed for twins. The other girl had a thin oval face and large striking eyes. She would have been pretty if it weren't for that crooked smile. Perhaps, Zhu considered, she was pretty in spite of it.

It didn't matter. These were ghosts living only in the past. The only thing that mattered now was moving forward. On the back of the photo was an inscription in black marker: *Ahui and Meili and annoying brother. Primary school graduation. Age 10.*

Zhu flipped the photo back to the desk and left the room. A part of him thought he should take the photo with him. It was the only picture he had of his sister. Another, more urgent part of him couldn't handle the guilt that rose up and gnawed at him every time he looked at it, so he left it where it belonged: in the past. He felt the tears coming, then, as he opened the bathroom door.

Instantly, his nose was hit with the strong odor of death. Without a sound, a mostly skeletal figure toppled out onto him from the dark. It wrapped both hands around his arm holding the doorknob and nearly tore a piece out. Taken completely by surprise, Zhu fumbled for his machete, lost his balance, and flailed backward.

He threw a punch on instinct and knocked it down, sending it tumbling into a heap on the floor. Zhu shook his bruised hand; punching bone was not pleasant. Annoyed, he stomped over to the fallen jiāngshī and kicked aside the arm stretching out for him. He reached for his machete . . . but hesitated.

For a moment, recognition stayed his hand. Whoever it was in its life had already been old before it died. Was it the narrow eyes or the tattered braided hair or the glints of gold in the teeth? Something he couldn't quite get his mind around. Before his head could play any more tricks on him, he drew his machete and brought it down hard on the jiāngshī's head, splitting its skull nearly in two. He moaned as cold realization, mixed with guilt and fury, took over. Zhu brought his machete up and hacked at the jiāngshī several more times until it was completely still.

The mixture of adrenaline and rage finally left his body, and he deflated. A chill passed through him as he stared at the withered and emaciated corpse, pathetic even by jiāngshī standards. There was no mistaking who this was. His ninety-nine-year-old grandmother, abandoned and left alone to die. Her final moments must have been terrible. That thought ate Zhu up inside. It must have been a difficult choice for his family to make. He had no right to be angry or to judge them, however. He hadn't been here. Maybe things would have been different if he had. Maybe he could have saved them. Maybe everyone would still be alive if it weren't for his absence. A choked hiss escaped Zhu's lips, and he stormed out of the bathroom and back into the living room.

By now, a small fire was burning in the stove, and a glow of warmth pushed back the damp air. Elena, nurturing it, looked up, puzzled. "Everything all right?"

He did his best to mask the welling in his eyes. "I need some fresh air."

"Hey xiǎodì," said Bo excitedly, brandishing a half-empty Styrofoam tray of black oval objects, as if he had found gold. "I found hundred-year-old eggs. We're going to feast tonight."

Zhu didn't reply as he stepped onto the balcony overlooking the Yuanjiang.

"Something I said?" asked Bo.

Zhu leaned over the balcony and watched the shore on the other side. The smell of fish and algae and dank rot filled his nostrils. A bloated corpse floated past a family of geese. Shortly after, another corpse floated by and then a dozen more, followed by a clutter of debris. He paid the ghastly image barely more than a thought. Probably a capsized boat. Sights likes this downstream along the rivers weren't uncommon.

Elena joined him on the balcony a few seconds later. Her arm looped around his waist, and she leaned into him. "Hey, is everything all right? You've been twitchy all day."

Zhu pulled her close and inhaled. She smelled like someone who had been wandering in the wilderness through mud and garbage for weeks, which was a given. It was a combination of sweat and dirt and something that honestly smelled a little like feces. But below all that, Zhu smelled her. It was wonderful. He gave her a small squeeze. "I'm just worried about going so deep into an urban area."

"First rule you taught me about survival," she reminded him. "Stay away from population centers. I'm kind of surprised you came up with this plan."

"We had no choice," he replied. "We haven't hit quota in weeks. We need a good scavenge."

"But all the way out here? How do you even know about this pot at the end of the rainbow?"

Zhu wasn't sure what that meant; Elena's American vernacular didn't always translate well in Mandarin. It was part of her charm. He sniffed the air. "Something smells like rotten eggs."

"Bo smashed a shelf for firewood that was coated with tar. We're cooking dinner now," she replied. "That stove is ancient. It looks like it came from the Ming dynasty."

He sighed. "What else is for dinner?"

Elena took on a haughty British accent that could pass for a bad mix of Singaporean and American cowboy. "Today's appetizer is stale water in a flask with a squirt of chlorine flavoring. The main course is peanut sticky rice wrapped in dried banana leaves. Dessert is a can of durian that you and Bo can share between the two of you." She paused. "We also have those hideous egg things Bo found."

Zhu made a face. "This menu is terrible. I want to talk to the manager."

"Of course, sir. You can lodge a complaint here." She gave him the middle finger, then switched to her pinky, which was the Chinese way, and then broke into a grin. "Seriously, though—if we're going to finally hit quota, the first thing I want to do with the points is get real fruit."

"Durian is real fruit."

"We can agree to disagree." She pointed at the horizon. "There's a fog rolling in. If it's still here tomorrow, we're going to be trapped in this village. We definitely shouldn't be exploring in the middle of it."

"It'll be gone by morning."

"How are you sure?"

"It will," replied Zhu confidently. He craned his head and looked back into the room. "What's Bo doing inside?"

"Reading his books."

Bo was the only one on the team who had been too poor to own any electronic devices prior to the collapse. Zhu carried a point-and-shoot camera and a small MP3 player loaded with music, while Elena had everything: camera, phone, MP3 player, and one of those fancy portable DVD players as well. All Bo had were books. On the one hand, that was fine, because he never had to pay the points to charge his entertainment, but it also meant he was often relegated to reading the same few books he had in his possession over and over again. Zhu had put his foot down about him carrying only one book at a time on scavenges.

"I wish I could read *Hànzì* better," said Elena wistfully. "What's the word for that sort of story again?"

"*Wŭxiá*, which means 'martial heroes.' It's where all those kung fu stories originated from. I can teach you to read better, if you'd like. After all, you did such a good job with my English lessons, before all this happened," said Zhu, searching for her hand.

"The apprentice has now become the master," she smiled, letting him lead her inside.

Dinner was exactly as described, sticky rice with peanuts and soy sauce wrapped with banana leaves. Zhu and Elena both gave Bo a little bit of theirs, since the big man was easily their total weight combined. She also gave him her share of the durian.

The woodstove leaked as much smoke into the room as it funneled out, but the team was willing to put up with anything to keep the chill away. They passed the time sharing their limited entertainment, listening to music on Zhu's MP3 player and clustering around Elena's small screen to watch videos. Afterward, Bo read aloud from his wǔxiá book while Zhu helped Elena with her Mandarin.

They huddled closer to the stove as night fell and the temperature dropped. It became too dark to read, so Elena regaled them with stories of her life in America, telling them how her folks would go boating nearly every weekend, and how they barbecued and strolled along sandy beaches and did something called "tubing" on a great river known as the Colorado. She told them about how her father took her and her brother Robbie bowhunting for white-tailed deer. Certainly explained why she was such a good shot.

Every time she talked about home, Elena's face would light up. It was obvious how badly she missed her family. Being so far away when the world had fallen apart must have torn her up inside. She hadn't heard anything from America since she and Zhu had evacuated from Changsha in the early days of the disaster.

Bo raised a hand as she tried to explain tubing to them again. "I don't understand." He ticked his fingers. "Your family has their own boat that you drive around for fun, not going anywhere or carrying anything. But then you also like to sit on tire tubes and float on the lake for fun."

She nodded. "It's not about actually going anywhere. It was about being together and enjoying the experience. Besides, there were always parties on Lake Travis. We'd cruise around and tie a couple of boats together and everybody just had a good time."

Bo looked a little confounded. Zhu didn't blame him. The two of them hailed from rural villages, Zhu from western Hunan and Bo from somewhere far up north. Both had left farms to find work in the city and ended up working next to each other on the assembly line in a factory. Zhu had met Elena shortly after when he was looking for an English tutor.

Bedtime music was a mix of *gǔzhēng* folk, classic Andy Lau, and Chinese death metal—the last one being somewhat of a recently acquired taste. Bo took the space next to the stove while Zhu and Elena shared a sleeping bag. One less sleeping bag to pack meant much more room for salvage to haul back to the settlement.

Zhu first checked the stove and added a few more pieces of wood from the shelf Bo had smashed with his sledgehammer. He checked the pipes once more to make sure the smoke was filtering out of the apartment. It would be a shame for them to survive the jiāngshī apocalypse only to succumb to smoke inhalation.

By the time he crept into the sleeping bag he shared with Elena, she had already dozed off. Zhu wrapped his arms around her protectively as she instinctively pressed her back into his chest. He blinked once, feeling the exhaustion weigh down his consciousness. He glanced to his side to see Bo still reading his book using his head lamp as a light.

"We have an early day tomorrow," he said.

The light turned off. "Okay, xiǎodì. Sleep well." The big man must have been exhausted. He was out within seconds, and soon his loud, labored snores that sounded not unlike a hissing jiāngshī filled the room.

To Zhu's dismay, Elena, nuzzling inside the crook of his armpit, added to the chorus, her soft breathing alternating with Bo's loud hisses. Together, they fell into a rhythm that was soon joined by the cicadas singing just outside.

Zhu continued to stare up at the ceiling of his childhood home well after this strange symphony had finally subsided. He wondered if jiāngshī slept, if they remembered any traces of their former lives, and if their souls were still in their bodies somehow. He mainly thought about his nǎinai sitting there all that time in the toilet, waiting for nothing.

He hoped desperately that the grandmother he loved and cherished had truly died alongside her body all those months ago and that her soul was now with the rest of her loved ones. She wouldn't have to wonder then, wouldn't have to worry, and most of all she wouldn't be lonely. The last thought he had before sleep swept over him was feeling guilty that he was allowed to escape and slip away into blissful unconsciousness.

2

THE TYPHOON
OF DEAD

The long line of jiāngshī shuffled, almost politely, single file down a narrow dirt path. Their leader, a scrawny teenager missing half his face, stopped when the nearby pond began to burp bubbles. The teenage jiāngshī grunted and stared, tilting his head to one side. The body behind him bumped into him, and then the one behind that did the same, setting off a cascade down the line until the forward momentum forced the first jiāngshī to start moving again. The line walked on, an eerie, near-silent procession.

Perched on a branch directly above the path, Ying Hengyen, leader of the Beacon of Light's wind teams, noted the scene with irony. In a way, what had just transpired was the perfect metaphor for the jiāngshī outbreak. A few walking dead were of little consequence, but add them all up and they become an unstoppable, uncontrollable force of nature, consuming everything in its path. Death, powered by mindless inertia.

The windmaster had originally considered staying in hiding and letting this line of jiāngshī pass, but decided there was no use in delaying the inevitable. The team would have to kill them now or kill them later on the way back. Might as well take the tactical advantage the current terrain offered.

He put his fingers to his mouth and let out a weak warble. He had spent most of the day neck-deep in cold bog water, so he was numb all over. It did the job, however. As soon as the noise left his lips, three figures rose from the water, each raising a long spear. The sharp tips of the spears found their marks in seven jiāngshī before the rest even noticed.

As soon as the dead turned their backs to him, Hengyen and Linnang dropped down from the trees directly on top of two jiāngshī, and then attacked the rest from behind. Hengyen, wielding two long daggers, hacked expertly, taking down four. Linnang, the newest member of the wind team, was fighting next to him with a large ax. They chopped and stabbed, slowly retreating up the heavily forested hill as the once-orderly line dissolved into a feral mob. The two men took position behind several brambles and picked off the jiāngshī that got caught.

The rest of Hengyen's wind team surged forward, using their long spears to carve up the others. When the jiāngshī turned their attention on them again, they would retreat into the water, where the clumsy dead moved poorly.

The path and pond were soon littered with body parts and stained with blood. Hengyen and Linnang came out of the brush and checked the downed jiāngshī, finishing off any that were still moving. Within a few minutes, the wind team of five had killed more than five times their number. All except for their "leader," who had continued to wander farther down the trail, oblivious to the fact that his retinue had been slaughtered.

Linnang pulled out a throwing knife and aimed. Hengyen drew his knife at the same time. Linnang's blade flew from his fingertips first, arcing through the air and missing the young jiāngshī's head by a handspan. The jiāngshī turned around to face them just in time to receive Hengyen's blade in one eye.

Hengyen patted the newest member of his wind team on the shoulder. "Spare a second. Save a life."

"Yes, dàgē." The young man blushed in embarrassment.

Hengyen turned to the other three on his team who were climbing out of the water, offering his hand to each to pull them up. The team quickly regrouped and continued up the trail that cut along one side of the gorge. In the distance directly ahead of them was a highway bridge that spanned the chasm. A steady stream of jiāngshī was crossing it. Even from a distance, the sounds of their moans and movement filled the air. Every once in a while, a jiāngshī would fall over the side and plummet to the rocks below with a loud crack, like hail striking a tin roof. The sounds reverberated throughout the gorge, echoes lingering in the air.

They moved quickly, staying alert as they passed into the shadow of the bridge. The ground at their feet was littered with bodies: jiāngshī that had stumbled off the roadway above. Most had been crushed beyond recognition, but a few still stirred, raising their twisted and broken limbs at the wind team. Hengyen's people finished any they found as they passed with efficient, mercenary strikes.

Six months ago, this ghastly site would have churned Hengyen's stomach. Now it was just another day scouting east of the Beacon of Light. One of the first instructions Hengyen gave every wind team recruit was to scavenge in the direction of the setting sun. To venture east was to invite death. To the east lay the remnants of the big cities, where the outbreak had begun, and where the jiāngshī numbered greater than the stars in the heavens.

His wind team was the only one allowed to venture in this direction, because they had a more important job than making a quota. Hengyen was one of the few remaining professional soldiers, and his sole objective was to ensure the survival of the Beacon. For the past few weeks, there had been a drastic uptick in jiāngshī flowing in from the east. He and his team of crack scavengers were the only ones with the experience and skill to walk into jiāngshī territory and investigate what was going on.

Since the beginning of the outbreak, Hengyen had fought on the front line against the dead. As a captain of one of the elite Falcon Commando Units in the Armed Police Force of the People's Liberation Army, he and his men were some of the first on the ground when the city of Hangzhou fell into chaos and panic. The only information they received were scattered reports of people infected by a terrible virus that caused them to go insane and attack others.

At first, the government called it a sickness, so Hengyen and his men did everything in their power to neutralize the "sick people" without harming them. That had been their first mistake. It wasn't until Hengyen witnessed firsthand a child no older than six tear out his mother's throat and then sink his teeth into one of his soldiers' arms that he realized what he was truly up against. His soldier died and then rose a few hours later, killing half the men in his hospital ward.

After it became apparent that the dead could not be contained, the Chinese authorities tried to evacuate the city instead of immediately calling for air strikes and decimating the carriers. That had been their second mistake. Containment was impossible. The cities were too heavily populated. The infection spread too easily. Within days, the dead and desperate survivors had overrun most of the quarantine checkpoints in the major population zones. Within weeks, the government had lost contact with every major city in eastern China. Since then, the communication blackout had spread westward, city after city, province after province, until eventually the military had run out of country to defend. Now, Hengyen wasn't sure how much military was left.

The wind team hurried beneath the bridge and pressed on, careful not to accidentally fall victim to the corpses dropping around them. They hugged one side of the gorge until they reached a shallow path that snaked up the eastern wall. Directly above them was a rock formation that rose a few stories above ground level, which provided a perfect vantage point for the surrounding area all the way to the city of Changde. Hengyen had discovered this particular path and outlook during his many scouting trips. He used to come by himself to track jiāngshī movements from the city, but over the past few weeks the crowds of jiāngshī had grown thicker, and it was simply too dangerous now for anyone to travel alone.

Hengyen ordered everyone but his lieutenant Wangfa to stay at the base of the gorge. The path was so narrow, the only way to cross was to shuffle up laterally with their backs to the stone. Even then, their toes hung out over the side. He had already lost one man to a fall. There was enough death going around. He didn't want any more lives wasted.

The two men began to move up the path. This was Wangfa's first time scaling the lookout. Hengyen thought it was important that his second in command became accustomed to it in case anything ever happened to him. Wangfa was the only other surviving member of the Falcon commando unit. The two more often than not didn't see eye to eye, but he was an able soldier and a competent officer. Hengyen trusted the man enough; whether or not he liked him was irrelevant.

In a previous life, Wangfa hadn't been command material and was in fact under investigation for excessive use of force and brutality, but the outbreak wiped his slate clean. China had already lost its best and brightest. The survivors had to make do once their ranks were depleted, so Wangfa was given a second chance and summoned back to active duty.

They had nearly climbed out of the gorge onto the same level as the plains when the narrow path ended. The rest of the way was connected by ropes and hooks that Hengyen had set up on a previous trip. Hengyen could hear the buzzing of the jiāngshī wandering around on the other side of the rock formation. Two months ago, the plains on this side of the gorge were all but devoid of jiāngshī. That was no longer the case. Hengyen reached the top first and helped pull Wangfa up. They crawled on their bellies to the edge of the stone formation and stared at the valley below. Wangfa gasped, while Hengyen could only look silently on and exhale slowly through his gritted teeth.

There wasn't just a mass of jiāngshī down on the plain below. They spanned the entire horizon in every direction. The number of dead were more vast than Hengyen could possibly have imagined. Even worse, they were on the move, funneling down the main road across the bridge.

"There must be hundreds of thousands here. A million," he whispered, a chill passing through him. For the first time since the early days of the war with the dead, hopelessness twisted his stomach and gripped his heart.

No force could face such an assemblage of dead and hope to survive. This would truly be the end of the Beacon of Light.

In the months since the war with the jiāngshī began, Hengyen had seen and done it all. Every turn had put him up against insurmountable odds and impossible decisions. During the first days of the outbreak, he had risked rescuing a squad of men from Changsha before calling in bombers despite knowing there were still civilians on the ground. He had ordered the death of every injured soldier in a military hospital because jiāngshī had broken through the perimeter and there wasn't time to evacuate. Hengyen's commitment and confidence had never wavered. The Living Revolution was all that mattered. He knew what he was fighting for.

"That road leads straight to the Beacon," said Wangfa in a hushed voice. "This many jiāngshī in one place will smash everything in their way."

"We have to divert them somehow."

"How, sir?"

"I don't know yet, but we'll find a way. The Beacon and the Living Revolution depend on it."

A shout from back down in the gorge caught their attention. They scrambled to the other side and saw Linnang waving furiously. One glance farther down the gorge told Hengyen what it was about. Thirty or so jiāngshī were stumbling through the ravine toward his team. If they didn't get down immediately, the two men could be trapped.

He grabbed the rope and swung his legs over the side. "We have to go now."

Hengyen repelled down to the path in seconds, but the way across the narrow ledge couldn't be rushed. He calmly surveyed the wave of the dead rushing past beneath his feet.

The first jiāngshī were felled easily enough, but like everything else about them, it was rarely the first that you had to worry about. Hengyen and Wangfa had only made it halfway down the path when the main body of the cluster reached the beginning of the path. It writhed like a many-limbed demon, groaning and gnashing along the path. His heart swelled at the sight of his wind team battling furiously with their primitive weapons. They didn't abandon him.

In his haste to rejoin his team, Hengyen lost his footing. He pitched sideways, flipping head first toward the ground. Three of his fingers managed to clutch the ledge, and then he lost his grip, falling two stories to the ground below. It came at him quickly, and he felt a hard crunch on one side of his body. A dull roar filled his ears, and his mind momentarily blanked with pain. The world stuttered, first slowing to a crawl and then speeding to catch up. Wangfa appeared at his side a moment later, pulling him to his feet. Then the roar burst like a bubble, and a cacophony of sounds slammed into him. He gathered his senses and found a battle raging all around him as Wangfa half dragged, half carried him to safety.

Hengyen shucked off his second in command and took charge. "The jiāngshī are clumsy. Use the terrain. Make them come at you."

He barked several more orders, marshaling his wind team back into a cohesive unit. He pulled Weizhen and Haihong back and called for everyone to gather close. The jiāngshī were hampered by the uneven terrain and the boulders and debris littering the ground. Their numbers were proving a disadvantage as the dead tripped over each other in their hastiness to consume the living. As long as the team stayed calm and followed orders, they should be able to whittle this large group down. In a short time, over half of the jiāngshī were already slain.

Out of the corner of his eye, Hengyen saw Linnang dragging behind, breaking the line. The newest member of the team was shouting incoherently as the jiāngshī surged around him.

"You corpses are nothing! Just bones and rags." He sank his ax into a skull. "This is for my *bà*." He slashed another, ripping its jaw loose. "This is for my *dì*. This is for my girlfriend, and my scooter. And my university; I got accepted to Fudan two days before the stupid outbreak. I studied two years for the entrance exam!" He continued to rattle off a long list of grievances.

"Linnang," Hengyen barked. "Pull yourself together. Pull back."

Linnang was so caught up in his bloodlust he didn't realize that the jiāngshī had surrounded him. He continued to rattle off a long list of grievances as he continued to hack away. Blood and guts soaked his shirt and arms as he swung his weapon in wide, looping arcs. The ax bit into the waist of a jiāngshī, nearly severing it in two. When Linnang tried to pull back, the blade got stuck in bone. He lost his grip on the handle and stumbled backward. He reached for it again.

"Leave it," yelled Hengyen, plunging his two daggers into the chest of a particularly fat and resilient jiāngshī.

Linnang finally realized his peril. The jiāngshī chasing after them turned and converged on the straggler. He could still have fled, pushed his way through the two or three dead blocking his escape. Instead, however, he panicked and drew his pistol.

"No!" screamed Hengyen. He raced toward the youth, but it was too late. Linnang unloaded his pistol, firing half a dozen times and dropping that many jiāngshī around him. The two men froze as the loud discharge from the gunshot continued to resonate throughout the gorge. Hengyen scanned the top of the ridge above as the lingering sound of the gunshot faded away. Nothing. Not a jiāngshī or even a dust cloud in sight. It appeared they had gotten lucky.

Hengyen rounded on Linnang and snatched the pistol out of his hand. "What did I tell you about discharging your weapon, especially with an army of them nearby?"

Linnang's hands were shaking. He loosed a nervous chuckle. "I'm sorry, Windmaster. I saw that you were all farther back and panicked."

Hengyen breathed a sigh of relief and poked him in the head. "Next time use your head. Fortunately, there was no harm this time, but . . ." His voice trailed off as a low rumble reverberated throughout the gorge, followed by a chorus of thin hisses and groans. The noise began to crescendo.

Something appeared to fall from the sky out of the corner of Hengyen's eye. He spun toward it and just caught the tail end when a body smashed into the rocks just a few meters from where he stood.

Haihong blanched and pointed toward the ridge line. Lines of jiāngshī appeared on the ledges on both sides of the gorge, attracted by the noise of the firearm. Several more stepped toward them and fell in, tumbling to the rocks below. More jiāngshī followed, except many in the second wave were able to scramble to their feet. The ones that had fallen first cushioned their fall.

Hengyen fought back his natural urge to make this a teaching moment and quickly signaled for an orderly retreat. He began to carve his way back toward the way they had come. The jiāngshī were raining all around them now. Many that crashed to the ground didn't get back up again. Just as many did, however. The bodies began to pile up at the feet of the steep cliffs.

One jiāngshī whose fall was cushioned by the dozens that fell over the ridge before it tumbled down a slope of bodies and somehow landed on its feet. It didn't miss a step as it lurched forward, arms outstretched, its neck bent in an unnatural angle. Hengyen was preoccupied barking orders at his team when it barreled into him and grabbed onto his arm.

The windmaster slipped his free hand underneath its elbow into an arm lock and spun it to the ground before burying his dagger into its skull in one smooth motion. Another came at him from his blind side. Hengyen swung his foot out and swept its feet from under it before clamoring to his feet and waving frantically for the rest of his team to retreat.

One jiāngshī got ahold of Linnang, sinking its rotting teeth into his arm before tearing off a bloody chunk. He screamed, batting the decayed creature in the head. A second jiāngshī managed to wrap its blackened hands around his leg. Another grabbed his hair.

Then the feeding frenzy began.

His screams pierced the air as he disappeared under the mass of bodies. Hengyen drew his gun and searched for his fallen man, hoping to get a clear shot to put him out of his misery. All he saw was a mess of flailing limbs and sprays of blood.

He signaled to the others. "Fall back."

The remaining members of the wind team broke off and fled. Hengyen led the way, careening from side to side as more jiāngshī rained down on them from above. One body nearly fell on Weizhen. Haihong tripped and took a nasty spill when another body landed directly in front of her.

The wind team continued at a full sprint for nearly a kilometer before Hengyen signaled for a stop. He stared back in the direction they had come. The gorge would soon be cluttered with jiāngshī. It would take weeks and manpower they couldn't spare to clear it if he wanted to use that stone formation as a lookout point again.

"What do we do next, Windmaster?" asked Wangfa.

Hengyen shook his head. In any case, that concern was for a future date. "We head home, double time. Drop all nonessentials. We have to warn the Beacon that a typhoon is coming."

3

QUOTA

Zhu's wind team set out the next morning at the crack of dawn. Just as he predicted, the heavy mist of the night before had mostly dispersed by first light. Breakfast had been the remaining hundred-year-old eggs—something Elena hated more than she hated durian. But since they were out of sticky rice, she ate every piece offered to her.

Zhu led them up the stairs to the top floor of the building, and then dropped down from a side window to an adjacent roof. They moved carefully along the edge of the pagoda-style roof, snaking to a corner and then climbing on all fours up to the roof's center ridge.

The going was slow and treacherous, the tiles slippery from the previous night's mist.

"Blow through as if you were never here," he muttered, carefully watching his footing. It was a common wind-team saying hammered into them during training.

As they moved deeper into the village, the streets below were increasingly filled with jiāngshī. Almost all of them stood perfectly still, completely undisturbed, as if they were part of the Terracotta Army. It brought Zhu back to his restless thoughts last night: Do jiāngshī sleep? Do they dream? Regardless, it was important they remained undisturbed, because agitation was infectious. The last thing the wind team needed was to get distracted by a sea of agitated jiāngshī. A swoop of low-flying cranes were passing by overhead when Zhu heard a squawk behind him, and saw Elena sliding down the steep roof feet first as her hands pawed against the tiles. He dove after her, but even as his body skidded down the rough tiles, he knew he wasn't going to make it. Then, to his surprise, Elena managed to stop her descent, and he found himself skidding past her. The edge of the roof was coming at him quickly. He visualized plummeting headfirst into a sea of jiāngshī, and then his slide came to a sudden stop.

He looked back and saw her stretched out, gripping a handhold with her left hand and a fistful of his pants with her right. How she had managed to save them both was beyond him. Zhu cautiously picked himself up and crawled to her on all fours. They climbed back up to the ridge of the roof together. Bo helped them to their feet.

Zhu grasped her arm tightly. "Good save."

She held up her fingers and wiggled them. "At least those years of mountain climbing in the Guadalupes count for something."

He checked her tennis shoes, which were worn down almost to the insoles. "We need to get you a new pair of shoes," he muttered.

"Size six, please. Pink, preferably."

He chuckled. "I'll see what I can—" Zhu stopped abruptly and turned toward the horizon. For a second, he thought he saw movement on the top floor of the building on the other side of the street. He scanned the rooftops, but detected nothing further.

Bo followed his gaze. "What is it?"

Elena, squinting, reached for her bow.

Zhu scanned the roof for several more seconds before letting it go. "It's nothing. I thought I saw someone. Stay alert."

The team moved deeper into the village with increasing caution. They continued to the end of the block to a defunct power line stretching across the street. Zhu went first to make sure it would hold his weight. Wrapping his arms and legs around the cable, he hung upside down and shimmied across, avoiding looking down at the river of dead below. The number of jiāngshī on the ground near the center of the village was so thick, the ground was no longer visible. Nearly at the other side, he made the mistake of looking down to find his footing only to come face-to-face with the mass of roiling jiāngshī, their fingers contorted into claws reaching for him.

The jiāngshī had finally noticed them, and the sheer madness of their feral rage made him limp. His mind reeled. Zhu had managed to wall off his emotions after the outbreak. It was the only way to survive the horrors of this reality. He made himself believe that the jiāngshī weren't dead people risen. No, they were just creatures that needed to be avoided or killed. He had to be strong to take care of Elena. But after what he discovered last night at his grandparents' home . . . he squeezed his eyes shut. He sucked in several shallow, quick breaths as his body trembled.

Zhu didn't know how long he hung on the cable, just that suddenly something stabbed him from behind, not hard enough to break flesh, but certainly enough that he let out a shocked howl. He looked down the wire and saw Elena behind him. She had her legs crossed over the wire and was holding on by one hand. In her other hand was her short spear.

His surroundings ebbed back into his consciousness. His arms suddenly burned, and blood rushed into his head. "I'm all right," he shouted as he made his way to the other side. He dropped to the roof carefully and then caught Elena as she fell into his arms. He held her even tighter than he had held the rope.

"Thank you for coming for me," he whispered in her ear.

"Don't scare me like that, asshole." Her voice trembled. "You were just hanging there for a whole minute. What were you doing?"

They were still embracing when Bo made it across. The big man tapped both their shoulders. "I have no one to hug." Elena made her cooing sound and moved as if to pull him in as well. Bo held his hands up. "No, that's not what I meant. I just want to go."

That was probably a good idea. They'd already wasted too much time here. "Come on," Zhu said. "It's not much farther."

"What's not much farther?" asked Elena. "What is this place?"

"Just a place I heard might be good for salvage." Zhu led his wind team down to a narrow alley that connected to two busy streets. Luckily, the jiāngshī were more scattered here. He pointed at a door on the ground level. "It's in there."

They dropped down at the exact same time in between a small group of jiāngshī. Zhu jumped the two on their left while his teammates handled the remaining three on their right. Zhu's machete whipped upward, slicing open a jiāngshī from naval to neck. The thing lurched forward even as the left half of its chest peeled away from its body, exposing several broken ribs and a dark red-and-purple mass of flesh, which he could only assume was a lung. He pulled the machete back, and found it momentarily stuck in between two ribs. The jiāngshī pawed at him with its one good arm. Zhu brushed it aside and planted a foot on its chest right at the purple mass. He pushed with his feet and pulled simultaneously until he wiggled the blade free.

That momentary delay proved costly as the other jiāngshī dove toward him. Zhu tried to duck out of the way but the thing plowed into him, wrapping its arms around his waist. This jiāngshī was a big boy, extra large and extra plump, who towered over Zhu and was nearly half again wider. He writhed as the jiāngshī wrapped its arms around his, trapping them to his body, and then watched in horror as it opened its jaws and went for his shoulder. The jiāngshī bit down. Zhu screamed.

Elena screamed as well. "No! I don't have a clear shot."

Zhu squeezed his eyes shut and clenched his teeth, fully expecting to have his flesh torn apart, feeling the spray of his own blood on his face. Then, that would be it for Chen Wenzhu. That was how the outbreak spread. If someone survived a jiāngshī's bite, they were doomed to die and return as one. There had been several instances of people surviving a bite by having their affected parts cut out or amputated, but that wouldn't help Zhu now. He was sure there was no way to cut off his shoulder.

Even worse than death, once he became a jiāngshī, he would attack the living and continue to spread this curse. The thought of him injuring people close to him pained him deeply. Elena or Bo would have to put him down . . .

Instead of his prediction, however, all Zhu felt was a dull ache on his shoulder, almost like a massage. He pried open one eye and studied the jiāngshī more closely, and realized it used to be an old man. Where his teeth should have been were greyed, glistening gums. This jiāngshī must have been missing his dentures! It continued to gnaw futilely with its gummy mouth.

An arrowhead burst out of his chest. The jiāngshī's body shook, but he stayed focused on trying to chew on Zhu's shoulder. Zhu managed to pry one arm loose and press it against the jiāngshī's neck to push him back. Another arrow went in through the back of his neck and out the front, piercing the flesh in between Zhu's thumb and index fingers.

He stared wide-eyed at the close call. A few centimeters to either side and he would be missing a finger. He turned to the source. "Hey, watch it."

Then Bo was there, grabbing a fistful of the jiāngshī's hair and pulling it off Zhu. The big man threw the heavy corpse to the ground and smashed his sledgehammer down on its head.

Elena was by Zhu's side a moment later. Near panic showed on her face as she pulled his shirt down to search for injuries. His shoulder was disgustingly wet, but the skin remained unbroken.

Both Zhu and Elena deflated with relief and held on to each other.

They stayed still for several moments as the adrenaline dumped from his body. Being out in the wilderness was always dangerous, but this was one of the closest calls he'd had with death, and it was merely by dumb luck that he'd survived. "That was close."

"Too close." She pulled back and poked him hard in the chest. "You have to be more careful, Chen Wenzhu. If you turn into a jiāng-shī on me, I swear I'm not going to put you down. I'm going to keep you around like a pet and call you Zhu Zhu."

"That doesn't sound too bad," he replied, half joking. "I'm sorry. I am unfocused today. Have a lot on my mind."

"You want to talk about it?"

He looked around. "Later. Now's not a good time."

"I'm holding you to that." She waggled a finger at him. "It's a good thing you have Bo and me to watch your back. Don't press your luck, mister."

He pointed back at the door. "Bo, can you break us in?"

"I'm on it."

Bo got to work on the door. He hefted his sledgehammer and swung it like a baseball bat at the door knob. The sound of the impact echoed with a dull thunk. Nothing happened. Bo frowned. He hit the door again several more times, making an impressive amount of noise with each blow but getting them no farther inside.

Elena tugged at Zhu's sleeve. "We're attracting an audience."

Jiāngshī had gathered on both ends of the alley to investigate the commotion. They began to stream toward the wind team one by one. Bo hammered the door harder and more furiously, but only succeeded in making more of a ruckus and attracting even more curious jiāngshī. The two mobs closed in on them.

"Save your energy," Zhu said to a huffing and puffing Bo after he dropped the sledgehammer to catch his breath. "We're going to need it."

"We can't fight this many," said Elena. She was right. This many jiāngshī in this confined a space would overwhelm them in seconds. She looked up at the narrow window above the door. "There, help me up."

Zhu laced his fingers and boosted her up to the window. Elena pulled out her knife and smashed the glass with the butt.

"They're coming," said Bo.

"I just need a few more . . ." Elena cleared the glass shards and disappeared inside.

Bo swung his sledgehammer at the closest jiāngshī, collapsing its collarbone with an audible snap, while Zhu waited for those coming from the other side to get closer. He would be able to kill two or three at most before the rest overwhelmed them. Behind him, Zhu could hear the door jiggle. He stabbed a jiāngshī in the face and retreated, his back bumping up against Bo. There were only a few meters of space now between the two groups.

"Listen, xiǎodì," said Bo. "Both of us don't have to die. I'll push you up to the window."

"All right." Zhu didn't hesitate. The dead may be slow, but they never hesitate. That was one of the first lessons ingrained into every windrunner during training. They all had to accept the reality that they would inevitably fall sooner than later, and end up joining the enemy's ranks. The question was if it was a good death.

As Windmaster Hengyen often quoted, "If you waste time fighting over the bill, you both end up paying the price."

Bo leaned his back against the door and laced his fingers together. He glanced at the encroaching jiāngshī and sighed. "This is how it happens in my dream as well. Take care of my *xiǎomèi*."

Zhu stepped up on Bo's hands. "I'm sorry."

Bo shrugged. "Cut the limb to save the body. Kill the man to save the team. Sacrifice the army to save the Living Revolution." Another slogan.

As soon as Zhu began to rise up toward the window, the door swung open and both men spilled inside, a tangle of kicking and flailing limbs. Elena slammed the door behind them and locked it again.

She hovered over them worriedly. "Are you all right? Anyone bitten?"

Zhu, finding himself sprawled on top of Bo, rolled off. He began to laugh as the relief poured out of him. Bo sat up and soon joined in.

"I wouldn't have fit through that window anyway," said Zhu.

Bo chuckled. "I know. I thought they would eat their fill of me and forget about you." Outside the door, the sounds of groans and scraping fingernails rose as their laughter diminished.

Elena helped them both up. "Where are we? Zhu, how did you know about this place?"

He didn't answer, instead scanning the room and letting his eyes adjust to the darkness. They were in a large mechanic's garage. The faint outline of what looked like a tractor missing its wheels sat on a lift. On the far side was an old delivery truck. Along the back wall were neat stacks of boxes of what looked like supplies. The air smelled stale, which was good. That usually meant this space was enclosed. As far as he could tell, he couldn't smell the dead. Maybe they really got lucky this time.

This was the right place, just as he remembered. From before . . .

But today, his wind team had hit the jackpot. He scrambled to one of the shelves and dug through the contents: a carton of coolant, strings of lights, a drawer of power tools. He cut open a cardboard box and raised a fist. "Oil cans."

Elena's face lit up. "Those are worth extra points!"

They split apart, scavenging for supplies in the dank room. They made their selections, balancing a given item's value against its weight. It was still a two- to three-day trek home, so they couldn't be too greedy. Zhu sent Bo to check the truck. Car parts were urgently needed, so they would fetch a lot of points. He sent Elena to load up on cans of oil and working lights and began to clear the cabinets, grabbing power tools and parts. One of the mechanics back at the Beacon had a request for a functioning motorcycle alternator. Elena scanned the boxes, looking for anything even remotely familiar to the characters for "motorcycle."

Zhu and Bo picked the place clean of the most valuable items based on what they could carry. They had to pass on several valuables, such as a carton of car batteries and several containers of gasoline, due to their size and weight. Ever since the grids fell, power was always in demand, but these would be far too heavy for them to carry all the way back to the Beacon. Other scavenge, however, like cans of oil or screwdrivers were worth their weight in gold. As if gold was even worth anything anymore.

The delivery truck engine on the other side of the garage turned several times, then rumbled to life. Bo climbed out of the driver's side and closed the hood triumphantly. "Xiǎodì, this thing still runs. I just put in a fresh battery and everything works. It'd be a shame to take the engine apart. Maybe we can load up all the stuff and drive it home."

Zhu shook his head. "Wishful thinking. We'll never make it through the river of jiāngshī. Just get what you can carry."

Bo's face fell. "Fine." He turned off the engine and disappeared around the back.

Zhu was about to check on Elena when a cry cut through the garage. One of the metal shelves dividing the garage toppled over, spilling its contents. Bo's flashlight went skidding across the floor, spinning its light.

Zhu beamed his own light toward the sounds. Bo had somehow run into one of the shelves and knocked it over. He had fallen onto his backside into one of the openings, and his feet were flailing in the air. Zhu was about to let out a chuckle when he noticed a scatter of movements just past where Bo had fallen.

A chorus of guttural groans filled the garage. Just past him, the delivery truck's cargo doors were swinging on their hinges, and a steady stream of jiāngshī tumbled out of the truck onto the floor, like lemmings off a cliff. Judging by their black helmets and conical hats, they must have been a mix of police officers and farmers.

A jiāngshī with riot gear would be tough to crack with the primitive weapons they wielded.

One of the long-dead police and a burly jiāngshī wearing a leather apron picked themselves up and began to drag their way toward Bo. The big man kicked the officer off balance, but the aproned one fell on top of him. Bo managed to grip its neck and keep from being bitten as the jiāngshī clawed at his face.

Zhu quickly grabbed his scavenge-laden duffel and hurried to help his friend. Elena reached Bo first. She pulled back her spear and stabbed the jiāngshī in the back of the head. Zhu was there a moment later, his machete expertly slashing two more dead as Elena helped Bo to his feet. He cut down another jiāngshī in a dress but nearly stumbled over a stack of tires that had fallen over.

Elena and Bo retreated toward the door as the garage crowded with more jiāngshī.

"No," yelled Zhu. "We can't go back out into the alley."

Elena spun around wildly. "There's no other way out."

She was right. Other than the garage doors, the only other exit was on the opposite wall, which required them to fight through the entire room. More metal squealed as another shelf toppled over, and the mass of jiāngshī rushed at them. One of the shelves fell on top of the tractor, pushing it off the lift, crushing several jiāngshī next to it.

Zhu looked up. There was a row of narrow windows just under the ceiling. He pointed. "Up there. Climb!"

He cut down a jiāngshī in mechanic's garb and then tested the shelf leaning on the tractor. He began to run up it, using each metal level as a step. Several arms reached up through the opening, grabbing at his leg. A bald jiāngshī who could have passed for Grandma Maribelle's husband bit down on his shoe. Zhu tried to get grandpa off, but the jiāngshī held on tightly, growling faintly like a Chongqing bulldog. This one actually had teeth and was quickly working his way through his sneakers. Zhu finally gave up trying to shake grandpa loose. He kicked his shoe off and let the jiāngshī keep it. He reached the top of the shelf and gestured for the others to follow. "Hurry!"

Elena got there first. She stared at the gap between the toppled shelf and the one still standing along the wall below the windows. She shook her head. "I can't."

Zhu grabbed her shoulders. He gave her a rough kiss and stared into her eyes. "You can. I'll be right next to you, but I can't go until you go first."

Elena nodded. "You'd better be right behind me, Chen Wenzhu."

She took a deep breath and jumped the gap, one foot landing on top of the shelf and the other just missing. A hand grabbed her ankle, and she nearly fell over the side, but then Bo was there. He swung his long sledgehammer and dismembered it at the elbow. Elena pulled her leg up and kicked the severed hand off her ankle as if it were a large, horrifying insect.

Zhu waited for Bo to scramble up to where he balanced. The shelf teetered with the two grown men standing on its edge. "Go, xiǎodì," Bo told him.

Zhu shook his head. "You let me go first in the alley. Your turn."

Bo also didn't hesitate. He leapt the gap and joined Elena on top of the shelf against the wall. The force of his jump, however, pushed Zhu's shelf away from the wall. Zhu teetered as it shifted beneath his feet. He dropped down to all fours to maintain his balance, still fighting off the grasping hands of the jiāngshī trapped beneath the shelf. Their increased flailing only added to the shelf's instability, causing it to slowly slide off the tractor.

Zhu had only a second to react as it tottered on top of the churning mass of jiāngshī. Just as it was about to fall to the ground, he jumped, his fingers just managing to grab the top of the delivery truck. He pulled with every ounce of strength he had and climbed onto its roof.

"Zhu!" Elena screamed, reaching for him through the window.

"Xiǎodì!" yelled Bo at the same time.

Zhu didn't have the strength to speak. He waved at his wind team and gestured for them to go on without him. He watched with a sinking feeling as Bo smashed the glass and tried to coax Elena through. When she refused to budge, he lifted her up and forced her through. The last thing Zhu saw was Elena's arm reaching for him before they both disappeared.

"Good man," muttered Zhu, hanging his head. "Take care of her."

He hadn't kept his promise to Elena, but at least she was all right. He was trapped but alive, for now. Part of him wondered if it would be better just to die. He closed his eyes and sat up. They were crowding one side of the truck and pushing against it, reaching mindlessly for him. Zhu considered just jumping down, accepting his fate, and letting them rip him apart. Certainly it was better than starving to death on top of a dusty box truck surrounded by the stench of jiāngshī. He drew his machete. Perhaps it would be better to open his veins.

He stared at the hood of the truck. That's when it hit him. He looked at the other side of the truck and found it empty.

"I hope you left the keys in there, Bo," he muttered.

Zhu took a deep breath and jumped down to the floor. Fortunately, the door was unlocked, and the key was still in the ignition. He muttered a prayer and turned the key. The truck whined several times. A jiāngshī appeared at the passenger side and began to pound the window. Another began to lift itself onto the hood. Several more joined in. A crack exploded and snaked across the windshield.

Zhu gritted his teeth. "Let's go. Let's go. Please start."

Some greater power must have answered his prayer as the engine finally rumbled to life. Zhu punched the accelerator. The truck squealed and came to a sudden stop against the garage door. He ran over a few jiāngshī moving forward, then backed up again. And again. Back and forth. Finally, the door tore off its hinges, and the truck was free.

The truck pulled out of the garage and clipped the corner of a brick building on the other side of the alley. Zhu swerved into a small parking lot, plowing over several more bodies along the way. He turned the truck toward the road, noting the groups of jiāngshī all along the path.

Zhu tried to weave his way between the clusters. A group of them could stop the truck just as easily as a brick wall. He had to escape this area as soon as possible. More importantly, he had to stay off the roads. Unfortunately, there were only a few ways in and out of the village, and all of them would be heavily crowded by jiāngshī and abandoned cars.

The truck ground against the side of a wooden building, collapsing the roof, then rammed aside two other cars as he turned to avoid a small crowd of jiāngshī. It rumbled down the side of a grassy hill and broke a large branch hanging low from a nearby tree before struggling onto a dirt path. He crumpled another car on his way out and finally broke free.

For a second, he considered turning around and going back for Bo and Elena, but a glance over his shoulder told him the jiāngshī were riled up and converging on his position, drawn by the noise and smoke. From buildings and alleys they emerged, shambling toward him with familiar groans and snarls. There was no way he could sneak his way back into the village. If anything, the best thing he could do for his wind team was lead the ones chasing after him as far away as possible. He gave the lumbering vehicle more gas and it rumbled forward.

Zhu had almost reached the outskirts of the village when he came upon a crowd of jiāngshī clustered near the main road and adjacent to a field leading out of the village. He turned sharply right, nearly tipping the truck over as it plowed through the tall grass and the dead. The cabin shook as bodies bounced off the truck.

It came to a stop in a rice field, dipping down abruptly into the mud, nearly causing Zhu to fly through the windshield. He slammed against the glass and bounced violently backward, his head snapping against the headrest. The world swayed and he saw triple of everything.

He blinked several times to fight off the dizziness. "A seatbelt would have been smart," he grumbled. He looked out the driver's side window and saw a jiāngshī wearing a conical hat and plain shirt lurching across the mud toward him.

Zhu was in no condition to fight. He scrambled to the passenger side and threw the door open. He stood a little too fast. The world was still spinning as he stepped out of the truck, and he pitched face-first into the mud. The freezing water bit into his face as he was momentarily submerged. It woke him from his daze, and he pushed himself onto all fours. He checked his duffel and looked around for an escape. Forcing himself up to his knees, Zhu tested his balance. He was still groggy, but everything was beginning to sway slightly less. He wiped the mud off his face and stopped.

Standing close by were two figures, both dressed in heavy country clothing. At first he thought they were jiāngshī. He reached for his machete, then stopped when one of them pulled out a club.

Zhu threw up his hands. "Wait," he pleaded, his words muffled from a mouthful of mud. "Who are you? I need help—"

But Zhu never finished the sentence, as one of the figures walked up and brought the club down across his temple.

4

STRANGER IN A STRANGE LAND

Elena fought Bo for as long as she could. She punched and clawed and slapped, but Bo was a rock, quietly insistent as he dragged her away from the broken skylight. When she nearly squirmed out of his arms, he just picked her up like a sack of rice, switched shoulders, and carried on.

"Put me down. We have to go back for him, asshole! Let me go, *húndàn*." Asshole and húndàn were repetitive, but that was how she'd first learned Mandarin. "We can't abandon him." She cursed a string of expletives in a mixture of Mandarin and English.

He finally put her down, but kept a fistful of her coat in his grasp. "He's gone, Elena. If you go back, you'll be gone as well."

Tears welled in her eyes. She held them back. Elena hadn't cried since the first month of the outbreak, when all she had done was cry. She had promised herself that she was done feeling sorry for herself, that crying didn't do anyone any good, and that the next time she cried, it would be tears of happiness when she saw her family again.

She drew in a deep breath and muttered. "I'm fine now."

Bo didn't let her go. "You promise you won't try to run back?"

She shook her head, muttering under her breath. "I promise, asshole."

"You promise you won't hit me again?"

She stared at the angry lines cutting across his cheek. "I'm sorry about your face."

He shrugged and let her go. He looked thoughtful. "What's an 'asshole'?"

Elena replied with a straight face. "It means 'good friend.'"

He nodded. "I am a very good 'asshole' then."

She sat at the edge of a roof and looked back the way they had come. She slapped Bo's hand away when it hovered near her coat again.

Bo knelt in front of her and clutched her arms with his large hands. He became serious, the usual jolly slow-talking doofus replaced now by someone thoughtful and sober. "Listen, xiǎomèi, I had a big family in Liaoning: wife, children, brothers and sisters, uncles and aunts, and more nephews and nieces than I could count. When the province fell, half of them died the first week. The other half died trying to rescue those who could no longer be rescued." He shook her gently. "Zhu's gone. The best thing we can do is to keep on living in his honor."

"What if he manages to escape?"

"Then he'll find his way back to us. To you."

"But—"

A loud screech shattered the air, followed by a thunderous crack from the direction of the garage. Elena exchanged startled looks with Bo, and the two scampered back the way they had come just in time to see the delivery truck turn the corner and speed away down the street. She flinched as it plowed over jiāngshī like bowling pins and plowed into the wall of a building.

She tugged Bo's sleeve. "Come on."

———

It wasn't hard to track Zhu. All they had to do was follow the wreckage and the tracks. They made their way along the roofs until they ran out of buildings, and then continued down the length of a brick wall that reached the edge of the village. She spied the truck in the distance, tilted forward in a rice field.

Finding the truck was the easy part, but getting to it proved far more difficult. The rice paddy they had to cross was littered with dozens of jiāngshī. It was an open field with no cover to hide in and nowhere for them to climb up to or crawl below. This made the several-hundred-meter trek extremely dangerous. At least at first.

Elena and Bo quickly discovered that this particular rice field was a sunken depression where water pooled in a basin. The water came up to her knees, making it a difficult slog to cross, but it was even worse for the dead. As hard as it was for them to walk across it, the jiāngshī almost seemed stuck in place. It made steering clear of the jiāngshī here relatively easy, although one thing they still had to watch out for were the jiāngshī they couldn't see, the ones completely submerged in the water. It took them an hour to weave their way to the truck with Elena continually prodding the ground ahead of her with her short spear.

It was late in the morning by the time they reached the truck. It had taken them much longer than they had hoped. As soon as they reached the dry part of the field, Elena broke into a sprint. She noticed a jiāngshī stuck in the mud close to the truck futilely walking in place. It faced them with an angry moan, attempted to change directions, and promptly fell flat on its face. She brought the business end of her spear down on its neck as they walked past.

Elena's hopes fell away when Bo swung open the driver's door to find the cabin empty. They found fresh blood on the windshield and seats. Elena circled the truck, cursing at the ankle-deep water. If it had been just a little less, they could have tracked Zhu's footprints.

"At least he's alive," said Bo, looking underneath the truck. "That's something."

Elena bit back her disappointment. Yes, it *was* something. Certainly better than finding a corpse, or worse, Zhu as a jiāngshī. The thought of having to put him down sent chills through her body. He was alive, and that meant everything. He might not even be that badly hurt if he walked away from the accident.

"His duffel is gone," she said.

"Good! He's probably heading back to the Beacon at this very moment."

Elena brightened. That made perfect sense. It had taken them over two hours to reach this field from the garage. Why would Zhu have stuck around? The two of them had moved carefully through the village to circumvent the jiāngshī. What reason did Zhu have to expect them to find him? She would be making her way back home too if she were in his shoes.

Elena looked east toward the horizon. "He'll be following the flags. If we hurry, we can catch up."

Bo looked up at the main concentration of light behind the thick rolling clouds. "It looks like rain again, and the day is half over. Maybe we should hide in the cab until it passes. We can head back first thing in the morning."

Elena shook her head. "No, we leave now. It's still early enough. We can make it to the sanctuary by tonight."

She left no room for objections. Elena knew she was being a little rash, but Zhu wasn't around to disagree, and Bo wasn't exactly the type to argue. She also didn't like the idea of leaving Zhu on his own, no matter how skilled someone was at surviving in the countryside.

They set off for the Beacon immediately. Elena led them out of the rice field and down into a narrow ravine that ran alongside the lone paved road leading out of the village. The trip directly back to the Beacon normally took three days, depending on the weather, but she hoped to make it back by the following evening if they pushed hard. Part of it was because she harbored the hope of catching up to Zhu, but also because they were now one pack down and still had to carry the scavenged supplies home. To make room, they kept just enough food and water for one day's worth of travel.

They used the roads as a guide but also made sure to only follow them from afar. Nearly every single stretch of highway, road, and trail connecting the population centers was cluttered with bumper-to-bumper traffic jams of abandoned cars and wagons. Inside many of the vehicles and immediately surrounding them were jiāngshī who filled up the rest of the roads and spilled out along both sides.

Elena and Bo kept a good fifty-meter distance safely away from the roads, only moving closer if they had to cross it, usually by finding a cable line that passed over the road or through the sewer tunnels that passed underneath. That was why it had taken their wind team so long to make it to Fongyuan after they left the flag paths. It would sometimes take an entire day to cross a road safely in an uncharted area. Fortunately, all the hard work had been done on the initial journey here, and the two simply had to backtrack the way they came following the flags they had planted previously.

The two broke away from the road and waded through a waterlogged field just as the sun was beginning its descent across the sky. The grasses here grew above Elena's head, so she could only see as far as the end of her short spear. It was times like this when she wished she had a real weapon instead of a sharpened broomstick. Zhu had offered to buy her a long knife with some of their points, but Elena valued food and clothing more than a better way of killing the dead. She also wasn't comfortable fighting up close, preferring the range capabilities of her bow and arrows.

It would have been easy for them to get lost, since Zhu usually led the way. Fortunately, they found the first yellow flag dangling from a branch well before they began to lose light. They would have been in serious trouble if they had missed it before dark.

There were dozens of wind teams operating out of the Beacon, continuously working to keep the camp running and the people fed. In the few months since they had started scavenging, the teams had created a system of tying yellow flags to frequently traveled paths to help map the region around the Beacon. It helped cut down on deaths and made it much easier to expand further out on runs.

They followed the flags through the marsh, navigating a maze of reed flowers and clumps of damp earth. The breeze overhead caused the water to ripple and the grass to sway. Sounds of wildlife came alive all around as dusk approached. Elena began to lose focus. A person could stay alert for only so long. She was slightly comforted by the fact that the marked paths had been cleared of jiāngshī many times, because it also meant they were getting close to home.

Bo tapped her on the shoulder and pointed to a jiāngshī hope-lessly trapped within the tall weeds. The poor thing was so water-logged, its gray bloated body was practically sagging off its bones. Elena aimed her spear and gave it a quick poke. The sharp point en-tered through its eye, piercing its head like an overripe melon.

The yellow flags led them out of the marsh and over a craggy hill down the side of a cliff, circumventing several known clusters of jiāng-shī. Elena and Bo reached the end of the rocky hills, crossing a long rope bridge to a thick forest in the valley below. The din of moaning dead flitted up through the foliage. They climbed one of the giant an-cient trees and continued moving from tree to tree using a system of ropes connecting the branches. Jiāngshī from the neighboring village of Duogai had spilled into these woods. Combined with the thick foliage, the ground below was impossible to clear, so Hengyen, the leader of all the wind teams, had devised a different strategy for crossing the forest. It had taken half of the wind teams and most of the surviving military garrison two weeks to plan, cut, and construct the sky bridge. Casualties were high, but it enabled the wind teams to scavenge westward, which was crucial, since it was practically impossible to travel east toward all the large cities.

After some miles had passed beneath their feet, Elena paused and stared at the horizon as she and Bo stepped out of a sewer pipe that ran under the main highway. The fading sunlight on the mist blanketing the green mountains in the distance was breathtaking. It was moments like this that made her heart skip, and she would momentarily forget about the tragedies that surrounded her. China was once again this magical place she had first fallen in love with during a class on Chinese mythology.

Hunan was considered one of the most beautiful provinces with its lush primeval forests, towering mountains, and many meandering rivers. It also held a particularly important place in Chinese history. This region was the backdrop of many legends of tragic heroes, mystical creatures, and celestial beings, as well as the famous Dragon Boat festival. It was the birthplace of the philosopher Wang Fuzhi, the artist Qi Baishi, and the founder of the People's Republic of China, Mao Zedong.

China was the most perfect place in the world for Elena to spend her gap year before starting law school at the University of Texas. She had had big plans of becoming fluent in Mandarin and working in international business in Asia. All her dreams were dashed now, or, at best, put on hold. Elena wasn't sure if this was the end of the world, but it sure felt like it. Her place should have been by her family's side, but she ended up being halfway across the world, far from her loved ones and everything she knew.

She wondered again how her parents back at home were dealing with all this. Elena had not heard any news from the States since the first days of the outbreak. She had managed to get ahold of her mom when reports of the outbreak first came on the news. Her mom didn't think anything of it, and assured Elena that the entire family was safe and symptom-free.

"We can't wait for you to come home," was the last thing her mom had said to her. "We miss you so much, darling."

That was the final time Elena heard from her family. The phone lines and Internet went down shortly after, as did all contact with the outside world. If things back home were anything like what was happening here in China, she feared the worst.

She hated the feeling of being completely helpless. As long as there was an ocean between her and her family, there was nothing she could do to help them or to even find out what fates befell them. For her, that was the absolute most painful part of this ordeal: the not knowing.

"Think positively, girl," she muttered. Her folks probably skipped town at the first sign of trouble and were waiting out the outbreak at the family cabin in Santa Fe, or at worst they were holed up at her uncle Braff's ranch in Marble Falls. Who knows, maybe the United

States was able to get it quickly under control and was already working on a cure. No matter what, she was intent on getting home one way or another. She just had to survive a little longer until rescue arrived, or she found her own way home.

Elena and Bo reached the tiny village of Duogai by sunset, racing ahead as the last sliver of orange rays disappeared over the horizon. Duogai had once been a vibrant fishing village, unique in that half of its buildings sat directly over the waters of a small lake. Now, the streets leading into the village, as everywhere else, were filled with lanes of abandoned cars and packed with jiāngshī in between.

Elena stayed true to her wind-team training. If she and Bo had arrived even twenty minutes later, they probably would have opted to sleep in the trees. They were cutting it close. They followed the yellow flags wide of the road to a shed behind a row of buildings, and climbed up a dumpster onto the shed's roof, then across a row of buildings that continued out onto the lake.

Light from the departed sun bathed the landscape in angry rust. In a few minutes, it would be dark and too dangerous to walk on these uneven, slanted roofs with pipes and broken tiles waiting to trip them. One slip and fall into the green murky waters was certain death. The wind teams had learned from a few of the survivors of Duogai that nearly half of the village had loaded themselves onto boats in the early days of the outbreak in the hopes of waiting it out. Inevitably, death reached them as well, and now half of the village stood at the bottom of this shallow lake. Anyone who fell in would instantly be pulled down to join them.

Elena and Bo reached the second-to-last building nearly a quarter of the way into the lake a few minutes after night had curtained. She went first, lowering herself from the roof to the balcony and then entering into the living room. This was one of the more secure rest stops the wind teams used. Surrounded by water on all sides, they were safe from any crowds of jiāngshī passing through. The windows and doors were barred, giving them the rare place outside of the Beacon where they did not have to constantly look over their shoulders. Desperate survivors were just as great of a threat as the living dead. In fact, owing to the fickleness of human nature, they were often worse.

She did a quick search of the two rooms and returned a little crestfallen. No small part of her had convinced herself that she and Bo were going to drop in here and find Zhu already next to a blazing fire, half-drunk from a bottle of plum wine that he had found somewhere. Just in case, she checked the walls carefully for any markings or drawings of a pig. During the early days of the outbreak, before the two of them reached the Beacon, they created a way to communicate with each other. Zhu's zodiac was a pig, Elena's a horse. If one ever needed to give the other a message, they would draw it on the walls. There were no pigs, so Elena scratched out a rough image of a horse with her small utility knife.

Bo built a small fire at the hearth, and they settled in for the night. The two ate the last of their food in silence, sharing one small flask of potable water. They had barely spoken the entire day, both feeling Zhu's absence acutely.

Elena tried to keep their minds off him. "Hey, Bo, you always say you're from up north. Where exactly?"

"Liaoning Province," he replied, chewing what little food they were having for dinner slowly. "Near the North Korea border."

"How did you end up in Hunan?" she asked.

He shrugged. "The job took me there. I was supposed to be a shift manager, but refused to bribe the right supervisor, so I ended up on the assembly line next to Zhu."

"What did you guys make?"

"Whatever they told us to. The last thing we built was knockoff headphones. It was Zhu's and my job to laminate the letters. That was when he got the idea to study English so he could make more money. Maybe even go to America to do business one day." He beamed a grin. "You could say that I'm the one that hooked you two up, since I was the one who encouraged him to find a tutor, xiǎomèi."

Elena smiled back, but it was a little forced. If Bo took the credit for her and Zhu dating, then Bo should have to take some responsibility for her being trapped here in China right now. No, that wasn't fair to either of them. What happened to her was a consequence of her decisions, her responsibilities, her fault.

The conversation was short-lived. Elena soon found herself fighting sleep, feeling her exhaustion weighing down her consciousness. She didn't even know why she was resisting the rest. She unrolled the sleeping bag she usually shared with Zhu. She knelt before it, pausing a moment before getting in. It looked particularly lonely.

Before she crawled inside, she decided to pray. She hadn't been deeply religious since high school, but end times like this had made her a little spiritually needy. Elena sat on her knees and pressed her palms together.

"Dear Lord, hey, just checking in. We haven't chatted as much as I would have liked, but as you know, things have been crazy. I'm still here though. I'm still fighting, and I have you to thank for that.

"I really need your help right now. Zhu's lost out there somewhere, missing, maybe hurt, maybe worse. You probably have your hands full right now, but I'd really appreciate it if you could do this one favor and look out for him. He's not a believer, but he's a really good guy." She paused, and choked. "He might be all I have left in this world. I don't know what I would do if I lost him."

She clasped her hands even tighter and dug her nails into her flesh. "If you can also take care of Mom and Dad and Robbie, that would mean everything to me. Like, I don't know how Mom can deal with all this. She's such a clean freak and this whole world is such a mess now. I hope she doesn't drive Dad crazy." Her chuckle fell apart into a sob. "And you know Dad feels like he always has to fix things. I hope in your wisdom you keep him safe and don't let him try to do too much. Just survive. And Robbie, just take care of that dummy. Don't let him take stupid risks. He's still a kid. We'll all get through this and be together again soon. Thank you. In Jesus's name, amen." Elena looked off to the side. "One more thing. I'm piling on favors, but please look out for Bo too. He's got a good heart, and he's already lost so much."

The last of her prayers lingered in the air a few moments before fading like wisps into the ether. Elena loosed a long breath and let the silence settle back over the room. It was so dark she couldn't even see the ceiling. Elena had hoped to feel uplifted. The prayer was spoken in earnest, but she somehow still felt hollow. She still felt empty inside. As much as she desperately wanted to believe again, and tried her damnedest to open her heart to God, the dead rising and killing everyone in sight really didn't help matters. Still, it couldn't hurt to try, and she needed all the help she could get not just to stay alive but also to not let her soul fall into despair.

The worn sack was usually snug like a cocoon, even a little claustrophobic. Now, there was too much room and it made Elena miss Zhu more. She tossed and turned for a while and was still awake well after Bo had finally stopped reading his book. They had stayed up too late and were going to suffer for it in the morning. She stared at the ceiling, listening to water lapping against the stilts below. Something, possibly a boat or a plank, was butting up against the wooden beams below the building with a rhythmic thunk. Elena turned for the tenth time and did her best to push away the thoughts of this reality she was trapped in. Stuck in a foreign land. Thousands of miles from home. Surrounded by death and decay.

She tried to keep her spirits up, turning her thoughts to things that made her happy: sunbathing on her daddy's boat, helping Mama set the table, playing the drums in the church band, working at Camp Longhorn in the summer, and going to high school football games on Friday nights. She was camping again, wading in Knaus Spring, dove hunting with Dad and Robbie. She would always have to snap the doves' necks for Robbie if he didn't make a kill shot. All these happy thoughts helped keep her sane and grounded, kept her from falling into despair.

The last thing she remembered before her consciousness faded into oblivion was Zhu sitting across the table from her at their favorite restaurant in Changsha about a month before the outbreak. They had been leaning forward over the table and holding hands, both on the verge of tears. Then, in a moment of impulsive inspiration and love, Elena took out her plane ticket and tore it up.

She next spoke those fateful words that even in sleep brought forth a spike of anger, guilt, and regret. "I'll rebook the flight. I can stay until the end of the summer."

But now, in this little wooden house over a death-filled lake, every ounce of her wished she had made a different choice.

5

THE WELCOME

Zhu's eyes fluttered open. A series of moans escaped his lips. The first one because his senses had returned to him, and he suddenly felt as if someone had hammered an iron spike directly into his brain. The second groan was because he opened his mouth to voice his discomfort and the act of moving his jaw had caused a fresh ripple of pain to wash over him.

Zhu squeezed his eyes shut and bit down on his lips as he waited for the waves of agony to subside, and then assessed his situation. His head pounded and his jaw ached, but nothing felt broken, although he might have a loose tooth. His entire left side was numb and wet.

His wrists were raw and bound together behind his back. Other than that, he was really thirsty. Hungry too. How long had he been out?

Zhu cracked open one eye again and blinked. He was facedown but on his side, with one cheek half-submerged in a shallow puddle. His entire line of sight consisted of mud and the trunk of an old tree. He craned his head toward the sky. It was night. He appeared to be in a field of short weeds, mostly trampled. Panic gripped him. Being out in the open like this at night with the dead all around was basically a death sentence.

Then he remembered what had happened. The two cloaked figures. Survivors! The club. They hit him . . . but why had they left him alive? His blood ran cold as the answer came to him.

Vultures. That was the name for people who refused to join the Living Revolution, who insisted on surviving independently from the Beacon.

Rumors of cannibalism among the vultures were rampant. They must have kept him for their larder.

Fresh fear coiled around Zhu's guts. The potential of death by jiāngshī—and the possibility of becoming one—was a reality he had long come to terms with. However, the thought of being eaten by other people, of becoming food, was magnitudes worse. The jiāngshī were mindless beings, forces of nature like a wildfire or an earthquake. People who willfully ate the flesh of others . . . they were monsters.

Zhu had to escape. He rolled onto his back and sat up. He was in a camp of some sort. A small fire burned just outside his line of sight. He could see the glow and a thin trail of smoke rising into the air. His captors were foolish for setting up camp in the open like this, easy prey for the dead.

He began working on his bonds and was surprised to find it wasn't rope that bound his wrists, but cloth. The knot was tied well. The harder he pulled, the more it cut into his wrists. It didn't take him long to realize his attempts were futile. He searched the ground for something sharp: a rock, a stick, anything. Then he decided to just flee. He preferred to take his chances running into jiāngshī with his hands tied behind his back than stay there as a captive to cannibals.

Zhu got his knees underneath him and scrambled to his feet. He took off, making it about five steps before he heard the sound of chains jingling. Something yanked at Zhu's wrists, nearly dislocating his shoulders as he flew violently back to the ground. He gasped like a fish on land.

There was rustling from behind. Footsteps. Was it cannibals, or jiāngshī? Zhu couldn't tell, not that it would have made any difference. Both boded poorly for his survival. He closed his eyes and stayed still.

He heard two voices, young by the sound of them. They were discussing being hungry. The voices fell to a hush as they approached him.

"Do you think he's a monster?" one of them said.

"Nah. He's skinny like one, but he doesn't look dead."

The footsteps came closer.

"What are you doing?" the first voice said, alarmed. "Bà said don't talk to him. Just put the plate down and go."

A memory flashed into Zhu's head. He was seven or eight; he had wrapped his legs and arms around his yéye's leg as his yéye dragged him into the kitchen with his hands around a white hen's feet. Zhu was wailing and pleading, his screams echoing throughout the farm house.

"What did I tell you about giving them names?" his father had growled, shaking Zhu loose.

"Pick another one," young Zhu had wailed. "Báibái is my favorite."

"They're all your favorite. Now stand still and watch."

Young Zhu had felt the ripples of horror pass through him as his yéye pinned the chicken's neck to the cutting board and raised the butcher knife. The worst was afterward, after Báibái's head had been severed from her body, when the blood had made his yéye's hand slippery and the body had slid from his grasp and begun to run headless around the kitchen, spraying blood in its wake. That image was seared into Zhu's brain.

Back on the forest floor, something sharp poked into his back. Zhu held still.

"What are you doing?" the voice said.

"I think he's dead," the second replied. A boy.

He poked Zhu again. The second time, Zhu rolled toward the voice and kicked his feet out, sweeping the boy's legs from underneath him. He was a teenager, skinny, probably fifteen or so. The other boy was obviously his brother; twelve, if that. The older one fell next to Zhu with a startled cry, and Zhu climbed on top of him, pressing one knee onto the boy's chest and the other on his neck.

He turned to the younger one. "Cut me loose. Let me go or I'll break his neck." The younger boy backed away and looked like he was getting ready to run. "If you go, your brother will be dead by the time you return," said Zhu.

The younger boy drew a small knife. His hands shook. "If you hurt him, I'll kill you."

"Probably," replied Zhu. "But not before I kill your brother. Free me, and everyone walks away. I promise."

"Don't do it, Huangyi," the one under Zhu's neck gurgled. "Run, get help!"

"You leave and your brother dies." Zhu paused, and then glanced at the two brothers. Old memories jogged his head. Now that he thought about it, they looked familiar. He frowned. "Wait a minute. Your names are Huangyi and Huangmang? Do you have a sister?"

Huangmang, the older one with his neck under Zhu's knees, scowled. "How do you know my *jiĕ*?"

A sigh escaped his lips. "I'm Chen Wenzhu. My family ran the convenience store. We had the chicken farm in the back."

Huangyi, the younger one, looked unsure. "*Gē*, what should I do?"

"I left the village over five years ago to work in the city. Huangyi might be too young to remember. I remember he barely came up to my waist." Zhu slowly moved his knee off the boy's neck and lightened the pressure on his chest. "Huangmang, you used to deliver packages of noodles to our store, remember?"

"Yes, the convenience store. I remember it, *shūshu*," said Huangmang, recognition finally dawning. He squirmed out from under Zhu and scrambled to his feet, backing away a bit. "It's good to see you."

"It's all right," Zhu tried to look unthreatening. "It's dangerous out there these days. Can you cut me free?"

"Yes, shūshu."

Zhu stood and turned to offer his binds. "Are there others from the village here?"

The first blow across the back of his head staggered him. The second made his legs go limp. He crashed to the ground face first, his head ringing. He rolled onto his back to face the two and tried to speak. No words escaped his lips.

"Huangyi, go get jiě and the elders," said the older boy.

"What happened? Didn't you say you know him? What did he say his name was again?"

Huangmang shrugged. "I don't care. I'm not taking any chances."

"I—" Zhu began.

"Shut up, húndàn!" Huangmang kicked him in the ribs, doubling him over. "You threaten my little brother? I'll beat you to death!"

Zhu decided to spare himself more injury and stayed silent. Huangyi returned a few minutes later. He brought with him several adults, each of them wielding assorted farming tools. One, however, held a hunting rifle. They dragged him to his feet. A boot to his backside sent him stumbling forward.

The group paraded him through a lightly thicketed area with tall grass dotted by occasional trees. It was a cloudy, moonless, and starless night. The only light shining their way was a small torch the lead man carried. A jiāngshī could step out of the darkness and be upon them before anyone could react. This suggested they were in a secure area. Zhu craned his head around. The group did appear relaxed. They had to think they were safe, but how was that possible? Even a veritable fortress like the Beacon was surrounded by walls. His investigative glance was rewarded with a sharp rap across the back of the head.

They entered a large clearing lined with rows of tents and makeshift wooden sheds. A bonfire was dying in the middle of what looked like a public sitting area. A pen on one side kept several dozen hogs, geese, and a lone, bony cow. There was an expansive garden on the other that looked well tended.

Several people sitting near the fire and at the table stood up, their gazes following him as he was led deeper into the camp. The crowd grew until they reached a large tent adjacent to the dining area. Two men and a woman were waiting, probably the village elders. All three looked as if they had just been awoken, and none seemed pleased about it. Zhu was shoved roughly into one of the chairs.

The elder on his left, a scrawny bald man with a lumpy head, yawned and spoke irritably. "I thought we were going to decide the intruder's fate in the morning."

"We were," the man in the center replied. Unlike his associate, he had a full head of long white hair and a beard to match. "He attacked two of our boys when they went to feed him."

"That makes our decision easy," the bald one remarked. "Just put a spike through his head and be done with it."

"Why did Jincai bring him into the grove anyway?"

"He drove a truck right up to the entrance. Jincai didn't know what to do with him."

"We're not killers," said the woman for the first time. She was the oldest, with a bent back and thinning gray hair tied in a bun. She also looked the most alert of the three. "One of the boys says this man claims to be from the village."

The hairy old man squinted. "I don't recognize him."

"I left for Changsha five years ago," Zhu said quickly. "I'm old Chen's son."

The three studied him dispassionately. The bald one crossed his arms and turned to the others. "Did Chen have a boy? I thought he had two girls."

"You're thinking of Chen the butcher. He had three girls," said the woman. "There was also Chen who ran the store."

The three began to squabble as if they were playing a game of mahjong.

"Wasn't Chen the one who ran the gambling ring?"

"No, that was Jiurang."

"Who is Chen then?"

The bald one shrugged. "Does it matter if he's from the village or not? Jincai says he's from the Beacon. If we let him go, he will lead soldiers back to us."

All three seemed to agree on that. They were still contemplating his fate when someone new nearly took the decision out of their hands. A young woman dragging one of the boys by the wrist stormed into the tent. There was murder in her eyes as she shook a finger at him. "Huangyi, is he the one?"

The younger boy, eyes wide like a startled rabbit, only nodded dumbly.

Before Zhu could open his mouth, the woman lunged at him. He stiffened when the cold tip of a blade pressed against the soft part of his throat, breaking skin. "You threaten to hurt my brother? I'll kill you." She was about to plunge it deeper and solve all their troubles when her eyes flared. "Wait, I know you."

It took a moment in the dim light for everything to click into place in Zhu's head. The large eyes, the slightly crooked mouth, the thin oval face. His jaw dropped, and he found himself at a loss for words, even though his life depended on what he said next. He finally managed one.

"Meili?"

6

THE BEACON
OF LIGHT

Elena waved, and the brightly garbed men and women waved back. The Heaven Monks were standing on a crop of boulders near the edge of the forest corralling a group of bound jiāngshī into a clearing. Their order was an offshoot Taoist sect that had risen from the shattered remains of the old world. Several groups of them operated in the area around the Beacon, and could regularly be seen herding jiāngshī like cattle. Nobody knew exactly what the monks did with them, but as long as they were helping thin the dead's ranks, nobody cared.

One of the monks, the leader by the looks of it, put his hands together and bowed. Elena bowed back. There were at least three or four sects of Heaven Monks operating in the area. She was pretty sure she had run into this particular cluster before. Zhu knew all of them by sight and was on a first-name basis with all their leaders. He was affable like that, always quick to make a friend.

Survivors operating outside the control of the government were technically illegal, but the Beacon tolerated the Heaven Monks because they helped keep the yellow-flag paths clear of jiāngshī. Once, during a particularly bad jiāngshī storm from the south, the Beacon had even opened their doors to give the monks shelter.

Elena and Bo continued on, walking on top of an eight-foot stone wall that followed the road for several kilometers. The jiāngshī in this area were noticeably sparser, which was a sure sign that they were finally close to home. A few of the dead ambled up to the wall and grasped at them, but the wall was just tall enough to keep anyone standing on it out of reach, and there weren't enough jiāngshī around to knock it down.

Elena and Bo reached the end of the wall by midmorning. They jumped from the bridge onto a row of vans and trucks, then leapfrogged to a utility pole. They climbed up the pole using the notched grooves as a ladder. From there, they moved from pole to pole, walking on wooden planks placed over the cables. The wind teams had fondly nicknamed this segment Lightning Lane. It took them another hour or so to reach the top of the hill overlooking a large flat plain next to the Yuanjiang River.

Along the shore of the river was a series of ugly metallic buildings that rose several stories into the air. They were built on the site of a water-purification plant that the military had taken over during the first months of the outbreak to safeguard the fresh water. Since then, the plant had grown into a full-blown military camp and was now the seat of government for the Hunan Province. At least, whatever was left of it. Dozens of container crates stacked two and three high lined the perimeter.

They had finally reached the Beacon of Light.

"Home sweet home," she muttered. They weren't out of the woods yet. "Come on."

The final stretch of the journey was over the razed land that surrounded the Beacon. They had to scale a large transmission tower and ride a makeshift cable transport into camp. Elena was silent throughout the ten-minute trip over the aptly named Charred Fields.

Below her was a burned-out stretch of land with a series of deep trenches cut into it. It looked like a battlefield at the gates of hell, the site of a great war between the living and the dead. One which seemed destined to last forever.

Jiāngshī, attracted by the sounds and lights of the settlement, converged on the Beacon from every direction at all times of the day. They would be met with barricades and teams of spearmen who filtered the dead into the trenches where they could be safely killed from higher ground. Once the jiāngshī were neutralized, the spearmen would close out certain tributaries so cart teams could retrieve the bodies and bring them to one of the burn piles that dotted the landscape. This had to be done every day from sunup to sundown, and was often assigned as punishment for petty crimes, disloyalty to the Living Revolution, or falling short of quota. The last one was especially pertinent to Elena. Zhu's wind team had so far managed to avoid cart duty, but they had had to take up spear duty twice now in as many months.

The rusty gate from the cable transport swung open once it came to a stop over the perimeter wall. The two climbed out and stepped onto the container crate. The metal parapet was a swarm of activity. Soldiers of the Living Revolution manned the fortifications as if they were in some medieval castle repelling invaders. In a way, that wasn't far from the mark.

Men and women were positioned every ten feet. Half were watchers who used bullhorns to call out any jiāngshī who had escaped the trenches. The other half were armed with bows. Children, some as young as seven, acted as runners, carrying messages, water, and provisions. Some of the teenagers and older citizens were sent to the fields to strip valuables from corpses and to reclaim spent arrows. Everyone had a role, and everyone did their part in this human hive. Always for the good of the people.

Overhead, a loudspeaker blared slogans of encouragement, and not a few veiled threats about responsibility and guardianship. The contemporary China Elena had known was nothing like the one she had learned about in books. It was modern and exciting and fueled by innovation and capitalism. Since the outbreak, however, she had seen the government and its people retreat and entrench into defensive rhetoric; habits that had birthed this nation were now wielded as a method of control.

When order began to slip, the government in Beijing had declared a second revolution, or a Living Revolution in this case. It was every citizen's duty to combat the threat of the jiāngshī by working together to fight off the infection plaguing the Land Under Heaven. Or something like that. Mandarin could get awfully flowery, and Elena's grasp of the language hovered somewhere around second-grade level. Zhu had interpreted it for Elena when the message was broadcast on the loud speaker.

Elena and Bo walked across a construction catwalk and joined the line of people waiting to go down a set of stairs to the ground. She began scanning for Zhu, although the odds of spying him among the mass of humanity below were slim. Still, she held on to the hope of finding him in line at the quotamaster's or eating at the mess hall.

The main encampment within the Beacon looked as one would expect in this new, terrifying world: part military base, part refugee camp, part prison, and entirely downtrodden and miserable. The majority of the settlement was a combination of tents and wooden sheds that wouldn't have been out of place in the worst slums in the world. It was said that the Beacon housed approximately three thousand people inside an area spanning three football fields.

Shipping containers made up the remainder of the more permanent structures. The side of the settlement near the river held the water purification systems and the few permanent concrete buildings occupied by the government. That was where the military and provincial secretary had set up the regional capital of Hunan after the old provincial capital, Changsha, fell to the jiāngshī.

Elena left the catwalk and threaded her way through the thick crowds along the muddy paths. Smoke, sulfur, and benzene filled her nostrils. Clusters of people huddled around burning metal drums. A loud tapping like someone hammering a pipe in one block was replaced by the sounds of hissing steam and the cry of an infant at the next.

Above that cacophony, the loudspeaker barked the updated Mao-isms, words of encouragement, and sayings straight from the glory days of the Revolution, blaring through tinny speakers like a late-night infomercial.

> Let one million flowers bloom to put to rest our restless dead!
> To volunteer to fight for the Living Revolution is a sacred duty.
> Birth more children. Every life you bring to the world is another blow
>   to the dead.

It sounded a lot more lyrical in its original tongue. Elena would have thought many of the sayings were poetic, even beautiful, if they hadn't kept blaring these slogans nonstop at every odd hour of the day. After a while, it became mostly background noise, but it was effective. Whenever a particular slogan came on, her brain automatically recited it in her head. It was what had made her ask Zhu to train to be on a wind team rather than stay in the Beacon all day doing other tasks that they considered more "appropriate" for a foreigner.

The two joined the queue at the quotamaster's tent. There were twenty or so wind teams ahead of her. Again, no sign of Zhu. She closed her eyes and tapped her foot impatiently as the line crawled forward. The last thing anyone felt like doing after spending days, if not weeks, out in the wild scavenging was to return to the Beacon and wait in the queue for the quotamaster to judge how well they had done. It was almost always less than expected, never mind the fact that every single one of them had risked their lives to get these supplies to keep the settlement running. All Elena wanted to do now was drop her scavenge off, get something hot to eat, and finally take a hot shower. Hell, she would have settled for a lukewarm one at that.

A small commotion erupted farther down the path. Several wind teams huddled their heads together and pointed. The crowds parted and saluted. Shouts of *dàgē* rang through the air. That could only mean one person. Ying Hengyen appeared a few seconds later. His face was grim and haggard, and his left arm was in a makeshift sling. He must have just returned from a hard time in the wild.

The rest of his elite wind team looked even worse. Their clothes were torn and bloodied. Whatever they had just gone through must have been brutal. That was when Elena realized what everyone around them was whispering. Hengyen's wind team was short a member.

"It's Linnang," said Bo quietly. "He just transferred in two weeks ago."

"I wonder who will take his spot," she replied.

Even in his condition, Hengyen took the time to stop every few steps to greet familiar faces, patting people on the shoulders and shaking hands like a politician working a line. Elena caught herself standing a little taller, a little straighter. She was intimidated by Hengyen. He had trained many of the wind-team leaders and was revered among the ranks. She had only met him once, when Zhu had brought her to him to ask for permission to train her for his team.

To Elena's surprise, he stopped at her and Bo. "Bo, you're looking healthy."

Bo sucked in his gut and straightened up. "A nourished body promotes a strong back, dàgē."

Hengyen grinned, patting him on the shoulder. "Nourish it too well and you end up just pulling your own weight." He continued on to Elena. He broke into passable English. "And how are you this day, Elena Anderson?"

"I'm well. Thank you for asking." She switched to Mandarin. "I'm ready to do my part."

He nodded and looked to either side of them. "Where's Wenzhu?"

Elena hesitated. "I don't know" did not sound like the right thing to say.

"He'll be along," said Bo quickly. "He had to take care of something out in the wild."

Hengyen did not look satisfied with their answer. "It's never wise to get separated. Please let him know I wish to speak with him."

"Yes, dàgē," both of them replied.

Hengyen continued down the line. When he was out of earshot, Bo leaned in to her. "What do you think he wants to talk to Zhu about?"

She shrugged.

"I bet Hengyen wants him to take Linnang's spot on his team," said Bo.

"Good for him." Elena bit her lip. She didn't really mean it. She had never considered being part of any wind team other than Zhu's. That wasn't what she had signed up for. He wouldn't abandon her to join Hengyen's wind team. Would he?

There was nothing as close to a group of rock stars at the Beacon as Ying Hengyen's team. Considered the elite of all the wind teams, each member was given a bedroom, allocated the best weapons, and all the food they wanted. Most importantly, they were exempt from quota.

Half the people desperately wanted to join Hengyen's wind team. The other half wanted nothing to do with it. The downside to joining the best wind team in the Beacon of Light was that it got the most difficult assignments and, as a result, turnover was high. Elena was in the latter camp, not that she was remotely qualified. It wasn't worth throwing herself in danger like that just for the best weapons and all-you-can-eat buffets. Now, if they threw in unlimited hot showers . . .

It took a little over half an hour before Quotamaster Ming got around to rummaging through their things. She and Bo stood there patiently while the seemingly always-sweaty stout man with the receding hairline and generous midsection opened their duffels, neatly stacking the contents onto the table. As he counted the cans of oil and double-A batteries, his fingers on one hand waggled in the air as if he were casting some magic spell. Zhu had told her the first time she witnessed those strange movements that the quotamaster was doing math with an imaginary abacus. When Ming finished going through the bag, he signaled to his assistant, who scrawled some numbers on a small whiteboard.

Ming next moved on to Bo's bag. He gave the power drill a dismissive look but raised his eyebrow when he pulled out the dremel and the alternator. He squinted and held the alternator up for a few seconds, and then fixed on the two with his beady eyes hiding behind his thick tinted glasses, no doubt wondering where they scored these supplies. Finally, he did more math with his fingers and then jotted a number on the whiteboard.

"Not bad," he said, grudgingly.

Sure enough, Zhu hadn't steered them wrong. It was a better-than-expected scavenge for them. The supplies from the mechanic's garage fetched a lot of points, enough to keep them afloat for a while. Maybe even buy some fruit. She also needed a new pair of boots, which really meant she could trade her existing pair in for something a little less worn down from storage.

After a quick meal on a bench in the general mess hall, Elena and Bo parted ways. Curfew was only an hour away, and neither had the points to go anywhere that stayed open after dark. Elena went on to the wash tent, using some of her hard-earned points for warm water, and luxuriated for the entire four minutes allocated her. She dragged her time out for as long as possible, waiting until the water attendant cut her off, and the shower reluctantly released the last few warm, precious drops.

The temperature had dropped drastically by the time Elena was dressed. A light drizzle had passed through between the time she reached the Beacon and left the wash tent, leaving the paths a little muddier than usual. She sighed. It was as expected. Between the rainy season and the cramped living conditions, there wasn't even a way to keep the dirt and grime off her in the short jaunt from the wash tent to her pod.

Elena hurried on, taking a roundabout way near the perimeter container walls where the traffic was slightly lighter. She passed by a group of children standing in a neat row, each wielding dull wooden broomsticks. Tied in front of them were five jiāngshī with their jaws torn off and their hands bound behind their backs.

An instructor carrying a stick walked back and forth behind them, barking *"Lān! Ná! Zhà!"* over and over again. The children, ranging from seven to twelve, practiced thrusting with the broomsticks, striking the dull ends into the bodies of the jiāngshī in time with the instructor's commands. One of the jiāngshī, its flesh more intact than the others', lunged forward, causing the little boy in front of it to yelp and drop his stick. The jiāngshī had moved so abruptly that Elena caught herself reaching for her dagger. The poor boy was given a sharp rap across the shoulders for dropping his weapon. She shook her head sadly as she passed. This was the new normal, at least in this part of the world.

Elena returned to her pod, which was in one of the dozens of container crates that had been converted into living quarters. The pods were stacked five-high along both the side and back walls of each container, looking an awful lot like the cages used at the pet shelter she had volunteered at on weekends a lifetime ago. A few of the women were playing mahjong near the front of the container. They paid her little more attention than a slight shift of the eyes. Two were huddled around a small television playing a soap opera recorded on old VHS tapes. They had played it so many times Elena could almost recite the entire series. Competing music was playing from a couple of cages. Everyone else was either already sleeping or reading books or magazines. Old gossip magazines were especially popular, for some reason, despite the fact that the subjects of the las-civious articles were likely dead and gone.

She plugged her electronic devices into the charger and scribbled a point on a piece of paper. They were technically on the honor sys-tem in the Beacon, but everyone closely watched everyone else. After all, not paying your points was a betrayal to the Living Revolution. Getting reported for cheating could put you on Charred Field duty or worse.

Elena threaded her way through the crowd toward the back of the container, wishing that some of these women would spend more of their points on showers. Her pod was on the top row in the far corner. The lower-level cages were given to the older women who had trou-ble climbing up. It was always a pain to get into her cage, but being in the corner afforded her a little more privacy than most.

Her pod was just wide enough to lay flat on her back and *almost* long enough for Elena to stretch her legs out. She pitied tall people. A thin mattress stuffed with hay served as bedding, and a small chest at the head of her pod held all her possessions in the world. Her posses-sions on *this* side of the world, she corrected herself. She had a bed-room and garage full of stuff back at home.

Elena tossed and turned on her rumpled mattress, trying to find a comfortable position. She stared at the lone picture of her family on one of their boating trips taped to the wall of the cage and fought off the tears welling in her eyes. No, she hadn't lost it yet, and she wasn't going to. "Soon," she whispered, stroking her mom's face. "Just have to hold on a little longer."

The yellow lights on the ceiling blinked twice. A message

blared over the loudspeaker about how important sleep was for the soul, and how it was everyone's duty to rest their bodies in service of the Living Revolution. A few minutes later, someone stopped by their container and slid the main door shut, enveloping them in darkness.

7

THE LIVING REVOLUTION

What about Lankui?"

"The old man?" Hengyen shook his head. "He got pulled off wind teams after two months when they discovered he had an engineering degree. They chained him to a desk at the purification plant before he could lodge a protest."

"Pity. He was a savvy windrunner. Only person who would rather scavenge than work in an office and sleep in a bed every night," said Wangfa.

"He'll do more good for the Living Revolution behind that desk." Hengyen continued down his mental checklist. "What about Hufeng?"

Wangfa shook his head. "She's pregnant. Secretary Guo will never allow it."

"'Women hold up half the sky,'" Hengyen quoted. "It should be up to her to decide."

"Stop quoting Chairman Mao at me all the time."

Both men stared at the opposite wall.

"I miss air-conditioning," Wangfa muttered, wiping his brow.

Hengyen, fanning himself with a cardboard flap torn off a box, nodded. It was a particularly humid day and the settlement felt like a huge, dirty sauna. The clothing on his back was damp. The blanket he slept under was damp. Even the cook-fires smoldered from the moisture.

The building they were in had working air-conditioning, but it was only on in specific rooms. Hengyen had a sneaking suspicion that this was the *real* reason Wangfa had offered to accompany him to the meeting. The two sat on a bench along the wall of a barren hallway. The squat two-story building had been the purification plant's administration center. It now served as the capital building for all of Hunan Province. It had ten rooms, and only half were in use, by order of the secretary.

"What about one of the Xing twins, the nice one?" asked his second in command.

"There's only one twin left. The other one died two days ago while trying to siphon fuel from a van when a jiāngshī crawled out from under it and bit his ankle."

"Which one died?"

"Luhong."

Wangfa grimaced. "That was the nice one. His brother is a terrible person."

"From what I hear, he's even worse now."

The door next to them opened, and a stick-thin man in a pressed suit with large-rimmed glasses and slicked-back hair emerged. Hengyen and Wangfa jumped to their feet and saluted.

Secretary Guo smiled and patted Hengyen's shoulder warmly. "Comrade, it's good to see you've returned safely. Come in, come in."

The secretary led them into his office, a spacious and well-kept room. Both men sucked in a deep breath of the cool air.

The office housed an ornate wooden desk and a beautiful traditional lounge set tucked in the corner. On the wall behind the desk were portraits of Chairman Mao and Jiang Zemin, the current—and possibly last—president of China, whose whereabouts were currently unknown.

It was rumored that during the evacuation of Changsha, the provincial governor had ordered his entire office, furniture included, loaded onto a plane. The governor and his staff, along with most of the senior party officials in the province, had perished when the jiāng-shī overran the airport. One of the dead got sucked into the turbine while the plane was trying to take off. The plane never left the tarmac, and those on board never deplaned.

Guo, who in normal times was far down the line of succession, was now the acting provincial governor of Hunan. He had rallied the remnants of the military and the government and led them to the Beacon. He had instilled hope and order, and kept the settlement together when almost everyone else had given up. Secretary Guo kept the idea of the Living Revolution alive by persistently hammering the message into every person's heart. Hengyen admired his single-mindedness and tenacity, even if he didn't agree with every decision the secretary made.

Even though the secretary was technically only the *acting* provincial governor and did not hold rank in the People's Liberation Army, he was a great man, completely loyal to China, the Communist Party, and to the Living Revolution. It was important for everyone at the Beacon to know that the government was still in control. It was Guo's idea to reach back to their roots during this crisis and reclaim the old party dogma to inspire and guard the people.

The secretary circled around the desk and sat. He plucked a slice of orange from a plate and peeled the skin off, then slid the plate over to his guests. "Please, sit, sit. What news from Changde?"

One of the first things Guo had done was allow military protocol to fall by the wayside. Most of the survivors here were not military, and the secretary felt it was more important to inspire loyalty and strengthen bonds than it was to maintain a strict command structure. Hengyen did not necessarily agree with the decision but understood its wisdom, so did as ordered. He still saluted the secretary, however. He would always salute.

"Secretary," he began. "It's as we feared. Something has stirred the jiāngshī from Changde, and they are now moving en masse. A large group of jiāngshī is sweeping down the main highway. They're traveling at roughly a quarter to one kilometer a day, so they'll reach us by month's end."

Guo at first didn't seem to register the seriousness of the matter.

He looked thoughtful as he picked up another slice of orange and peeled away the skin. "This sounds serious. How many more windrunners do you require to turn it aside? We can always enlist some of the settlement's guards to assist."

Hengyen shook his head. "There are not enough windrunners or guards in the entire Beacon of Light for the job. Sir, the mass of jiāngshī is enormous. There are hundreds of thousands of dead. The largest typhoon I have ever witnessed."

"Then we'll have to just redirect some of our efforts to improve our fortifications."

Blunt honesty was often the best course of action. Hengyen spoke in a measured tone. "Once that typhoon reaches us, it'll smash through our fortification within hours."

"What are our options? Can we fight them off?"

Hengyen shook his head. "There are simply too many. If we put every man, woman, and child in the Living Revolution to work, it would not be sufficient. Our only hope of survival is to abandon the Beacon of Light."

The realization on the secretary's face came slowly and drastically as his eyes widened and tension etched deep lines into his face. Hengyen could almost see his thoughts spinning frantically in his head. Guo wiped his hands on a red handkerchief and pointed at the map on his desk. "The Beacon is a kilometer away from the highway. What are the chances the typhoon misses us completely?"

"None, Secretary," said Wangfa. "The dead are so numerous they span the horizon. Add the noise and lights from the settlement, the jiāngshī are bound to find their way to our doorstep."

"What if we were to shut the settlement down and keep silent until the typhoon passes?"

Wangfa made a face. "It will take weeks for this typhoon to pass. We would starve long before then."

"They will also be attracted to the jiāngshī already in the Charred Fields," added Hengyen. "Even if we wait out the main body, we'll have a sea of dead surrounding us. We have no other choice."

A long silence passed as Guo studied the map. He finally spoke, "Comrades, do you know why I named this run-down facility the Beacon of Light?"

"No, Secretary." In truth, they did know, but both men knew it wasn't their place to answer rhetorical questions.

"The people look toward *us* for inspiration and guidance in these perilous times," the secretary recited for probably the hundredth time. "Our purpose here is not just to eke out a meager existence until the cursed dead claim our lives. We are not here to scavenge for scraps from the corpses of our cities. We exist to stand tall. The Beacon is the symbol of the Living Revolution. We are the ones who draw the line. Our struggle, our very existence inspires hope in every survivor as far as the eye can see. We must show the people that the Living Revolution has not succumbed to this plague. We must show them hope, inspire them to strengthen their resolve, not to surrender to the darkness. We fight until our last breaths for the Land Under Heaven."

The secretary was a true patriot. His words were spoken directly into their souls, as if to lift their very hearts. Hengyen noticed Wangfa nodding along with every proclamation. Ever the skeptic, Hengyen was not so easily swayed. It was a good speech, although he personally thought that Guo would do well to vary it up a little. As flowery and inspirational as the secretary's words were, it didn't change the facts. Numbers did not lie. Reality defeated hope every time.

"I understand the significance of the Beacon," Hengyen said slowly. "With all due respect, Secretary, the issue is not the people's dedication to the Living Revolution." He paused, choosing his words. "The Beacon is indefensible against these numbers. Even if we manage to keep the typhoon off our walls, it will simply surround us and starve us out. These are impossible odds."

"Impossible is a symptom of a lack of creativity," declared the secretary.

Hengyen bit his lip and struggled to keep his expression even. "You are right that it is more than just these walls and buildings. These we cannot move. The Beacon is the people who reside inside. We can move and save the people. Hope and inspiration may sustain their hearts during the outbreak, but we need to save lives."

Wangfa was staring at the map. "What if we find a way to turn the typhoon aside? Change the course of their flow?" He traced his finger along the highway and river. "If we destroy the bridges and roads here, here, and here, the typhoon may wrap around the Yuanjiang River and flow south instead, avoiding the Beacon entirely."

Secretary Guo's face brightened immediately. "There you go, Comrade Wangfa. Find a solution. Surrender is not an option. We will use whatever resources the Beacon has at our disposal to defeat the jiāngshī."

Hengyen was dubious. After months of fighting the jiāngshī, he knew better than to try to divert a mass of this size. Wangfa's idea had a low chance of success. Even worse, it would cost them valuable time and resources they could otherwise direct toward evacuating.

It was Hengyen's solemn duty to follow orders, but it was also his duty to avert disaster. He stood his ground. "Secretary Guo, you've entrusted me with keeping the people safe—"

"Enough," snapped Guo. "My decision is final. We are not abandoning the Beacon. The Living Revolution will not cede more ground to the dead. You will find a way, comrades. We cannot afford to lose the water-purification plant."

That was the crux of the problem. Clean water was difficult to supply for the thousands of souls within the Beacon's walls. In many parts of the country, the rivers were tainted by the bodies of the dead. Still, what was the point of clean water if everyone who had access to it was dead or starving?

Guo must have noticed the look on Hengyen's face. He looked toward the door, as if checking to see if anyone was outside eavesdropping. "This is confidential. This information cannot be leaked until we verify it, but . . ." He leaned in. "We've received a signal from the Central Military Commission. It's taken them months to recover from the initial shock of the outbreak, but party radio channels have communicated that the People's Liberation Army has regrouped and is finally beginning to stem the tide of the dead."

Both Hengyen and Wangfa were stunned. The two men gasped and exchanged a quick, wide-eyed glance before remembering their place. After months of being completely in the dark, Hengyen's staunch, unfailing faith in the country had started to crack. "Is it true? How far away is the main body? When will they reach us?"

"It's true," said Guo. "But there are many thousands of kilometers and millions of jiāngshī between us and the People's Liberation Army. The CMC is reclaiming the country province by province. It will take some time before they reach us, but help is coming. Until then, we must remain resolute." He came around from behind his desk and put his hands on Hengyen's shoulders. "In times of difficulties, we must not lose sight of our achievements, of what we have built here at the Beacon of Light. Comrade Ying Hengyen, you are the hero of this settlement, the living embodiment of the Beacon of Light. Everyone here admires and respects you. They follow your lead and stand by your side in battle. This typhoon now threatens to snuff out the Living Revolution. It is our solemn and patriotic duty to stand against this tide of darkness to keep this light shining for future generations. Can you do this for your people?"

Hengyen had no other choice. Reconnecting with the main body of the army would change everything. He glanced down at the map again. "Perhaps if we were to blow these two bridges and block off these roads here, Wangfa's plan may have a chance. However, we have to be careful not to corral them into the gorge. The dead move like water, and all rivers flow to the path of least resistance. We block one section and the dead may flow directly to a path leading to the Beacon."

"I leave the planning to you, Hengyen," said Guo, walking them to the door. "You will have the Beacon's every resource at your disposal."

Hengyen saluted. "Thank you, Secretary."

No sooner had they left the office and Guo's earshot, than Hengyen stopped Wangfa in his tracks. "What was all that about?"

"Sir? I don't understand." The expression on his second in command's face said otherwise.

"Next time you want to suggest a plan, run it by me first."

"My apologies," replied Wangfa. "It was a moment of inspiration. I did not mean to speak out of turn."

If they had been back in the Falcon Commando Unit, there would have been severe repercussions. But they weren't. Good soldiers were rare these days, and taking initiative should have been commended, not punished. It wasn't a bad plan either, just one that was due more diligence before being brought to the secretary.

"Let's meet this afternoon to go over the details," he replied.

Wangfa nodded. "Have you decided on Linnang's replacement?"

"Prepare more names for me," Hengyen ordered as he walked to the door. He wouldn't have minded finding a cooled office and staying indoors for the rest of the day, but he was hungry. As he stepped outside, a curtain of humidity blasted him. He ignored the drops of sweat that began to pour down the sides of his face.

As much as his stomach growled, Hengyen took his time, making sure his steps were calm and measured. His role was to ensure the security of the Beacon, and to be present for the people he protected. If people saw the head of security in a hurry, they would automatically assume the worst. The people were skittish enough. He made sure to make eye contact with the other residents, giving a reassuring smile here or a wave there. He never wanted to appear unapproachable or too important for the people he worked alongside of to foster the seeds of the Living Revolution. Cries of "Dàgē!" filled his ears. Several came to shake his hand. A vendor offered him sweets. A woman brought her child to meet him. It filled Hengyen's soul to see the people alive and vibrant. It always did a soldier's spirits good to know what and who it was he was defending.

The walk also helped him clear his mind and gather his thoughts. His father used to fondly say that wandering legs could unravel problems that a focused mind could not. Hengyen had found this true whenever he was faced with a problem. By the time Hengyen reached the cafeteria, he had found an answer to at least *one* of his problems.

He greeted the cooks by first name, which was a trick he had learned early in his military career. The cooks especially appreciated it, and showed it with bigger helpings. Not that it really mattered for someone in his position, but old habits were hard to break. There was never a reason to break good habits.

He sat down at a table reserved for officers and party members at the end of the tent. A girl he didn't recognize—she couldn't be more than seven or eight—brought him a plate that was easily three regular rations' worth. It was almost embarrassing. He thanked her, and then whistled for her to come back when she turned to leave. He took the guava and two buns from his plate and held them out. The hunger was raw in her eyes, but she refused shyly.

Hengyen winked. "Our little secret. Take some home to your folks if you like." He instantly regretted those words. There were too many orphans at the Beacon. It was unkind of him to bring it up, in case her parents were among the dead. The little girl didn't seem to mind as she accepted his gifts and stuffed a bun into her mouth.

"Thank you, dàgē," she said, through full cheeks.

Hengyen watched the girl leave to continue her work. It must be difficult for someone to have to serve food to others when they were themselves so hungry. He had just about finished his meal and was reviewing the previous day's quota report when Elena Anderson came in for lunch. Seeing her reminded him of the other problem he had found a solution to during his stroll.

He glanced down at his leftovers. He honestly couldn't eat another bite. After months of eating half rations, a body got used to the smaller portions. Still, wasting food at the Beacon was practically a crime. He sighed and stuffed the rest into his mouth quickly, then hurried over to the other end of the tent.

Elena Anderson was sitting alone staring at her camera when Hengyen arrived at her table. "May I join you, Ms. Anderson?" he said in his broken English.

She looked up and froze before finding her voice and replying in her native tongue. "Oh, of course, Windmaster. I'm sorry. Please, sit."

Hengyen switched back to Mandarin. He knew just enough English to ask to use the bathroom, demand surrender, and to request to be taken to the Chinese embassy. "I reviewed your salvage from yesterday. Ninety-two points. Nicely done."

"Thank you," she replied, blushing. "Wenzhu was the one who found the spot."

"Has he returned yet?"

Elena shook her head. He could see the strain around her eyes. Something was wrong. "Is he in trouble?" she asked.

"On the contrary," he replied. "I have an opportunity for him. As you probably know by now, I have an opening on my wind team. I think Wenzhu would make a fine addition."

She hesitated, not looking as if she was taking the news well. "I thought your wind team was only for those in the military."

"It was," he admitted, "but with everything going on, there aren't many soldiers left. In any case, I prefer brightness and competence to military experience." He paused. "Will that be a problem?"

Elena's face had tightened even more, which was all he needed to know about what she thought of his offer. The two windrunners were close, too close. They should have been separated and put on different teams, but it hadn't been a problem yet, and there was already enough sadness and distress going around that Hengyen wasn't in a hurry to add to it. Still, it was probably for the best.

"No problem at all," she said carefully. "I'm sure Wenzhu will be honored."

Hengyen stood up. "Please let him know that I would like to speak with him."

"Wait," Elena reached out and grabbed his wrist. Just as quickly, she let go. "I need to beg a favor."

There was something about her tone. "I'm listening."

"I know we just returned from a scavenge yesterday, but I'd like to go back out tomorrow."

"Three days minimum between scavenges," replied Hengyen. "That's the rule. While I commend your diligence, team exhaustion is a real danger. Every wind team we lose deprives the Beacon of an important resource."

She looked apprehensive. "Actually, I would also need to be exempt from quota for this trip."

Hengyen sat back down. "What's wrong?"

Elena told him about her team's last scavenge. She claimed not to know why Zhu had chosen that particular village. Two days' journey was the absolute limit for most teams. Three led to diminishing returns. Hengyen came to a conclusion as soon as she told him about the empty truck in the rice field.

"I'm sorry," he said gently. "I don't need to tell you how dangerous the field is. If Zhu hasn't returned by now, he's likely passed. He could have died anywhere."

"I just want to go back and search the village," she said. "Just a few days. I know the exact flag path he would take. I want to check out some of the surrounding sanctuaries. If we don't find him after a few days, then I'll accept that he's gone."

Hengyen considered her request. He respected her desire to search for her missing teammate, even if it was for the wrong reasons. He could also tell Elena wasn't one to let things go. However, allowing a wind team to return without meeting quota set a bad precedent. "This village where Zhu disappeared is the same as where you found the ninety-two points?"

"Yes, dàgē."

Hengyen drummed the table with his fingers. "Did you clean out the scavenge site or is there more?"

"Much more, but we attracted several jiāngshī on our way out."

"Can you clear it?"

Elena hesitated. "Yes."

"Very well. Here's my offer: I'll allow you to leave whenever you are ready and instruct Ming to give you a week's worth of supplies. You can go to the village and search for Wenzhu. If you don't find him, return with another ninety-two points worth of scavenge. Agreed?"

"Thank you, dàgē."

"I hope to see Wenzhu safe and well. Now if you'll excuse me . . ." Hengyen stood up to leave. "Good luck, Elena Anderson."

Hengyen left the tent and headed to the capitol building. He had a lot of work to do. He thought he had solved one of his problems today, but he was pretty sure Wenzhu was no longer an option for his team. It was highly unlikely that Elena was going to find one man out in a wilderness full of jiāngshī, but against his better judgment, he was giving her this opportunity for closure. Her best-case scenario would be to find him as a jiāngshī and put him out of his misery. The not-knowing ate some people up inside.

The problem of replenishing his wind team could wait for now. Hengyen had to deal with something much more pressing. The lives of everyone at the Beacon, possibly the entire Living Revolution in this region, were at stake.

8

HOMECOMING

Zhu spent the rest of the night trussed up in the animal pens along with the oxen and pigs. The elders had conceded his identity, but it was too far past their bedtime for them to make any other decisions, including about his accommodations. When Zhu had been a boy in the village, he had thought that farms smelled fresh and clean, while the big city was full of fumes and garbage. How quickly had urban life changed him.

The pen smelled as one would expect, given the pens were full of liquid manure and rotting plants. His bed for the night was a pile of damp hay mixed with mud. At least, he hoped it was mud. It was still a marked improvement over where he had woken up. He spent the dark hours huddled next to a sleeping cow, which provided some much needed warmth. Meili was kind enough to stop by with a thin blanket that he ended up using as insulation against the wet and itchy hay.

By morning, Zhu woke up caked in muck and submerged in several centimeters of water. It had rained, and the cow had pushed him off the blanket. Zhu tried to stand up, only to be reminded that one of his wrists was bound to a wooden post.

Meili returned shortly after he awoke with a pot of tea and a change of clothing. She untied him and poured him a hot cup to warm his chilled bones. His morning bath involved a ladle and a bucket of icy rain water. The clothes were too generous around the shoulders and waist and too short at the legs, but they were clean.

When he was presentable, Meili brought him to the heart of the village, if one could call it that. By his count there were probably two hundred or so souls living in the assorted tents and cabins. The majority were middle-aged or very young. There were surprisingly few people his age. Everywhere they went, the people met Meili with a smile and greeted Zhu with suspicion. Their eyes followed him. Whenever she introduced him as someone she had grown up with, they would interrogate him about his childhood as if trying to catch him in a lie.

Zhu thought he saw a few familiar faces, but he couldn't be sure. It had been a lifetime since he had been a sixteen-year-old setting off to the big city for secondary school. He had tested well enough in the national exams to attend a third-rank senior middle school. His parents had sacrificed much for him to get a better education, but things didn't work out as planned. Being one of the brightest in his village didn't carry over to a better school. Failing to score well enough to attend university, Zhu went to work at a factory right after he graduated to pay his parents back. The rest was history.

As Zhu walked through the small crowds, he was struck once again by how relaxed everyone was. There was a wooden watchtower near the center of the village, but other than that, he saw no security. Children ran through the soggy grass and older people sat around a fire and gossiped, as if the world hadn't completely fallen apart. Their destination was a large tent that was home to Meili and five other women. They sat down at a small circular table in the center of the tent, and she watched as he slurped down several bowls of congee.

"This place is strange. It feels like . . ." He couldn't quite put his finger on it. ". . . like the outbreak never happened. How is that possible?" Zhu barely managed to get any words out as he inhaled the food. He was already on his third bowl, which would have cost him dearly to purchase at the Beacon.

For the first time in as far back as he could remember, he could feel himself letting his guard down. He hadn't felt like this since before the dead began to rise. Even back at the Beacon, people had to stay alert. Zhu never realized how exhausting that was until now, when he felt like he could finally stop looking over his shoulder.

She nodded. "We've been blessed, at least up until now. The elders plan to move us soon."

Zhu surveyed the open field and grove of trees surrounding their tent. It had been a long time since he had seen an area this large without dozens of jiāngshī nearby. "Why would you move? This place looks like paradise. Where are we? How are you keeping the jiāngshī out?"

"Remember that valley south of our village? The one that's almost completely enclosed by the rice fields terraced up the mountains?"

He nodded, now recognizing some of the hills he saw on the horizon. It was an unused field nestled between rice terraces on all sides. There was only one winding path cutting over a tall hill to reach the land depression, and it was easily defensible. In many ways, it was the perfect place to isolate the village from the rest of the world.

Something about it joggled his memory, however. There had always been a good reason it was unused, why it was forbidden for children to play here. He walked to the edge of the tent and felt the wet grass squishing under his feet. He counted the layered terraces that rose like the steps of a ziggurat all the way to the top of the hill. Small streams from the night's rain trickled off each level to the one below it like a cascade of thousands of tiny waterfalls. It was beautiful.

He craned his head back toward her. "The rainy season. That's why you're leaving."

Meili nodded. "By this time next month, this entire field will become a lake."

"Where will you go?"

She looked pensive for some reason. "We're not sure yet. We've sent teams in every direction. We've heard back from only a few. It's almost the same anywhere else. There's jiāngshī everywhere. Xupin, one of our scouts, returned from the north with promising news. The Precipitous Pillars in Zhangjiajie are mostly free of the dead."

That made sense. The breathtaking national park was home to

some of the most majestic peaks and rock formations in the world. The ground level was thick with vegetation and trees while giant, almost alien pillars of rock that seemed to defy gravity rose as high as mountains into the sky. "Chopsticks for giants" was what he called it when his family had taken him to Zhangjiajie as a child. Save for the tourist areas, the terrain at the park was tremendously difficult to traverse, making it easily defensible against the clumsy jiāngshī. Even a storm of jiāngshī would not be able to penetrate deep into the park. Outside of the small towns surrounding the park, nobody lived there, so there wouldn't be too many dead. It would make a good home for the village.

"Only one scout returned?" he asked. "What happened to the rest of the team?"

"They stayed north to look for a place to settle." Meili hesitated and then leaned in. "Wenzhu, Ahui is with the north team."

Zhu stared at her dumbly at first, and then his hands began to tremble. His mouth opened; nothing came out. Her words hit him so hard his mind was having difficulty deciphering their meaning.

He hadn't dared think about his family, at least not since the early days, when he had frantically tried to reach them every way he knew how and had received no response. When he learned that the village had been wiped out, he had mourned for a few hours and then pushed the thoughts out of his mind. It was all he could do the few months after the outbreak to keep himself and Elena alive, running from horror to horror, fighting off vultures and jiāngshī alike. It wasn't until they found a home in the Beacon that they had managed to start living again.

In a way, believing they were dead had freed him to survive. There simply wasn't enough room in his head to worry about his family and surviving in this new world. Now that freedom twisted into crushing guilt.

"She's alive?" was all he managed to utter. His eyes watered. "I thought . . ." He couldn't finish the sentence. "Why didn't you tell me earlier?"

"I wanted to tell you when we were alone, after you got some rest and food," she said.

"How . . . how is she? What about the rest of my family?"

Meili shook her head and put a hand over his. "I'm sorry. When the village fell, Ahui and your mother were the only ones to flee with the survivors. And—".

He jumped to his feet. "Is my *mā* here?"

She bowed her head. "She caught pneumonia shortly after we arrived. I'm sorry. Ahui told me your father was bitten getting her and your mother out of the neighborhood. She said your nǎinai was too old and refused to leave. They tried—"

Zhu buried his head in his hands. "What about my cousins?"

Meili pursed her lips. "They were in the neighborhood where the outbreak first breached the perimeter. No one from there survived. We only managed to escape because we were next to the river and fled into the boats."

She caught Zhu up on the years he had spent away from his home. He dug through his memories and asked about all the people he had grown up with. Most people his age had moved away to the larger cities long before the jiāngshī appeared. Those who had stayed had been taken by the army to work on the Beacon of Light. That left no one else for him to remember.

"They say you're from the Beacon," she finally said quietly. Her words sounded less an accusation and more a disappointment. "Is that true?"

He nodded. "It's the seat of government in Hunan. We're doing everything we can to save the people and this country."

"That's not how the village sees it," she replied. "When the dead first woke, Fongyuan was prepared. The elders ordered a fence built. They enacted a strict curfew and ordered no one to travel in groups of less than three. For a while, the village was safe. We didn't have any incidents. When Changsha fell, the army came one day and drafted young people to help build what you call the Beacon of Light. More soldiers returned a few weeks later to take a few more. We never heard from any of them."

Zhu knew what had happened, but he dared not say. He had heard stories about the fate that had befallen the workers, although he hadn't been there to witness it. He and Elena had arrived at the Beacon well after construction was complete. The previous governor had ordered a military base built as a backup in case Changsha fell. Most of the army had been busy losing ground trying to stem the tide of the jiāngshī, so laborers were gathered from the surrounding villages. It was supposed to be temporary, but an outbreak erupted in the camp. The army had to clean up the mess and complete the construction.

"This is a hard time for everyone. There was much confusion," he said, lamely. "The Beacon is doing its best. If there is no one in control, then we've truly lost our country to the jiāngshī."

"Well," she continued, visibly upset by his response, "when we lost all our strong and able-bodied people, we could no longer protect the village. The jiāngshī overran the village a few weeks later."

"There is no way to fight the tide of the dead except through the concerted and organized effort of everyone involved," replied Zhu. "I've seen thousands of them all in one place sweeping across the land."

Meili shook her head. "Perhaps, but we were never given a chance to try. Eventually, all the survivors packed what we could and fled here, where it's safe."

"How did you escape mandatory enlistment?"

"Is that what you call it?" she asked bitterly. "Such a nice word for slavery. Your family hid Ahui and me when the army came looking for workers." The anger in her voice was palpable. "Huangyi and Huang-mang hid in the forest. They took my uncle and cousins."

Zhu was conflicted and uncomfortable with her animosity toward the Beacon. Talking about this also obviously evoked deep anger in her. He decided to change the topic. "Do jiāngshī ever wander in here by accident?"

Meili seemed relieved to talk about something else as well. "A few, but the village is ready to deal with them. Come, I'll give you a tour. You're our guest now."

"Does that mean I don't have to sleep in the animal pen tonight?" She gave him a playful smile.

Meili took him around the valley, showing him how the villagers had turned it into a self-sufficient community. Zhu was surprised by how many seniors were here until Meili explained how the village had prepared for the jiāngshī. The elders, having anticipated this need when the outbreak was first spreading across the coast, had made plans to use this valley as a safe haven. The cabins and furniture were built hastily. Supplies were stockpiled: dried, smoked, and fermented meats and vegetables, dozens of bags of rice, hand-wrapped dumplings, banana-leaf food bundles, even hundreds of packages of instant noodles. All were stored here in advance, which likely saved many lives early on.

That, of course, created other problems. How would a village with over half of its population too old or too young to survive the journey travel through jiāngshī-infested lands? Meili assured him they had it handled. She brought him to Wu Chima, who was the head of security for the village. He had also been Zhu's ping-pong coach. Chima proudly showed him the barricade and wooden gate at the end of a winding path, as well as the three watchtowers dotting the valley. The village was protected by a team of twenty guards, and the watchtowers were manned by children.

"In the months since we came here," Chima proclaimed proudly, "we've only had half a dozen jiāngshī and only one casualty. Our security tackles all problems before they happen."

"How are you preparing for the move?" asked Zhu.

"We'll be ready," Chima replied, as if speaking it aloud made it a fact. "We have six rifles and we're going to train more guards until we double our number."

Zhu nodded and shook hands with several of the guards. Most, like nearly everyone else in the village, were slightly too young or slightly too old. They all reminded him of new wind-team recruits with the way they held on to their weapons. It was just a slight awkwardness and unfamiliarity in the way they carried them. Windmaster Hengyen often said that he could always determine a person's skill just by the way they stood at attention.

Just as they were about to head back to the village, the young man standing watch on top of the barricade barked out an alarm. Chima and the two guards with him hustled to the gate. Zhu and Meili joined them soon after and peered through the gaps in the barricade. Two jiāngshī were slowly ambling up the slope. They must have been attracted by the conversation and smoke from the fires.

"Jincai, Li, you two with me," Chima piped, hefting a fishing spear over his shoulder.

"Do you need help?" asked Zhu.

The former ping-pong coach waved him off. "It's all right, young Zhu. We have it well in hand."

Zhu peered through the barricade as the three men walked up to the two jiāngshī. They looked like fisherman, one young and one old, and possibly related. Both dead were waterlogged and bloated, their flesh gray and sagging off their bones.

The boy named Li poked at the old fisherman with his pitchfork. He began to bark for help when it continued walking forward, pushing him backward.

"Plant your feet," Zhu muttered.

The one named Jincai had a little more success. His first swing cut deep into the base of the younger fisherman's neck, knocking it to the side like a ragdoll. He shot a look at Zhu as if to check if Zhu was watching. He flourished his weapon and followed up with the same swing, biting it slightly deeper into its neck. And then promptly got the ax stuck. He yanked futilely several times, until it came free with a disgusting, wet noise. But the sudden release made Jincai lose his balance, and the young man tumbled to the ground. The jiāngshī continued to advance on him.

Chima came to Jincai's rescue, charging the young fisherman with his spear, hitting the jiāngshī in the shoulder. The thrust caused the jiāngshī's torso to turn sharply from the blow. Chima, misjudging the impact of the glancing blow, continued his forward momentum and shot past the jiāngshī as he stumbled down the slope.

Zhu caught himself reaching for a staff leaning against the barricade. The three eventually recovered from their initial attack, finally putting down the two jiāngshī with a lot more work than should have been necessary. They returned to the barricade beaming, patting each other on the shoulder.

"See," said Chima. "It was a mighty battle, but my men are ready for anything." The two boys nodded vigorously.

Zhu kept his opinions to himself. The Beacon expected all their guards to be able to easily handle multiple jiāngshī at a time. Needing three to take on two would have meant Charred Fields duty for the unlucky team members. These people needed better teachers, not more guards. Doubling the number of untrained amateurs only resulted in twice the number of people who didn't know what they were doing.

These people were going to get torn apart once they left the safety of this valley. This haven was a blessing, but it had also made them complacent, overconfident, and delusional. With the jiāngshī threat getting worse by the day, he had little faith in these soft villagers being able to travel hundreds of kilometers through gales and storms of jiāngshī to reach the Precipitous Pillars.

The villagers who had eyed him with suspicion warmed up once they learned that he was Ahui's brother. From the stories they told, it seems his quiet and dutiful sister had blossomed into a loud, opinionated firebrand. She had been the one who had pushed the elders to find a new home, and had also been the first to volunteer to lead a team to explore the dangerous wilderness. By dinner, most had welcomed him into their circles, shared their food, and even slaughtered a chicken. A fleeting memory of his childhood pet chicken Báibái flashed through his head, which was often the case whenever he ate poultry. That was quickly shoved aside the moment his teeth tore into the drumstick's flesh. It had been many weeks since Zhu had tasted meat, and he savored every delicious morsel.

After the sun set, darkness curtained the field quickly. The watchtowers and the burning embers from the central bonfire were all that illuminated the village, save for whatever light the stars could lend. Zhu sat next to Meili as they conversed with the villagers after the evening meal. There were faces young and old, chatting, laughing, and showing little concern for the horrors of the outside world.

For a blissful moment, he forgot about the jiāngshī and the sickness falling across the country, and was transported to simpler times when life was small and peaceful. It had been a long time since he had last walked outside the walls of the Beacon feeling as safe as he did right now. It had been even longer since he had last felt like he belonged anywhere.

Zhu didn't notice himself huddling closer and closer to Meili as the number of people gathering around the bonfire shrank in proportion to the dying flames. He caught himself staring at her more than a few times. So much of her reminded him of his sister. Not because the two were in any way alike, but because they had been inseparable as children. Zhu didn't have many memories of his little sister that didn't involve Meili. Their parents had often joked that it'd be easier for everyone if they just betrothed Zhu and Meili and made her officially family. Both children had strenuously objected at the time.

Nothing ever did happen between them. In the end, he wanted to move to the big city and she wanted to stay close to home. Zhu wanted to do more than run a convenience store or be a rice farmer, and Meili wanted to be with her family. Now he wondered if he had made the wrong choice.

The bonfire eventually withered into barely more than glowing embers. Meili got to her feet and brushed the dirt off her pants. She offered a hand, which he accepted, and led him to the outskirts of the village. As they strolled through the light brush, a creeping feeling settled into his bones, but Zhu couldn't quite figure out what it was or why he was feeling it. It wasn't until they had lost sight of the village that he realized that he wasn't armed. If a jiāngshī came out of the darkness now, they would be defenseless.

His mind ran in circles as his past collided with his present. As much as a part of him longed for what had been and what could have been, he also drifted back to Elena. Was she all right? Had she made it back to the Beacon? He loved her. More importantly, he owed her in a way he could never repay. His heart and mind tugged him in two directions at once.

"We're here," she said in front of a lonely wooden hut in a small clearing. The hut, resting on four cinder blocks to keep it off the wet ground, wasn't much to look at, just several uneven pieces of wood lashed together by chicken wire beneath a tin roof. A torn piece of canvas over the doorway rippled against the breeze, causing the entire structure to creak and groan.

"What is this?" he asked.

"This is where you'll be sleeping tonight," she said. "I spoke with the elders. They've come to the conclusion that you are indeed Ahui's brother and that you're not a threat."

"Much nicer than the cattle pens," he replied. "Thank you."

"Tomorrow, can you show us how you got into the village?" she asked. "We could use some supplies."

He nodded. "It's the least I can do."

Before he could say another word, Meili wrapped her arms around his waist and pulled herself into him. "It's really good to see you again, Wenzhu." Before he could react, she let go, stepped away, and disappeared into the night.

9

SEARCH

Hengyen was as good as his word. The next morning, an hour before dawn, Elena and Bo reported to the supply tent and found a week's worth of supplies waiting for them. The quotamaster had his arms crossed when they arrived and scowled as he filled their duffels.

"Dàgē said you two are exempt from quota," he huffed, "but you're not exempt from me. I know exactly how much you are packing. I better get at least as much back when you return. If not, don't bother returning at all."

"That Ming is a hard-ass," Elena grumbled as they left the tent. "Ming the Mean. Ming the Jerk."

"He is merciless," Bo added.

Elena translated his words into English and shot him a grin.

"What?" asked Bo, puzzled.

"Never mind." Elena had learned early in her stay in China that most people knew a surprising amount of English. An even greater number had solid listening comprehension even if their fluency was lacking. Just last month, Ming docked her half of a scavenge when she called him a "crap stain" in English. That was when she had discovered that Ming's American name was Wilbur, and in his previous life he had attended NYU on a full ride majoring in international relations and minoring in English literature. One thing was for sure: whatever he had learned as an international-relations major sure as hell wasn't being applied toward his dealings with others.

To their collective surprise, they were allocated a shotgun with twelve shells. Prior to the jiāngshī, the Chinese government had kept tight restrictions on gun ownership, reserving guns primarily for the army and law enforcement. Firearms were a rarity in China, even more so since the outbreak. The armory at the Beacon was decently stocked due to the military unit that had been based here, but Ming and Hengyen rarely allowed wind teams guns. Not only was ammunition in short supply but gunshots also tended to work like siren calls in attracting hordes of the dead.

Hengyen was giving orders at the training grounds when Elena and Bo set out. Elena caught his eye as they passed. She waved and silently mouthed her thanks. He gave her a curt nod before turning his attention back to the crowd. Something big was going down. The other wind teams had been abuzz all morning. The rumor was that they were all heading east. Whatever it was, Elena was glad she and Bo weren't involved. The last time Hengyen had gathered this many people for a job, it had been to clear the forest half a day west of the Beacon. That expedition had suffered heavy casualties.

Elena and Bo walked up the stairs to the top of the container walls and climbed into the cable transport just as first light bathed the landscape. The battle at the Charred Fields was starting to pick up. The survivors avoided fighting at night, but the jiāngshī did not sleep. She watched as the morning rotation left the gates to meet the dead that had swelled into the fields overnight. The first wave, armed with long spears, corralled the jiāngshī into the trenches. It wasn't long before their lines broke as the jiāngshī converged. The spear team fought their way back to the gates, but not before losing three of their number. A few seconds later, another group of spearmen appeared and attacked the jiāngshī, but they struggled to even push them away from the walls.

Elena bit her lip as she saw one spearman, a boy who couldn't have been more than fourteen, get dragged to the ground. She resisted the temptation to draw her bow and start raining arrows. In reality, though, she could empty her entire quiver and not make a dent. She scanned the rest of the fields. It wasn't her imagination. The number of jiāngshī flooding the Charred Fields was growing steadily. Her gaze lingered on the battle until the cable transport crested the hill. The car shook violently as it stuttered along the final stretch over the forest, swaying back and forth as the motor at the station labored to bring them in. The car finally bounced off the guard rail and came to a rattling stop.

Bo slid the creaky door open. A touch of vertigo passed over

Elena as she stepped onto solid ground. The ride was getting worse and worse. It reminded her of a lesson her dad had instilled in her as a little girl: loose nuts and bolts are always telling you something. Never let them get away. Wiser words were never spoken. She reckoned it wouldn't be long before a very necessary piece of the lift rattled off, breaking the entire contraption.

She set that worry aside: it really wasn't her problem. She turned away from the sputtering motor and resolved to remind the mechanics upon her return.

Elena stepped to the edge of the platform. Her gaze followed the zigzagging path of the sky bridge on the electric poles above ground. Her heart fluttered. She had walked this course dozens of times, but this would be the first time she would lead a team. It was just Bo—not much of a team really—but there was a stark difference between being a team member and being responsible for even just one life more than her own.

"Where to, xiǎomèi?" asked Bo. "How are we going to find Zhu? There are four flag paths he could have taken from the village."

Elena pulled out her map. "That's true, but there are only seven sanctuaries in between. He would have marked wherever he stayed. Let's hit all the ones between here and Fongyuan village. If we see a drawing of a pig, we'll know he was there." And that he's alive, she added silently.

"And if we don't find him?" he asked.

"Then we're in the perfect place to scavenge."

Bo grimaced. "Through that garage filled with jiāngshī? That doesn't sound like a good plan."

She shouldered her pack and began to climb down the ladder. "Let me know when you have a better idea, big guy."

———

The first leg of their journey, along the sky bridge, was relatively uneventful. Like the cable transport, some of the poles were starting to show significant wear from constant use. These things weren't built for groups to walk along them every day. It was just a matter of time before one of the cables snapped or a pole fell over. What would the Beacon do then?

More jiāngshī littered the ground than ever before, and the seasonal rain was starting to make them look melted, like action figures that had been held over a fire. Elena caught a whiff and had to stop and gather herself. The smell of decay was worsening too. She ended up losing her breakfast over the side of the bridge.

She stared as her vomit splashed down into the muddy ditch below. Her first thought was irritation at losing much-needed calories. Her second was fascination as what initially looked like a large mud monster with assorted limbs rearing up from the muddy deep.

It looked like a bunch of body parts glued together crawling out of the ditch and blobbing its way toward the pole, shaking it. A chorus of moans followed, almost like an off-key a cappella performance. Several jiāngshī stuck to the mud mass began to climb over the bodies of other jiāngshī until they reached halfway up the shaft. The bridge shook from the stress and the moist ground and began to lean toward the side.

Bo grabbed her by the sleeve and pulled her along. "Keep moving before that thing finds a way up here."

They hurried along, running haphazardly across the narrow wooden planks. It wasn't until the mud monster was out of sight that they finally slowed to catch their breath. Elena could still see the cables along the bridge trembling. Hopefully the thing wouldn't bring the entire bridge down. They'd be in trouble then.

"Everything is falling apart," she muttered. "What do we do if the bridge collapses?"

"The secretary will think of something," replied Bo confidently. "We've made it this far under his guidance. He'll see us through."

Elena had little optimism left in her once-deep well. There had been too many failures, too many broken promises. She recalled missing the last flight home because of emergency road closures. From the American Embassy falling a few hours before she was scheduled to evacuate to not being able to afford the price of a ship heading to the States, it had been one painful disappointment after another. Now she had very little hope left to cling to. Especially if Zhu was truly gone.

Elena wiped that thought from her mind. He had to be alive. There were a dozen reasons why he hadn't returned to the Beacon yet. Maybe he was injured or captured by vultures. Maybe he was taking time away from the pressure to produce back at the settlement. It wasn't unheard of for entire wind teams to find a comfortable sanctuary and hole up for a few days. As long as you were back at the Beacon, you were spending points and under constant pressure to get out and scavenge again.

The two reached the horse ranch, the location of the safe house closest to the Beacon, by early evening. They did a quick sweep of the premises, clearing three jiāngshī that had wandered in. The horses were long gone and the ranch was halfway up a steep, winding hill well off the main road, so only a few jiāngshī ever found their way here.

Elena was surprised by the strange and sickening scent of burnt meat in the air. She didn't know where it came from, but it lingered in the pens, in the well, at the barn, everywhere. There were also several strange gray mounds that rose chest-height in two of the horse pastures. She didn't give it much thought and headed into the attic of an old barn that served as another sanctuary. After a short search, she concluded that there was no scrawl of a pig.

Elena didn't let this dishearten her. Zhu hated this sanctuary. It was too far out of the way of the flag paths, and the nearest water supply was tainted by the bodies of the previous owners, who had ended their lives in some sort of suicide pact. The real reason, however, was that Zhu was deathly allergic to horses. When they had camped out here, his face puffed up and itched for days. They only ever used this sanctuary if there was no way they could make it back to the Beacon by nightfall.

Elena and Bo retired early to the upstairs loft of the barn, making beds among the dry stacks of hay. Bo read his wǔxiá book while Elena leaned against a traditional vector window and stared through the open gaps up at the night. Her fingers curled against the circular patterns layered against the wooden frame. She had hoped to see a few constellations, but thick rolling clouds likely laden with rain had covered the stars. Lightning cracked in the distance.

She looked up anyway, thinking perhaps at that exact moment her folks were doing the same. It was her parents' birthdays around this time. At least she thought it was, give or take a few weeks. Her mom and dad were born days apart, and they always invited the entire neighborhood over for a barbecue to celebrate jointly. She fought down the urge to take out her camera and go through photos of her family. They were going to be gone from the Beacon for a while: she had to conserve the camera's power.

Elena eventually dozed off with her face against the vector window. Before she lost consciousness, she felt Bo stoop nearby and drape a horse blanket over her. The hay scratched her skin, but she appreciated the gesture.

No sooner had she nodded off than she was awakened by a shout. It was several loud voices, actually. Yelling and . . . chanting?

She was instantly alert, one hand reaching for her knife while the other pawed for the shotgun leaning against the wall close by. Bo had been roused as well and was peeling his sleeping bag off like a caterpillar's cocoon. He crept next to her as they scanned the darkness near the front of the barn. It was pitch-black, but there were people out there. Strange voices. Shouts and . . . there was that rhythmic singing again. Elena couldn't quite make out the words. Mixed in with human voices was the unmistakable, loud cacophony of jiāngshī. Scores of them.

Elena froze. What was going on out there? Had a group of vultures moved onto the ranch? Had they accidentally stumbled across a river of jiāngshī? Of all the luck. She jumped when several silhouettes scattered in the field in front of the barn came alight, bathed in flame. One after another, people, by the fives and tens, became walking torches. The smell of burning flesh filled her nostrils. The fire spread, soon illuminating the entire field.

No, those weren't people. Jiāngshī. They were trapped in the pens with the gray mounds from earlier. Their groans were soon overwhelmed by the crackling roar of the fire as it spread from body to body. A figure walking the perimeter of the pen carrying a fuel canister was dousing the jiāngshī with some sort of fuel, presumably. Each of the dead burst into flame, one by one. Just outside the pen was a cluster of people, living people, standing in a row chanting loudly with their arms raised to the sky.

"Heaven Monks. This must be what they do with all those jiāngshī they round up." Bo tilted his head and listened more closely. "Some sort of cleansing ritual?"

Relief flooded Elena. She had assumed they were dealing with vultures, which meant the two of them would have had to either flee in the middle of the night or stay hidden in the barn and try to wait them out. More plumes of flame and smoke shot into the air as several monks stepped up and tossed more gasoline into the pen. The jiāngshī, bodies burning like dozens of candles on a cake, lumbered forward until they bumped against the wooden fence, their hands grasping at the monks. A few fell, succumbing to the flames, but more took their place.

The chanting grew louder. Several of the monks reached out as if trying to lock hands with the dead. The way the Heaven Monks treated the jiāngshī was respectful, even tender. Elena's eyes brimmed with tears. The scene that was unfolding below here was oddly touching. She could tell they truly believed that they were putting tortured souls to rest. Sending spirits to heaven on columns of thick, acrid smoke. In a way, the singing and dancing, the waving of the arms . . . the ritual reminded Elena of her own church. She found herself swaying along with them.

Bo peered at her. "You aren't planning on joining these monks, are you, xiǎomèi?"

Elena answered him with a small smile. Of course she wasn't. She couldn't deny that there was a void in her soul that gatherings like this filled, but this wasn't her religion. This wasn't her congregation.

The chanting faltered and the singing became fragmented. Elena turned her attention back to the ritual and saw what had happened. The wood at one section of the pen had caught fire and splintered. The chorus turned into screams.

The burning jiāngshī poured through the gap and fanned out toward the monks, each a giant burning candle flickering wisps of smoke into the air. Everything they touched burst aflame. The sickening smell of cooked flesh and burnt wood soon wafted into Elena's nostrils as the fire spread. Elena watched, horrified, as one jiāngshī wrapped his arms around a robed monk. The woman's cries joined the chorus of screams as the flames jumped to her heavy robes and crawled up her arm. Her panicked wails turned to ones of agony as she futilely tried to bat at the jiāngshī holding on to her. Her struggles weakened and she collapsed to her knees as the jiāngshī bit into her chest.

One monk punched a jiāngshī with a series of martial arts moves and managed to break its neck, but his close proximity to the burning dead set his own clothing on fire. As he tried to bat away the fire, two other jiāngshī pounced and sandwiched him together. One grabbed his arm and the other bit into his cheek. The three bodies seemed to melt into one as they succumbed to the flames. More, encumbered by their large bulky robes and unable to defend themselves, fell as the jiāngshī descended on them. Only a few of the monks were armed with long poles, but they were quickly overrun. It became a slaughter.

Elena dashed to her duffel and returned to the window with her bow in hand. She tossed Bo the shotgun.

Bo caught it but made no move to use it. "What are you doing?"

"We need to help them."

"I don't know if we should get involved," said Bo. "Remember what we're here to do. This is not our mission."

"It'll be even more dangerous if the jiāngshī burn the barn down. Come on." Elena kicked out the wooden vectors of the window and drew an arrow.

She was about to let it fly when Bo put his hand on her wrist. "We might need your arrows later on."

He was probably right, but Elena wasn't going to just stand there while people got slaughtered. With a hiss of disgust, she drew her short spear and headed to the ground floor. She was pleased but not too surprised to find Bo a few steps behind her. As much as he might disagree with her actions, he was dependable. She hoped it didn't get him killed.

The Heaven Monks were startled to see a wind team charge into the fracas, but quickly accepted their help. Bo smashed the chest of the nearest jiāngshī, and Elena headed toward an older woman holding a giant ax known as a *pǔdāo* that was nearly as tall as she was. The woman swung the ax expertly, using the momentum of her swings to lop approaching jiāngshī in half.

Fighting next to her was a tall, imposing young man who was ineffectually trying to beat away two jiāngshī with a broomstick. If anything, he was helping put out their fires. He yelled and fell back when his weapon caught fire, leaving the old woman alone and dangerously surrounded.

Elena fought her way to the old woman's side, watching her back but staying away from the ax's looping swings. Her caution didn't seem necessary. The old woman looked as if she were dancing, spinning and lopping off jiāngshī heads left and right. Elena almost wanted to just stand there and admire the woman's work, but three burning jiāngshī were bearing down on her.

She slashed the nearest one across the chest with the point of her spear, barely slowing it down. The skin of this one, a relatively fresh jiāngshī by the looks of it, was bubbling and melting off its body, exposing its rib cage and cooked intestines, some of which were trailing along the ground. It was times like this Elena wished she had a longer weapon. The short spear was easier and lighter for someone like her to use, but it forced her to fight up close, and the heat from the jiāngshī was too intense to make it an easy thing. The smoke stung her eyes and nostrils.

Fortunately, the old woman solved Elena's problems. She came up behind the three jiāngshī and decapitated two with one swing, then plunged the sharpened edge of the pǔdāo clean through the back of the last one, carving away half of its rib cage. The old woman eyed Elena with almost an amused squint before she moved on to the next jiāngshī. In a matter of minutes, the Heaven Monks managed to rally enough to kill the remaining dead that had escaped the pens. The purifying fire finished off the rest.

Elena found a small patch of clean grass under a fir tree and rested her weary body. Bo sat next to her and pulled out his handkerchief to clean his sledgehammer. A little while later, the leader of the Heaven Monks, the same white-haired man with the flowing beard who had greeted her a few days before, approached them. He laced his hands together and bowed. "Thank you for your assistance. I am Master Jiang Ping. I lead this sect."

Elena returned the bow. "Glad to be of help. How are your people?"

"We have many injured, and we'll bury a few of our brothers and sisters today," he replied, "but at least they will be sent directly to heaven and not trapped in an earthly shell. What brings you to this place?"

"We were just staying here for the night."

Jiang Ping studied them more closely. "You are members of Chen Wenzhu's team. But young Wenzhu is not here?"

Elena nodded. She appreciated being recognized, although it wasn't that hard. There were only two Caucasians on the wind teams, and Darragh O'Brien was old, bald, and a real mean jackass.

Jiang Ping reached his own conclusion. "I'm sorry for your loss. He was a good man. I hope he finds his way to heaven."

"He's not dead. We're searching for him right now. Can you help us?" she continued quickly. "We were separated in Fongyuan village two days west. He was alive at his last known location. He may be injured."

The look of pity Jiang Ping gave her was the same as Hengyen's. "I'm sorry, but we cannot return the aid you have given us. This is a cruel world we live in now. I wish you the best but advise you to make your peace."

Elena bit back her retort. The Heaven Monk was trying to be kind. He was probably right, and this was a fool's errand, one that put both Bo and her at risk and wasted resources.

Elena and Bo spent the rest of the night helping the Heaven Monks clean up the mess. Elena tended to the wounded while Bo helped carry the bodies to a funeral pyre. By dawn she felt like she had been up for a straight week, but they had to set out. Daylight was precious and they could not afford to lose an entire day. The sect was good enough to share food and supplies. They even gave Bo a book, much to his delight. Jiang Ping found them again as they were setting off to offer them a small basket of fruits. Elena's mouth salivated. That was worth its weight in gold to her. The monk looked thoughtful as he spoke. "I may have something that could aid your search for Wenzhu. There is a small enclave living near Fongyuan, survivors from the village hiding in a nearby valley. We trade with them regularly."

Elena perked up. Of course. That could explain how he had just disappeared without a trace. "Why didn't you tell us this earlier?" she demanded.

"They wish to stay hidden for good reason, especially from those at the Beacon," he replied. "I warn you, they do not view strangers kindly. Tread lightly when you go. I wish you luck."

As Elena and Bo headed away from the ranch, Elena mulled over what the monk had said. It made the most sense that Zhu was with the village. That, or dead, and he couldn't be dead. "Come on, Bo," she finally announced. "Let's go straight to the village."

"What about the other sanctuaries?" he asked.

"No use in trying to find needles in a haystack."

He frowned as he tried to parse out a meaning. "But aren't sewing supplies worth extra points?"

"Never mind."

10

STOPPING THE TYPHOON

Fifty windrunners from ten teams.

Thirty guards from the Beacon's walls.

Twelve engineers from the treatment plant.

Nearly a hundred souls putting their lives in Hengyen's hands. Not since the fall of Changsha had Hengyen led this many people into battle. He had to be careful. There was no way the Beacon could recover from losing more than half the wind teams.

Secretary Guo had likened this war to the legendary and heroic Long March during the Chinese Civil War, when the Red Army had retreated northwest to recover and regain their strength in the fight against Chiang Kai-shek's nationalist forces.

"The jiāngshī threaten our homeland like the Kuomintang did," he had declared to the assembled group before they departed. "It is our duty and unity of purpose to follow in our ancestors' courageous footsteps in routing these invaders so that the seeds of our rebirth can thrive."

It was a rousing speech, one that got the troops to their feet. Hengyen, being an actual student of military history, had raised an eyebrow at the comparison. If the Beacon had *actually* been anything like the Long March, they would have been heeding his recommendation and packing up the settlement this very moment. But then that was why the secretary was the politician and leader and Hengyen was the military man: he knew how to use rhetoric to get the people to act against their best interests.

In any case, the decision had been made. The secretary went with Wangfa's recommendation, so it was now Hengyen's role to try to stop the tide from washing over them.

Hengyen watched as his lead teams fanned out along the narrow passage in the ridge as they fought their way toward the Yuanjiang. They had to clear out the hundreds of jiāngshī that had fallen in from his last foray, but they had no other choice. It was almost always the wrong tactic to attempt to subdue the jiāngshī with large numbers of troops. Time, however, wasn't on their side. The main body of the typhoon was less than ten kilometers away from the Beacon. Five weeks, maybe less if something urged them on.

Wangfa came up from the rear. "The wagons are having trouble keeping up."

On top of all these people he had to take care of, there were also several tons of explosives loaded up across three wagons. It was a mixture of military-grade explosives, grenades, C-4, and dynamite. Anything the engineers could get their hands on.

"Tell the engineers that if the wagons can't keep up, they should distribute it evenly among everyone else. I'll carry the first portion."

Wangfa did not look enthused about carrying explosives in his pack, but he nodded and shuffled away. No one looked pleased, for that matter. But to Hengyen's grim satisfaction, the efforts in keeping the wagons rolling were redoubled and they were soon maintaining a steady pace.

Progress was slow. Individual wind teams had the luxury of sneaking past some jiāngshī and killing only when necessary. They were fortunate that they were moving along a well-worn path, one that had been cleared many times before. Anywhere else, they would have been faring far worse. Their parade was still forced to stop every time they encountered a group of jiāngshī that numbered greater than ten, which basically meant they were stopping every hundred meters.

They reached the first night's campsite shortly after sundown. It took a little longer than Hengyen had planned, but considering the dozens of small battles they had waged to get here, he was pleased with their pace, especially considering they only suffered one injury along the way, which happened to have come from one of the guards accidentally slicing another on the arm with a pike. The injury wasn't life threatening, and there was no jiāngshī taint, and so even Hengyen allowed himself to smile along with the rest of the retinue's laughter.

When order returned, he sent the woman home with the guard who had inflicted the injury as an escort.

The Beacon group cleared out a tiny one-street village and commandeered several small boats to cross the chest-deep shallows. Their destination was a small island nestled in the middle of the Yuanjiang. Perhaps island was a bit charitable; it was barely more than a lump of rock, sand, and tall resilient weeds, with no resources or shade. But it afforded the column a protective buffer against the migrating jiāngshī that dotted both shores. It had never been inhabited, except recently by a small group of refugees that had fled here to survive the outbreak. Now all that remained were the ruins of their camp and their jiāngshī wandering aimlessly across the sand. These were dispatched easily enough.

The guards quickly set up a perimeter while the rest of the expedition got to work setting up camp. Hengyen walked the breadth and width of the small island, parsing out orders setting up a watch rotation. He eyed a group of jiāngshī staring back at him on the other side of the river. The guards on watch should have plenty of time to deal with any jiāngshī trying to cross over.

After he was satisfied with their defenses, he returned to the heart of the camp and huddled near a campfire while a windrunner brought him lukewarm tea in a tin. He sipped it slowly and gestured for Wangfa and Qingwei, the head engineer, to join him as they went over last-minute instructions.

The initial plan had been to destroy three bridges and four roads, which would completely sever the flow of jiāngshī from Changde to the Beacon. They realized right away that controlled explosions at many locations were impossible. They barely had enough explosives and manpower for three, so their target was now two bridges and one road. Hopefully the rising Yuanjiang would do the rest of the work.

"Did you notice any unexpected difficulties when we passed under the bridge earlier?" he asked Qingwei as he drew a large X in the sand, which marked the bridge spanning across the ravine.

The head engineer shook his head. "It's a little farther from the camp than I thought, and there are a lot more jiāngshī than I anticipated, but as long as your windrunners are watching my back, it shouldn't be a problem."

Hengyen turned to Wangfa and drew two lines, a wavy one indicating the river and a straight one running parallel to it. He circled several points of interest in between them. "There are a few small settlements here, here, and here that weren't on our map. We don't know what's there, but it may be better to follow the river up to here, before cutting back inland to reach the main road connecting to the primary highway that runs directly to the Beacon."

Wangfa frowned. "That's a big detour for this many men. It'll add half a day to our travel time." He poked at the main road leading to the highway. "I think the best thing to do is lead my team straight up the gut on the main road, clear away all the jiāngshī, and then head back the same way we came."

Hengyen didn't love that idea, but Wangfa's thoughts weren't without merit. While it was an uphill climb and battle up that road, Wangfa *was* leading the largest team, which meant they were the best equipped, but it also meant they would have the most difficulty trying to sneak past any large groups of jiāngshī.

"What about you, Windmaster?" asked Wangfa. "Any changes to your plan?"

Hengyen glanced at the river. "The rapids don't seem as hazardous as I feared. I'm not going to wait until morning. My team will head out tonight over water."

Qingwei frowned. "Is that wise? Travel is extremely dangerous at night."

"We'll need those extra six hours if we hope to return to the island by tomorrow evening and head back to the Beacon with everyone else."

Hengyen was leading the smallest team with the most dangerous job of blowing up the bridge farther down the Yuanjiang. Hengyen hoped that every team would be able to complete their part of the mission and return to the island by tomorrow evening, so they could all head back to the Beacon the next day. Mainly this was for Hengyen's team's benefit. The journey back to the Beacon would be much safer if they traveled in large numbers. Because their objective was the farthest away, his team needed as much time as possible to complete their mission. In the event any of the teams were wiped out, everyone else had standing orders to wait until the morning after and then head directly back.

Hengyen finished up the meeting, wished Wangfa and Qingwei luck, and then sent word to his team about the change of plans. He pulled them from their current tasks and ordered them to catch a few hours of rest. They would head out shortly after midnight.

——

The sky was pitch-black when Hengyen's team boarded one of the small fishing boats and drifted downstream toward their target, a small bridge near Wuqiangxizhen village. He had only four others on his team: Weizhen, Haihong, and two engineers, Lankui and this other young man whose name Hengyen kept forgetting. Something about the boy's voice grated on his nerves and made his mind blank. Besides, fresh kids like him rarely survived their first mission, so why bother?

The team huddled beneath the cloth canopy as Lankui steered the rudder. They had just navigated around a sharp bend when their fishing boat nearly crashed into a crop of rocks. This part of the river was choppy and the small group were jostled around as if they were riding a roller coaster. Water sprayed into the boat as they narrowly avoided a capsized sailboat, cartwheeling away from the hull and spinning into an eddy wall. They nearly capsized themselves as Lankui struggled to regain control. Hengyen saved the young engineer from going overboard when he lost his balance and nearly tumbled over the side. He got dunked into the water headfirst before Hengyen managed to grab a fistful of his shirt and pull him back in. Hengyen couldn't help but break into a grin as he watched the young engineer sputter and screech like a wet cat. It had been a long time since he'd had "fun," if he could call it that. This was as close to fun as he'd gotten since the beginning of the outbreak.

Lankui finally got the boat under control and they drifted past another stranded boat, this time a water taxi. More than a dozen jiāngshī screeched from inside the passenger area of the boat as they passed. No sooner had the wind team managed to get around it than they encountered another obstacle, this time a capsized tugboat.

They passed more and more boats, forcing them to weave carefully as through a maze, one that changed constantly, opening new paths and closing others as the currents pushed the boats around. The sounds of jiāngshī groaning and teeth chattering joined with the rhythmic thunks of the boats clunking against one another and the waves lapping against the hulls. It was inevitable that they would eventually hit a dead end.

They found the source of the congestion shortly before dawn. A great big barge had crashed into one of the bridge's foundations and capsized, creating a blockade beneath the bridge preventing anything bigger than a canoe from passing. There were now a hundred or so meters of ships between them and the bridge they intended to blow up.

"What's the plan, dàgē?" Haihong asked.

Hengyen scanned the banks. Both sides were teeming with jiāngshī. "Pack our gear. We go the rest of the way on foot."

"On foot? But, dàgē, we are far from shore," said the other engineer. Hengyen clenched his teeth. That high-pitched whiny voice . . .

Without a word, Hengyen stepped up on the rim of the small craft and hopped to the next, an upturned rowboat. He landed with a loud bang, thin metal flexing and groaning beneath his feet. Several jiāngshī on the shore turned their crooked, ruined heads in his direction. Hengyen stabilized himself against the moving platform, took two great steps, and hopped to the next boat.

Whiny's eyes widened as he stared at the row of gently moving platforms. "There has to be another way, dàgē," he pleaded. He was a young man who had made a brave show of volunteering for the job when the call first went out. It seemed it was easier to be brave in front of a crowd of his peers than in front of the dead.

Hengyen turned around halfway, glancing at Whiny. "Follow my orders, stay close, and nothing will happen to you. The Living Revolution depends on us." Hengyen turned to Haihong. "Look after the fragile engineers. Make sure nothing happens to them." He leaned in as he passed on his way to the front of the boat. "Watch that one carefully. He looks ready to panic and run."

He must have not spoken softly enough. The other engineer, Lankui, who had run with the wind teams until the secretary learned about his engineering degree, grinned. "Fragile, eh? Don't worry, dàgē. I'll keep him in line. Hey! Dummy! Don't you know you should be more afraid of the windmaster than the dead?" Whiny blanched.

Hengyen nodded. "Thank you, Lankui. How does it feel being back out in the field? I heard about you fighting jiāngshī in the Charred Fields last week. Staying sharp?"

Lankui saluted lazily. "Yes, dàgē. I volunteered to maintain the wall's eastern fortification. We've gotten into several good scraps."

From what Hengyen heard, Lankui was underselling it by calling the action a "scrap." One thing was for sure, the encounters were becoming more common. He slapped Lankui's shoulder. "I'll leave the young man to you, then."

Lankui distributed the packs laden with C-4. He made a face when Weizhen shied away. The old engineer slapped the bag several times, causing the windrunner to jump. "These things won't blow up if you drop or shake them. They need detonators to have any fun, so relax."

Hengyen scanned an adjacent barge, then a small ferry on the other side of the boat. He decided to take his chance on the barge, believing there would be fewer jiāngshī there than on a ferry. He maneuvered his current fishing boat next to a ladder on the side of the barge and grabbed the first rung. No sooner had he planted his feet on the deck than he saw broken tents on the main deck area and realized he had chosen poorly.

It might have been the angle of the moonlight, but the closest jiāngshī looked almost surprised. Had it raised an eyebrow at him? Its graying skin hung off its bones like swamp moss. A broken tibia jutted from a blackened slit in its leg. The thing managed to shuffle a step forward before Hengyen buried a dagger in its skull through the soft mentum of the chin. Past the falling corpse, several more jiāngshī appeared and began to crowd him. Hengyen had no choice but to stand his ground. He dispatched two before the rest of his team got onto the deck.

Hengyen helped Lankui up and then urged his team on. "We need to move."

They ran to the bow of the barge, which was jammed up over a small yacht. Haihong swung over the side and dropped to the lower deck, then helped the engineers while Weizhen stood guard. The jiāngshī on the deck crowded closer. Weizhen lodged his spear in the gut of one, somehow getting the point stuck in the bone. He yanked back, throwing the jiāngshī around, but was unable to free his weapon. Another jiāngshī came from his side and tried to take a bite out of Weizhen's arm. Hengyen's dagger sliced through the air and severed its limb at the elbow. He pulled his man back and pushed him toward the edge.

"Go." Hengyen jumped over the side as soon as his windrunner disappeared, landing heavily on the yacht's deck. The impact rattled his bones, but he was on his feet an instant later, looking up at the barge to make sure none of the jiāngshī had followed them down. Fortunately, the barge's rails prevented that. He turned his attention to the rest of his team just in time to see Haihong kill a skinny bikini-clad jiāngshī.

"Boat's clear," she replied, yanking her short sword loose.

Weizhen was holding and studying his forearm.

"Are you all right?" Hengyen asked.

"It bit me, but . . ." He paused, concern all over his face. "I don't think it's deep. I think I got lucky."

The scratches looked light; they had barely broken the skin, but there were still traces of red. Hengyen had seen similar seemingly minor wounds end up killing a person and turning them. Still, he was not ready to amputate one of his best windrunners on the basis of scratches. "Watch it carefully," he instructed. "If it's not better by evening, you know what we have to do."

Weizhen's already worried and pale face grew even whiter. He nodded. "Yes, dàgē."

Hengyen turned to leave but then noticed Weizhen still standing there, staring at his minor injury. There were times when Hengyen had to be a cold, calculating commander to his reports. There were other times when he had to act like the big brother everyone called him. This was one of those times. He shook the young windrunner's shoulders. "Listen, son, worry is a poor companion. We have enough problems coming for us. Don't invent more.

There's nothing we can do about it right now, so focus and hope for the best, understand?"

Weizhen nodded. "I just don't want to be a burden on the revolution."

He was barely older than a kid, but a good man. Hengyen stole a glance at Whiny. If only he had ten Weizhens instead of a hundred Whinys at the Beacon.

"As long as you fight by my side, you will never be." Hengyen then shrugged. "Besides, we may all be dead by tomorrow, so why go looking for trouble?"

They continued to the other end of the boat, stepping onto a junk and then a large catamaran, putting down what looked like an extended family. Hengyen experienced an unusual moment of hesitation before he buried a dagger in the face of what had once been a little girl, cleaving her face in two, spilling her brain onto the floor. He was usually far past the point of caring who these people had been in their previous lives. The Living Revolution needed steel and resolve.

Children, however, still gave him pause every now and then. For some reason, children that had turned into jiāngshī still carried their innocence. Not even the curse of these monstrosities could wipe that away. Hengyen had never had any children of his own, but his thoughts sometimes wandered back to his family in Beijing: his parents, brother and sister, his many nieces and nephews. All were dead. Every child's face reminded him of that loss. Some would call it a weakness, but Hengyen considered it a small reminder that through all this horror, he hadn't lost all his humanity. He was going to need that one day when this was all over.

The team continued jumping from boat to boat. They passed through a clutter of fishing boats lashed together, fought their way across a tour boat, and even managed to cross a submarine. Hengyen wouldn't let himself imagine the horrors below deck.

They reached the barge that had run aground on the bridge's foundation in the middle of the river by early afternoon. He called for a break, and the tired team collapsed onto the pitched deck. They had been on the move and fighting for over seven hours. Whiny was dead on his feet, and both windrunners were unsteady. Even Hengyen was feeling the effects of the long trek. Surprisingly, only Lankui seemed fresh, even eager to continue.

Hengyen and Lankui jumped down off the barge onto the gravel shore to inspect the foundation supporting the bridge. "Will it work? Can you blow it?" he asked.

Lankui shrugged. "Does it really matter? I'm not a demolitions expert. I'll do my best to blow it up and not blow us up at the same time. That's all I can promise."

"That's not exactly comforting, but that's good enough for me." There wasn't much more Hengyen could ask for. These days, everyone had to work with what they had. They went over the logistics of what the engineers needed to get the job done, then they headed back to the tugboat to make final preparations.

"Give us two hours, possibly three," declared Lankui. "Keep food in our bellies and the dead off our backs, and I guarantee something will explode. Preferably not us." Hengyen couldn't help but grin. There was something refreshing about dealing with another person who didn't fear death.

"Actually, there might be a problem with that." Lankui held up a small metal box. "This is a short-wave detonator with a range of fifty meters."

Hengyen didn't need any more explanation. The original plan had just been to plant the explosives and head back. They had anticipated that the shores would be filled with jiāngshī and unusable, but they hadn't anticipated all the boats and debris cluttering the bridge on their return.

"We don't know what will happen once the bridge blows," continued the engineer. "The resulting explosion could sink half this fleet, or it could uncork the bottleneck and sweep everything downstream. To say nothing of how large the radius of the debris field could be."

"Now you're sounding like an engineer. But neither sound like great options," muttered Hengyen.

Lankui hesitated. "There's a third way that is probably best. Once we prep the explosives, everyone starts heading back upstream save one person. That guy stays to push the button once the others clear the area."

Everyone spoke at once.

Hengyen shook his head. "The Beacon can't afford to lose good engineers."

Lankui smiled. "We can afford to lose our dàgē even less."

Weizhen raised his scratched arm. "I'll stay, Windmaster. I'm done for anyway."

"I can think of no greater honor than to lay down my life for the Living Revolution," said Haihong.

"I'm not doing it." Whiny was really living up to his nickname again. "I don't want to die."

"I'm not sacrificing anyone," Hengyen finally snapped. "How far away do we need to be to be safe from the explosion?"

The old engineer furrowed his brow. "As far away as possible. Maybe a hundred meters?"

Weizhen frowned. "But you said the range of the detonator is only fifty."

Lankui shrugged. "Nobody said life was fair."

"Can we even survive at fifty meters?" asked Haihong.

"I don't know. Look, I'm actually a software engineer, and there are no computers at the Beacon. The only reason I'm an engineer at all is because my uncle taught at a technical college and got me in." Lankui shook his head. "You young people keep asking the wrong questions. It doesn't matter if we can survive at fifty meters, because to actually blow this bridge up, fifty is the farthest we can go."

"He's right," Hengyen crossed his arms with finality. "It doesn't matter. Blow it. We'll figure the rest out later. The Beacon's survival depends on our success."

It took the engineers two hours to plan out the best ways to cause the most damage to the bridge. They came to the conclusion that the foundation itself was too thick and sturdy for their limited supply of explosives and decided that the best way would be to focus on some of the bridge's more vulnerable joints.

The rest of the wind team kept watch over them. No jiāngshī came. The thunderous buzzing overhead continued, but the roving dead were completely unaware of the living working below. The dozens of other jiāngshī trapped on the boats were foiled by each boat's railing. The few that managed to find an opening or tip over the side fell into the waters and were quickly swept downstream. The watch was calm, even boring.

That left one problem for Hengyen to solve: how to escape the blast without sacrificing anyone.

The solution came to him just as the engineers were finishing up. He was sitting on the gravel edge of the water watching the small bits of wood and random debris float by when he shot to his feet and hurried back to the team.

"We'll blow it downstream," he announced. "We'll loosen one of the smaller boats, and then float downstream. Once we're fifty meters away, we blow it."

The younger engineer raised his hand. "What if we die from the blast?"

"Then we're dead. Next stupid question," snapped Lankui.

"Not all of us are old farts like you. Some of us would actually like to make it back to the Beacon!"

"I swear I'm going to kill you myself."

"Dàgē," said Haihong. "This cuts us off from the island and takes us directly away from the Beacon. How will we get back?"

"We find a good landing point and then we walk."

"That's a long way away," Whiny huffed. "We'll never make it."

Hengyen waved off any further discussion. This plan wasn't up for debate, and it wasn't like they had an alternative anyway. He sent his two windrunners to find a boat while the engineers finished their work. Their escape craft ended up being the life raft of a pleasure boat. It was meant for only four occupants, but it served.

It was early evening by the time the raft and the explosives were ready. Smart money may have been on waiting until next morning, but Hengyen was impatient. He did not intend to lose an entire day waiting for more sun. The team jumped in and began to drift away from the bridge. Lankui clutched the detonator tightly in his hands while Whiny and Haihong paddled.

"Are you ready?" he asked when he estimated that they were roughly fifty meters away. Truth was, it didn't seem far enough at all, but he couldn't risk it. If they drifted too far from the bridge, they might not be able to fight against the current hard enough to get back within range.

"I've been waiting to blow something up my entire life," replied Lankui.

"Now is your chance. Make it count!"

Lankui grinned like a schoolboy and pressed the button on the unit.

A burst of fire rolled sideways from under the bridge, sending a plume of dust into the air. The water under the raft roiled as the concussive blast sent shock waves across the river. Debris rained down upon them, sending sharp fragments of rock and wood into the water nearby. Haihong suffered a nasty cut from a sharp sliver of wood, while a chunk of concrete the size of a fist glanced across Weizhen's face, nearly toppling him over the side. Only Hengyen's quick reaction prevented him from falling into the water.

Then the waves came, first tipping the raft to one side and then hard to the other. The five occupants of the craft sized for four slid and bounced, and then the craft capsized. Hengyen didn't have time to suck in a breath before he found himself underwater. His lungs burned, but he forced himself to stay calm as the currents batted him around. He glanced at the river floor and caught a few rotting jiāngshī with weights tied around their waists staring up at him, arms raised and hands grasping. He would be deathly curious how those jianghis got there if it weren't for the fact he was close to death himself. His body was just beginning to convulse when his head finally broke the surface.

He sucked in a large gasp of air and caught a quick glimpse of yellow out of the corner of his eye. He made his way toward it and clasped onto a rubber handle. Haihong had managed to keep ahold of the raft the entire time. Weizhen's head broke the water's surface a few seconds later. Hengyen scanned for the two engineers and caught sight of them downstream. Whiny was flailing his hands weakly while Lankui was slumped over a wooden board farther downstream.

Hengyen ordered his team to swim toward them, but everyone was mostly at the mercy of the currents. At one point, he realized he could not reach both men. Whiny was closer, and Lankui still hadn't stirred. As much as he hated to make the decision, Hengyen did what he thought was right. He ordered his wind team to guide the raft to the young engineer.

It took most of his remaining energy to reach him. Already spent, the three windrunners kicked and paddled across the rapids toward the other side of the river. The water brimmed with large pieces of floating debris, some slamming into the raft and ping-ponging them around the rough waters. A tugboat narrowly missed running them over as it sliced past, its wake sending them back almost to where they started. Their arms burned, legs kicked, and chests heaved, but the river had other ideas.

They were almost within arm's reach of Whiny when his head went under water and failed to come back up. For an instant, Hengyen considered letting him go as a loss. His sense of duty wouldn't allow that, however. Gritting his teeth, Hengyen let go of the raft and dove after him, battling to dive against the currents that wanted to send him back to the surface. Hundreds of small fragments, several sharp and moving quickly, pelted his body, some slicing open his skin.

Hengyen finally got hold of the engineer's sleeve and yanked him up. The two fortunately broke the water's surface near the raft. He didn't think he had enough energy left to drag them both much farther. Haihong and Weizhen pulled the engineer to the raft, and then together they rode it until it finally washed up against a boulder in the middle of the river, giving them a chance to right it.

By the time they did, everyone was exhausted. Haihong and Weizhen climbed in first, and then helped Whiny in. Hengyen rolled inside and fell onto his back, coughing and sputtering water. He closed his eyes to catch his breath, and then opened them to the gray skies that threatened to dump more water on them.

He turned his head to the engineer curled into a ball next to him. "Are you all right, son?"

Whiny, whimpering, began to cry. "Please just get me back to the settlement. I want to go home."

Hengyen gnashed his teeth at those tears and sat up. He scanned farther downstream. Lankui's body slowly disappeared from view. He had either sunk into the water or was now too far. The old man was gone.

Hengyen closed his eyes and muttered a blessing for another lost hero of the Living Revolution, then pushed that loss out of his mind.

He looked back at the bridge and was sharply disappointed to see it still standing. Part of the structure directly above where they had planted the explosives had collapsed, narrowing the jiāngshī's path, but there was still space to cross. They were still streaming through. At best, all Hengyen's team had managed to do was slow them down.

"Dàgē?" asked Haihong, in between deep gasps. "What do we do now?"

Hengyen looked to the setting sun and saw the dozens of jiāngshī on both sides of the shore staring at them. He shook his head. "Dry up. Rest and get some sleep. We set off for the Beacon at first light."

11

INNOCENCE RECLAIMED

Zhu woke with a start. A shadow had passed through the cracks between the loosely fitted wooden beams. Momentarily disoriented, he pawed for his machete and found it outside his reach. Instinct took over, and he rolled ungracefully off the cot, landing hunched on all fours on the floor.

There was a soft rap on the wall next to the piece of cloth draped over the entrance. "Chen shūshu , are you awake? We were supposed to have the lesson this morning. I can come back." Huangmang's face popped under the flap. He froze when he saw Zhu crouched like a feral tiger waiting to pounce. "Chen shūshu, are you all right?"

It took a moment for Zhu to remember he was in a safe place. He blinked at the boy who had bruised his ribs a few days ago. A long breath loosed from his mouth as he relaxed.

"Of course." He forced a smile on his face. "I overslept. Let's go."

Huangmang led Zhu to an open field where a bunch of eager youths and a few of the guards were waiting. Zhu had spent the past two days teaching them some of the techniques and tactics the wind teams employed. He taught them how best to fight the jiāngshī, and, more important, how best to avoid them entirely. None were old or large enough to scavenge on their own or take on a jiāngshī by themselves, but they could make an effective group if they worked together. Even more important was that when they finally did grow up, they would have the skills necessary to keep the village functioning.

That last thought left a sour taste in Zhu's mouth. He had abandoned the village once already.

Zhu spent half the morning teaching his class of villagers, ranging in age from eleven to fifteen and from fifty to sixty-five, how to climb trees and poles using rope and homemade spurs. He spent the second half teaching them how to fight the dead as a group with spears, showing them the parts of the head a barely sharpened stick could pierce without requiring too much strength. The class had cut long poles and were practicing pinning him to a tree when the lunch gong sounded. Zhu watched the ragtag group drop their poles and wipe the sweat off their faces. They had been working hard all morning, eager to impress him, soaking in everything he told them.

"How did we do, Chen *shīfù*?" asked a boy Zhu could tell had once been quite heavyset, but had since lost substantial weight quickly and in an unhealthy manner.

Zhu couldn't help but smile every time one of them called him master. "Very, very well. You'll be ready to kill jiāngshī very shortly."

"Could we join your wind team then?"

"Absolutely," he lied. These kids wouldn't make it through their first night in the field with the jiāngshī. Then again, most people couldn't until they actually did. In this day, everyone had to grow up quickly or join the enemy.

He was walking with his class toward lunch when something lurched out of the shadows. He was caught unawares as a pair of hands clapped his back. If he had been out in the field, or the Beacon for that matter, he would be dead. It had been a long time since Zhu had been able to let his guard down, so much so that feeling safe was no longer his default. In the field, one either slept lightly or ended up dead. In sanctuaries, the threat of vultures was constant. Even at the Beacon, there were occasionally bullies and thugs who dishonored themselves by trying to steal others' food and meager belongings.

The people at the village, however, felt like a real family, a tight-knit community that trusted and looked out for one another. They weren't trying to find ways to take advantage of the situation. There was no need for points or incentives to work, and they certainly weren't forced to labor for some revolutionary cause. These were people who had known each other their entire lives, and now that things had gotten bad, were taking care of each other. Zhu badly missed this comradery in his life.

"Hey." Meili grinned, bounding alongside him. "How's the kung-fu school coming along?"

"They'll be ready to help the village." He lowered his voice. "One day."

He waved goodbye to his students and joined Meili at one of the lunch tables. Several of the villagers waved. Even Hong, the grumpy bald elder who had initially wanted to beat his skull in, gave him a friendly nod as he passed. His work over the past two days had earned him the goodwill of the villagers. To Zhu, it was payment and gratitude for the kindness, food, and shelter they'd given him. It felt much more like a penance; one he gladly paid.

Lunch was a bowl of rice with string beans, egg-drop soup, and a tiny helping of duck. The village was blessed with fields of wild rice that had continued to prosper even while everything else fell apart. The old woman who served Zhu the bowl of soup even smiled, which was a stark turnaround from earlier. The first day he had joined the line, she had threatened him with her wooden ladle, scowling and muttering under her breath as she slapped half the amount of slop on his plate she gave everyone else. He didn't complain.

He spent some hours with Meili, peppering her with questions about the village, trying to fill in the gaps of lost time from the years he had been away from his family, his friends, his community. Would things have been different if he had stayed? Probably not, but maybe he could have helped carry his nǎinai to safety. Maybe he could have made the difference for fighting off the jiāngshī and saving the village. Instead, he had been hundreds of kilometers away, spending the money he was supposed to send home trying to impress a woman he knew would eventually return to her rich and comfortable life in America. A woman who was now waiting for him at the Beacon.

Zhu and Meili sat on a tree stump at the edge of the dining area. He was still uncomfortable with the many sideways glances the villagers threw at him.

"Everyone is talking about you." Meili sounded amused.

"I wish they would stop," he replied, burying his face in his bowl.

"You know how villages are. Everyone gossips. Especially now that they all know you're Ahui's brother. They're curious."

An elderly couple approached them. The woman, with gray thinning hair and wrinkles etched into her entire body, stared at him with intense eyes. The man, completely hairless and hunched over, was the opposite, his skin stretched across his thin body, making him look almost skeletal. He couldn't seem to tear his gaze off the ground.

"Excuse me, *xiànshēn*," the man bowed deeply, using the most formal term for "mister," and avoiding his gaze. "Are you from the Beacon?"

Zhu was embarrassed that the elderly were treating him with such respect. He stood up and bowed quickly. "Yes, *lǎo* xiànshēn, I am. What can I do for you?"

"I was," he stuttered. "Well, my wife and me . . ." The old man choked, seemingly having a hard time getting the words out.

"We were wondering if you saw our children," the woman said quickly. "We have a son and daughter: Xingjian and Yangyi. They were taken to the Beacon of Light to work. They are twenty-seven and twenty-five. Xingjian is tall, like you. He has a strong jaw but a very large forehead. He's not very bright but very sweet. Yangyi is strong for a girl, but short and fair." They continued rambling off details that only parents would know but Zhu would never have noticed. Their talk became more desperate, and then they began to argue about conflicting details.

Zhu listened patiently, letting the elderly couple have their release. When they finally took a moment to catch their breath, he spoke gently. "I'm sorry, I haven't seen them. I assure you, if they are still there, I will keep an eye out for them when I go back." Meili glanced at him out of the corner of her eye.

The couple's reaction was of both disappointment and hope. He hated to feed them false hope, but he wasn't sure if it was a kindness to tell the truth. The attrition from the Beacon's construction was terribly high. Zhu knew of maybe two dozen who were still there. It did seem to encourage the old couple, however. The man finally met his eye, and the woman rubbed his arm up and down with her calloused hand, thanking him profusely for being so noble.

No sooner had the elderly couple left than a middle-aged man searching for his nephew, his last surviving relative, took their place. Immediately after, three children looking for their older brother. A woman looking for her husband. Even a little girl searching for her dog. The list went on. Zhu gave them all the same story: he wasn't aware of this person, but he would ask around and keep an eye out when he returned.

Once the last of them was gone, he deflated back onto the stump. There was something draining about lying. He studied the soggy grass intently. "I didn't know the Beacon took so many people."

Meili's voice was low. "The soldiers conscripted all nine of Lan Bi-ying's grandchildren. None returned."

"Who's that?"

"The egg-drop-soup lady."

Zhu looked up toward the food line where the old woman with the wooden ladle continued to serve hungry villagers. He couldn't even fathom that number. She must have sensed him because she looked his way. A smile appeared on her face, but there was nothing joyous about it.

The two sat in silence for several moments. Zhu stirred the dregs of his soup. "No wonder everyone hated me," he muttered.

"Are you really going to go back to the Beacon of Light?" Meili finally asked. Her hand touched his shoulder. "You don't have to, you know. You've been gone for years, but you're still part of the village. If you prove to the rest of the village that you belong and can help us, I'm sure they'll consider letting you stay."

It was true. These were his people, his community, his family. This was a chance to absolve some of the guilt that had festered in him ever since the beginning of the outbreak. He couldn't fix everything, but he could make things better. He could try. The village needed him now, more than ever.

Zhu shook his head. "My heart wants that badly, but I can't stay. I have to go back to the Beacon. The Living Revolution needs me. Someone has to stop the jiāngshī. We can't allow the dead to take over the country. It's our duty to protect our lands. It's our duty to the living and to the ones we have lost."

There was also someone else living he had to go back to. It wasn't just because he loved Elena. Some debts could never be repaid. He had abandoned people he cared about once. What did it say of him if he did so again? Especially someone whose choices, made for him, had cost everything.

"What about Ahui?" asked Meili.

Zhu had no answer for that. He had abandoned her too. He loved Elena, but Ahui was family. His heart and mind teetered. As he watched three young children playing in the adjacent field, his thoughts drifted to memories of his mostly happy childhood. Long hours playing xiàngqí with his yéye, his nǎinai making soy milk, Ahui and Meili chasing him through the narrow alleys between buildings. Dreams of better and more peaceful days. No jiāngshī, no destroyed villages, no living in cages, risking his life for points and the privilege to do it over and over again.

"I have something for you." Meili pulled out his camera and machete wrapped in a paper bag, and held it out.

Zhu thanked her, collected the items, and turned his camera on. It was still at approximately the same power level, which meant they hadn't rummaged through it. They had confiscated it the day he was captured and were shocked to discover that it had power. As far as he knew, there had been no electricity in the village since the day it fell.

His mind wandered back to the picture he had found on Ahui's desk back in their room. Now he regretted not taking it with him. He would have to make a special trip to retrieve it. On a whim, he wrapped his arm around Meili's shoulder and pulled her in close for a picture.

Meili made a startled, wide-eyed face when he snapped it, her crooked mouth midgape. "Wait, I wasn't ready. Delete it and take another."

They ended up taking six more until she was satisfied. Zhu was loath to delete anything these days unless absolutely necessary, so he kept them all. The two were horsing around and snapping several more photos when Guan Jincai and Lu Shenyang ran up to them. They were two of the few healthy young adults in the village. The pair had managed to hide in the forest with a few others their age when the Beacon's soldiers came.

"Meili," Shenyang said breathlessly. "Some people have entered the old village." Shenyang was the lookout. It was her job to warn the village if any vultures, scavengers, or traders came to Fongyuan. She was the one who he caught a glimpse of that first day in the village, and was the one who had tracked him all the way to the rice field.

Meili immediately took charge. "Vultures?"

Jincai shook his head. "I don't think so. They look organized and well-armed. I think they're from the Beacon." He was the tall, strapping man who, Zhu had learned, was the one who had clubbed him across the face and cracked his tooth at the rice paddy.

"Did they see you?" asked Zhu.

"Of course not." Shenyang bristled.

She actually wasn't as good at sneaking as she thought she was, but Zhu could bring that up another time. For now, they had a problem on their hands.

"Where are they now?" asked Meili.

"At a garage near the center of town," said Jincai. They spent half the morning working their way there. They're trying to clear it now, but I think they've run into some trouble. They're making a lot of noise and attracting a lot of jiāngshī toward the garage. I think they're trapped now."

That was probably a wind team all right. He was heartened by the news. He had been worried about Elena and Bo ever since they got separated. They must have made it home safely with enough scavenge for the Beacon to send another team. Still, whoever was there now were still his comrades, and if they needed help, it was his duty and moral obligation to do what he could. He pulled his machete from his pack and strapped it around his waist. "Lead me to them."

"Absolutely not," said Meili. "You'll expose the village."

Zhu was torn. The villagers, for obvious reasons, wished to remain hidden from the Beacon of Light. Zhu, on the other hand, still considered himself a proud member of the Living Revolution and had mixed loyalties. "We don't need their blood on our hands," he replied.

She crossed her arms. "Every time the village has dealt with the Beacon, they have killed and stolen from us. If they want to scavenge the village, we won't stop them, but we won't help them either."

Meili was adamant. It took some convincing, but Zhu finally agreed to her way. He was their guest. He finally decided to do what was best for the village and trusted the wind team's skills. "Meili's right. Leave them alone. Windrunners know how to handle themselves." He broke into a grin. "Besides, I've seen the way you help people from the Beacon. I'm sure they would appreciate not getting clubbed."

Jincai blushed and broke into a wide grin. "Sorry, Zhu."

"Keep an eye on them, but don't expose yourself," instructed Meili.

The two teens nodded and were about to head back out when Zhu hesitated, and then asked, "Did you manage to get a good look at them, by chance?"

Shenyang nodded. "There were two of them. A large, fat man, and a small woman with blond hair."

Zhu's chest tightened. "Damn it. And they're in trouble?" He jumped to his feet, Meili's orders slipping from his mind. "I have to go."

He had his machete in his hand and was halfway to the valley entrance before anyone even knew what he was doing. Zhu was sprinting down the winding path leading out of the valley when he realized that he had company. Jincai had kept up with him, while Shenyang and Meili were a few steps behind. He stopped abruptly. Jincai, who was easily half a head taller and broader, nearly barreled him over and knocked him out again.

"Stay here, please! I know these people," he said quickly. "They're my friends. If they're in trouble, I have to help them. I promise I won't betray you."

"What are you doing?" Meili demanded. "You're risking the entire village, Wenzhu."

"I'll take care of this. I'll come back as soon as I can. Do not follow me." Zhu turned around and sped off again before any of them could stop him.

12

REUNION

Elena shifted on the traditional stone slab bed. She didn't understand how anyone could sleep on something so hard. It was supposed to be good for one's back, but if that was the case, a person might as well sleep on the ground. Hell, soil was bound to be more comfortable than stone.

Elena would know. She had spent the past hour sitting on it staring at the pictures on the wall. She and Bo had arrived this morning at the same apartment Zhu had brought them to the first time they visited the village. Something about this place had nagged at her and piqued her suspicions. It was how Zhu had chosen this particular apartment out of all the others. It was how anxious and sensitive he became when they were here. Something about this place had really gotten to him.

She finally figured it out after staring at all these photos. Many were faded and unclear, but she finally recognized Zhu's familiar face on a scrawny youth in three of them. This place belonged to Zhu's family, or at least one of his relatives. This explained why he was on edge when they arrived, why he was so shaken after he killed that jiāngshī in the bathroom. Goodness, what if it had been his relative?

In all the time they had dated, Wenzhu rarely spoke about his family—which, to be honest, she didn't mind not knowing about and hadn't pressed the issue. Why should she? This relationship was never supposed to be a real thing. It was a summer fling in a faraway locale with a handsome, albeit slightly nerdy, boy on the other side of the world. They were supposed to create a magical experience together, and then she would return home and treasure these memories for the rest of her life. That was it. No strings attached. Why ruin a good thing by getting serious?

Now Elena understood that Zhu didn't feel that way. She was ashamed to admit that he had treated their relationship much more seriously. In return, she had made the fatal mistake with summer flings and had actually fallen for him. Even when they did get serious, though, and she had shared stories about her family, he was still close-mouthed about his. At first she thought it was because he was ashamed of his poor, uneducated, and rural upbringing, Now she knew the reason Zhu didn't talk about his family: guilt. This was his family, and he had returned to find them gone, and probably dead. He even had to put down one of them.

Elena didn't blame him. If she were in his shoes, she would have felt the same way. Well, unless the jiāngshī in question was her uncle Graham. That guy was a piece of work.

Elena resisted the temptation to take one of the photos out of its frame. It wasn't hers to take and keep. She kissed her finger and pressed it against one of his pictures, and then went into the next room.

Children had obviously lived here. Did Zhu? She brushed her hands against the desks, noticing the disturbance on the otherwise fine layers of dust. Who were those two girls in that picture with him? His sisters? She closed her eyes and inhaled, nearly choking on the thick soot lingering in the air. She felt almost like she was invading his privacy coming here. In a way, she was.

Elena had decided to use this apartment as their base of operations during their time here at Fongyuan. This place was already cleared of jiāngshī, safe from vultures, and free of Mother Nature's wrath. In truth, she had hoped to find Zhu here. In any case, they had three days' worth of supplies to do so. That or find the village and get their scavenge.

She and Bo had decided to set up camp first, grab some lunch, and then hit the garage. Get the trivial stuff out of the way first so they could concentrate on the real task at hand of finding Zhu.

The plan for the garage was simple. Bo would lure the jiāngshī away with a distraction, and Elena would drop down and clean the place out. *Simple as cobbler*, as her mother would say. They had mapped out a reasonably safe route along a stone wall that ran parallel to the garage and then armed Bo with a wooden spoon and a pot. Elena would then climb onto the garage's roof and wait for his signal. With a little luck, she would be in and out of there without having to stab a single one of the rotten bastards.

———

After their lunch, they set out for the garage.

Everything started out exactly as planned. Bo's clanging reverberated through the entire valley. Elena, kneeling at the roof window, watched as the jiāngshī standing around in the garage perked up and turned toward the commotion. At first, she feared his distraction was working too well. It cleared away not only the jiāngshī inside the garage but just about every single dead within a hundred meters. Even at a distance, she could see Bo's eyes widen in fear as the jiāngshī converged on him. Bo was a brave man, and he continued to beat the pot as he hurried down the wall like the Pied Piper with the jiāngshī in tow.

Once the coast was clear, Elena crawled through the narrow window and dropped down. Inside, she found three jiāngshī that hadn't joined the chase. The first was still trapped under the tractor from the last time they were here. The second was missing its legs and had its arms crushed, so was making little headway. The third had been foiled by one of the toppled shelves, bumping its knee into it over and over again. Elena put all three out of their misery with swift, efficient jabs to their temples, as casually as if she were taking out the trash.

She was about to get to work when she realized her mistake. The shelf that was directly below the open window had toppled over, and there was now no way for her to get back topside. She cursed. She should have planned for this, and was kicking herself for forgetting such a basic survival rule: never neglect to secure an escape route. She glanced out the hole in the wall that had been the garage door. It was a fifty-meter sprint out of the hole to the nearest place to climb to safety. There was no way she was going to be able to lug two duffels' worth of supplies that far without getting bogged down.

Thankfully, inspiration hit soon after. Elena grabbed a carton of filters, three boxes of spark plugs, some cans of oil, and a few other things on the mechanics' wish list. She had made a point of specifically asking them what they needed in order to get maximum points for this trip. Once one duffel was fully loaded, she placed it directly under the window and tied the straps to a nylon rope. She tied the other end to the fletching of her arrow and then drew it, quietly muttering a thank-you to Bo for convincing her not to waste all her arrows at the ranch. It was a tight shot, but the arrow sailed effortlessly through the window and disappeared onto the roof. Elena broke into a satisfied grin. Zhu would have been proud. Windmaster Hengyen might have even nodded in approval.

She began filling the second duffel, loading it up with car batteries. It was a special request from the engineers, so the usually merciless Ming was offering big points. These things were normally too heavy to scavenge, especially from two days away, but that was what a big guy like Bo was for. She realized quickly that these batteries were not only heavy but also dense. Four in a duffel was already too many, and she was forced to drag it on the ground. She opened cabinets and drawers, searching for light items that could fill the empty space: filters, plastic bags, gloves.

That was when she made a second mistake. In a moment of carelessness and overconfidence, she assumed she was opening a closet door. When it opened, she was met with darkness and a rancid odor that made her stomach twist. An arm shot out, followed by a chorus of choking rasps. Then the door flew all the way open, knocking Elena off her feet. Windmaster Hengyen always told them to assume the worst behind every door. Elena had forgotten that lesson and was now paying the price.

She crab-crawled backward as jiāngshī spilled into the garage. Within a breath, six of them were climbing and pushing over each other to get to her. Their numbers doubled, and then doubled again. At that point, it didn't matter how many dead there were. Elena clambered to her feet and rushed to the exit, where, as luck would have it, a small group of jiāngshī was straggling past just as she reached the broken garage doorway.

Elena skidded to a stop. The jiāngshī changed course and converged on her. She kicked the chest of the lead jiāngshī, a teenager still in his school uniform, and shouldered another—his classmate— aside as she careened toward the tractor, then plowed blindly into the lone still-standing shelf. Her head rang and she staggered sideways, blinking, trying to keep moving as the room swam. She knocked some boxes off the shelf trying to get around it, and found herself completely surrounded.

Elena reached for her spear and grasped air. She must have dropped it during her tumble. Strike three. At this point, she was questioning if she deserved to get out of this alive. There were five more jiāngshī for every one closing in on her. She bumped up against the shelf again as she retreated. Panic crept up her body and tightened its grip around her throat. For some weird reason, flashes of Custer and Crockett and every other desperate last stand popped into her head. Elena Anderson wasn't going to die to these stupid dead things without a fight!

She grabbed the nearest box—it was empty—and bounced it off the uniformed student's head. She grabbed the one next to it and hurled it to similar effect.

"Why do they bother stacking empty boxes?" she yelled, tossing another. Oh, it was because her wind team had cleaned them out the first time they were here. Fortunately, there wasn't time to feel foolish. Elena stared at the shelf. Another of Windmaster Hengyen's lessons rang in her head: *There is always a way forward, a way in, and a way out. If you can't find one, create one.*

That was when it hit her. Of course. Elena dragged her body through the shelf to the other side. She fell to the ground roughly and rolled to her feet, leaving the jiāngshī staring at her through the narrow shelf. She shouted triumphantly and then extended the middle finger on her right hand at the grasping dead.

"Don't mess with Texas, asshole. You don't know who you're dealing with, you dumb—"

The rest of her thoughts escaped her as she stared up at the shelf teetering on its edge, slowly headed in her direction. The metal frame squealed as the jiāngshī on the other side pushed against it, trying to reach her. The boxes and assorted tools and items sitting on it began to slide off. A cardboard box smacked her square in the chest. This one was unfortunately not empty and knocked her onto her backside. An electric drill fell off the shelf next, the drill bit chipping the concrete inches from her head.

More items began to rain down. An empty paint can bounced off her forehead. A toolbox upended its contents, spilling screwdrivers and wrenches on her. A pair of plumbing pliers bloodied her nose. A box of nails nearly blinded her. Then the shelf toppled over her and emptied the rest of its contents on top of Elena. She did her best to cover up. Hot pain knifed up her leg as part of the shelf bit down onto her ankle. She held down her scream and tried to squirm free, but her leg was trapped. The harder she pulled, the deeper the metal cut into her flesh.

"Stay calm, stay calm," she whispered, feeling her hot breath in this claustrophobic space. There was always a way out. She just had to figure it out. If not, Bo would come back for her. He would never abandon her. Not like they had abandoned Zhu in this very same place. Elena really hated this garage.

She laid her head back down and looked off to the side, noticing a sliver of light along the floor. It was the door leading to the alley, the one she had used to climb in the first time. She snaked one hand into the box above her head and wielded it as a buckler against the grasping swipes of the jiāngshī. With her other hand, she managed to curl her fingers around the bottom of the door. If she could pull herself free, maybe she could sneak out that way. If there weren't another ten jiāngshī waiting on the other side.

The rustling around her continued, and then briefly, it sounded like the jiāngshī had moved on. Elena froze. Maybe if she stayed still enough, the jiāngshī would get bored and wander off. She didn't dare make a sound, she didn't dare breathe.

A sudden hard blow to the side of the box knocked it away from her face. A jiāngshī, a long-haired young woman missing part of her forehead, looked down at Elena with empty black eye sockets. Elena stared back; it was like looking into the abyss. It bent over and reached for her with clawed fingers. Elena swore as she grabbed its wrist with one hand and batted at it with the other. At the same time, she wondered how this thing could see without eyes. Elena managed to punch the jiāngshī square in the nose, caving it in. Its head began to leak through nearly every opening, oozing chunks of brain matter, blood, veins, and broken bits of bone.

Elena gagged as all of this splattered onto her face. She turned aside, squeezing her eyes shut and pursing her lips, careful not to ingest any jiāngshī gunk while simultaneously trying to clear her vision and fight the jiāngshī off as its innards rained down upon her.

In the distance the sound of Bo banging the pan grew fainter. At least he was still alive.

———

Zhu sped toward the commotion. He didn't know what the hell Elena and Bo were doing, but from what he observed, it was clearly a bad plan. The ruckus was so loud it had probably attracted every jiāngshī in the village. He wouldn't have been surprised if these two managed to whip up a storm.

Zhu was about to turn toward the edge of town to follow the

noise when he stopped. He knew exactly what their plan was. Why was he following the diversion? He reached the edge of the village and crept through the thickets, sneaking by a dozen jiāngshī shuffling along a stone wall as if they were on patrol. He found a relatively quiet corner and ambushed two jiāngshī, lopping off the head of one and pulling the arm off the other, throwing it off balance. He took a leg out from under it and brought the point of his machete down on its face.

He began to make his way toward the garage when the banging picked up its beat and became more frantic, then stopped altogether. Sounds of screams replaced it, not of pain and suffering, but of terror. It was Bo, and he was in trouble!

Zhu changed course and sped straight toward his friend. Elena was smart and competent enough that she probably didn't need his help right this very moment, but Bo definitely did. Zhu ran haphazardly against the steep spines of the roof, sliding down one side and hurdling across a narrow alley, one foot barely catching the edge. He scrambled onto all fours and kept running. Bo's panic continued to fill the air.

Zhu found him in a few seconds. He had climbed onto an old water wheel at the edge of the river and was balancing precariously at the top as jiāngshī surrounded him. The wheel swung back and forth, causing him to balance unsteadily as the jiāngshī crowded closer in.

Zhu, hunched on the nearby roof, waved his arms. "Bo!"

The big guy, hands clutching the paddles to maintain his balance, looked up. He looked confused and then brightened. "Xiǎodì, you're alive!" He removed a hand to wave, but thought better of it and grabbed back onto the wheel to hold on for dear life.

"Jump into the water," yelled Zhu. "Hurry!"

Bo shook his head. "I can't swim."

"I thought you were from the country," he yelled back.

"Lake water is always so dirty."

Zhu couldn't believe it. "You really aren't suited to survive an apocalypse," he muttered. Finally, he raised his voice again. "Jump. I'll fish you out."

Bo stared at the murky green water, then back at the jiāngshī as if trying to decide which he preferred. He made a face. "You promise?"

Zhu nodded urgently. The joints of the water wheel were starting to crack and splinter. It would likely be a matter of seconds before the wheel either crumbled or toppled. Bo took a few false starts before finally holding his nose and mouth with one hand and stepping off. He plummeted straight into the water just as the jiāngshī pushed over the water wheel. It toppled directly over where he landed, and for a moment Zhu feared it had crushed his friend.

He let out a relieved breath when Bo's large round head broke the water's surface farther downstream a few seconds later. "Help! Help, xiǎodì!" he screamed, his arms furiously pounding the water.

Zhu gave himself a running start before he jumped off the end of the roof after his friend. The shock of cold was momentarily paralyzing, and then he swam after Bo, who was getting swept farther downstream. It didn't take long, but by the time he reached Bo, he was exhausted. Bo's flailing didn't help. The larger man grabbed onto him and dragged both of them underwater for a few seconds. His panicked grip was viselike as he anchored Zhu down.

Zhu ended up punching at Bo, trying to stave off drowning. His feet touched the muddy river floor and he pushed, then stood up. The water only came to his neck. Bo continued to struggle, grabbing at his arm and chest. Zhu finally got his friend's attention with a quick slap across the face.

"Ow," Bo cried. "That's not—"

"Stand up," Zhu ordered.

Bo obeyed. The water came up only to his chest. "Oh." He smiled sheepishly, and then enthusiastically embraced Zhu again. "Xiǎodì, you're alive! I was sure Elena was going crazy."

The embrace was bone-crushing, but Zhu felt the same way. He hadn't realized how much he had missed his wind team until he saw Bo. "Where's Elena? Is she at the garage?"

"She's scavenging while I lured the jiāngshī away," Bo nodded. He smiled proudly. "I'm the distraction."

"You sure are. We need to talk about that tactic," said Zhu. "Later though. Where are you supposed to meet?"

"Back on the roof above the garage."

"All right, let's go."

They continued wading upstream against the fast-moving currents back toward the center of the village. Along the way, they attracted a sizable following of jiāngshī, many who tried to wade in after them. Fortunately the dead were far clumsier in water than on land. Most at some point lost their footing and were swept away downstream. Zhu and Bo were able to easily pull away from the remaining sure-footed ones until they found a safe stretch of land.

It took them another fifteen minutes to find a way back onto the rooftops. By the time they reached the rendezvous point, the wind had changed, growing chilly as it blew down from the mountains. Both were wretched, exhausted, and shivering in their damp clothes. Bo had lost his sledgehammer and was now wielding a thick branch.

Zhu stared at the arrow on the roof piercing one of the tiles. He picked up the rope tied to it and followed it straight to the window where, after a short yank, he pulled up the duffel tied to the end of it. He poked his head through the window. The garage was dark. There were still a few jiāngshī inside, but most had wandered out into the lot.

Bo stayed on the roof while Zhu used the rope to lower himself down. He sneaked up on the four jiāngshī on one side and dispatched them quickly. His heart stopped when he crouched in the corner where everything seemed to have fallen over. There was blood everywhere, on the metal shelves, soaked into the cardboard boxes, splattered against the walls. It was still fresh, still wet. This slaughter couldn't have happened more than an hour ago, probably less.

Zhu closed his eyes. He was too late. It had taken too long to find Bo and get back here. He had failed Elena again. By the looks of it, it had not been a painless death. A choked sob escaped his lips and he fell to his knees, his head buried in his hands. "I'm sorry," he moaned.

A tin clattered to the ground. Zhu jumped to his feet as a silhouette stumbled forward. Another jiāngshī, hidden in the corner. This one was covered in coagulated blood. Pieces of organs, sinew, and muscle were caked to its body. Its face was smeared red with dried flesh from its recent feast. Zhu curled his lips and raised his machete angrily, ready to take his grief out on this monster.

The jiāngshī's eyes popped open suddenly. There was an unusual spark in its blue eyes as it stared and reached for him. It opened its mouth and a small but familiar voice spoke to him. "Oh my god, Wen-zhu, is that really you?"

Zhu stared at Elena for several moments. The machete that he had almost buried into her skull slipped from his fingers. She was completely unrecognizable, covered in guts and entrails, looking akin to a sun-shriveled corpse. She smelled like one too.

None of that mattered. He rushed into her arms and held her tightly, guts and all squishing between them. "I can't believe it's you. You're okay. I was so worried."

"You're the one worried?" Her voice was muffled, buried in his shirt. "I thought I was never going to see you again."

The two probably would have kept standing there for another hour if a cough hadn't interrupted them. Bo, head poking in through the window, waved. "Hi Elena. What happened to your clothes? You look like a mess. I'm glad to see you're all right, but you two should get back up here before more jiāngshī find us. You two can finish your reunion later."

Zhu reluctantly let Elena go and led her to the rope. It took some effort to get her to the safety of the roof. The jiāngshī were still wandering around on the other end of the garage and just outside. Her hands and body were slick with blood, so she couldn't climb the rope. She was so exhausted that he wasn't sure if she would have been able to regardless. They ended up tying the rope around her waist for Bo to haul her up while Zhu kept watch on the ground level.

After everyone was safe, they hurried back to Zhu's family's old apartment, which was where Elena and Bo had set up camp. Then they spent the next hour cleaning up. Bo found some leftover laundry detergent while Zhu risked sneaking to the back alley to load a bucket of sand to scrub off all the stubborn dried gunk that had caked onto their bodies. Afterward, Zhu and Bo broke down a couch and bed for tinder for a small fire in the living room. All three were wet and exhausted, but relieved and happy to find each other again.

"How did you survive the jiāngshī?" Zhu asked Elena as he wrapped his arm around her waist and held her tightly. She hadn't stopped shivering until just a few minutes earlier.

She shrugged. "There was one on top of me. I literally tore the thing apart with my bare hands, and all its guts just splattered on me. After I killed it, I thought its friends would pounce on me. I was still trying to catch my breath when the next one appeared. It stared at me and then walked right past, as if it couldn't see me at all. That's when I got the idea to smear myself with more jiāngshī guts. As long as I didn't make any sudden movements, I became completely invisible to them."

"Why did you stay in the garage?" asked Bo.

"By that time, you had stopped banging the pan," she replied. "I was too tired to try to climb back onto the roof, and I wasn't sure if this disgusting camouflage actually worked in a crowd of them. Wasn't too excited to find out, so I stayed put." She turned to Zhu, squeezing his hand. "What about you? Where have you been?"

Zhu should have expected this. He should have been ready for these questions. For some stupid reason, he wasn't. "A couple of vultures robbed me and left me for dead. I managed to find shelter in one of the houses."

"Why didn't you head back to the Beacon, xiǎodì?" asked Bo.

His hesitation was brief. "They smashed my head pretty bad. It took me a while before I could think clearly. After I recovered from the concussion, my head was groggy and I needed to recuperate." Zhu touched his forehead gingerly, reacting with exaggerated pain when he grazed the lump from the villager's club.

It was a lame excuse, but Bo appeared to accept it. "But you're ready to come home now?"

Elena shifted her weight away and stared at him pointedly. There was a glint in her eye. "You are coming back with us, right?"

He had always expected he'd return to the Beacon. Just not this soon. His mind immediately flashed back to the village, to his students who were expecting him, to Meili. Fongyuan was not only his home but also his identity. It was as much a part of him as his mind, his hands, his voice. The few survivors here were his community, his neighbors. His people. He had thought all of this was lost, but here they were, waiting for him, asking him to not turn his back on them again. He really could help the village. Be the difference between their survival in reaching the Precipitous Pillars and succumbing to the outbreak. Fongyuan needed its son now, more than ever.

It wasn't just Meili and his students, it was Ahui as well. She was alive! As far as he knew, his sister was his only living relative. Could he live with himself again if he abandoned her a second time? Staying with the village could be his only chance to see her again.

But then there were Bo and Elena, his dearest friend and his lover, who had risked their lives alongside him, saving his life countless times. He wouldn't be breathing now if it weren't for them. Could he abandon them? And what about everyone at the Beacon of Light and the Living Revolution?

If Zhu was being honest with himself, even with the recent discovery of his village, he wasn't sure if he should stay. In order to protect the village, to hide their existence, he had to return with Elena and Bo to the Beacon of Light. In order to aid the Living Revolution, he had to return to the Beacon. His heart may selfishly have wanted to stay, but his truth and his honor demanded otherwise. As much as his heart begged him to choose one path, it was his mind who forced him to choose the right one.

Zhu swallowed a sigh and nodded. "Of course. I can't wait to go back to the Beacon."

13

THE LINE DRAWN

Only Hengyen and François made it back to the Beacon of Light. Hengyen had finally bothered to learn Whiny's name this morning, but only because his other two windrunners had died and it felt awkward not knowing what to call his last remaining companion. In hindsight, he'd have much preferred to keep the nickname.

François had insisted he be called by his English name even though Hengyen was pretty sure it wasn't "English" at all. The last few hundred meters through the dead-infested Charred Fields nearly finished them off. By then, after five days of barely any food and little water, Hengyen was scarcely more alive than the jiāngshī around them. If it weren't for the Beacon sending a contingent of guards to meet them at the eastern edge of the Fields, he doubted they would have survived that last leg.

He glanced to François—who had been nothing but a hindrance this entire mission—and resisted the urge to stick a knife through the boy's throat, if anything just to shut him up. It was a terrible injustice that good people died while this sniveling coward still breathed.

The moment the two stepped through the small gates leading into the container crate forming the base of the wall, François collapsed to his knees. Hengyen honestly felt like doing the same, but they were surrounded by guards, and a cluster of people had formed just inside the entrance. Apparently, word had spread quickly that he was returning. As touching as it was to know that people cared, he personally would have preferred they all continued about their work.

"Did the main body of the team return?" he asked.

"Yes, dàgē," replied the guard.

Relief lifted Hengyen's spirits. "All of them?"

"Most." The guard furrowed his brow and revised his assessment. "Maybe half?"

Half wasn't a good number.

Hengyen entered the Beacon amid cheers and scattered cries of "Dàgē!" He ignored them as he scanned the crowd, then turned to the nearest guard. "Get François checked out at the medical tent. Take me to the secretary immediately." He turned to the crowd. "Know this. Ling Weizhen, Wang Lankui, and Tian Haihong are heroes of the Living Revolution. Their names should be remembered for a thousand years." The crowd cheered three times in unison respectfully.

Hengyen looked away. There was nothing glorious or heroic about their deaths. Haihong was killed the first night after the bridge job, when François, while searching for firewood, led the dead straight back to camp, arms waving and screaming and making so much noise he likely attracted all the rest of the jiāngshī in the area. Weizhen perished the next day while they were trying to cross one of the jiāngshī-infested roads. The young windrunner was already weakened and running a high fever from that infected scratch on his arm. The three had nearly made it across the four-lane highway when he stumbled. Hengyen went back to help him, but that delay proved costly when a group of jiāngshī appeared and cut off their escape. That was when Weizhen had sacrificed himself by throwing his body at that group, buying Hengyen and François time to escape to the other side.

In any case, the Living Revolution needed their heroes. They needed to be inspired and keep their hopes alive.

"Do you want to rest first, sir?" asked the guard. "You must be hungry."

He was actually starving, but there were more pressing things on his mind. He caught one last glimpse of François being led away. He hoped he would never have to see the boy again. The guards escorting him to the administration building were unnecessary. The crowds parted before him as if he were an emperor, some even going as far as to bow deeply and bring their hands together in thanks and blessing. Hengyen would have stopped this foolishness if he weren't so tired.

"The rumors were that you had perished," the guard closest to him explained. "Some of the people held a vigil for your safe return. We were starting to lose hope."

Hengyen grunted. "We shouldn't be wasting candles."

To his surprise, instead of being escorted directly to the administration building, he was taken to the showers. "Secretary Guo's orders," said the guard as one of the cleaners brought him a fresh set of clothes. "He's asked to see that you're well tended to before your meeting."

More likely the secretary didn't want his nice furniture soiled, but Hengyen wasn't going to complain. He looked in a mirror before he stepped into the shower and didn't recognize the face staring back at him. His short hair was matted and ruddy from dried blood. The mirror displayed more dirt than face, and his sunken eyes made him look skeletal. He tugged at his shirt and found it sticking to his body like a second skin.

Hengyen took his time showering, letting his horror and exhaustion wash away. He hung his head and was mesmerized by the layers of grime and blood swirling into the drain. The lukewarm water pelted the crud on his body, struggling to dislodge the gunk that almost felt like a part of him. A small chunk of flesh fell, splattering a ring of red. He stared at it, wondering what body part it was and who it had come from. How many people's remains were on him? Ten? Twenty? A hundred? Was he washing away the very last of their existence in this world?

When he finally felt too guilty for wasting warm water, he stepped out of the wash tent, dressed in some clean clothes provided by the guard, and was escorted to the administration building.

He was hit with a blast of cool air as he entered the secretary's office, which chilled him to the core. Hengyen saluted the secretary sitting behind his desk. Guo was scowling. Hengyen turned to find Wangfa, who rose from the couch off to the side.

The two men clasped arms. "Wangfa, I'm glad to see you," he said.

"We thought we had lost you, sir," his second in command replied.

"Are our objectives still standing?"

"The explosives were insufficient to destroy the bridge, and we were not able to fight through to cause the cave-in on the highway. You?"

"We managed to only blow part of it." All three objectives failing was worse than he had anticipated. "How many losses?"

"The bridge team lost one-third. I lost half."

Hengyen grimaced. This was nearly the worst-case scenario. He turned back to Guo, who was coming around the desk. "We have failed. Please accept my deepest apologies."

"The apology is not accepted," replied Guo. "The Living Revolution is the struggle of our generation. It was not meant to be easy. If my best must atone every time we fail, then that is a failure of leadership and trust."

"Thank you," bowed Hengyen, humbled.

"However," the secretary continued, rather dramatically as he stared at both Hengyen and Wangfa. He focused more on Hengyen. "It is our duty to ensure that these errors are never to be repeated. The plan to deflect the typhoon away from the Beacon was flawed. Mistakes were made. Wangfa wanted to destroy the main bridge along the highway. Perhaps if we had focused only on that, the mission would have succeeded."

"Destroying that one bridge would have done nothing, secretary," Hengyen protested. "It would have at best slowed the typhoon down, maybe bought us a few days."

"And now we have destroyed nothing and bought no time at all," Guo shot back sternly. "However, that is all in the past. We must move on to our next course of action."

Hengyen nodded and began speaking briskly. He had spent many hours during his long trek devising a plan. "We need to begin preparations to evacuate the Beacon. If we follow the Yuanjiang River, we can protect our rear. Wind teams can move ahead to carve . . ." He stopped. Guo and Wangfa had exchanged sideways glances and were looking at him expectantly.

Guo's words came slowly and carefully. "I reviewed our organizational structure while you were away. Too many things lately have been falling through the cracks. Ming says our stores aren't keeping up with our burn rate, and the wind teams are not operating at optimal levels. The tension between the windrunners and guards have steadily worsened. I realized that we have been burdening you with too much responsibility. You're stretched too thin, Hengyen. No one man can handle everything on your plate."

Hengyen stood at attention. "I do not disagree, secretary. As you are well aware, casualties among my wind teams are high. It has been a priority to—"

Guo interrupted him abruptly. "I have promoted Wangfa to the Beacon's head of defense. We have been discussing our next step."

Hengyen stiffened, his eyes narrowing as he involuntarily clenched his fists. He maintained his composure, if barely. "If the secretary has lost faith in my abilities, or believes I have failed the Living Revolution, I will tender my resignation."

"No, no," said Guo hastily, waving his hands. "Your resignation is not accepted. You are still vitally important to the revolution."

"Yet you have deemed it fit to strip me of my rank, lower my standing among those under my command, and plan the defenses of the Beacon of Light while I was away."

The secretary's voice softened. "Do not think of it as a demotion, comrade. The Beacon of Light needs her windmaster to be fully committed and focused on leading our wind teams. The Living Revolution still requires your services, Ying Hengyen. Would you actually abandon her in our most dire moment of need?"

Of course Hengyen would never do such a thing. He knew this. Guo as well. It still stung. However, duty before pride. "Very well then. So, what is our plan, Defensemaster Wangfa?"

His former lieutenant nodded and gestured to the large map on the wall. For the first time, Hengyen noticed the markings spread around the settlement. New trenches, wooden stakes at the perimeter, choke points behind the walls . . . it was well-conceived and carefully laid out.

It was also a complete fairy tale.

"So you plan to defend against the typhoon," he shook his head. "This won't work, Secretary. It might hold off the jiāngshī for a few hours, perhaps a day, but they'll break through. Even if they don't, they'll simply starve us out. The jiāngshī have eternal patience."

Wangfa crossed his arms defensively. "It can work. We have a few weeks to set up these defenses. We will put the entire base to work."

Hengyen pointed out the window. "There are hundreds of thousands of dead out there. More jiāngshī than there are clumps of dirt in the Charred Fields. We have what, three thousand souls? And most can't fight. And this!" He gestured dismissively at the fortifications marked on the map. "How do you even plan to build this fantasy? Even if you enlist every person in the Beacon to dig these trenches and put up these fortifications, it will take months. The jiāngshī will be at our doorstep in three weeks."

"That is your job to figure out," Wangfa shot back. "Your wind teams will need to enlist those in the wilderness to aid the Beacon. We need hundreds more for construction and for the front line if this is to work."

"It won't work whether you have fifty or five hundred more bodies."

"Then draft a thousand!" snapped Wangfa. "Grab every breathing body from here to Chongqing if you must."

"Draft . . . ?" Hengyen was taken aback. He ticked off his fingers. "Let me get this straight. You want to capture vultures, integrate them into the Beacon, and then simultaneously leverage their labor to build up our defenses? How are you going to get them to cooperate after we enslave them? Where do we house these people? How will we feed them? Who will watch over them? How are you going to deal with these vultures when they rebel? Because they will unless we keep them chained. On top of that, how will our existing wind teams—already stretched thin—find the time to capture all these vultures while also keeping the settlement fed? For that matter, where will we get all the raw supplies we'll need to build all these lofty fortifications? Have you thought any of this through?"

Wangfa gritted his teeth. "We're still working on the details."

"Working on the details?" Hengyen rarely let his temper get the best of him, but this was more than he had been prepared for. He roared and shook his finger at Wangfa. "This is sheer idiocy. This is suicide. You have no plan! Our only chance is if we pack everything and get out of the typhoon's path!"

The secretary slapped the table. "Enough. We are not abandoning the Beacon. This is our home. It is the symbol of our defiance of the dead. We are also not abandoning the water purifier. It's the only reason we've been able to keep this many people alive. We will hold firm until the People's Army arrives to relieve us. That was their orders. This very spot is where we will draw the line. We will obey the party and the military, or we will die defending the Living Revolution. You two will work together like brothers of the Living Revolution. If not, I will send you both to work the Charred Fields for the rest of your days. Is that clear?"

The two men glared at each other for a long moment.

"Yes, Secretary," both replied.

Guo fixed them with his own steely gaze before the fire finally left his eyes. He took on a more measured tone. "The day those alive begin killing each other is the day the Living Revolution is truly dead. You both have your responsibilities. Work harmoniously to see them through. You've both failed me once. Do not fail me again. Now get out of my sight."

14

THE RETURN

Zhu didn't know why he was nervous when the wind team returned to the Beacon two days later. He watched the cable transport with growing apprehension as it clanged to a stop on the platform. Maybe it was because he wasn't sure how he would be received after being considered missing. Maybe it was because Elena pointed out the loose gears rattling as the gas engine wheezed to pull the transport in. Or maybe it was just because he couldn't quite bring himself to look Elena in the eye every time she pressed further about what had happened to him.

He half expected guards to be waiting after they disembarked from the transport. Dereliction of duty was a serious offense at the

Beacon, whether for a truant windrunner, a guard who fell asleep while on watch, or for a garbage man who skipped a day of pickups. The last one was especially egregious. Apparently nothing made a society fall apart faster than improper waste disposal.

Thankfully, none of the guards paid him a second glance as he climbed down to ground level. The few civilians who recognized him waved and greeted him as if nothing had happened. Even other windrunners didn't realize he had been gone for the better part of two weeks. The Beacon didn't miss a beat at all.

The one person who did miss him terribly, unfortunately, was Quotamaster Ming. He saw Zhu approaching his tent from far down the block. He stopped the salvage line, stood up, and planted his fists on his hips. "Well," his voice carried all the way across the field. "If it isn't the prodigal windrunner. Nice of you to finally join us. Everyone step aside. Let Chen Wenzhu through. We shall see what the young prince has brought us."

Fifty pairs of eyes tracked them as Zhu, face crimson, cut to the front of the line. Elena and Bo tried to shield him by stepping up to Ming first and presenting their scavenge. At two duffels, it was a handsome haul with several important and necessary components. Ming barely took his glare off Zhu the entire time he was sorting the inventory. The quotamaster was going to make an example of him.

Ming made a show of adding up the points. He shook his head. "Not bad, but not good enough. This doesn't meet quota for three people, especially considering the supplies allocated to your team, Elena Anderson, and the fact that Windrunner Wenzhu took an extended leave."

Bo gaped while Elena scowled. She planted her hands on her hips and hissed. "Zhu was injured and needed help. Windmaster Hengyen personally allocated these supplies—"

"Hengyen is only in charge of the wind teams now. I own the quota," Ming snapped. "Fifty—"

"My team was the one who got this scavenge," Zhu cut in. "They shouldn't be punished for their sacrifice, and I shouldn't be rewarded for their contributions to the Living Revolution." He pointed at the supplies scattered across Ming's table. "The points belong to them."

"Zhu, no!" Elena pleaded.

"We're a team," added Bo stubbornly. "We share our scavenge."

Zhu was adamant, however. His wind team had risked everything to find him. He would take a bullet for them. Or, in this case, throw himself at the mercy of Ming the Terrible.

Ming's expression turned shrewd. "Is that so? Look at you, Chen Wenzhu, so very righteous. Very well, then," he waved Elena and Bo off. "You two can go. Seventy-eight points apiece. As for Wenzhu, you not only stole time from the Living Revolution, you inconvenienced your comrades. They had to risk their lives to rescue you. How dare you make your brothers and sisters shoulder the extra burden! Have you no shame? For that, you will pay the penance of a full week in the Charred Fields. Report to the field master at dawn. Of all the selfish . . ."

While Ming berated him in front of the wind teams, Zhu kept his eyes downcast and studied the muddy ground, letting the abuse wash over him. At this point, the quotamaster was simply putting on a show, humiliating him not only as a lesson but as a display of power, and an assertion of Hengyen's waning influence.

Zhu did his best to take accountability for his actions. He *had* been delinquent. He *did* put his wind team and his comrades in a dangerous position. He deserved all of this. However, things felt different now. As much as he tried to accept his punishment, he was already mentally checked out, not only from Ming's dressing down but also from the Living Revolution.

The difference was knowing that Ahui, Meili, and those in the village had survived. Before Fongyuan, Zhu was a loyal revolutionary, a true believer in the living's cause to retake the land from the jiāngshī. Now . . . now all he could think about was wondering what Meili and the rest of the hidden villagers were doing. Were his students disappointed when they found out he wasn't there to teach class? He had only stayed with them a few days, but he hoped his presence had made a small difference with their survival. He hoped they understood why he had left them, that he hadn't had a choice. At the very least he hoped Meili would tell Ahui that her brother was still alive.

Zhu closed his eyes and imagined his sister's reaction. He couldn't envision her doing all those things the villagers said she did. Chen Ahui, a leader and fierce warrior? Leading a team to find the village a new home? He couldn't even imagine what she looked like now. The only picture he had in his head of her was the one from the photograph of her and Meili as teenagers. That faded photo was the last thing he had taken from his family's place before they set out for the Beacon.

"Wenzhu!"

He snapped back to the present, finding Ming standing centimeters from his face, yelling and shooting spittle. The quotamaster had worked himself into a special kind of frenzy when he realized Zhu was no longer paying attention. Zhu swallowed the sigh climbing up his throat. "Yes, Quotamaster?"

"You've already wasted everyone's time. Get out of my sight. If I hear that you are even a minute late tomorrow, I'll feed you to the dead myself."

Zhu bowed low and beat a hasty retreat, hoping that a little show of humility would soften Ming's anger, but also because he didn't want the quotamaster to see his eyes roll. He hurried away to wash off two weeks of wilderness. It was too late for a meal, but the showers never closed, and the pond bath he had taken at the village hadn't done much for him.

After the shower, he returned to his pod. He couldn't remember the last time he had slept here. It certainly didn't feel like home anymore. Now that he thought about it, had it ever? His cage on the top level halfway down the length of the container was just a place he slept between scavenges. He felt like a dog in his kennel, waiting for the next time he would be let out to hunt.

His cagemates offered small waves and nods as he passed. Most here were older men without families, or at least men who no longer had families, so they kept to themselves. This particular pod housed several of the purification plant engineers, which made them a little less rowdy than the crates that housed guards and laborers. There were pods reserved for windrunners, but Zhu found them disquieting. Half of the cages were always empty, and there were strangers moving in nearly every day. A danger of the occupation.

Zhu stopped by the charging station. He pulled out his camera and was about to plug it in when he hesitated. It had only been a few days, but the urge to go over the photos he had saved was overwhelming. He slid to the floor next to the small table and began to scroll through the photos of Meili: the funny face, the peace sign, the comedic attempt at a smoldering look.

It wasn't Meili specifically he was looking at, although she took up the entire screen and he admitted to himself she was pretty. It was the idea of being in a place that felt like home instead of what surrounded him now. The ribbed metal ceiling and the matching ugly rusted walls. The men next to him like animals in pens. The sweat and stink of the enclosed space. Their hopelessness pervasive. This place was a tomb. The entire base was a graveyard.

"Hey, you."

Zhu looked up and saw the reason he had come back. Elena had also showered and was wearing a dress. He hadn't seen her wear one since before the outbreak. She must have spent her points on it. He rose to his feet and pulled her in for an embrace. "You look amazing."

"What were you looking at?" she asked. "Did you get a new video?"

"Oh, nothing." Zhu hastily stuffed the camera into his pocket. "What are you doing here?"

Her eyes lingered on his pocket, and then she shot him a playful, pointed smile. "Are you busy tonight?"

Her question went over his head, as many of the things Elena said often did. Zhu wondered if he had forgotten something or whether there was some place he needed to be. He had his penance tomorrow; he couldn't miss that. There was also the matter of Windmaster

Hengyen wanting to speak with him. Elena had told him about that on their way back, although she seemed reluctant to tell him why.

She offered a hand. "Come with me."

Zhu desperately needed sleep. "Can it wait?" He stopped himself. After all that she had done for him. Selfish fool. "Of course. Where to?"

"You'll see."

Elena led him out of the pod and guided him to the north edge of the Beacon, away from most of the residential areas. Dusk had fallen, so Zhu stayed alert. Crime wasn't a common problem at the Beacon, since valuable possessions didn't really exist anymore, but one couldn't be too careful after dark.

She led him to the dead end of an alley flanked by the doors of three container crates meeting at the corners, and spun to face him. She smirked. "You owe me, Chen Wenzhu."

Zhu had the fleeting impression that he was about to get robbed. "How do I repay you?"

Elena grabbed him by the front of his shirt and pulled him toward her, placing her mouth over his. Zhu lost his balance and nearly sent them both tumbling into the mud. "I bought permission from the administrators for a night. I even paid extra for a suite," she drawled suggestively, waving a long rusted key lazily in the air. "I thought we could use it today."

Ten seconds ago, Zhu was tired and unsteady on his feet. A surge shot through his body and he quivered, suddenly wide-awake.

There were a few love suites at the Beacon, but most people couldn't afford them. Not only was the privacy alluring, there was a real bed inside the container, much more substantial than the thin foam padding that they used in the cages. His wide eyes must have been enough of a signal for Elena. She turned and inserted the key into the padlock and twisted it with a satisfying click. The latch unlocked with a hollow ring, and then the door creaked open.

Elena turned back to Zhu, attempting a not-quite-successful sultry look. Not that he cared at this moment. It was the thought that counted. She beckoned suggestively with a finger. "Come on—"

He had already lifted Elena off her feet, cradling her as if they were newlyweds going into a honeymoon suite. The inside of the container was plain, just a bed barely large enough for two. On one side were a nightstand and a candle, the only source of light. Zhu laid Elena gently down on the bed and lit the candle.

A yellow glow illuminated the dim interior, giving the room almost a romantic feel. The bed—a real bed with cushions—cradled a shadowy Elena. He was about to join her when she pointed a toe in the air. Zhu looked backward and hurried to close the door behind them.

It was as if they had completely cut themselves off from reality. All outside sounds became muffled. The whooshing rush of the purification generators was missing. The barking dogs and the calls of the night watch disappeared. The constant low buzzing of the jiāngshī was gone. There were no loudspeakers blaring revolutionary slogans, no prying eyes from the next cage.

Zhu pawed at the door, just to make sure it was locked. They were finally alone, just the two of them. No jiāngshī, no vultures, no neighbors or comrades. A charged silence followed. Elena stood, her fingers fumbling with the buttons on the front of her dress until it split open down to her navel. Zhu froze; he was nervous, as if it were their first night together. It had been months since the two had last been intimate. Between being mentally drained from sorting through the horrors of this world and the sheer physical exhaustion of trying to stay alive, there had been little time for tenderness.

The dress slipped off Elena's shoulders. She breathed in, her chest rising slowly. It all came back to Zhu in a rush as he nudged her toward the bed, kissing and pulling and stumbling. She squawked lightly as they tumbled onto the mattress in a tangle and clawed their way toward the headboard. Zhu tore himself away and yanked awkwardly at his shirt, popping the buttons off. Elena, eyes intent with desire, went for Zhu's pants, alternating pulling both sides down until they loosened off his hips. That was when he lost his balance and fell on top of her. Their mouths met. She smelled of soap and rain water, and hope, if there were such a scent.

A small, breathless sound escaped her lips as she lightly raked her nails across his chest, tracing her fingers along his many scars. The one on his shoulder from a pack of wild dogs. The gash on his neck from when a vulture had gotten the jump on them. The ugly starburst on his side from an arrow—friendly fire during the search of an abandoned house. Elena had been outside. Two arrows struck the jiāngshī, and it was only because Zhu was squirming as he tussled with the monster that the third nicked him instead.

They became a tangle of limbs rolling across the bed, knocking off pillows, bunching up blankets, and accidentally sweeping the candle off the side table. Darkness curtained the room.

Elena looked alarmed as she craned her head. "Is the candle okay?"

"I'm sure it's fine," Zhu replied in a muffled voice as his tongue worked his way up the base of her neck.

She laughed and pushed him off. "They'll never let us use the suites again if we burn the place down."

The timing couldn't have been any worse, but Zhu obliged. He rolled off her and crawled to the edge to make sure they weren't setting the room on fire. The floor was of course metal, like the rest of the container. He stretched out to pick up the candle and place it back on the table where it belonged.

When he rejoined Elena, they lay side by side, their faces so close they shared the same air. The faint light fell upon her, bathing the curves of her body in an orange luminescence, like the sunrise over the rolling hills of these lands. Zhu sighed and took a mental picture. He wished he could use his camera instead to remember this moment forever.

But then Elena pounced on top of him. Her fingers were calloused and firm on his chest as she guided him inside. He didn't remember her touch being so coarse before the outbreak. So many changes, even the smallest things. Zhu suddenly found it difficult to keep his train of thought. His body became flushed, his mouth dry. Their eyes stayed locked. Time slowed to a crawl. They played for an eternity, changing positions, laughing and reconnecting. The world they lived in no longer existed for these few moments.

The end came for them together. It was like a long walk up a hill, and then a sharp exhilarating plummet off a cliff. His knees buckled, and he momentarily forgot the world around them. He fell onto the bed next to Elena, his body drenched in sweat as he sucked in humid air. When he got his bearings, he felt drained, but content.

Elena rolled to her side and ran a finger down his damp chest. She spoke softly. "I didn't know how much I loved you until I thought I lost you."

Zhu froze. She had never said "love" to him before. Neither had dared. He loved her as well, but he had never imagined a future with her. Before the outbreak, they had an understanding that she would eventually return home. Afterward, there was little room for love.

"I love you too," he replied simply. The words came surprisingly easily, although a sting of bitterness still scratched the back of his mind. They loved each other, but not enough to give up their pasts.

Even now he couldn't imagine a future with Elena. His heart was with her, but it was also with his village. She would never go with him if he decided to leave the Beacon and join them. Doing so would mean giving up hope of ever returning to her family. He could never ask her to give that up. As much as she said she loved him, he knew Elena would leave him the moment she had the opportunity to go back to America.

She eventually fell asleep in his arms, her chest rising and falling as she curled against him. Zhu stayed wide awake, staring at the ceiling, guilt scratching in his head until he too fell into an exhausted slumber.

15

IN DEFENSE OF
THE REVOLUTION

Elena woke at the first sound of the morning loudspeaker. She scrunched up her face and groaned, pulling the thin sheet over her head. She hated those damn speakers. There were a dozen spread over the Beacon, making it so loud she could hear them clearly even in their metal cocoon.

Every morning, without fail, the entire base woke to the loudspeaker playing the Chinese national anthem, which was followed by twenty minutes of slogans: "The dragon rises with the dawn to feast on the still-slumbering sheep." "Too little sleep robs the body, too much sleep robs the Living Revolution." And then her personal favorite: "Only the healthy flower that blooms with the sun will find the strength to meet the challenges of the day." Because flowers had to worry about the dead trying to eat their brains.

Elena watched as Zhu zipped up his jeans. She marveled at how much he had changed in such a short amount of time. When they met, his scrawny body was a blank slate, his skin was milk-pale and the only mark on him was inflicted by a chicken who had objected to him taking her eggs many years ago. Now, he was sunbaked and wore more scars than she could count. He was still slender, but his body was taut with stringy muscles, the result of hundreds of hours of stress and strenuous activity, and not enough food.

Zhu threw on his shirt and grimaced at the loose buttons scattered on the bed from the night before. "I don't have time to get this fixed."

"Don't look at me. I can't sew." Elena rolled onto her stomach. "You should go fight jiāngshī with your shirt hanging open. I think it's sexy."

Zhu walked over to the bed and bent down. Elena met him halfway up for a kiss. "I'll be back by evening."

"Be careful out there. I just got you back." She changed her mind. "Wait, I'll walk with you. I need to start my day."

They left the stuffy suite hand-in-hand and were blasted by a cool mist hanging in the air. A fog had rolled in overnight, and a fine layer of dew now settled over the ground. The sun, hidden behind several layers of clouds, was a dull yellow climbing up the horizon.

Elena walked Zhu to the base of the wall, where a group of about fifty had gathered. Most of these people were assigned here as punishment for various infractions: breaking curfew, stealing food or water, sleeping on watch, speaking poorly of party members, et cetera. Most of them would work in the Charred Fields for a day. More than that for repeat offenders. The more serious offenders—the rapists, murderers, spouse beaters, drunken brawlers—were on permanent Charred Fields duty, forced to work every day. There were only a handful of them. Most didn't last longer than a few weeks before either the jiāngshī or sickness got to them.

It wasn't surprising that Zhu was the only windrunner paying penance today. Windrunners were usually too valuable for such work. The people who knew who he was must have assumed he had committed some grievous wrong.

A guard handed out several long weapons, mostly cut spears and pitchforks, but also several traditional weapons. Elena didn't know which kung fu school, armory, or traditional opera troupe they had scavenged these ancient weapons from, but she was glad for any implement that made slaughtering jiāngshī easier. Zhu opted for a blood-stained and rusted man-catcher: a long pole with a wide U-shaped two-pronged fork attached to one end. The local police called them riot forks, and used them to control crowds or to subdue someone from a safe distance.

Zhu gave it a few practice thrusts before hefting it over his shoulder. He turned to Elena. "I'll see you tonight?"

"I'll wait for you here when you're done," she replied, kissing him quickly before he was corralled into a squad and marched to the entrance of a container crate that led to the fields on the other side. Once the doors on this side closed, Zhu and the rest of his assigned squad would open the outer gate.

Elena went up the catwalk to the parapet and watched Zhu's squad on the field begin to fight in a ragtag formation, herding the jiāngshī into the trenches. She wasn't very worried about him. He could handle himself out there. What she worried about were the people next to him, the ones who weren't used to being out among the dead, the ones who frightened or fatigued easily.

At that moment, Elena was specifically thinking of a middle-aged woman with stringy, thinning hair pulled back into a ponytail fighting next to Zhu. She was thrusting a crooked tree branch timidly at the jiāngshī as if she were poking a piñata. The woman seemed ready to run at any moment, which would leave Zhu's left flank unprotected.

Elena scowled at the sad bunch of pushovers her boyfriend was saddled with. She wouldn't put it past him to choose to fight next to that timid woman in the hope of helping her survive the day. Zhu was good like that. That's what she liked about him, but she also didn't necessarily approve. Kindness was rarely rewarded these days.

She spectated a while longer as his squad corralled the jiāngshī into a cluster and then pushed them into a pit. The field master managing the squad doused the dead with gasoline or oil and lit them up. Within an hour, there were a dozen such pits burning in the fields. Long columns of smoke choked the air, clouding the sky with soot and ash.

The loudspeaker, blaring its usual slogans, paused to summon all off-duty windrunners and guards to a mandatory meeting. Elena had seen enough anyway, and was glad to finally be away from the walls. The growing stench permeating the air was terrible. She hurried down the catwalk stairs and continued toward the heart of the base.

The smell of cooked flesh was replaced by one of humanity living in squalor. She was minimally comforted by the fact that she knew she would get used to it within a few minutes.

The meeting was already underway by the time Elena reached the sitting area. She found Bo, which wasn't difficult; he was nearly a full head taller than everyone else. The big man grinned and made space for her.

"What did I miss?" she asked.

"The usual," he shrugged. "Windmaster Hengyen always starts with the good news. Wangfa was promoted to master of the Beacon's defense."

Wangfa was one of those guys who never gave her the time of day. In his eyes, if you weren't military—or Chinese for that matter—you weren't worth speaking to. The two men were standing on a table in the center of the dining area, speaking to the group of guards and windrunners who weren't on duty or scavenging. It was a smaller group than she expected, but they were still depleted from the mystery mission that they had been sent out on last week while she was looking for Zhu.

The windmaster was standing on top of a table still singing the praises of everyone there, making a point to call out individuals for certain deeds. Elena even got a little bit of a nod for leading her first scavenge and pulling in valuable resources. Then Hengyen eulogized the fallen. The crowd became respectfully somber yet also slightly restless. Every one of them knew it could just as easily have been their names being recited. Several scanned the crowd, probably taking note of the unfamiliar faces while searching for missing friends. Since windrunners were always coming and going, it could be weeks, if not months, before they learned that someone had made the ultimate sacrifice.

"Now," he continued. "You must all be wondering why we've called you here. As many of you know, there have been rumors of a typhoon bearing down on the Beacon of Light." He paused. "One so large it blights the land all the way to the horizon. I only wish I could dispel those rumors, but I have seen it with my own eyes. It's endless. A million of our former brothers and sisters, stolen from us, are now cursed to fight their comrades."

A wave of mutters and curses swept the crowd. If anyone knew the threat of the jiāngshī in great numbers, it was people who risked their lives every day. People began to talk among themselves. The consensus sounded like they wanted to run, but there was a very vocal group among the guards who demanded they stay and fight.

"What do we do? Where do we run?"

"We can't run. There's no escape from the dead. We have to make a stand."

"You fool. We can't fight a thunderstorm. The only thing we can do is take shelter."

"Coward! Where the living go, the jiāngshī follow. We must make a stand for the Living Revolution."

"How dare you!"

A scuffle broke out within arm's length of Elena and Bo, and quickly spread. It appeared the divide was between the windrunners and the guards. Bo, ever protective, moved between her and the melee and raised a ham-fist threateningly at anyone who dared venture too close.

A gunshot pierced the fracas and sent everyone into a stunned silence. Even Windmaster Hengyen appeared startled and annoyed when he noticed the smoking pistol in Wangfa's hand. Hengyen continued speaking. "The decision has already been made. My brothers and sisters of the Living Revolution, we will cede no more ground to the jiāngshī. We will stand. We will triumph. Or we will die fighting."

An uneasy silence passed among the crowd of wind teams. Some men and women were nodding along with a steely look, but many others were not as convinced by the windmaster's words. Restlessness and uncertainty rippled through the crowd.

"There is one more thing." Wangfa hurriedly stepped in front of Hengyen and broke into a wide grin. "Secretary Guo has confirmed that he has been in contact with the People's Liberation Army. Order is slowly being restored across the country, and it is our duty to hold the Beacon until they relieve us."

The two leaders had buried the lede. A great cheer broke the stunned silence, and grew to a deafening roar as the guards and windrunners, at one another's throats a moment earlier, now cheered and clapped each other on the backs. Bo had both fists raised in the air, and Elena got caught up with everything and ended up following suit, throwing her arms around his waist as they both jumped up and down. Someone started singing "March of the Volunteers," and it became a chorus.

Elena found herself humming along. She didn't know all the words, but it was definitely one of the snappier national anthems. If the army was still intact, that meant the rest of the country might be as well. If the tide was turning against the jiāngshī here in China, then maybe there was still a way to get home. For the first time in recent memory, Elena embraced that hope, just for a moment.

It was just a matter of time. She just needed to see this through.

Something about the two leaders caught her eye. Wangfa was enjoying the celebration a little too much. He basked in the glory on top of the table as if they had already won. Hengyen, on the other hand, looked like he had just bitten into something rotten. He crossed his arms and waited patiently until the song ended, then waited some more until the chatter died.

"We haven't won anything yet, brothers and sisters," he said into the silence. "The People's Liberation Army is on their way, but we must survive long enough to receive them. That means the Beacon of Light cannot break. We *will* not break. We will stand firm and cede no ground to the dead. We will fight them with all our strength."

More cheers followed.

The windmaster's tone changed, becoming grimmer. "Sacrifices will be made by every member of the Living Revolution. The typhoon will smash into our walls like ocean waves against the rocks. We must be prepared. We must strengthen our defenses, raise the walls, sharpen stakes, cut deeper trenches. Our stockpiles must overflow, our food supplies must overflow, and our hearts must be made of steel. We are willing to lay down our lives for the Beacon of Light to stand. This is our Long March, my comrades. Not every one of us will survive, but the ones who do will be golden.

"All of us will be pulling double shifts, and every soul will contribute to the defense. For the windrunners, the scavenge outputs will need to be vastly increased. Point requirements are now tripled. No more mandatory rests between scavenges.

"Furthermore, the Living Revolution will no longer tolerate the vultures on the outside to reap the fruits of our struggle. It is by our hands that the Yellow Flag paths are kept clear of the dead, all while these parasites feed off our accomplishments. All survivors outside of the Beacon will be brought into the fold in order to aid our defenses. It is now all wind teams' duty to report and bring forth anyone they find. No exceptions."

A new series of mutters swept through the crowd, especially among the windrunners. Capturing people changed the nature of a windrunner's role. All of them knew someone out in the wilderness. Some friendly, some not, some who bartered supplies or offered shelter. There was an ecosystem of survivors out there, one predicated on relationships and the shared need for survival. There was no turning back once these fragile trusts were disrupted. Elena personally found this new development distasteful.

One of the windrunners raised her hand. "Dàgē, I know a settlement near Dafu Lake with sixty people, most elderly."

"Every person," said Hengyen, grimly. "Man, woman, child. Anyone who can chop down a tree, carry wood, carve and sand a shaft, wield a spear. No one is exempt. If the group is too large for a wind team to bring in, then notify me to coordinate a raid. It's past time we unify the people toward our common goal."

"Until our needs are met for the upgrades of our defenses," Wangfa added, "every person brought in will count toward maximum quota. Any information leading to the capture of people will receive points as well."

Another windrunner raised his hand. "I know a family living on a barge on Yuanjiang River."

"There is a large group of vultures who raid near the base of Kiyu Mountain."

"There's a bunch of Christians living in an abandoned factory two days south."

More windrunners began calling out information they had about groups living in the wilderness in the hopes of getting credit.

Bo raised his hand. "Heaven Monks live on the horse ranch halfway up the San Mountain."

Elena's mouth dropped and she threw the hardest elbow she could into her friend's ribs. "Why did you do that?"

"What?" He winced, giving her the same look their family dog Winnie had when nine-year-old Elena had stepped on her tail. "The windmaster said 'everyone.'"

"Not our friends, or good people, and especially not people of . . ." The words died in her throat. Did it matter if someone still had faith in this world? Were they to be admired or ridiculed? She scowled. "Well, our team isn't going to do it. There's no way. You hear me?"

"Hey, Big Bo," one of the women standing next to Wangfa called, gesturing for him to approach. "You had raised your hand? Give me the information so I can credit your team."

Bo looked conflicted, but it didn't matter. It was already too late. She watched as he gave her a last helpless glance and weaved his way through the crowd to report what he knew. More windrunners, also wanting credit for identifying groups of survivors still in the wilderness, began crowding around the notetaker.

Elena took this opportunity to slip away. More than any other moment in the last few months, now she felt that she needed a drink. Even the sweet-sour plum wine would do. Anything to wash this bitter taste out of her mouth. She wasn't sure if it was from the ash in the air from the Charred Fields or just bile from her disgust.

On her way back, Elena treated herself, paying a little extra of her recent earnings to purchase some American-style pizza for lunch. It tasted like it was made by someone who obviously had never eaten pizza, but it was a nice change of pace from her usual diet of rice and scallions.

Afterward, she returned to her cage to listen to music on her MP3 player. She played through the same ten albums for the umpteenth time each, and spent the rest of her afternoon seeking solace in her worn, pocket-size King James Bible. A going-away present from her pastor father, it was one of the only things she had managed to save from . . . before. Elena never realized how much she had taken it for granted until desperate times like this, when she really needed a source of hope. She took comfort in the fact that if her parents were still alive and safe, they would be reading the same book. Now, more than ever, she wanted to believe that wasn't such a big "if."

Elena pushed away her dark thoughts. Her folks had to be alive, working with their neighbors to keep the community safe. They were probably worried sick about her just like she was about them. It was the not-knowing that was always the worst.

Someone appeared at the doorway to her pod and knocked on the metal walls. "Elena Anderson, may I speak with you please?"

Elena bit her lip. She recognized the voice immediately. "Yes, Windmaster?"

Hengyen walked inside. He looked exhausted up close. Not just tired but stressed in a way rest wouldn't relieve. "Ming told me the good news. You found Wenzhu. You did a service to the Living Revolution. Your bravery will be remembered. Do you know where he is at this moment? I stopped by his pod, but he was not there. I have something I need to discuss with him."

"Yes. He's serving his penance now. He should be finishing up soon."

Hengyen looked annoyed. "Penance? Ming can be hard. He fails to see past the numbers. That man is using an ax to shear grass." A small smile sprang to his face. "Why don't you and I be there to meet him when he completes his duty?"

Cold dread came over her. Not only were they headed into the greatest fight of their lives but Zhu would now be taken away from her for Hengyen's wind team. Feeling totally drained by the last hour's pronouncements, Elena barely managed to answer, "Of course, Windmaster."

The two exited her pod and moved along the paths parallel to the south wall where Zhu was working the Fields, passing through the narrow maze of container tunnels along the outer edges of the Beacon. The engineers wisely realized that the containers made excellent choke points in the event of a breach. The problem was they made getting anywhere through the thick crowds difficult for the living as well. Fortunately, walking with the windmaster quickly resolved that problem. The crowds parted for him as if he were some sort of holy man, waving and bowing as they passed. Elena felt like a celebrity just walking next to him.

They made it to the gate right before sunset. Hengyen stepped away to speak with a few of the engineers while Elena waited at the entrance where the fieldworkers returned in a weary single-file line. Each looked as dead as the creatures they had been fighting. She recognized the incompetent woman who had been fighting next to Zhu earlier; Elena was mildly shocked she had survived. Zhu was not among this group, however. She waited as more people filed in. Her worry began to build. Had something happened? Was he hurt, lost, worse? She began asking questions, starting with the incompetent ponytailed lady. She was clueless even though she had fought alongside Zhu all day. The more people Elena asked, the more she began to panic. It wasn't until she found the fieldmaster, literally the last person to come in from the Charred Fields, closing the gate behind him, that she learned what had happened.

The fieldmaster was barking orders to his subordinates when she approached him. He shrugged when she asked about Zhu. "You mean that windrunner? Ming told me to make sure that guy paid a little extra dues, so I put him on cleanup duty as well. He's scouring the corpses for valuables as we speak, along with a couple of other criminals."

Elena was apoplectic, "You did what?!"

The guy eyed her and smirked. "Isn't that what you windrunners do best, picking through the dead? Besides, he'll finally learn what it's like to have an honest day's work." The relationship between guards and wind teams had always been tense.

Hengyen stepped into the conversation. "Is that how you run your detail, Wang?"

The fieldmaster stiffened, and he suddenly developed a stutter. "Win . . . Windmas . . . master. How can I help you?"

"Go find Wenzhu and have him brought to us immediately."

Wang saluted and sprinted off into the field. Elena watched the fieldmaster speed off, actually worrying that he was running so quickly and carelessly through the Charred Fields that he might hurt himself. He returned a few minutes later with Zhu following close behind. Elena resisted the urge to throw her arms around him as they passed through the container walls.

Zhu gave her an appreciative look and then saluted Hengyen. "Windmaster."

"Paying your penance, I see?" asked Hengyen.

"It was my privilege and honor to serve the Living Revolution."

"Really, how was it?"

"It was terrible, Windmaster."

Hengyen chuckled. "And a waste of your skills, Wenzhu. I have an offer for you, for you both actually. There is a new threat to the Beacon of Light. The secretary has ordered us to confront and defeat this threat at all costs. Not only do we need to continue scavenging, we must," he paused as if searching for words, "*recruit* the vultures out there to assist in our cause. Our wind teams must work differently from this point on. The teams will have to be larger, more organized. The work will be more unpleasant, and so will require the most wise, competent captains. Zhu. I want to make you one of the leaders of these new teams."

Hengyen's Shanghainese accent was strong, and Elena didn't quite register everything the windmaster had said. It was clear that Zhu was getting a promotion, but what was that about "recruiting" the vultures from outside the walls?

Zhu's face was painted with uncertainty. He looked anything but ecstatic about the promotion. "It will not be easy convincing the vultures to help us. Many avoid the Beacon of Light for good reason."

"There is never a good reason to avoid working with the Beacon of Light," said Hengyen sternly. "We are the last hope for the Land Under Heaven, Zhu. Does the Living Revolution have your support?"

Zhu bowed deeply. "Of course, Windmaster. It is my honor to serve."

"Good. Stop by my office later today. We'll organize the teams and start the raids tomorrow."

"Excuse me," asked Zhu. "What happens if the vultures refuse to join us?"

Hengyen gave him a hard look. "Then we enlist them into the Living Revolution by force."

16

RAID

Zhu took in a deep breath as he intentionally strolled casually across the empty field toward the formerly abandoned grain silo. The vegetation around it, approximately fifty meters in radius, had been burned away. His first thought as he approached the squat building next to the silos was that the vultures should have burned three times the area surrounding the silo to establish a better perimeter. The second was that there should have been someone sitting atop the building to keep watch since silos didn't have windows. What was the point of even establishing a perimeter if it wasn't guarded?

The third was that none of it mattered, because Zhu was going to be a backstabbing asshole. He waved.

A rail-thin young man, missing an arm below the elbow, was chopping firewood in front of the squat building. He squinted and was about to reach for a rifle leaning against a stack of cords when he stopped. A smile broke on his face. He waved back. "Good morning, Chen-shūshu."

It was the Smoker leader's son. Zhu couldn't remember the boy's name. The Smokers were a small settlement of refugees from several of the northern villages. They had banded together during the outbreak and made a home in these large abandoned grain silos. They had used the massive warehouses to smoke meats, dry fruits, and store other foodstuffs from the surrounding communities, usually taking a very fair fee. Many people—including the Beacon—not only used their services but also stored a fair amount of their preserved food here. These people were harmless, well regarded, and even considered essential by many in the region.

Unfortunately, the Smokers were also vultures.

"Is your mother here?" Zhu asked.

"Of course. I'll fetch her right away."

Zhu watched the boy run back inside the main building. He was a good kid: polite, respectful, and earnest. A movement off to the side caught his attention, but Zhu kept his eyes focused on the doorway.

Jiafeng emerged at the doorway a moment later. She was a squat, middle-aged woman with her hair pulled tightly back. There was a fair amount of gray in her hair, and her skin was a deep sunburnt brown. She was wearing an apron. From a distance, Zhu could almost mistake Jiafeng for his mother.

"Hello, Wenzhu." She smiled. "Where have you been? How are things in your big city?" The Beacon of Light was anything but a big city, but to many from the tiny villages it was probably still the biggest population center they'd ever seen.

He forced a cheerful smile onto his face. "We're still breathing."

"Well, come on in. A couple of hunters brought in five deer three days ago. Paid for the work with the fawn. We'll clear a plate."

Zhu squeezed his eyes shut. He really hated himself right now. "I'm actually here on official Beacon business."

He quickly spouted off the secretary's orders regarding vultures, laying out the threat of the typhoon and the need for bodies to help with the defenses. Jiafeng's smile slowly turned the other way as he rambled on. Finally, she cut him off.

"What if we refuse?"

"That's not an option," he replied miserably.

"I just made it one." Jiafeng tried to retreat back into the building, but before she could, Zhu's team of ten windrunners appeared from around the corner. One of them blocked her escape and kept the door open while the others rushed inside.

Zhu walked up to her. "I'm sorry." Jiafeng, hands on her hips, just glared at him. He couldn't help feel like a chastised schoolboy.

Zhu studied the ground intently as the rest of the Smokers were marched out of the grain silo single-file. He probably should have been paying attention in case one of them tried to make a break for it, but he was having trouble meeting their gazes.

Next to him, Taijian, a young windrunner who was recently promoted from the guards' ranks, continued to count aloud as they passed by: "Twenty-one, twenty-two, twenty-three . . ."

He should have been happy. The raid on the Smokers' settlement was thankfully brief and nonviolent. The Smokers just dropped what they were doing and surrendered. They were simple farmers and tradesmen, not fighters or predators. The wind team didn't even need to draw their weapons.

The windmaster had initially agreed to leave these people alone, but he was overruled by both Secretary Guo and Defensemaster Wangfa. They needed as many people as possible to build up the Beacon's defenses and man the walls. The two made it very clear that there could no longer be any exception. All survivors needed to throw their shoulder behind the Living Revolution.

Zhu was aghast when he first received the wind teams' new directives. Vultures were now considered high-value scavenge. Fighting the dead was one thing; fighting other living people felt like doing the jiāngshī's job for them. To have to capture people and bring them back to the Beacon of Light for forced labor was beyond the pale. This was not what he had signed up for when he joined the Living Revolution as a windrunner.

Several Smokers who recognized him called out and pleaded with him, asking for or demanding an explanation. Zhu, face crimson, bit his lip and continued to stare intently at the ground. This felt deeply like a betrayal, regardless of the technicality that they existed illegally outside of the Living Revolution.

"Zhu," Taijian reported. "Thirty-two total."

"How about their stores?" he asked, thankful to have something else to look at. More important than the individuals themselves were their extensive food stores.

The young windrunner gestured toward the six carts of smoked meats being loaded. "It's a great scavenge, even with the new quota rules. We scored big today."

Jiafeng began to yell when she saw that the wind team was confiscating the food. "You can't take that." She broke free from the windrunner trying to bind her hands and rushed to Zhu, leveling an accusing finger. "Wenzhu, you know all this food belongs to the hunters and farmers who brought it to us. They're paying to have it preserved. If you steal it, hundreds will starve."

The windrunner caught up to her and pulled her into a headlock, dragging her back to the line. "If you care so much for their well-being, tell us where they are and we'll make sure they have food in their bellies and roofs over their heads." Several others laughed.

Zhu did his best to ignore her screams. "Finish up. I want to be back at the Beacon before nightfall. Make sure all the silo doors are closed and secured." He was about to walk away when he hesitated, and then turned to Jiafeng. "Hopefully you'll soon return to find these silos just the way you left them." That was probably a lie, although Zhu desperately wanted to believe that after the threat of the typhoon had passed, they could send everyone home.

Jiafeng spat on the ground. "You're worse than the jiāngshī, Wen-zhu. They're monsters, but you, you're the devil. You have a choice."

The windrunner cuffed her across the side of the head and knocked her to the floor. "Watch your mouth, vulture."

"Hey," Zhu snapped. "She is now a sister of the Living Revolution. Treat her like one. Else you will have me to answer to."

While they were all distracted, Jiafeng's son, the polite, skinny young man missing an arm, head-butted the windrunner holding him. Blood exploded from the broken nose, and the windrunner collapsed into a heap. The young man took off, pushing another windrunner down and sprinting for the trees.

"Run, son!" screamed Jiafeng as she was dragged down to the ground.

The young man bumped and startled Elena as she walked out of the silo. She hesitated and then raised her bow. Zhu could tell this was a little Bobby situation all over again as the arrow sailed wide left. She found this work just as distasteful as he did.

Taijian stepped up next to him, raising a hunting rifle. Before he could shoot, Zhu pulled his arm down. "Our job is to recruit for the Living Revolution," he snapped. "Not add to the enemy's ranks. I'll take care of it."

He nodded, pivoting his aim to the remaining vultures. "Be careful."

Zhu took off after the young man, crashing haphazardly through the thickets. Thorns and branches whipped his face as he just managed to keep the escapee in sight. Plowing blindly through the trees like this was foolish and extremely dangerous. It was a sure way to fall into a gust of jiāngshī. Zhu wasn't doing this for his own benefit though, and certainly not for the Beacon's quota. What mattered to him was saving the young man from his panicked and rash decision. If Zhu didn't get to him first, the jiāngshī inevitably would.

Soon, the boy's pace slowed. Zhu was a mere ten meters away when a jiāngshī, likely attracted by the noise, stepped into the boy's path. He panicked and tried to change course, and ended up clothes-lining himself on a low branch. He landed heavily on the ground, writhing and clutching his neck, hacking and spitting. The jiāngshī lumbered toward him.

Zhu wasn't going to get to the boy before the jiāngshī took a bite. He did the next best thing, drawing his machete and lobbing it with all his might. The machete sailed lazily through the air, its handle bouncing off the jiāngshī's head. The impact was enough to knock the jiāngshī off balance, buying the boy a few seconds to roll away, still grabbing at his throat with his remaining arm.

Then Zhu was there. He soccer-kicked the staggering jiāngshī in the face hard; the thing's neck snapped back with a satisfying crack. Zhu picked up his machete, walked over to the gray, twitching mass, and plunged the blade through its empty eye socket.

He let the blade sit in the skull for a few seconds and then yanked it out. The boy recovered his wits just in time to see Zhu approach with his machete in hand. He crab-crawled backward, kicking at Zhu with both legs, and then opened his mouth, presumably to scream.

Zhu quickly covered the boy's mouth and pinned him down, hissing in his ear. "Here are your choices. If you stay here, the jiāngshī will get you. I won't let that happen, which means I'll have to kill you. You can accept that, or you can come with me. You'll have to serve the Beacon, but at least you'll be alive. More importantly, you'll be with your family and the other Smokers. You can still help them if you stay with them. Do you understand?"

The boy nodded and mumbled something. Zhu slowly pulled his hand away from his mouth, ready to slap it back on. The boy spoke. "Why can't you just leave us alone? We never did anything to you." That was the truth. Perhaps that was the problem.

"A typhoon is coming. The dead will wash over this province unless we stop them," Zhu replied. "The only way we can do that is if we all work together." He softened his tone. "Come, let me take you back to your mother. She will need you now more than ever."

His words seemed to get through to the boy, and they returned to the silos without incident. Jiafeng looked simultaneously appalled and relieved when they emerged from the forest. Zhu handed the young man off to a windrunner with explicit instructions to treat him well.

He wandered to the edge of the clearing and sat down on a boulder, burying his face in his hands. "This is for the Beacon's survival, for all of our survival," he muttered over and over again. No matter how many times he repeated it, it didn't feel any more true.

Someone patted his shoulder. He knew instantly from the soft touch who it was. "Are you all right?"

He clutched her hand tightly. It made him feel better, a little less alone, less like a terrible person. "I'll be fine," he replied. "I'm just drained. This is our third raid in as many days." He had barely slept at all. In his dreams, the faces of the vultures were now mixing with the faces of the dead, except now he was running into these people in their captivity at the Beacon.

Elena threw her arms around him and held him tightly. "We're almost done. Just hang in there a little longer. Once the army gets here, everything will be all right. There is light at the end of the tunnel."

Zhu wondered if that were really so. He had grown so accustomed to this new, hellish world. Could they ever hope to go back? If they did, what would it mean for Elena, who yearned for her family and homeland?

"Come on, we're ready to get out of here. The sooner we get home, the better." She pulled him to his feet and led him back to the main body of the raid.

The wind teams, their wagons laden with supplies and prisoners, were about to depart for the Beacon of Light when a contingent of guards appeared. To their surprise, Defensemaster Wangfa was leading them.

"This wind team has new orders," he said, surveying the convoy. "You're being sent on another raid. My guards will take over this detail and escort our newly repatriated citizens of the Living Revolution back to the Beacon. We're also commandeering the silo for Beacon use."

"But, Defensemaster," Zhu protested. "This is a large convoy. There are several dangerous areas that require windrunner skills."

"It's only a two-hour journey. My guards can manage." Wangfa gestured to the men around him. Ever since he became defensemaster, Wangfa had slowly turned the guards into something more in his own image. Whereas windrunners depended on finesse, stealth, and skill to accomplish their tasks, these new guards under the defensemaster's leadership wielded intimidation and brute force to keep the people in line.

Many of his guards were drawn from the ranks of the local toughs and bullies. They tended to be louder, more abrasive, and quick to resort to their batons and clubs. Zhu also considered them cowards, or they would have tried to become windrunners as opposed to pushing around the people behind the safety of the settlement's walls. A tinge of fear and tension now constantly hung in the air back at the settlement. While the secretary claimed to disapprove of the guards' new harsher tactics, he also commended Wangfa for keeping order and keeping the crime rates low.

"In times of war, some freedoms must be sacrificed for the greater good," the secretary had declared when the harsher rules and early curfews were enacted.

"You're far out of your jurisdiction, aren't you, Defensemaster?" asked Zhu.

Wangfa eyed him dismissively. "You are hereby ordered to make your way to the horse ranch sanctuary. The Heaven Monks lived too long on the periphery. Secretary Guo charges your wind team with rounding that Daoist rabble up."

Elena sucked in her breath. Zhu didn't move, save for his hands curling into fists.

"Defensemaster Wangfa, our peace with the Heaven Monks has existed since the founding of the Beacon. They are a valuable ally that would be lost if we forced them into the Beacon."

Wangfa looked at him pointedly, and lazily placed a hand on the ax head hanging off his waist. "Then find another way to . . . *convince* the Heaven Monks to rejoin society. But one way or another, your duty is to bring them in. Do you have a problem with that, comrade?"

A tense moment followed. Zhu masked his sigh and bowed his head. "Of course not. I serve the Living Revolution."

———

Elena studied Zhu out of the corner of her eye as they walked up the winding road to the horse ranch. She worried about him. He hadn't been the same since Fongyuan. Something must have happened in the time they were separated, and he clammed up and became pensive every time she asked. If she didn't know better, she would have thought he was hiding something from her.

The situation with the windrunners and the vultures only exacerbated his mood. Since the first raid on the vulture settlements over a week ago, his temperament had steadily deteriorated, becoming waspish and unpredictable. He wore a near-constant scowl, and she often caught him staring off into the middle distance.

Elena could sympathize: the act of rounding people up and putting them to work at the Beacon was certainly distasteful. That said, she also thought the vultures needed to be held accountable. It wasn't a coincidence that there were several vulture settlements within a day's journey of the Beacon. From a steady supply of purified water, to the Beacon guards constantly clearing the streams of jiāngshī, to the build-out and upkeep of the flag paths, the vultures had enjoyed the benefits of the Living Revolution without working for them. It was always Beacon labor and Beacon lives at risk. Elena, and many others, had long grown tired of this unfair arrangement.

Back in Texas, Elena had been raised in a tight-knit community. Her family's homestead was surrounded on all sides by cattle ranches.

Whenever a neighbor lost one of their cattle, everyone would pitch in to help find the lost animal. It was always a neighborhood effort, one freely offered and accepted because everyone knew they could be the ones sending out a call the next day.

It was only right that these freeloaders started contributing to the Living Revolution, especially with fighting off this oncoming typhoon. Besides, if the typhoon destroyed the Beacon of Light, then everyone in Hunan province was doomed.

Zhu didn't see things that way, and people were starting to notice. If he didn't get it together soon, Windmaster Hengyen would have to do something. If Zhu wasn't careful, he could end up laboring next to the people they had been capturing.

They reached the horse ranch by late afternoon. Elena had hoped to find it abandoned. Regardless of how she felt about vultures in general, she didn't relish the idea of capturing a religious group, especially one she had fought alongside less than two weeks ago. It all hit a little too close to home.

Unfortunately, luck wasn't with her. Smoke rose from the chimney of the main house. Several carts, including a wagon with a cage on top, were parked neatly off to the side. A monk was on guard at the second floor of the barn where she and Bo had stayed. More disconcerting were the fifty or so jiāngshī corralled in the pens off to the side. It appeared the Heaven Monks had not been deterred by the recent problems, and were still performing cleansing rituals.

Master Jiang Ping and a small group of Heaven Monks were waiting for them at the front steps to the main house, all wearing their red-and-gold robes. Standing by Jiang Ping was the old woman she admired so much, still looking like a badass with her huge pǔdāo, staked to the ground next to her. Elena recognized several others whom she had either fought next to or helped tend to after the previous battle here with those escaped jiāngshī.

Elena initially shrank back and hid behind Bo as the elderly monk approached to greet them. It was the wind-team leader's job to inform them of the terms for their surrender, but Zhu looked like he was in another world. Bo was about to nudge him when Elena decided to take matters into her own hands.

Elena stepped up and took charge. She bowed. "Master priest."

Recognition lit his face and he offered her a friendly smile. "Hello, Elena Anderson. What can we do for you today? If your people require rest, we will happily share our space and food with you. Be warned, however, we have nearly a hundred jiāngshī in the pens. A cleansing ritual is scheduled for tonight. Your wind teams are more than welcome . . ." His voice trailed off when he finally sensed the tension in the air. The monks behind him must have noticed as well, because their hands drifted toward their weapons.

"What is the meaning of this?" he asked softly.

Elena respectfully informed Jiang Ping of Secretary Guo's directive, trying to make it sound like she was delivering an official statement. She was honest, telling him about the typhoon and the consequences of not complying with the will of the Living Revolution. She emphasized that the Heaven Monks would be well rewarded for their loyalty, and that there was a good possibility that they could operate autonomously after the immediate threat was over. By the time she finished, she was nearly begging the monk to comply. "The living should be working together. We all want the same thing. Please, consider our offer."

Jiang Ping did not hesitate. "What you propose is not an offer, Elena Anderson. It is an ultimatum. Your Beacon would take us from our holy duties shepherding the jiāngshī to heaven so that we can work like oxen." He ran his fingers down his ample beard. "I am sorry. This is not acceptable. Please send my regards to the secretary, but the Heaven Monks will not be joining you. I wish you luck in your battle ahead." Jiang Ping bowed slightly, then turned his back to her.

He retreated back to the porch before Elena found her voice. Her tone hardened. "It is I who is sorry, Master, but your refusal to serve your country and the Living Revolution is not an option either. This is your last chance." She undid the strap and let the shaft of her short spear slide down her palm. She took a big step forward.

Master Jiang raised an eyebrow and flared the front slit of his coat dramatically, assuming a defensive posture. The kindly old face now held a look of steel. For the first time, Elena noticed the straight sword in its scabbard dangling off his waist beneath his outer robe. She realized by the way he was standing that she was dealing with someone who knew how to use it.

The monks behind the master adopted similar poses, their weapons flashing out. On Elena's side, the windrunners did the same, all except for Zhu, who still had his hands in his pockets. Bo, who had recently traded up for an even bigger sledgehammer than the one he had wielded before, stepped next to her, bouncing the monstrosity in his hand. For a second, Elena had a flashback of one of those old Samurai Sunday movies, except with the old Western standoff music layered over it.

"Don't do this," she pleaded. "Today does not have to end in violence."

"The choice is yours to leave."

Elena bit her lip. The master had called her bluff, and she had folded rather easily. Truth was, she had never cared that much for the Living Revolution to begin with. Serving it was just a way to survive and a means to possibly get home.

"What do we do?" one of the windrunners asked as confusion ran among their ranks. Everyone looked to Zhu for leadership, but he wasn't giving any, looking indecisive and miserable.

Elena threw an elbow into his ribs, snapping him out of his stupor. "Say something," she hissed. "Fix this."

She appeared to have been successful. He grimaced and made a show of snapping his machete into his sheath. "I signed up to kill jiāngshī, not shed the living's blood. Come on—"

It was too late, however. Zhu's leadership had already eroded with this group. Taijian, eager to prove his worth, stepped forward and brandished his broadsword. "No, I'm not paying penance because of your cowardice. We have our orders. Listen, you crazy freaks." He marched forward and leveled his blade at the master. "We have made it clear—"

The young man managed three steps forward before an arrow sank into his chest. The poor sap stared at it, puzzled and confused. He grasped the shaft, as if he didn't believe he had actually been shot, and summarily collapsed in a heap.

Another of the windrunners drew a rifle and began unloading in the direction of the archer in the barn. The shots rattled the air, blasting a dozen holes in the side of the structure. A moment later, the man with the rifle fell to a dagger thrown by someone standing on the porch.

Pandemonium broke out. The windrunners—most didn't have guns—drew their weapons and charged, only to be met in melee by the monks. Elena caught Zhu standing in the middle of the chaos out of the corner of her eye. He still hadn't drawn his weapon and was waving his arms wildly, trying to get everyone to put down theirs. Neither side was listening, and the Heaven Monks especially didn't care that he was unarmed.

One of them, wielding a giant spiked mace, charged him from behind. He would have crushed Zhu's head in if Elena hadn't gotten there first. She pierced the monk in the ribs below the armpit just as he was about to reach her boyfriend and drove him sideways into the ground. She twisted the spear in her hand and violently yanked it from the monk's body. She turned toward Zhu, who was still oblivious that she had saved his life. She was about to yell at him to wake up when several more monks attacked.

Swords clashed against spears, clubs against staffs, and, in Bo's case, his giant sledgehammer against the little old lady's pǔdāo. Elena had learned from Bo that the pǔdāo was known as a horse sword, used primarily to cut the legs out from under cavalry. The large weapons clashed and clanged. On the surface, the two looked completely mismatched. Bo was a hulking man, and the head of the sledgehammer arced in wide loops around his body. There was nothing graceful about swinging the sledgehammer with such force that it didn't matter if someone blocked his attack. Realizing this, the woman didn't try blocking the big man's attacks, but managed to dodge and deflect, moving in tightly controlled arcs like a dancer. Every time the sledgehammer whistled at her, the blade of her sword swung up to gently guide it out of her way.

Elena was right that it was a mismatch, but not in the way she had expected. After the first six or seven swings, Bo's exhaustion became evident. Meanwhile, the old woman looked as if she hadn't even broken a sweat. Then, as Bo's hammer missed once more and sank into the soft earth, he hesitated just slightly before yanking it back up. That was when she struck, chopping downward with the pǔdāo and slicing him on the forearm. He howled a surprisingly high-pitched squeal as blood sprayed from the gash. Bo dropped his sledgehammer and clutched his arm.

Elena rushed to his aid. She was too far away and too late, however. The old woman leaped, and the blade of her pǔdāo flashed through the air, threatening to sever Bo's head from his body. The tip of her blade missed him by a hairsbreadth, but then she jabbed with the butt end. Bo gasped as it punched into his generous midsection, doubling him over. The old lady whacked him once across the side of the head and then stepped in front of his fallen body, ready to make the killing blow.

That was when Elena reached them. One moment the old lady had the pǔdāo raised high over her head, the next Elena's spear pierced her back and came out through the front of her chest. The old woman shuddered, and her large weapon slipped from her fingers. She staggered and gripped the shaft, and then she turned to Elena.

"Oh my god, I'm so sorry," Elena cried. "I wasn't thinking and, and..."

"Deliver me to heaven, please," the old woman gasped as she fell over.

"Lǎopó!" Master Jiang Ping screamed, rushing to the woman's side.

Elena froze, forgetting to breathe for a few seconds. She hadn't realized the woman was the master's wife. How could she have? Bile crept up her throat. She hadn't meant to kill anybody. She wasn't even thinking. Her friend was in trouble. She had tunnel vision and just acted. "I..." Words failed her.

The usually kindly master's face hardened. He drew his straight sword and leveled it directly at her. Elena stood there, frozen, as the blade flicked the air like a snake's tongue. The sword was beautiful, shiny, and intricate, with patterns of flowers and dragons wrapped around the guard and hilt. More pressingly, it moved in the monk's hand as if it were an extension of his body.

Within the first clash of their fight, Elena knew she was in big trouble. Jiang Ping was faster and stronger, and his movements were more fluid. She was armed with only a short spear, the plain shaft uneven and bumpy, hewn from oak with a rusty spearhead sharpened on a wet wheel. When she fought with it, her only thought was to stick things with the pointy end.

The fight between them could hardly be called that. Jiang Ping advanced with the sword. Elena tried to poke him with her spear, but he moved too fast. His sword whirled in front of her and suddenly her thigh, shoulder, and hand all exploded with pain. The spear flew from her grasp, flipping into the air and sinking point-first into the soft ground well out of reach.

Elena collapsed onto her backside and watched as the grim-faced monk advanced. Tears rolled down his face as the tip of his sword pressed into the skin over her heart. "You do not belong in heaven."

Just as the blade was about to pierce her chest, someone came barreling toward them, tackling the monk to the ground. It was Zhu! The two men landed hard on the stone ground and rolled several times as they struggled for control of the straight sword, with Zhu finally ending up on top. The blade hovered between them for several seconds as Zhu, both hands on the blade, pressed downward. He was larger and stronger than Jiang Ping, and the blade inched lower and lower. Finally, with an anguished scream, the point cut down into the monk's neck, slicing through skin and flesh.

Jiang Ping couldn't even muster a cry as he choked on his own blood, his arms and legs thrashing. Finally, after several seconds, he went limp. Zhu stayed straddled on top of him, his body shaking, his fingers bleeding from holding on to the blade.

Elena grimaced as she scrambled to her feet. The battle had ended as quickly as it had begun. Most of the monks were not fighters, and they quickly surrendered once their leaders fell. She made sure the other windrunners were getting things under control, and then she went to check on Zhu.

She winced as she limped to where he still knelt. His face was blank as he stared intently at Jiang Ping's lifeless eyes, his head half severed from his body. When she touched his shoulder, he shrugged her off. She hesitated, and then clutched his hand. When he tried to shake her off again, she squeezed his hand even tighter.

"You had no choice," she exclaimed. "He was going to kill me. You saved my life."

A sob wracked his body. "Did you know what Jiang Ping and his wife did before they became monks?"

"No."

"They were opera singers. They put on makeup and masks. They danced and acted in plays. They performed theater for people in the villages. These were their costumes. They stopped by my village once when I was a child. I spent the entire summer pretending to be Sun Wukong, the monkey king. They spent most of their lives bringing people joy, and then they spent the rest of it trying to send them to heaven. And for that, we killed them." He held up his bloodied hands. "What are we doing anymore?"

17

MORAL CHOICES

Zhu sat on the river's edge, watching the reflection of the morning sun. The day smelled like flowers and dew, with not even a hint of rot in the air. His vision blurred, and he blinked. He had been so focused on the shimmer that he had not realized his eyes had watered. He sniffed and wiped the tears off his face with his sleeve, taking several deep breaths, doing his best to pull himself together. It wouldn't do to get discovered kneeling here under the willow tree sobbing like a little boy.

It had been ten days since the wind teams began raiding vulture settlements. Ten days since Zhu went from a man who found food and supplies for the Beacon's survival to a man who captured people and forced them into labor. For some reason, these raids—sometimes two or three a day—were all a haze, but he remembered the face of every single person he had helped imprison at the Beacon. For every head he brought in, Ming would wash him with points, more than he could spend. If points were currency, Zhu was rich. For some reason, that made it worse.

A figure sprinted up and knelt next to him. "Zhu, the raft is ready."

Zhu nodded. "Any change on board the ship?"

The windrunner, Chow, shook her head. "Still just sitting there like a beached whale in the middle of the river. It must have dropped anchor or run adrift. No lights, no movement."

Zhu got to his feet and brushed the sand off his hands. He signaled to the rest of the team. "Load up. I want us on board before the sun is off the horizon."

Yesterday, a group of laborers had run across the ferry sitting in the middle of the river. They had thought it abandoned and sent two men on a canoe to investigate. The men were last seen climbing up a set of stairs and entering the bridge. After an hour, the head guard decided he couldn't risk sending any more men and returned to the Beacon. Last night, Windmaster Hengyen tasked Zhu with raiding the ship.

Zhu and his team of nine had set out before dawn, staying as close to the flag paths as possible before breaking off toward the river. This was his first raid since they returned from that disaster at the horse ranch three days ago. He was operating without Bo or Elena, who were both recovering from their injuries. Zhu hadn't realized how much he depended on them for emotional support until they were no longer by his side.

The wind team pushed off on a rubber dinghy and, staying in the shade of the trees leaning over the water's edge, made their way around the river's bend. The ferry came into view a moment later, wobbling lazily on the slow-moving current. It must have been some sort of exotic tour boat in its previous life. It looked like a floating castle, three stories tall with traditional roofs and dynastic green-and-red etchings along its hull. A large dragon's head missing its lower jaw formed the prow of the ship. Its boxy aft rose high above the water at an awkward angle. Zhu realized the ship was listing heavily to both fore and starboard sides.

He motioned for the team to paddle around to the back of the ferry, sliding up against its shadowed side. Chow was scanning the decks through a pair of binoculars. There was still no movement on board. Zhu found that strange. Most settlements this out in the open would at least have someone standing watch.

They crept up the ladder one by one, taking position under a row of large, square portholes. There was little sound other than the occasional creaking of wood and water lapping against the hull.

Zhu signaled and mouthed quietly. "Groups of two on the stairwells. Sweep from the top."

He signaled to one windrunner to stay with him, and they crept hunched over toward the nearest entrance. The first room was a sitting area with three sections of wooden benches. The two crept across to the other side, checking for signs of life, or jiāngshī. Finding none, they were about to move on to the next room when he noticed a large bathtub, looking very out of place near the front of the room. He ordered his partner to watch the door while he investigated.

The tub was resting on an elevated platform, almost like an altar. The windows that curved around it were blown out for some reason, and shattered pieces of benches were displayed ornately around the tub in a flower pattern. At first, Zhu thought this was a cult, then the smell hit him: burnt wood, cooked meat.

He closed his eyes and exhaled, almost resigned to what he was about to see. He was not disappointed. The first thing he saw in the tub was a hand cut off at the wrist, and then a head, hair shorn off, all near the bottom of the mostly-drained tub, along with what looked like sliced wild onions and potatoes and several small pieces of bone. The broth was dark red and had a slightly viscous look to it. At least now he knew the fate of the two men the head guard had sent yesterday.

Zhu peeled away from the grisly scene in the tub. "Cannibals. Alert the others. We're not bringing anyone back to the Beacon."

The windrunner nodded and was about to jog away when Chow came sprinting up the nearest stairwell. "Zhu, we caught them by surprise while they were still sleeping. We captured them but you need to see this."

Zhu pointed at the tub. "I just did."

Chow blanched and covered her mouth with her hand, but she shook her head. "No, this is something else."

She led them down to the stairs to a lower level. They passed through several doorways to areas that were now being used as living quarters. Signs of cannibalism were everywhere: skulls, femurs sharpened into tools and weapons, flayed skin that appeared to be drying for leather. The smell here could be the worst that Zhu had ever experienced, and it worsened the deeper they moved into the vessel. The rest of his wind team was waiting in the mess hall with the cannibals tied up against the wall. All of them looked pale and half in shock. Cannibalism, no matter how many times they encountered it, was still difficult to take in. There was no place at the Beacon of Light for monsters like this. A line had to be drawn.

Zhu was about to order his people to clean up when he realized why everyone on his wind team looked so unsteady. This was a nest of children, ranging between the ages of eight and fifteen by their looks. All were emaciated and terrified, covered head to toe in dried blood, grime, and who knows what else. How long had they lived like this?

"What do we do?" asked Chow. "We can't leave them."

"We can't bring them back to the Beacon," someone else added. "The only humane thing to do is—"

"We should bring them back," said Chow. "They're just children."

"My little girl is not going to play next to a cannibal."

The windrunners began to bicker. One drew his club.

Chow moved between him and the closest child, her hand grasping the handle of her hatchet. "Don't you dare."

"What are you going to do next? Defend jiāngshī?"

"We're not killing children!" Zhu finally roared. "This is the world we live in now. We've all had to do terrible things to survive. These poor kids did as well. It doesn't mean all hope is lost. We bring them back with us." He turned away from the ugly scene, mainly to hide his disgust with everyone and everything around them, but also to blink away the stinging in his eyes. It wouldn't do for his team to see his tears. "Chow, make sure they're well enough to travel. We will treat these children like children."

"Yes, Zhu." She put a hand on his shoulder as she passed by. "Thank you."

"We'll need to watch them closely." Zhu turned to the rest of the windrunners. "Search the rest of the ferry for useful supplies. No food whatsoever. I don't care if you discover crispy fried duck hanging off a rack."

"Come children," Chow spoke in a kind voice. Zhu had nearly forgotten she was a grandmother who had lost her entire family during the outbreak. "We're going to take you to a new home. You'll have clean food and water and—" Her words were cut short by a scream.

Zhu whirled around to see one of the children, who looked about eight years old, with her teeth around Chow's throat. The windrunner screamed and batted at her, but the girl was locked on. Zhu jumped on top of the girl and pulled her off Chow, but only succeeded in helping the cannibal rip out a large piece of Chow's throat. Zhu rushed to the windrunner's side and tried to press down on the wound, but it was too late. Chow gasped, her mouth opening and closing as she struggled for air, every breath gushing blood out of her wound.

He looked up just in time to see a boy with a butcher's knife charging him. He had nearly reached Zhu when a windrunner stepped in between them and slashed the boy across the abdomen with a sabre, spilling his intestines onto the floor. More weapons flashed in the rest of the windrunners' hands. Children screamed. Blood sprayed across his back.

Zhu cradled Chow's head in his lap as her eyes darted left and right. Fear and panic gripped her when she realized that her death was looming. Zhu squeezed her hand and kept his gaze locked onto her until, slowly, the life faded from her eyes and she stared off into nothing. Zhu muttered a choked prayer and closed her unblinking eyes as her body went limp. He didn't wait long to finalize her death with a swift, efficient plunge of his machete.

The massacre was mercifully short. By the time he looked up, all the children and another of his windrunners were dead. Zhu pulled out his knife and pushed it through Chow's temple. He stood over her body and surveyed the carnage. Blood was everywhere. Small bodies, tiny limbs, innocent faces.

"Make sure none of them rise again," he ordered, and then stormed out of the room. Feeling short of breath, Zhu fled topside onto the deck. He sucked in several labored gulps of air before slamming his fist into the metal hull, sending a dull gong reverberating across the ship. He struck it two more times before turning his back to lean on the wall. He slid down and crumpled into a shuddering mess on the floor. He buried his head in his hands as he replayed that grisly event over and over again.

All he could think of was what he could have done to save Chow's and the children's lives. Every decision he had made ended in people dying. Now both Chow and the children were dead. A part of Zhu wished he had made the wrong choice—he would gladly accept the responsibility—but now he realized every choice was the wrong choice. There were no good choices, no better outcomes. Nothing he did made a difference. This was the world they lived in now.

The children had just been hungry. The Smokers had just wanted to eke out a living and be left alone. The Heaven Monks had just been following their spiritual path. All the vultures had just been people trying to survive.

Dagang, the windrunner who had saved his life by gutting the boy like a fish, found him a few minutes later. "We cleared the rest of the ship. The little brats won't hurt anyone else anymore. What are you orders?"

Zhu continued to stare off into the trees. Finally, he answered. "Gather the wind team. We're leaving the ship immediately.

"What about the scavenge?"

He shook his head. "Forget it. We burn the ship to ash."

Zhu spent the rest of the day in a daze. He skipped his mission report to Hengyen and found an isolated spot near the purification plant to stare at a rusted metal wall. There were dried blood and bullet holes on it. The rumor around the Beacon was this was where the military had executed deserters during its construction. Not that this mattered to anyone anymore.

He had spent the entire trip back to the Beacon running over every decision he had made ever since life had fallen apart. Those Smokers could have been his neighbors. The Heaven Monks could have been from his village. Those kids could have been his nieces and nephews. He stared at his distorted reflection in one of the dented water tanks. He didn't recognize the person looking back at him anymore.

Zhu had always justified his actions by thinking about the greater good. Even capturing hundreds of vultures over the recent days had been for the Living Revolution, for the people. It was the only way any of them could cope with the horror of this world, but all of this felt like too much.

Whatever patriotism he had owed to the Living Revolution, he had more than served. It was time for him to return to his village and find his family. There was nothing left for him at the Beacon of Light. He was pretty sure Bo would come with him. The man was always a more loyal friend than patriot. Besides Bo, however, there was still Elena.

Elena had never cared much for the Living Revolution, but it was her only tie to whatever was left of the Chinese government, which meant her best and likely only way of ever getting home. Abandoning the Beacon would mean resigning herself to living the rest of her life in China. That would make Zhu happy, but he knew deep down that it wasn't what Elena wanted. He had been the reason she stayed in China in the first place, and the guilt of that fact was added to his emotional load.

He also didn't know if he was willing to leave her at the Beacon if she refused to go. The thought of abandoning her to the typhoon sent palpitations through his chest. Still, he realized he had no choice. He had to leave the Beacon, tonight if possible, so he resolved to convince Elena to do the same.

Now that he had made up his mind to leave, Zhu felt a weight lift off his shoulders. He left his hiding spot energized, relieved, with fresh determination. The first thing he did was use the majority of his available points to purchase supplies: weapons, a solar battery charger, salts, clothing, shoes. Anything that he and the village might need once they no longer had access to the Beacon. It wasn't like he had any reason to hoard points. When Ming raised an eyebrow at the requisition list, Wenzhu explained that he was personally rewarding his wind team for reaching one hundred vultures captured. Though skeptical as always, Ming seemed to buy it.

He spent the rest of his points purchasing a love suite for the night. It was the only place he knew of where he could speak to Elena in complete privacy.

Zhu stopped by the infirmary. One of Elena's injuries had become infected and was festering. Windrunners were vitally important to the Beacon, so the medics were treating and monitoring it closely. She was sleeping when he arrived, so he left a note for her to meet him at the suite.

Then he waited. He had considered buying a bottle of plum wine with his remaining points but he barely had enough left for a meal. He spent the afternoon going through the photos he had taken at the village. The more he looked at them, the more he realized this was the right decision. He was looking forward to leaving the Beacon. He had hope.

He was still flicking through the photos when Shanshan, one of the guards watching over the prisoners, barged into the suite. "Zhu, you have to come!"

Zhu quickly put his camera down on the bed and covered it with a blanket. "What is it?"

"It's the Heaven Monks. One threw himself into the fire. The rest overpowered the guards and took over the containers housing the smithies. They're threatening mass suicide unless we free them. Wangfa is instructing the other guards to just kill them all and string their bodies on the parapets to dissuade any further rebellions. You have to talk them down! Hurry!"

Zhu leaped off the bed and followed her out of the suite. He immediately saw the thick plume of charcoal-colored smoke drifting up toward the gray skies. The loudspeaker was screaming for water brigades, crying every patriots' responsibility to preserve and defend the settlement. Zhu and Shanshan joined the throng of people carrying buckets and containers toward the source of the smoke. Everyone knew what was at stake if they couldn't get the fire under control. It would be a death sentence for not only the Beacon of Light but also for the Living Revolution.

There was already a water line working furiously by the time they arrived at the smithies. Buckets were being passed back toward the front while children ran with emptied ones back to fetch more water. Guards standing watch over the work were barking for the people to work faster, chastising any who spilled their buckets.

It was fortunately not a large fire, and most of it was contained within individual containers. Zhu crept his way toward one of the containers' entrances. He pulled his shirt over his mouth as the smoke stung his eyes. He kept creeping closer, carefully picking his way deeper through the charred wreckage. By the time he made it inside the first container, however, he knew that he was too late. All hope for the Heaven Monks was lost.

He stood at the entrance and stared at the dozen or so charred bodies melded together on the other side. Some were on their knees, their palms clasped together in prayer as their opened mouths continued to scream silently in agony.

"Is this all?" he asked one of the blacksmiths digging through the debris.

"There are four more containers of this," the man replied. "Damn vultures."

"Watch your tongue," Zhu snapped. He closed his eyes. "Send the guards in to clear the bodies. Make sure they put stakes through all of them."

Zhu stumbled away from the grisly sight, his eyes wet from more than the stinging smoke. These monks' deaths were on his hands. The least he could do was help send them to heaven.

18

THE SPLIT

Elena was having a rough day. Her head was fuzzy from a mild fever, and the skin around her infected shoulder itched something fierce. The nurse mashed some tiny, black, foul-smelling pellets that looked like rabbit poop into a paste with water and poured that down her throat. Now her breath smelled like rot, and the inside of her mouth tasted awful. She held up the cryptic note that Zhu had left with the head nurse. He said it was urgent that they meet right away at the love suite. As much as she looked forward to seeing him and putting the suite to good use, she was self-conscious about her rancid breath. Her kingdom for a breath mint, if those things even existed anymore. Still, love suites weren't cheap, and she was going to take every advantage of this opportunity.

The two hadn't seen much of each other since they had returned from the horse ranch. It had been a hard day for everyone, Zhu especially, even though she and Bo were the ones who had come out of it bleeding like pigs. Maybe this nice surprise was Zhu's way of apologizing for being so unbearable lately.

A group of guards rushed past as she weaved her way through the crowds. Several sharp shouts cut through the air as they pushed their way through the crowds toward a plume of smoke on the eastern side of the settlement. Elena didn't mind the commotion. Whatever it was had to be bad. In any case, any problem within the Beacon's walls was under the guards' jurisdiction. Short of the jiāngshī breaking through the walls, this was none of her business.

Humming, she hopped over a trickle of mud slurping down the slope serving as drainage and weaved through the maze of tents, makeshift shacks, and shipping containers. She frowned when she reached the block of love suites. The door to the suite on the note was open. Elena double-checked the note and peeked inside. No Zhu, but the bed appeared used.

Well, she had no qualms about hanging out on the bed until he returned. The infirmary cots were little more than linen wrapped over a plywood plank. Elena kicked off her shoes and, mindful of her injured shoulder, eased herself down. She stretched, swinging her arms and legs out as if she were making a snow angel. As she inched up, her foot pressed down on something hard under the blanket.

Curious, she pawed under the sheets and produced a red point-

and-shoot camera. It was Zhu's, and he must have snapped new photos. She had seen his entire library dozens of times before. The one on the screen was of him standing on a small ledge in front of several levels of terraced rice fields. His arms were splayed out and he was grinning from ear to ear. Elena couldn't remember seeing him this happy in months, possibly since before the outbreak. This was definitely a recent picture. When—and where, for that matter—had he taken this?

Elena slid her finger to the next photo. Zhu was sitting on a log next to a bonfire slurping soup. She frowned. Where had he gotten that? The following picture was Zhu surrounded by a group of kids. It looked like he was teaching them how to pin down a jiāngshī. There were several more of the same. Zhu in a pen wrangling an ox. Zhu skipping rocks along a pond. It was idyllic, almost, and a complete mystery.

Elena scrolled to the next photo, and nearly dropped the camera. It was Zhu with a strange woman. Their face was close together—cheeks touching—and they had their tongues out in a stupid way. The next was them both trying to look seductive, looking up toward the corner. The two throwing up peace signs. Making funny faces. The images went on and on, each one slicing another wound in her heart. She checked the timestamp of all the photos. They were all taken when he disappeared in Fongyuan. All this time she thought he was hurt or kidnapped, but he had just been with another woman.

"That cheating asshole liar!" Hot rage sparked in Elena's soul. It seethed and burned, consuming her memories. All that time she had fretted about his well-being, terrified that he was hurt, dead, a jiāng-shī. The lengths she had gone to in order to find him. The emotional space she had given him. The truth hurt so much worse.

Elena's hands curled into fists. She squeezed back the tears welling in her eyes. At the very worst, she had always tried her best not to blame him for her being trapped here, but it had always stuck with her like a splinter embedded beneath the skin. If it hadn't been for Wenzhu, Elena could very well have been spending her days with her parents and Robbie, sleeping in her own bed. Even if things were as bad over there as they were here, at least she would be with family. She had thrown it all away. For him. Elena's chest heaved and she bit down on her lip as a pained cry—half heartbreak, half rage—escaped her chest.

"When I find him, I'm going to kill him. And when he comes back as a jiāngshī, I'm going to let him live forever as a stupid walking corpse!" She clenched the camera and, without thinking, hurled it as hard as she could. It smacked the container wall with a loud echo like a gong. It fell to the floor faceup, the back screen webbed with cracks. Roaring, she stomped over and was about to smash it under her heel when she noticed several figures standing at the entrance. She froze.

There were six guards blocking her only way out. All with weapons drawn and ready to use. In any other moment, Elena would have been worried and more than a little frightened. Now she just wasn't in the mood. "What do you want?"

The guards looked taken back, and uncomfortable. One of them finally spoke. "Windrunner Wenzhu had reserved this suite. Where is he?"

"Hell if I know. What do you want with him?"

"We have orders to bring him in. There are things he needs to clear up."

"Get in line," she growled.

Another guard muttered something to the one speaking. He nodded and added. "We are to bring you in as well if we do not find him."

These guys weren't messing around. The only reason security would deploy six guards was to arrest Zhu. What had he done? Other than cheat on her? Only one way to find out, not that she had much of a choice.

Elena picked up his smashed camera and stuffed it into her back pocket. "I suppose you're going to arrest me too?"

"Not unless you want us to," the speaking guard shrugged. "We'll need your weapons."

"Why, if I'm not getting arrested?"

"Nobody meets with the secretary armed."

Now a tinge of worry touched her. This was serious. She slowly drew the knife at her thigh and the one at her ankle, and tossed them both to the floor in front of the guards. The group parted ways down the middle.

"I want all my weapons back after this meeting," she hissed as she passed by.

"Of course, windrunner." One made a move as if to grab her elbow.

"Touch me and you'll lose all your fingers."

The guy's hand stopped, and he ended up stuffing it into his pocket.

The parade through the settlement was a little embarrassing. Elena felt like a criminal on death row as they passed people going about their business and children playing and training. Every set of eyes fell on her as the six guards at her flanks barked for them to make room to let them pass. She wished they would shut up. The entire settlement would probably know about this within the hour. Rumors were bound to follow.

The scrutiny followed them all the way into the administration building. The hallways were cluttered. This was the first time she had come in here, and she was amazed by how normal things looked in the building, as if there were no apocalypse and society hadn't fallen apart just outside these walls. The guards escorted her to a door and ordered her to wait just outside. She could hear loud but muffled voices on the other side. Just like outside in the market, everyone threw sideway glances as they passed.

Thanks again, Zhu. Asshole. Piece of sh—

The door next to her swung open and a blast of cool air blew into her face. Elena's eyes widened, and the hairs on her arm prickled. She couldn't remember the last time she had felt air conditioning. The yearning for home almost brought a tear to her eye, however illogical that was. It just made her all the more terribly homesick, especially now that she realized that the only thing that meant anything to her here was a lie.

She was surprised to see Bo walk out of the room. His face was sheet white and there were stains under his armpits. What did they do to him in there? He looked shocked to see her and mouthed something silently. Elena couldn't make it out. Her Mandarin competency did not extend to lip reading. She watched as he was escorted down the hallway and out of sight.

Windmaster Hengyen appeared at the door a moment later. He looked grim-faced as he beckoned for her to follow him inside. Secretary Guo and Wangfa were there as well. The defensemaster looked as serious as the windmaster. What was all this about?

The secretary shot her a bright smile and gestured at the chair. "Come in, Elena Anderson. Please, don't be scared. Sit, sit."

What did she have to be scared about? She hadn't done anything wrong. But Elena was now terrified, and Guo's words only made it worse. She did as ordered and sat with deference to the leaders of the Beacon of Light. "How can I serve the Living Revolution?"

"Where is Chen Wenzhu, and when are you two planning on leaving?" asked Guo.

Elena was startled. "Leaving for where? I don't know what you're talking about."

"You expect us to believe that?" Wangfa demanded. "That he would not take his woman with him when he deserted?"

A scowl inadvertently betrayed her face. "I'm nobody's woman. I'm looking for him myself."

Hengyen looked thoughtful. "You don't know about his plans to flee the Beacon?"

She shook her head. "This is the first I've heard of it."

Wangfa looked ready to hang her up to dry. Hengyen and Guo exchanged glances before the windmaster finally spoke. "Earlier today, Windrunner Wenzhu went to the quotamaster and spent all his points on survival gear and rations for either a long journey or a large number of people."

Elena's mouth fell open. "What?"

Hengyen continued. "Usually when someone at the settlement does this, they are planning on leaving the Beacon or ending their life. Based on the items he procured, it's the former. People who no longer wish to be of this world do not purchase necessities to survive in the wilderness."

"There is little we can do to stop a man from being a coward," added Guo, "but desertion cannot be tolerated."

Elena's anger deepened. Everything made so much sense. "That asshole. He was planning on abandoning me."

Wangfa's eyes narrowed. He jabbed a finger into her face. "You expect us to believe that? I think you're covering for him. Tell us the truth, or you'll serve penance until your last day on this earth."

Now Elena was relieved that she didn't destroy the evidence. She pulled out Zhu's cracked camera and showed them the photos. Her voice cracked. "I found these today. Just now, actually. She sat there red-faced, humiliated as the three men looked over her evidence. The secretary and the defensemaster were carefully poring over every picture, including the ones that had nothing to do with Zhu's infidelity. The windmaster only looked at her thoughtfully.

"Well," said Guo finally after what felt like forever. "We have suspicious activity, and now we have a motive. Defensemaster Wangfa, have your men pick up Wenzhu and bring him here for questioning."

Wangfa nodded. "I'll send out a general alert across the loudspeakers."

Hengyen held up a hand. "Secretary, this evidence, while strong, is circumstantial. Zhu has been a loyal patriot to the Living Revolution. Shouldn't we give him the benefit of the doubt? He hasn't been found guilty of anything yet. What if this was just a series of unfortunate coincidences? There is no turning back if you publicly announce his arrest over the loudspeakers."

Guo considered the windmaster's request. "Very well. Bring Wenzhu in discreetly, Wangfa. Call it over the loudspeakers only if he resists or if you cannot locate his whereabouts. The windrunner will have plenty of opportunities to prove his innocence."

Wangfa saluted and left the room. Elena got up to leave as well, but the secretary motioned for her to stay put. She crossed her arms and waited. The minutes stretched on. She became restless, and caught herself staring at the sliced oranges on the secretary's desk. It had been a long time since she had eaten an orange. Elena must have been projecting her desires, but at some point, Guo slid the plate toward her. She thankfully helped herself to a few slices.

Finally, after what felt like an eternity, the loudspeaker came on announcing Zhu's arrest, declaring him a potential enemy of the state and the Living Revolution. All three in the room looked up. Elena's heart began to beat quicker. What was happening?

"It appears our windrunner is guilty," declared Guo.

"Or maybe Wangfa just couldn't find him."

Wangfa returned shortly after the announcement. He looked irritated but also a little smug. "We're too late, Secretary. By the time we located him, Wenzhu was already on the cable transport passing over the Charred Fields."

Hengyen frowned. "How did he escape? Why didn't the guards just pull the transport back?"

"He had an accomplice."

"Who would dare?" Guo demanded. "Bring the traitor to me immediately."

Wangfa shot Hengyen almost a knowing side-eye. "You have some housekeeping to do, Windmaster." He signaled toward the door.

Elena gasped and shot to her feet when two guards walked inside. Standing between them was Bo. His wrists were bound, and his shirt was torn and stained red. His body was a mess of red and purple, and his face was so puffy his eyes had been reduced to thin slits. A deep cut ran along the side of one cheek down his face until it split both his lips. He looked dazed on his feet.

She tried to move to her friend. "What have you done?"

Hengyen grabbed her arm and pulled her back. "Stay here if you know what's good for you."

"Don't tell them anything," said Bo, his words coming out mushy. Blood trickled down the side of his mouth.

Wangfa walked up to the big man and punched him across the jaw. Bo's knees buckled and he crumpled to the floor.

Secretary Guo walked over to her fallen friend, towering over him. He nudged Bo's body with a toe, and then he glanced over at Elena, once again shooting her that wide politician smile. "What else do you have to tell us, Elena Anderson?"

19

PREPARATIONS

Hengyen walked along the uneven terrain on the southwestern edge of the Charred Fields making final preparations. The fighting would be thickest at the southern walls of the Beacon of Light. He stood on top of a mound of soft dirt that was designed to melt into a mudslide and peered through a pair of binoculars at the main stretch of land in the Charred Fields. Satisfied, he made several markings on a map to update the latest fortifications.

The newest additions were two wooden angled walls slanted inward along both sides of the main road at the far end of the field. The engineers had worked night and day to design these to withstand as much direct force as possible, using the terrain, an intricate support structure, and outward-leaning leverage to impede the oncoming rush. The way the jagged points alternated, the jiāngshī would not only get impaled trying to pass, their bodies would help block the ones coming behind them. When the jiāngshī did eventually knock over the wall, the entire thing was rigged to collapse on top of them. The fields were now cluttered with fortifications, from sharpened wooden stakes to flammable tar pits to piles of dirt that when doused with water would cause avalanches of mud to further impede the dead.

Hengyen was proud of his windrunners. They had achieved what he had thought was impossible. This was the culmination of thousands of man-hours using innumerable resources. Not only had they managed to round up nearly a thousand vultures to aid in the Beacon's defense, the Beacon was stocked with enough food and supplies to keep the expanded population fed and clothed for two months.

It was a good thing they wouldn't have to wait that long. The secretary had confirmed that reinforcements were on their way. However, they were moving behind the typhoon, and rather than shatter their ranks needlessly against so many dead, the army was content to follow at a safe distance until the typhoon passed the Beacon. From the perspective of a military tactician, Hengyen saw the logic in this plan. However, it certainly didn't help the residents of the Beacon with the immediate threat. He just hoped there were still people left alive by the time the army arrived. By his estimation, at the rate the typhoon was traveling, the Beacon would have to weather this storm for about three weeks. That was a long time to hold.

Hengyen continued across the field to the settlement walls, calling out words of encouragement to the workers laboring in the humid conditions. Along the way, he passed a line of former vultures digging a trench. The vultures were divided into groups of four, with plastic binds linked around their waists. Hengyen looked past their sullen faces. He didn't mind that they hated him, just like he didn't hold their selfishness in looking out for themselves instead of helping their country fight the outbreak against them. Winning them over was optional and could certainly wait. What was important was that they were helping now.

He returned to the shipping-container wall and quickly scaled the ladder onto the parapet, which unfortunately was only one container-level high. Hengyen surveyed the field, checking the map's accuracy to make sure everything was up-to-date. There were now six wooden walls, a maze of deep trenches and hundreds of spikes staked into the ground. Any jiāngshī that wandered onto the fields would be subjected to a veritable meat grinder. There was no way the Beacon could actually combat the full brunt of the jiāngshī, but they didn't need to. The plan was to inflict so much destruction that jiāngshī bodies formed a natural barrier until the danger passed.

That was assuming their defenses didn't crack, which was anything but guaranteed. The settlement could at best leverage two-thirds of the population for its defenses. That was every man, woman, and child over twelve fighting around the clock.

If he were a betting man, Hengyen would not put money down on their survival.

The windmaster peered through the binoculars toward the horizon. Today would be the settlement's very first test. The vanguard of the typhoon had arrived, approaching in staggered waves about a week ahead of the main body. It was a manageable trickle, but their numbers would only grow. The key would be to hold their lines as the dead relentlessly broke against their defenses.

He signaled to the flag bearer standing close by, who began waving a long green flag known as the dragon's tail. The laborers still in the field began to pull back. They were soon followed by teams of windrunners who pulled away from the outer perimeter. Next was a long red flag, the dragon's tongue, which sent three hundred armed men, women, and children as the first shift to meet this vanguard.

Two people joined Hengyen on the parapet a moment later. He didn't bother turning around. By the scent of soap and sweat, Hengyen knew it was the secretary and Wangfa, respectively.

Hengyen handed the binoculars to the secretary.

"Only three hundred?" asked Guo.

"The numbers will grow as the main body approaches." Hengyen put two fingers into his mouth and blasted a shrill whistle, capturing the attention of a group of guards who had just been deployed onto the field. He jabbed a finger to their left. "Wrong place, Lo. Your team fights on top of the hill." Hengyen turned back to Guo. "My wind teams bought us some time. They put up several smaller blockades along the side roads, narrowing the jiāngshī's paths into streams. They managed to divert them from the Beacon in other places, potentially turning away thousands of jiāngshī."

Thousands diverted, thousands still on the way. They were putting Band-Aids on bullet wounds, but it was what was being asked of him.

"How about our personnel?" asked Guo.

"Six shifts at four hours nonstop. We can maintain this rotation for now, but will probably struggle to keep it up once we suffer casualties," Wangfa reported. "We could use a few hundred more bodies."

Hengyen shook his head. "My wind teams have already scoured every crevice and vulture settlement that we could find. We are literally out of bodies to throw in danger's way. We have to make do with the numbers we have."

"Perhaps not every crevice," said Wangfa. He held up a camera with the glass shattered. "I looked through Wenzhu's photos. There's a few group ones taken that had at least thirty in it. This settlement he has left us for could be sizable enough to make a difference."

Hengyen was dubious, especially with the typhoon already on their doorsteps. "But the defense . . ."

". . . can hold for a few days," Wangfa insisted. "Take a few of our best. Arm them with guns. Even if you only bring back those in the picture, it would be worth it."

"Do we even know where this supposed village is located?"

"No," said Guo, "But I know someone who may. Bo has so far refused to talk, regardless of how much the guards have tried to beat it out of him. Elena Anderson clammed up when we interviewed her, but I think she knows more than she's letting on."

"She's innocent. She is as much a victim as anyone. Zhu betrayed her."

"What if we're just not giving her the proper motivation?" Guo plucked the camera from Wangfa's hands. "Come, Windmaster, let's speak with your underling. Maybe she just needs the right incentive to remember some helpful details."

"But the typhoon is approaching now. My place is on the front line." Indeed, the first of the jiāngshī had just reached the far outer wall.

"Wangfa's place as head of defense is on the front line. He has done a splendid job with our fortifications. We're in good hands. Your duty is to acquire the resources the Beacon needs to maintain our defenses, or have you forgotten?" Guo waved at the battlefield. "Besides, this is just the appetizer. What did our scouts say? We have a week before the real threat arrives."

"Go ahead, Hengyen," said Wangfa, crossing his arms. "The walls won't crack in the first hour of the first day just because the great savior of the Beacon of Light isn't here."

Hengyen scowled and was about to shoot back a sharp retort when the secretary cut him off. "You're with me, Windmaster. That's an order. Let's go."

None of this sat well with him, but Hengyen had no choice but to follow. What else could he do? He was only a small cog of the Revolution. As much as he hated and questioned being pulled off the front line in the initial attack, the secretary was in charge and, short of staging a coup, Hengyen had to respect the chain of command. The day the Living Revolution fought with itself was the day the revolution died.

Besides, Guo did make a good point. As much as he hated to admit it, there was wisdom in the secretary's decision to divide his duties. The only reason why the Beacon was able to successfully acquire the resources they needed was because Hengyen had focused his energies on the task while leaving the construction of the defenses to Wangfa. There was no way Hengyen could have done both jobs adequately.

The two men went down the catwalk stairs and headed to the supply warehouse. While Bo had been put on permanent Charred Fields penance for his part in Wenzhu's escape, Elena was given the benefit of the doubt but grounded within the Beacon. She had been reassigned to assist Ming, who had reported discrepancies in his inventories. He believed someone or some group was stealing from the supply stores.

They found Elena taking inventory of the food in one of the tents. They could hear the quotamaster's grating voice even from half a block away. Ming's demeanor turned subservient the moment they walked inside, and he quickly barked for Elena to come when Guo asked to speak with her.

"How can I serve the Living Revolution?" Elena stared blankly at the ground. Her hair was ragged, she looked sullen, and deep lines circled her red eyes. The fire in her had diminished. She appeared utterly spent, and what remained was the husk of the once-assertive woman who was not afraid to stand out. Her lover's betrayal must have hurt her badly.

"We need your help," said Guo. "As you know, the typhoon is here. Wenzhu has abandoned you and Haobo to your fate, and joined his other woman in that traitorous hidden village. Do you know where it's located?"

"I'm sorry, I don't know where he is," she mumbled. The girl was a bad actress.

"I admire your continuing loyalty to someone who has wronged you so terribly," Hengyen said. "But the settlement requires more defenders. Thousands of lives depend on these fortifications holding."

"The walls are only as strong as the patriots who man it," Guo added. "Your friend Bo is paying the price for his loyalty to an evil person. Do not fall for that same trap. Help us, and I promise all will be forgiven. I will even extend my clemency to Ming Haobo as well."

Elena flinched, but still said nothing. The conflict inside her, however, was plain to see. She blinked and wiped her face with her sleeve as if she were struggling to breathe.

Hengyen shared glances with Guo. "That's a shame." He turned to leave.

"Elena Anderson," said Guo slowly. "Did you know that the city of Xi'an still stands?"

She shook her head. "No, Secretary."

He nodded vigorously. "Indeed it does. The military managed to quarantine the city and get its population under control before things got out of hand. It is now the temporary capital of China until we can reclaim the rest of our country."

"That's good news," she replied, not sounding enthused at all.

"The airport in the city is still operational."

She blinked, her eyelids flickering as she processed the meaning behind his words.

"Of course," Guo continued quickly, "it's currently reserved for military use, but I believe the government has been using the airport to reconnect to the rest of the world."

"Really?" A small spark appeared to rekindle inside her.

"I personally guarantee that I will do all that's in my power to put you on the next flight back to your home country. All you have to do is assist us in whatever way you can through this dangerous moment in the revolution. Help us locate Zhu and those villagers to bring back into the arms of the Living Revolution. Can you make this arrangement for the greater good?"

Hengyen stood back and watched their exchange intently. The smartest thing Secretary Guo could do now was not utter another word. He already had Elena Anderson eating out of the palm of his hand.

20

FINDING HOME

It took Zhu two days to reach Fongyuan. There wasn't time to pack his stash of supplies or grab any food. All he had were the clothes on his back and a small knife he kept strapped to his waist. Making the journey alone was hazardous enough, but doing it without any supplies had been nearly suicidal.

Zhu had stayed on the flag paths, but avoided the sanctuaries out of fear of running into another wind team. His days were damp, yet the sun scalded his exposed skin. The nights nearly killed him with cold and rain. He barely managed to get any sleep up in the trees as he suffered from a combination of falling temperatures, insects, and the constant fear of falling. The only food he managed to eat were a few edible sprouts and grubs that he foraged for along the way. This while thousands of mosquitoes and other insects attacked him constantly.

By the time he reached the village, he was more dead than alive. To be honest, he was surprised he'd made it this far. If it weren't for Shenyang on lookout, he might not have made it at all. She caught sight of him from her perch as he staggered half-conscious through the muddy rice field filled with stuck jiāngshī. He had grown lightheaded and ended up face-planting in a puddle. It took most of his remaining strength to push himself to his knees, but he had nothing after that. He didn't know how long he stayed in the wet field, futilely willing his quivering legs to straighten before she appeared by his side. Drowning in ankle-deep water would have been one of the more embarrassing ways to die. The last thing Zhu remembered was slumping against Shenyang as she supported him the rest of the way.

The next few hours were a blur. One blink, he was being half dragged, half carried across a rice field. The next, they were struggling up the hill toward the barrier in the hidden pass. She was screaming awfully loudly for help. Zhu remember wishing she were a little quieter. The next blink, he was surrounded by people. They were jostling him in a makeshift stretcher. Water was splashing everywhere. There were voices from every direction. Worried faces came into view and then faded.

At one point, a pair of calloused hands began prying his eye lids open and slapping his face. Zhu didn't have the energy to fight them off. Someone removed his clothes. The next time he blinked, he was so close to a roaring fire that half of his face felt blistered while his feet were so wet and cold he wasn't sure if they were still there. He was also completely naked underneath a wool blanket. Even half-conscious, Zhu felt embarrassed that someone had undressed him.

By the time he finally woke with his wits about him, it was dark outside. The fire that was roaring earlier was now just an angry smolder with bright tiny sparks dancing above it like fireflies. It hissed every time a drop of rain slid off the tent flap onto it. Zhu touched his forehead and felt damp sweat. He was still shivering uncontrollably even though his skin was hot to the touch.

He grunted as he forced himself to sit up. His body was stiff and ached all over as he stretched his arms and soaked in his surroundings. He was sleeping inside a tent. There was just enough cover over him to keep off the light drizzle blanketing the area. The bed he was sleeping on was a wooden pallet that gave him a little clearance above the ground so that he was not lying in water.

Meili was also here, curled with her knees to her chest on a plastic chair just off to the side with a blanket wrapped around her body so only her face showed. She was asleep; the sound of her breathing mixing with the rain pattering the earth had a calming effect on Zhu. He was about to call her name when he stopped. Just because he was awake didn't mean he had to ruin her rest.

He thought about getting up and stretching his legs but then remembered he was naked under the blanket. He found his clothes hanging from a pole on the other end of the tent, but decided against retrieving them. The man who had killed a hundred jiāngshī was afraid to be seen walking naked to the other side of a tent for fear that one of the villagers might spot him.

That was the moment Zhu realized he was really finally home. A smile broke on his face. He was back where he belonged, with the people with whom he belonged. The warmth expanding in his chest just now was hotter and more nourishing than the remnants of the fire burning next to him.

He stuck his head out from beneath the tent flap and stared at the starless night sky, being just able to make out the fast-moving clouds rolling by as cold drops of rain struck and rolled down his face. He was safe now, but what about Bo and Elena? Zhu hadn't gotten the chance to say goodbye to anyone.

When Bo had found him, he was helping the guards pull the burnt bodies of the Heaven Monks out of the shipping containers. The group had committed mass suicide through immolation after their demands had been rejected. Bo came running up to Zhu and before any of the guards could say a word, had yanked Zhu away by the collar as if he were an errant child about to be punished. His loyal friend was in a near panic and Zhu could barely make out what he was saying. It took Bo several tries to convey the warning that the guards were about to arrest him and that he had better flee the Beacon immediately.

At first, Zhu thought his friend was overreacting and tried to calm him down. It was a good thing Bo was adamant. His friend literally picked Zhu up like a sack of rice, carried him up to the parapet and stuffed him into the cable transport. Zhu didn't even get the opportunity to tell Bo to take Elena and meet him at the village.

The cable transport had just cleared the settlement's walls when he heard his name blared over the loudspeakers. That was when he realized his friend hadn't been overreacting. He had to watch helplessly as Bo fought off several guards who were trying to reach the transport's controls. The last thing he saw before the Beacon disappeared from view was a swarm of guards overwhelming Bo. His friend had just managed to keep them at bay long enough for Zhu to escape.

Zhu worried for him. At best, Bo would be severely punished. At worst, his strong, funny friend had sacrificed his life for Zhu. And what of Elena? Zhu hadn't gotten a chance to ask Elena to come with him. He hadn't even gotten to say goodbye. Was she paying penance for his betrayal to the Living Revolution? Did she think he had abandoned her?

His heavy thoughts must have been loud. That or he wasn't as quiet shuffling around as he thought. Meili stirred, and her eyes fluttered open.

She startled him when she spoke. "Are you awake?" She slipped into a pair of galoshes and splashed over to him, checking his forehead and cheeks with the back of her head. "Your skin is still hot. How are you feeling?"

On cue, Zhu's stomach grumbled so harshly his entire body shuddered. "I could eat."

"Of course, the cooks should be up soon."

Zhu was about to stand when he remembered his current state of dress. He pulled the front of his blanket tighter around his neck. "Could you please hand me my clothes?"

A smile grew on her face as she went over to retrieve them. "They're still wet. Hang on." She left the tent and returned a few minutes later with a fresh set of clothes wrapped inside a paper bag. "These are Jincai's. I think you two are about the same size."

Meili was a bad judge of size, because Jincai ended up being slightly broader and much taller. Zhu had to roll the pant legs all the way back to his knees, and the shirt hung off his shoulders like he was a little boy trying on his father's clothes. Still, they were dry and clean. Meili also gave him a pair of mismatching sandals for walking on the soggy ground. The left sandal was too narrow and pinched his toes, while the right was too large and slid around.

The rain had finally subsided by the time he was dressed, and the village was beginning to stir. The sun had not risen yet, but people were moving about starting fires and preparing breakfast. Zhu poked his head out of the tent and took a hesitant step onto the grass. His entire foot got sucked into the water. He scanned the field. Once his eyes adjusted to the darkness he realized that he was seeing more water than dirt.

Meili appeared next to him and threw her arms around his neck. "I'm glad you're back."

"I can't imagine myself being anywhere else." He really meant it.

Much had changed in the few weeks he had been gone. The center field that had previously been the heart of the village was now a shallow lake. A few of the more permanent structures were poking out of the surface. The villagers had moved to higher ground along the terraced edges surrounding the lake. Those areas too, however, were now mostly flooded. It was only a matter of time before they ran out of ground.

"You came back just in time," she explained as they walked along the edge of the newly formed lake. "We were planning on leaving in the next few days."

"Is the village prepared for the journey?" he asked as they moved to a plastic table elevated on a stack of pallets.

"Food and supplies, yes. Chima admitted he didn't realize how unprepared we were in the security department until you arrived and showed everyone how to survive. We've been trying to train more people, but we're nowhere close to ready. Now we're out of time and have no choice." She leaned in. "You *are* coming with us to the Pillars? That's why you came back, right?"

Zhu had hoped there would be enough time for him to go back to get Elena and Bo but, if he was being honest, that was no longer feasible. The Beacon had become a fortress. It was suicide to try to sneak back in, especially after his very public escape.

But, leaving them at the mercy of the typhoon? Zhu hated the impossibility of the world he lived in now.

His guilt was interrupted by a flurry of activity as his students charged their table and surrounded him. Excited shouts of "Zhu-shūshu" and "shīfù" filled his ears as the kids clamored to welcome him back. Some asked where he had gone, but most just wanted to know if he was staying for good this time. A few grumbled and asked why he hadn't said goodbye. Many wanted to know if he would teach them some jiāngshī-slaying moves.

A little girl tugged at his overly long sleeves. "Are you coming with us to our new home?"

Meili put her hands on the girl's shoulders and leaned in. "Well, Wenzhu, are you?"

A smile cracked open on his face. "Of course I'm going with you to the Precipitous Pillars. And you all better start warming up. You all have class this morning." His stomach grumbled. He added, "After breakfast."

21

FONGYUAN REVISITED

Elena let the pack slide off her shoulders. Wincing, she first hunched over and then arched her sore back, letting her aching muscles stretch. She had never realized how cumbersome ammunition was until she had to carry fifty rounds of it around her waist while hiking up and down mountains. Between that and the obscenely large assault rifle they had given her, it was like carrying half her body weight.

Hengyen had pushed the fifteen-member wind team hard, stopping only three hours during the night for a quick rest. It took them a little under twenty-four hours to reach Fongyuan, finally stopping to set up camp a quarter of the way up a mountain on the northern side of the village.

She would have thought that everyone would be allowed to rest after such an arduous trek, but the windmaster immediately deployed scouts to the village and also sent someone farther up the side of the mountain to maintain a lookout.

"I want to be heading back to the Beacon by tomorrow, whether we find this village or not," he announced. The windmaster was adamant they return to the Beacon before the main body of the typhoon reached it. He had been moody and irritable the entire trip, often pausing to look back toward the direction of the settlement. Hengyen had put up a confident front, but he was obviously concerned about leaving on this raid at this crucial time. The windmaster had made it very clear that it was only on Guo and Wangfa's insistence that he had agreed to come.

His rush was understandable. He was worried about the typhoon. They all were. They had departed the Beacon on the morning of the second day of the front of the typhoon. When they left, hundreds of jiāngshī were spilling into the Charred Fields every hour. There were already rumors that parts of the outer perimeter were under duress.

Elena leaned against a tree and scanned the rooftops of the village below. She had come to detest this cursed place. As bad as things had been before, it was this village that had introduced all the recent chaos to her life, a little over a month ago. Just seeing this place once again raised her hackles and made her tense like a cornered animal.

Although to be fair, if they hadn't come she wouldn't have ever learned what sort of a conniving asshole Zhu was. The secretary had shown her a mountain of evidence. Zhu had planned on robbing and abandoning the Beacon ever since his return. He had spent all his points and had his belongings packed and ready to go. Ming also believed it was Zhu who had been pilfering supplies. It appeared he was going to funnel everything to his new woman and her village before he left. To make matters worse, one of the guards involved in his capture claimed Zhu had set Bo up to take the fall so he could escape. Poor Bo was now facing penance for the rest of his life. The pain of his betrayal—not only to her and Bo but to the Living Revolution as well—was unforgivable.

A tiny part of her—the part that still loved him deeply—still balked at this revelation. This portrait of him everyone was painting wasn't the man she loved. Zhu was honest and trustworthy, caring and considerate. He would never do this to her and Bo. He was a good man. That part of her shouted that none of this made sense. However, that small voice that refused to believe the truth about him was shouted down by her rage. Every time Elena thought about her ex-boyfriend, she couldn't help but see red and get worked up into a fury.

When she managed to find a few minutes alone with Bo, he had emphatically denied everything that Zhu was accused of. He even went as far as to say Zhu wasn't trying to escape and that it had been he—Bo—who had forced Zhu to leave. The whole thing was preposterous. Elena was now seeing things with fresh eyes. Her cheating boyfriend had played everyone for fools, especially her. She thought about everything she had given up for him. From small things like her scavenge points and rations, to the monstrous fact that she had stayed in China for *him*. That fact rattled her the most: that she had inadvertently chosen to ride out the apocalypse with a liar over her own kin. The ache in her heart glowed and built into a hot, bitter anger.

Chen Wenzhu would pay, one way or another. Secretary Guo was even generous enough to offer a way for her to clear both Bo's and her names. "I have known Haobo ever since he arrived at the Beacon of Light. He is a good man with a kind soul, but he is not very wise and easily coerced and manipulated. That is why I am willing to forgive his crime if you redeem him." That was the main reason she had agreed to turn on Zhu and work with the windmaster to find and raid this village. She wanted to absolve Bo of these crimes.

Okay, that wasn't true. Elena couldn't let Zhu get away with his betrayal. She didn't consider herself the vengeful type—well, maybe just a little. But she could never live with herself if he got away scot-free. She had tried to convince herself that it was all about the justice and fairness of it all, but the truth was it was all about revenge.

It wasn't just because he was a cheating boyfriend; she had gone through those before. She loved him, but not only that, she gave up everything for him. Zhu was the reason Elena was stuck here in China, the reason she wasn't with her family, and the reason she was now forced to do so many despicable things.

So yes, she wanted to save Bo, but she *needed* to make sure Zhu paid for his crimes.

Of course the secretary's offer to send her home contributed to her decision, but it was really all about saving Bo. That's what she told herself. But just because she thought she was doing the right thing didn't mean it wasn't eating her up inside. It occupied her mind for most of the day.

The first group of scouts returned at noon. They hadn't seen any people but had discovered a caravan of mixed wooden wagons and hollowed-out trucks with the engines removed half-hidden beneath a group of willow trees. The beds were empty, but the footprints around the vehicles were fresh. Someone—more accurately, a big group of someones—was getting ready to move.

Elena was deep in thought when the second group of scouts returned with something even better: a prisoner. She quickly threw the strap of her rifle over her shoulder and joined the crowd of windrunners gathering around a young woman, really barely more than a girl.

"We found her hiding inside a partially caved-in roof in one of the houses," said the scout. The woman grabbed the girl by the rope bound around her wrist and gave her a hard yank. "Watch her mouth. The brat already thinks she's half jiāngshī. She tried to bite me when I stuffed the rag into her mouth."

At first, she looked like just a typical village girl. Soft and innocent compared to most vultures. Her clothes were relatively clean and fresh. She looked well nourished. Most telling, her eyes weren't wild or bloodshot, as were so many others'.

Elena reached for the girl's hand. The girl shrank away, terrified. Elena grabbed her hand more forcefully and felt her palm. "Calloused, but not torn or scarred." She lowered her face to the girl's eye level and flashed her palm. "I'm going to take the cloth out of your mouth. Don't try anything. You'll be dead before you can take a bite of me. Understood?"

The girl's eyes darted left and right. She nodded.

Elena admitted to holding her breath when she plucked the rag out. There was only one way to treat an amputated limb out here. "Now," she said in her most soothing voice. "What's your name?"

When the girl didn't answer, one of the windrunners slapped her face.

"Hey," Elena barked, pushing him away. "I got this."

The man raised his hand again, but Hengyen's hand on his shoulder stayed the blow. The windmaster nodded for Elena to continue. She acknowledged him and led the girl away from the crowd.

"Listen," she began, touching her chest. "I'm Elena. What's your name?"

"Shenyang."

"That's a pretty name." Elena brushed several loose strands of hair from the girl's face. "Shenyang, the Chinese government sent us. We're here to help. We need to speak with whoever is in charge at your village. Do you understand?"

The girl pursed her lips and made no indication of understanding.

"Do you know Chen Wenzhu?"

No answer.

"He's a friend of ours."

Still nothing.

Elena turned her to face the group of windrunners. "You want to talk to *me*, because those guys over there are monsters. They'll hurt you. I'm trying to protect you." She tilted her head at the windrunner who had slapped the girl. It took the guy a few seconds to realize what she meant. He eventually got her hint. He snarled at Shenyang and drew his knife. Not the most convincing performance, but it was enough to make the girl jump.

The charade went on for a while longer, but the girl didn't budge.

Finally, Hengyen pulled Elena back. "We're wasting time. The village will realize she's missing. Maybe they'll come looking for her. Maybe they'll go into hiding. Either way, that puts us in danger or compromises the raid. Either we get actionable information from her, or we tie her to that tree and leave her for the dead. Enough delay."

Elena bit her lip. Hengyen had made it perfectly clear that they returned to the Beacon within the next four days no matter what. That meant at best they had two, maybe three days at most to find Zhu and capture the villagers. Secretary Guo had also made it perfectly clear that Elena and Bo's pardon was contingent on capturing these villagers as well. The thought of losing her only way home made Elena's entire body clench.

So much for this good-cop crap that always worked in movies. Elena tried one last time. She drew her knife and stalked back to Shenyang. She held the knife to the girl's neck. "If you don't tell me where your village is, I can't protect you anymore."

Shenyang whimpered and squeezed her eyes shut.

"Damn it. You're really going to die for your stupid village?"

The girl had called her bluff. Elena lowered her knife and looked away. She had promised herself that the old woman with the pǔdāo would be the last. She didn't want to do this, but she had no choice. There was nothing left for her on this side of the world anymore.

Elena was dog tired. Exhausted by playing this stupid game of trying to be nice or do the right thing. Tired of feeling like everything was out of her control, and that nothing she did got her any closer to what she wanted most in the world. Just once, just once dammit, she wanted something to be easy. Why did everything have to be so hard? Her chest seized. Desperation and anger took over.

Without warning Elena's slashed her knife across Shenyang's face, her movement so quick most around them didn't even notice at first. That is, until they saw the blood sprayed across Elena's and the girl's face. Shenyang blinked, momentarily confused. Then the pain registered. She palmed her cheeks and screamed as blood spurted out of both sides of her face, soaking her hands and pouring down her arms and shirt. Her cries were cut short when Elena stoppered her mouth with a palm. With her other hand, she pointed the tip of her knife inches from her the young woman's eye. "One more noise out of you and I'll shove this clean through your skull. Do you understand?"

Shenyang made no sign that she did and continued her muffled scream. Off to the side, several of the windrunners shouted. At first Elena thought they were under attack. Perhaps the girl's people had found them. She turned to see a jiāngshī stumbling out from the trees. It was skinny and bald, wearing traditional clothing, which resembled a cross between a bathrobe and a potato sack. He had an overbite and what looked like two or three teeth left, which he was using to chomp repeatedly as he dragged a lame leg.

One of the windrunners cursed, drew a club, and walked over to the old dead man. Before he could bash its head in, Elena called out. "Stop. Leave it."

The windrunner looked at her curiously. When the jiāngshī changed course and lumbered toward him, he gave it a swift kick in the chest, sending it flying back. He raised his club as if to smash its head in again.

"Stop," Elena repeated. She grabbed the still sobbing girl by the hair and dragged her to the fallen jiāngshī. "Hold it down," she snapped at no one in particular.

The windrunner hesitated, but did as ordered as Elena pushed Shenyang's head down until it was only inches from the jiāngshī's snapping jaws. The girl's muffled screams would have otherwise been bloodcurdling.

Elena hissed in her ear, barely above a whisper. "Tell me what we need to know, or I will let this monster tear your flesh apart bite by bite. But I won't let it touch your face, because when we find your village—we'll find it with or without your help—I'm going to use their little Shenyang to keep them all in line or you'll turn them into jiāngshī as well. Do you understand?"

The girl was moaning and sobbing out of control. Elena had pressed her face so close to the old jiāngshī's that the blood dripping from her cheeks was falling into its mouth. The thing went crazy and was squirming so hard it almost broke free of the windrunner's grasp. Finally, Shenyang moved her head in something that resembled a nod, and Elena pulled her back up and tossed her roughly to the ground. She fell into a broken heap, sobbing.

Elena rubbed her hands together to hide the fact that she was trembling all over. She looked up to see the entire wind team staring back at her, eyes wide with shock and fear. Elena set her jaw as she walked away from the ugly scene, pausing as she stopped by the wind-master. "The girl shouldn't give us any more trouble. Let me know when we're ready to move."

She kept walking until she was well out of earshot. She hid behind a small cluster of fir trees and leaned against the trunk of an ancient knotted cypress, her adrenaline and resolve leaking out of her body. She clenched and kneaded her still-shaking hands trying to calm her nerves. Finally, with a frustrated snarl, Elena drew her still-bloody knife and tossed it into the brush. Then she buried her head in her hands and sobbed.

22

INTO THE FOLD

Zhu and Jincai were just coming back from the nest after Shenyang failed to return to the village that morning. The two had just crossed the river and were creeping through the tall weeds along the water's edge when they heard the first pops: fast and sharp, their echoes lingering in the air. Several more rattles followed. A jiāngshī standing a few meters away, a lanky bald man wearing fishing waders with a fishing pole still in his hand, turned toward the sounds. It made a guttural grunt that sounded almost curious to Zhu's ear and began to lumber in the direction of the sounds. Right to the entrance of the hidden pass leading to the village in the valley.

"What was that, shīfù?" asked Jincai, a few steps ahead of Zhu.

"Gunfire," he replied, his concern growing. "It's not far."

Jincai, leading the way, disappeared into the underbrush. The teenager was well acquainted with these surroundings and guided the two safely through the dense foliage. While the forested area near the pass had been mostly cleared of the dead, there was still a steady stream leaking in here from the main road a few hundred meters to the east.

Thinking of that reminded Zhu of the daunting journey ahead. With the caravan composed of old wagons and hollowed-out cars with the engines removed, there was no way they could travel on the dead-infested highways. Their only option was the winding back roads, which were hit-or-miss. They could be on an empty stretch of road for a hundred kilometers, or they could run into a storm of jiāng-shī. Their one advantage was that there weren't any big cities between here and the Precipitous Pillars, only small villages. Zhu preferred they avoid the roads entirely, traveling on foot and carrying their possessions on their backs, but that was not feasible with so few strong and healthy people in the village.

Zhu shook himself back to the current situation. None of that mattered right now. There was no point in thinking about tomorrow if no one survived to see it. He didn't know what they were facing. If they were lucky, someone was practicing with rifles at the village, although that was doubtful, considering the bullet holes at Shenyang's nest. It was more likely that a group of vultures had stumbled upon her and forced her to reveal the village's location. He prayed she was still alive.

They continued for another twenty minutes through the thickets, painstakingly moving from cover to cover. They finally reached the narrow winding pass that cut through the mountains into the valley. So far, there was nothing out of the ordinary except for two jiāngshī who were making their way toward the village.

Jincai pulled out his knife when Zhu stopped him. "Let them go first. We'll follow behind at a good distance. Anything that happens will hit them first."

In hindsight, it was probably a bad plan. The dead were notoriously clumsy, and walking uphill did them no favors. Zhu and Jincai waited in the shadows while the two jiāngshī spent almost ten minutes trudging up the small stretch of road. Zhu thought once they began down the hill, things would go a little faster, but the two jiāngshī stumbled and face-planted multiple times until they finally reached level ground. It was a frustrating exercise in patience.

Zhu sighed. "We probably should have just killed them."

Jincai only chuckled.

Zhu couldn't help but join in. They kept the jiāngshī in sight until the decoys reached the barricade guarding the entrance to the valley. It had been partially smashed, and the wooden gate at its center was torn off its hinges. It appeared abandoned. No one stirred behind it as the jiāngshī lumbered across the stretch of land leading up to it.

Zhu was about to step out from the boulder they were hiding behind when a man poked his head out above the gate. He was bald, with an ugly zigzag scar running across the crown of his head. There was a rifle slung across his back. Instead of drawing it, he drew a long spear and strolled up to the two jiāngshī, stabbing them each through the head.

Zhu's breath caught in his throat, and he quickly ducked back.

That was Raisin-Head Fang. He had often played board games with Zhu when they had down time. Fang was very competitive and broke the rules any chance he got, but he always shared his plum wine.

These weren't vultures. The Beacon had found them.

Jincai clutched his knife in his hand. "There's only one person there. I think we can take him."

Zhu grabbed the teen by his collar, shook his head. It was a good fifty meters across an open field to the barricade from their hiding place. Fang wasn't a great shot, but he'd have to be blind to miss them out in the open at this distance. Zhu nudged Jincai. "I'm going to distract that guy. When his back is turned, jump him."

Jincai frowned. "How are you going to do that, shīfù?"

Zhu took a deep breath, and then stepped out of cover. He waved. "Raisin-Head!"

Several deep creases matching the scar appeared on Fang's bald head. The rifle appeared in his hands and was pointing at Zhu an instant later. Zhu had made the right call not to charge.

"Wenzhu, is that you?" Fang squinted, temporarily lowering his guard before remembering that Zhu was a wanted fugitive. "Palms to the sky."

Zhu did as he was ordered, keeping his pace slow and his voice even as he approached the barricade, circling wide to the opposite side. "Come on, Fang. It's me. You know me. I let you cheat at mahjong."

"I don't cheat. You just suck. Don't try to make a fool of me, Zhu. I'll shoot you dead, and I'll kill your jiāngshī too."

Zhu kept his pace slow and his voice relaxed, deliberately keeping Fang's attention. Fang kept the rifle's muzzle trained on him. He did, however, slowly pivot his body until his back was turned away from Jincai. Zhu moved to the barricade and palmed the wooden walls. He could feel Fang's presence as the man moved up behind him. Zhu's machete hissed out of its scabbard and was tossed to the ground. The knife at the other side of his waist came next, followed by the one at his ankle.

Now, Jincai. Now! he thought.

Fang began to pat the rest of Zhu's body. "I didn't believe it when I first heard you were a deserter. That was a lousy thing to do to Bo."

"What did I do to Bo?" Zhu began turning his head and was rewarded with a hard jab of metal to the ear. "Eyes to the wall."

What is that boy waiting for?

The attack came a second later. There was a muffled cry and a curse. A high-pitched yelp and sounds of a scuffle followed. In the time it took Zhu to turn around, Jincai had jumped on Fang from behind, and the windrunner had flipped the boy onto the ground. Jincai was facedown and Fang had a boot planted on the back of his neck. The rifle had been tossed a few meters away.

There wasn't time to reach for it, so Zhu lowered his shoulder and plowed into Fang, knocking him off the boy. They crashed into the dirt and skidded downhill along the loose gravel. They rolled several times, pawing at each other's faces and necks. Fang was bigger and stronger than Zhu and ended up on top with a hand wrapped around his neck. Zhu tried to buck him off, but the larger man just leaned in and dropped an elbow on his nose. There was an explosion of red and Zhu's eyes teared up. He choked and coughed as blood spilled into his throat.

He tried to turn away, but Fang continued to pound on him. Zhu was already half-blind, and each blow only made it worse. His consciousness was blinking away when the pounding abated, followed shortly by the crack of a gunshot very close to his ear. The heavy pressure from Fang sitting on top of his chest lightened as the bigger man slumped off to the side.

Zhu wiped his eyes and sat up. He looked over at Jincai holding the barrel of the rifle like a club. He must have hit Fang across the head with it, and he must have hit him hard because the stock of the rifle had cracked and broken off.

Jincai looked pale, and his hands shook. Zhu was immediately confused. How had the teenager shot Fang, but then clubbed him with the rifle like that? Then he saw the red stain expanding along on Jincai's left arm and it all made sense. "Did you shoot yourself?"

The rifle slipped out of Jincai's hand and he fell to one knee, clutching his wound. "It went off when I whacked him." He hunched over, grimacing. "This really hurts."

"It's no fun getting shot," Zhu agreed, not that he would know. He quickly scanned their surroundings to make sure they did not attract any jiāngshī or windrunners. Once he was sure they were relatively safe, he tended to the boy. He pulled out a rag and tied a makeshift tourniquet for Jincai. "Try not to move it too much. We're going to have to get that bullet out later. Can you walk?"

Jincai nodded, wincing as he put weight on his injured leg. "Shīfù, please don't let me turn into a jiāngshī."

"Don't worry. You're going to be old and gray before you turn into one."

"What about the vulture?"

"Leave him. And he's a windrunner." Leaving Fang alive was probably a mistake, but Zhu wasn't ready to kill anyone in cold blood. Raisin-Head was still alive, unconscious with blood pouring from his ears. The smart thing to do would probably be to just cut his throat. The guy had threatened to kill him. Even so, Zhu didn't have the heart to kill an unconscious person he still considered a friend. If he managed to wake up before a jiāngshī caught scent of the blood dripping from his shattered nose, he deserved to live and fight another day.

Zhu picked up and checked the rifle, or what was left of it, and threw it to the ground. A working gun would have been awfully useful in this situation. They continued past the barricade, hugging the right side of the pass into the valley proper. The ground gave way to wet slop, and they waded ankle-deep. The sounds of running water were everywhere. The terraced fields had turned into miniature waterfalls cascading down the mountains from all sides. It was a tough slog, in every sense, but Zhu tried to focus on the positives: at the very least, it masked their movements from would-be pursuers.

Zhu's heart hammered in his chest; his worst fears were soon realized. A large wind team from the Beacon had somehow tracked the village down. Maybe he was followed, or they had tortured Bo. Zhu knew his friend wouldn't have given that information up voluntarily or easily. It didn't matter how the wind team found the village; they were here now. This was all his fault. Guilt and panic took hold, choking his breathing. He had doomed his village by coming back. Anyone killed, anyone enslaved, their blood would be on his hands. He had to do something!

A group of seven or eight windrunners were watching over what looked like seventy villagers sitting in a cluster on their knees. There were several dead bodies scattered about. Six by his count. He clenched his fist when two windrunners dragged Chima's broken body onto a pile of corpses and tossed it on top as if he were trash. One of them leaned in and pushed a blade into his skull.

Upon closer inspection, he realized that most of his students and the village guards were in that group. Where was the rest of the village? Where was Meili? Hopefully they had gotten away deeper into the valley. It had plenty of nooks and crannies. The wind team would never find them unless they swept the entire area, which could take days.

A familiar voice speaking loudly sent chills up Zhu's spine. "This is your last chance. Surrender the rest of your village. If you return peacefully with us to the Beacon of Light, your illegal actions will be forgiven."

No one spoke.

"We've confiscated most of your supplies for the Living Revolution," continued Hengyen. "Your people will starve if you abandon them here. Bringing them back to the Beacon is the only merciful choice. You have managed to survive out here so far because you have been lucky. It is commendable, but don't forget who you are, what country you belong to. It is time to support the Living Revolution and bring together the shattered remnants of our great nation. Tell us where the rest of your village is."

Zhu nudged Jincai, whispering, "We can't take so many by ourselves, but if we find the others, we might have a chance. Do you know where they could be hiding?"

"There's a grotto on the far side of the valley a quarter of the way up the hill," said Jincai. "We keep most of our dry supplies there."

"Let's go."

Just as they turned, Hengyen's powerful voice boomed across the clearing. "Chen Wenzhu: we know he has contacted your village leaders. You will lead us to him now, or suffer the consequences."

At the sound of his name, Zhu froze, heart thudding in his chest. His gaze met Jincai's and the two shared a moment of panic. The Beacon was hunting him; the *windmaster* was hunting him. As if the journey to the Pillars wasn't impossible enough.

Slowly, Zhu and Jincai backed away from the crowd and through the dense foliage to the grotto, picking their way from bush to bush. They were about to pass his little tent when he saw a figure crumpled on the ground in front of the entrance. At first, he thought it to be a corpse of one of the kids, but then it moved, raising its head.

It was Meili! Zhu's heart stopped. He stared for a few seconds. Zhu motioned to Jincai to wait, but the boy had already moved on and disappeared into the brush. Zhu decided he couldn't leave her like this and peeled away toward her. As he got closer, he realized her wrists and ankles were bound as she huddled in a fetal position. Meili looked his way as he approached. Recognition filled her eyes and she opened her mouth. She was alive! He broke into a sprint.

Meili shook her head weakly. "No, Zhu."

It was too late.

A figure stepped out from the shadows, and then the nerves in Zhu's face exploded in pain once more. The world flashed bright and turned sideways. He splashed headfirst into the shallow water, the shock of it prickling his flesh. The world faded black for an instant, followed by the feeling of drowning.

Gasping, Zhu pulled his head up just in time to see a grim, familiar face approaching him with a short spear in hand. "Elena, wait," he sputtered.

She swung her spear with both hands, striking his broken nose. Fresh waves of agony raked his body as he flipped up and crashed back into the water. His head lolled to the side just in time to see Fang appear with his hands wrapped around Jincai's throat.

"Hit me from behind will you, you little mutt," the windrunner growled, picking Jincai up by the neck and slamming him into the ground. He held the teenager's head under the water as Jincai flailed his arms and legs.

"Please, Fang, don't." Zhu's voice was such a weak whisper he barely even heard himself.

A shadow passed over him. Elena towered over his slumped body and pressed the sharp tip of her spear into his neck. There was hatred in her voice. "I wish I had never met you, Chen Wenzhu."

23

PARADISE LOST

The wind team set off on its return trek to the Beacon of Light as soon as they had the captured villagers organized into a column. Hengyen had no intention of wasting hours, possibly days, scouring the valley for the remaining survivors. Not with only fifteen windrunners, hands already full with sixty-two prisoners and all the supplies they had confiscated, which had to be carried on each person's back. There was simply no way to travel east with anything on wheels.

After the wind team returned with the minimum number of prisoners that Wangfa demanded, Hengyen planned to speed back to the settlement so he could join the defense against the impending typhoon.

Secretary Guo, he mused, would be most excited about the capture of Chen Wenzhu, and not the labor or supplies. Zhu's actions reflected poorly on the Living Revolution, and for someone who had escaped so visibly not to be brought to justice, well, Hengyen understood the need for punishment. But was it worth sending able-bodied troops on a mission so close to the crucible?

Meanwhile, the former windrunner had kept quiet, keeping his head down and not making eye contact with anyone. A few of the other windrunners had taunted and cuffed him around pretty violently, but Zhu made no move to defend himself. He took the brunt of their punishment until Hengyen personally stepped in. In a way, it was the proper reaction to his transgression. It was the right mixture of humility, shame, and quiet dignity. Hengyen could almost respect him for that. Almost. Hengyen had little sympathy for traitors and deserters, and he had hoped for more out of the man, personally. Zhu's betrayal stung the windmaster more than the latter cared to admit.

Elena, however, was content to shoot figurative daggers at him at every opportunity, glaring with an intensity that eventually made even Hengyen nervous. There were moments where he thought she was going to start a fight. He had to move her to the front of the column in order to keep her gaze focused outward for jiāngshī as they made their way through forests, swamps, and fields of tall grass.

This wasn't just reserved to the jilted woman and her lover either. Most of the windrunners and guards had subscribed to Guo's assessment that all vultures who were not supporting the Living Revolution were actively working against it. That every person who refused to throw their full support behind the revolution was adding additional burden to the true patriots who were. That had changed the tone of the relationship between those residing in the Beacon and those outside. Hengyen had to stop his windrunners several times from abusing these people.

In any case, Hengyen didn't have time for domestic squabbles and casual cruelty. They had a besieged settlement to defend. An hour didn't pass when he didn't wonder if they were returning to a ruin overrun by an ocean of the dead.

The windmaster's heart beat heavily as they followed the last flag path up the hill to the cable transport. They had been gone now for just under a week. It had taken a day to get there, a day to capture the village, and to his chagrin and extreme irritation, nearly five days to return with the prisoners.

When the advanced scout returned to report his findings, his face was pale and his eyes wide. Hengyen couldn't wait five more minutes to reach the top of the hill. "Well, how do things look?"

The scout's lengthy pause was not reassuring. "The Beacon of Light still shines."

"Still shines" did little to ease Hengyen's concerns. "Have the jiāngshī breached the walls? Are our people still fighting and standing firm?"

He nodded. "The wall appears intact. I can see people manning the parapets, but . . ."

Relief surged through Hengyen. That news was good enough for now. He patted the scout on the shoulder and jogged the rest of the way up the hill to get a look for himself. He heard the noise before he reached the crest; it sounded like a swarm of a locusts. What he saw with his own eyes would haunt him for the rest of his life, though at this point he was not so certain how long that would be.

The western side of the Charred Fields should have been the side with the smallest number of jiāngshī, but that did not seem to matter. Thousands of dead were crammed in the narrow stretch of land in between the cable transport and home. It was a literal sea of bodies in ragged clothing, outstretched arms that exposed bone and rotting flesh, the sound of hissing and moans amplified a millionfold, like a swarm of locusts that blotted out the land. Only a few patches of earth were visible here and there.

What made it even more terrifying was the way they moved in unison. When a noise or light or movement caught the attention of one jiāngshī, those around it also reacted. The slightest change in one of the dead caused a ripple through the surface of waving arms and heads, like an ocean wave from hell. The jiāngshī were intently focused on the settlement, their roiling masses surging and breaking against the walls with uniform momentum like ocean waves against a cliff.

It was even more frightening on the south, if that was possible. From his vantage, it was just one massive uninterrupted sea of dead. That meant all the fortifications they had erected over the past month had fallen in less than a week. If it had slowed the dead at all, Hengyen could not tell; it seemed as if the jiāngshī had simply washed over it all.

Nature could not be fought and defeated. It could not be tamed or calmed. Nature could only be admired, respected, and avoided. And when all else failed, surrendered to.

Hengyen scanned the top of the parapet. The walls on the west side appeared intact. A few gaps between containers patched with wooden fencing appeared to be holding under the pressure. Suddenly, an explosion and a plume of fire in the southwest corner lit the otherwise gray sky. Wangfa had already rolled out the explosives.

"Too early," muttered Hengyen. Or perhaps it was too late now.

That was when Hengyen noticed the column of smoke. It was coming from inside the settlement. He had been so focused on the Charred Fields that he hadn't noticed that the haze lingering in the air around them was the product of several roiling stacks of smoke rising like giant serpents into the skies.

He turned to the scout. "Get me over there immediately with the first group. Ferry the rest across in as few trips as possible. Once they get into the settlement, house our new comrades in the cells until we can sort out their roles. See that they're fed and cared for." He looked back at the main body still making its way up the hill. "Move Wenzhu into a jail."

"Yes, Windmaster."

The cable-car door slid open with a high-pitched shriek. Hengyen climbed inside with Fang and eight of the villagers. He patted the windrunner's shoulders. "How are you holding up, son?"

"Ready to fight for the revolution, dàgē!" Fang was all bravado, but the man badly needed medical attention. He was obviously not well. He had a massive lump from the blow to the back of the head from that villager boy he had killed. He had been complaining about light sensitivity ever since they left the settlement, and he had been having trouble with his vision. His eyes were now just thin slits on his face.

"Get yourself checked out right away," Hengyen instructed. "Do not stop by your pod. Do not get cleaned up. The next person you talk to is the doctor, understand?"

Fang nodded and continued to avert his eyes from the sun.

The gas-powered cable transport sputtered and kicked alive, squealing as it lifted off the platform. The violent vibrations under his feet sent shivers up Hengyen's spine. He eyed the loose bolts rattling the main hoist near the ceiling, clanging loudly against the iron frame of the car.

Several of the villagers gasped and cried out as the wooden platform below them gave way to a grisly and terrifying hellscape of thousands of jiāngshī reaching for them amid great clouds of dust. For once, Hengyen wished the loud banging of the cable transport were enough to drown out the guttural cries from the jiāngshī below.

Several villagers broke down sobbing, begging for them to reverse course. A few held each other tightly as if it were the end of the world, while others hammered their fists at the metal grating, demanding to be let out.

Hengyen spied a young woman comforting the others. She appeared to be one of their leaders, or at the very least someone who had her head on straight. He got her attention.

"What's your name?"

The look she gave him was of unabashed hatred. "Meili."

"I hope to see you all safely returned to your village one day. I want all of you to survive. To do so, we need to work together. Do you understand?"

She paused, and then reluctantly nodded.

"I'm going to depend on you to lead your people. Keep their spirits up and keep them in line, and I'll do my best to see them well taken care of. If you have any problems, you tell any guard that you need to speak with me." Hengyen held out his hand. "Do we have an agreement?"

She stared sullenly and didn't accept his hand.

"This typhoon of dead would eventually swallow your village whole. Your only chance at safety is to fight alongside your brothers and sisters at the Beacon," Hengyen all but pled.

"Safety? You call this safety?" She gestured out over the chasm swarming with dead. "My people *were* safe, until you kidnapped us."

Much as he tried not to show it, her words had hit on his very real concern that the Beacon was in dire straits.

Nothing he could do or say would ever make her accept him. It wasn't necessary. As long as she kept her people in line, that was all that mattered. After this crisis was over, someone like her would be important to help heal the wounds.

The cable car reached the end of its journey with another loud clatter. Hengyen stepped out and surveyed the area around the platform. It was heavily fortified for no apparent reason. It was manned by ten guards, all positioned facing toward the settlement, not out toward the Charred Fields. He tapped the operator on the shoulder. "Why are so many guards stationed here?"

"Deserters, Windmaster. Secretary's orders."

Hengyen swallowed his irritation. "Put these men to better use along the fortifications. From this point on, keep the loads to eight per car. I don't want to stress the motors."

He sent Fang off to the infirmary and gave instructions on the care of the newest batch of repatriated citizens. He stepped off the platform and scanned the chaos around him. The parapet was a hive of guards and windrunners mixed with conscripts. Everyone looked exhausted and sleep-deprived. Several injured lay along the walls.

A shout from the left caught his attention as one of the presumed injured rose up and bit the person next to him in the neck. Several guards swarmed the new jiāngshī, cutting it to bits, but not before it managed to tear the throat out of the woman next to it.

The two "survivors" were summarily decapitated and tossed over the parapet edge.

What the hell was going on? Their defenses were a mess! No order, no discipline. Panic and tension were heavy in the air, and it looked like everyone here was on the verge of cracking.

He stopped a passing guard passing by. "Walk with me."

"Yes, Windmaster," she replied, hastily following him down the catwalk.

"What happened here? Why are there fires? Did the jiāngshī break through?"

The guard shook her head. "The jiāngshī overwhelmed perimeter defenses two days ago. We retreated behind the walls, but not without many casualties and injuries. So many died the first night, and . . ." She pursed her lips.

Hengyen cursed, feeling déjà vu from the time he had lost the hospital coming back. "I saw us lose a man back there because we're being careless. Why haven't we established better procedures for triaging for the wounded?"

"I'm sorry, Windmaster. Things have been chaotic. We've suffered so many casualties that our rotations have had to be cobbled together. Some of our ranks were so devastated that we no longer know who is still alive and who is dead. Not only that, most of our supplies have disappeared and we haven't heard from anyone in charge in days." The guard looked as if she were about to break into tears. "My brother is a guard on the east wall. He leads a team of vultures on the first night shift. He says his people haven't eaten in two days."

"When was the last time you slept?" asked Hengyen.

She shrugged. "I don't even know what day it is anymore."

"Where's Wangfa?"

"The defensemaster is leading the fight on the southern wall."

They continued through the heart of the settlement toward the administration building. There were signs of battle everywhere. Tents and cabins had collapsed. Garbage was strewn about. Slumped bodies littered the path, many still wearing the blood-stained clothes they had fought in. Others cradled their weapons in their laps. Some looked as if they were simply too exhausted to make it back to their pods or tents and had passed out where they stood. Nobody would know if anyone here was dead until they rose as a jiāngshī.

There was no order, no direction, no leadership holding the people together. Hengyen should have stayed behind to lead the settlement. Regardless of his role as only the windmaster, he should have held firm. By the time the administration building came into view, Hengyen had worked himself into a silent fury.

"Get some rest," he ordered the guard before sending her off.

Hengyen stepped through the entrance of the administration

building and found it nearly empty. Puzzling. He would have thought all the leadership of the settlement would be holed up in here trying to manage the crisis. Instead, he found room after room barren of people.

No wonder things were falling apart. The body had no head. At the very least Wangfa should have devised a war room to oversee their defenses.

The door to the secretary's office was locked for the first time that Hengyen could remember. He raised his knuckles to knock, then decided there wasn't time for this. Apologizes could be made later, although he felt a sinking dread that they wouldn't be necessary. Hengyen stepped back and kicked the door open, sending pieces all across the floor.

He wandered inside slowly, taking in the details. The office was empty, as he had expected, but even more so than the other rooms. Whereas the other offices were empty of people, Guo's was bereft of a soul. The desk was there, as was the portrait of the Chairman. So was the map and the stacks of handwritten reports, a quarter of which were probably from Hengyen. Gone however were the personal belongings: a framed picture of Guo's deceased wife, the books on the shelf, even the bottles of alcohol in the cabinet. There was no longer any sign that this office held the seat of leadership of Hunan province.

Something clicked from above, and then cool air began to tickle the back of his neck. And of course the central air. Even in this desperate time, even with no one here, the damn air conditioning was on.

Hengyen walked around and sat heavily in the chair. He slammed his fist on the desk. The secretary had abandoned the settlement along with most of the senior leadership. Did they just panic when the typhoon arrived or had this been Guo's goal all along? No, this must have been planned if he had time to steal all the settlement's supplies.

He laced his fingers together, bumping them repeatedly against his forehead. Was the news about the army even true? Did Guo and his fellow conspirators use that lie to keep the settlement together long enough to pull off this theft and cowardly escape? No wonder Guo was so adamant about him personally leading the raid to the village. He needed Hengyen out of the way to pull off this crime. Guo knew he would never go along with their plan and would do everything in his power—including starting a coup—to stop him. For the first time, Hengyen cracked as his resolve and confidence withered. He should have seen this coming. The clues were there. Why had he been such a blind fool?

Hengyen stared out the dirty window at the gray skies. He could just make out the battle still being waged. Was the Living Revolution just a lie held up by weak men, or was it nothing more than a con perpetrated upon a group of gullible fools? Had any of this ever been real?

He closed his eyes. "I am the lone monk walking the world with a leaky umbrella."

What should he do now? What purpose did he have if everything was a lie? The Red Army was probably broken, the government gone, the country destroyed.

This was no longer the Land Under Heaven. Heaven had fallen, and with it the people, and that foolish dream of fending off the jiāngshī, of defeating death. The Beacon of Light was not the last hope of a people standing against the darkness. It was a tomb, an island of dirt and mud, waiting for the ravages of the dead to swallow it until the accursed living in this wretched world were finally snuffed out of existence.

All this time, he had blindly followed and obeyed people he thought wise, noble, patriotic. Now he realized, the rot the Living Revolution faced was more than the rotting flesh of the dead, but also of the corrupted souls of men.

Hengyen didn't know how long he sat in silence in Guo's office, staring out through the smudges of soot and grime on the window, listening to the distant chatters and screams of battle. It must have been hours. The sun was far along its descent by the time the sound of footsteps eventually broke through the low-level noise, loud, sharp slaps of boots on stone. They were followed by a woman's voice.

"Windmaster Hengyen, are you here? Windmaster?"

Hengyen swiveled in the chair and faced the doorway, wondering who was seeking out this fool. A moment later, the guard who had escorted him appeared. Her face was pale, her shirt wet with sweat. She obviously had not heeded his orders to get some rest.

"Windmaster, thank goodness I found you. You're needed. The southwestern corner just collapsed."

Hengyen grimaced. He was suddenly so tired. A voice in his head wanted to shrug off her words. What was the point of fighting if their fate was inevitable? He nearly told her this much. Then he saw the guard struggling to breathe, fighting to do her duty against these impossible odds. These people needed him to lead them, even if they were all doomed. Especially if they were all doomed.

"Firstly, do not fear hardship, and secondly, do not fear death," he muttered, rising to his feet. He spoke louder. "What happened?"

"The team on the corner was using explosives to set the jiāngshī on fire. One of the injured died and came back as a jiāngshī without anyone else realizing. He bit a guard and a grenade went off in his hands, detonating their entire cache and blowing apart the wall."

Hengyen was already striding out of the room before she finished her sentence. "Rally all the reserves. It is time for the People to make our stand!"

24

THE SIEGE

Elena had hoped to catch a few hours of sleep after that grueling raid on Fongyuan before she had to join the fight against the typhoon. Unfortunately, the dead and catastrophe waited for no one. The moment she crawled into her cage, the southwestern corner of the Beacon exploded, cratering an entire section of the wall. Elena and just about every other windrunner were summoned to the front line to plug it while groups of enslaved vultures hastily built a second line of fortifications.

Fortunately, the Beacon's architects had built another row of containers just behind the outer walls that functioned as backup fortifications as well as housing. The Beacon's defenders were holding so far, but barely. She had spent well into the night defending the doorway of a half-destroyed container. The bodies littering the ground were so thick the mud flowed red.

Fourteen hours later, Elena was still waiting to sleep. She was finally pulled away from the front line at dawn. She was essentially asleep on her feet when she tripped and nearly face-planted in the mud on the walk back to her pod. At first she thought her foot had gotten caught on a branch, and then she realized it was an arm. Then she realized the person the arm was attached to was still breathing. Elena was so exhausted she was tempted to just leave them there, but she stayed and waved down a medic.

She watched as two former vultures picked up the unconscious man—more a boy, really—and moved him onto a stretcher like a slab of meat. One of the medics noticed a tear in the boy's coat and checked it, uncovering a gash running from beneath his ribs all the way up to his armpit. It didn't look deep, but it was angry and red. They had to get him to the infirmary quickly—

Elena gasped when the medic shook his head, pulled out a knife and jammed it into the boy's temple. She grabbed the medic's wrist. "What are you doing?"

He pulled away with a shrug. "Windmaster's orders. We take no chances with the jiāngshī."

She glowered as the two dumped the body off to the side of the path and continued searching for survivors. They stabbed two more injured before disappearing around the corner. She stared at the carnage around her. It felt almost claustrophobic in its oppressiveness. Death had come to the Beacon, and there was no way out.

Even when Changsha was falling, the people were doing everything in their power to save lives. During the worst of the outbreak, human life still mattered. Now, lives were being discarded on the streets; people who weren't even seriously injured. The worst part was she had helped make this happen. She had voluntarily captured other people and dragged them to this hell. And for what? To serve as fodder for the jiāngshī and be tossed aside to die on the streets?

Elena retreated from the side street to a square and saw Hengyen giving orders to several windrunners around him. Eyes narrowing, she set her jaw and stormed up to him. She waited for an opening to speak with him.

"Windmaster, did you give the order to kill our injured?" The accusation in her voice was blatant.

He finished rattling off instructions to a guard next to him before turning his attention to her. "The infirmary is reserved for those who can fight the next day. Anyone else is a liability; a potential soldier of the enemy."

She gaped. "We're throwing lives away as if they're worthless."

"In the case of poisonous bite, cut the finger to save the hand; the hand to save the arm; the arm to save the body."

"I just saw those medics murder three people!" she screamed. "They could have lived!"

He looked grim as he leaned in and hissed in her ear. "Elena Anderson, chances are none of us will survive this week. If we don't prevent the jiāngshī from rising up in the streets and attacking us from behind, none of us will survive this *day*."

Elena felt numb. "I helped bring these people here to get butchered. This is my fault."

"It's not your fault," he replied. "It is just the way it is."

"If you think we're all going to die, why are we fighting? Why don't we evacuate?"

"The Beacon is surrounded. The only way out is through the cable transport that fits ten people at a time. There are still over four thousand souls in the settlement."

"Then we start moving ten at a time."

"What do you think will happen if word spreads that people are trying to leave? Whatever hold we have on our defenses will collapse, then it'll be wholesale slaughter. Even if we get all four thousand people out of the Beacon, what happens? That many people will attract every jiāngshī within twenty kilometers. They'll be slaughtered. At least here we have defenses and shelter." He shook his head. "Besides, there isn't enough time or fuel to move everyone. Who lives? Who dies? At least together we have a chance to survive the typhoon. We just need to hold out until the main body passes."

"Is the Red Army still coming?" she pressed.

For the first time, Hengyen's steely calm cracked. She had never seen the windmaster look tired before. He never showed weakness. "Does it matter, Elena?" His voice was low. "I don't think anyone is coming for us. We're on our own. Now if you'll excuse me, I have a settlement to save." He turned away from her, their conversation ended. "Where are supplies? Has anyone seen the quotamaster? Never mind. I'll go to the supply tent myself."

Elena was left standing alone. She had never felt so lost. She had nothing left to fight for, no family, no hope. In a moment of weakness, she even wished that she had Zhu, the lying bastard. She retreated, joining the throng of exhausted and injured people heading to the back line of the settlement while slightly less tired and injured people took their places.

As she dragged her feet up the red, muddy slope leading back toward her pod, someone caught her attention. It was the woman in Zhu's camera, the one she had used as a lure to capture Zhu. Elena had avoided her during the journey back to the Beacon. She didn't want to give the villagers—or her wind team for that matter—the satisfaction of seeing her pain.

The young woman was hunched over the body of a fallen windrunner. She checked his pulse and grimaced, brushing his opened eyes with her hand. The woman wiped her eyes with her sleeves and put her hands together in a prayer, and then jammed a screwdriver into his skull.

Elena's eyes followed her as she moved from body to body. She was gentle, respectful, not unlike the two medics. It made her like the woman even if it infuriated her at the same time. She finally made up her mind and walked to her.

The young woman saw her approaching and the blood drained from her face. She bowed her head submissively. "Windrunner."

Elena held out her hands. "Relax, I just want to talk. How are you being treated?"

The woman couldn't hide the hate that flashed on her face. "Do you really want to know?"

"Never mind. What's your name?"

"Meili, Windrunner."

"Call me Elena."

The woman kept her head bowed. "Is there something you need, Windrunner?"

"I want to ask you about Chen Wenzhu. When did you guys meet? Was it when he came across your village? Can you tell me about it?"

Meili frowned. "I don't understand. I've known Wenzhu for a long time. We're from the same village."

A tinge of doubt scratched at the back of Elena's head. "Were you 'childhood sweethearts'?" She said the last words in English, not knowing what the Mandarin equivalent was.

"I don't know what that means. Our parents wanted to betroth us as children."

Elena ground her teeth. What was she doing asking things she already knew? It was stupid and only reopened sore wounds. "This is stupid," she muttered.

"But we were never . . ." Meili fumbled over the words. ". . . sweethearts. Wenzhu's sister is my best friend. Her name is Ahui."

Something Meili said gave her pause. "Wait—Zhu's sister *is* your best friend? She's alive? Is she here, or still back at that valley?"

Meili clammed up again. Of course the woman wouldn't say anything, especially after what the wind team had done to her village.

Still, everything became clear. It hit Elena like a punch in the gut.

Zhu hadn't been with another woman so much as reconnecting with the people from his home village. He had found the very thing she longed so much for. Could she hate him for that? "What have I done?" She had been so angry she had fed into whatever fit that narrative. The secretary had fanned that rage. She had never given Zhu the chance to explain himself. Now they were all doomed. This was all her fault.

Elena clenched her fist. "Listen to me, Meili. I'm relieving you of your duty right now. Go find the rest of your people who are out right now and send them back to their cells. Can you do that and have everyone back in an hour?"

"But—"

"No time to discuss this. Go!"

Elena watched as the woman hurried off. She had to go see Zhu. She had to make things right. But first, there was one more thing she had to do.

25

REDEMPTION

Zhu sat in the corner with his knees pulled to his chest and stared at the scrawled lines on the ribbed container wall just outside his cage. The previous occupant had been in here for seven groupings of five, exactly thirty-five days. That meant this person must have either assaulted someone or disparaged a party member, and only if they had a relatively valuable skill. There was no way the Beacon would keep someone fed and taken care of for long without getting something out of them. If they had committed murder or were not a useful person, the Beacon would have sent them to the Charred Fields or banished them from the settlement.

He frowned. That made Ming setting him to penance all the more insulting.

The rest of the villagers were crammed in the shipping containers next door. At least they were there when they were not hard at work. The guards had wasted no time putting the villagers to work in shifts, forcing them to help build barricades, serve food, and clear bodies. Zhu had just returned from burning bodies with the second shift of villagers. Every six or so hours, half of the village would get pulled out of the cage with the threat that if they tried to escape or disobey, the rest of their kin would be killed.

He would much rather be fighting jiāngshī, but the guards deemed him too dangerous to give him a weapon. They put him in one of the private cages to prevent him from inciting a rebellion. He lay down and stretched his feet, staring at the ceiling. He didn't mind being in here. This dog kennel was essentially the same size as his pod and certainly less noisy. Less noxious, for that matter. At least these cells got hosed down periodically.

The problem with being trapped here with nothing to do was it gave his worried mind room to run. Death was probably coming to collect him soon, so he tried to spend his last moments in this world trying to make his peace. Unsuccessfully. Regret and shame filled his hours. He wished he could see his family once more and apologize for not being there for them. He wished he could make amends with Elena. He knew how much she had lost because of him. He wished he had never found the village so his people wouldn't be trapped here in the Beacon with the typhoon at their doorsteps. Most of all, he wished he could see Ahui one more time. Knowing she might still be alive warmed his soul. Knowing he was so close but would likely never see her again broke his heart.

When Zhu wasn't beating himself up about his poorly led life, he filled the rest of his brain space with the sense of impending dread and doom. The noise from just outside these thin walls didn't help matters either. Zhu could hear just enough to know things weren't going well. Occasional screams, shouts, explosions. Muffled, panicked conversations just outside his shipping container. Whatever information he couldn't glean from those noises, his runaway daydreams filled in. If reality was anything like his imagination, the Beacon was in deep trouble.

Zhu was just contemplating the worst scenario he could think of when the container door rumbled open. He called out to the lone guard tasked with watching all the prisoners. "Hey, Jianping; about time. I haven't pissed since . . ."

Bo's big lumpy head appeared through the entrance. His wide ear-to-ear smile lit up the otherwise dark room. "Xiǎodì!"

Zhu scrambled to his feet so fast he banged his head on the top of his cage. His fingers clasped around the bars. "Bo, you're alive! I'm so glad to see you." He did a double take. "What happened to your face?"

Bo grinned. "They took my points, and you weren't around, so I couldn't get a haircut or shave." The big man pawed at a faint five o'clock shadow around his mouth.

"No, I mean why is it all purple and bruised?"

The big man looked away, crestfallen. "Oh, it's nothing."

Zhu clasped hands with Bo through the bars. "I'm so glad you're all right. What are you doing here? Jianping said I wasn't allowed to have visitors. Did the windmaster change his mind?"

"Not that I know of." Bo became apprehensive and looked back toward the doorway. "Someone wants to see you."

Elena stepped into view. "Hello, Wenzhu."

Her face was red, and she looked worn down. Deep lines were etched into her forehead, and her hair was mussed and tangled. Her clothes were stained. Elena was still the most beautiful person he had ever seen.

Zhu scowled, his fingers tightening around his bars. "Here to finish me off, Elena?"

"Now, xiǎodì," said Bo. "Hear her out. She saved me."

"She led a wind team straight to the hidden village," snapped Zhu, not taking his eyes off her. "She doomed innocent people. My people!" He shook his head. "Worse, she believed the secretary's word over my own." Elena cast her eyes downward.

"She told me everything," said Bo. "That's why we came. We're here to make things right."

"You can't make things right!" he roared. "People died during the raid, and everyone who was captured will die here with the rest of the Beacon."

"They don't have to." Elena produced a key. "I can't undo my mistake, but I can do what I can to fix it. You can take the villagers and escape."

Zhu stared at the key. "How did you get that? What happened to Jianping?"

Elena held a bloodied knife in her other hand. "I'm not asking you to forgive me. I'm asking you to let me help you escape."

He didn't hesitate. "Open the gate." He didn't trust her. He doubted he ever could again, but it wasn't like he had a better alternative. What was the worst that could happen? It wasn't like she could betray him again. Well, she could, but he was basically already suffering through the worst-case scenario. Still, he half expected a wind team to burst in when she unlocked the door. When Zhu walked out, Elena backed away, fearing his wrath.

Zhu clenched his fist and turned away. "Where are the villagers?"

"They're being held in the group cells one container block over." Bo poked his head out the doorway. "We checked it before we came. One of the Xing twins is watching over them."

"Luhong?" Zhu gave his prison one last glance as the three left the shipping container and moved along its wall in single file.

Bo, taking lead, stopped at the corner and raised a hand. "No, he's dead."

Zhu's mouth dropped open. "Oh no. When?"

"Over a month ago, Zhu. Right after you went missing the first time. Elena and I got back just in time to attend a little ceremony for him. He was everyone's favorite."

Zhu sighed. "I really liked him. His brother, not so much."

"Tell me about it. At least we won't feel so bad about knocking him out." Bo pointed at the building in the far corner of a small clearing. "Your villagers are being held in there. The guard house is over there off to the side. The húndàn twin should be there with the keys."

"What does húndàn mean again?" asked Elena.

"Like what you Americans call an asshole." Zhu looked at the two buildings adjacent to their target. "What about the other vultures? We can't just leave them."

Bo frowned. "Wait a minute. I thought 'asshole' was a good thing, Elena."

Elena ignored him. "Zhu, I know what you want to do, but we can't bring everyone with us. I don't think we can even get all your villagers out."

Zhu looked as if he was going to argue, and then relented. "We have to try, at least."

The three waited until the coast was clear. There weren't many people walking about in this corner of the settlement. Most were vultures returning from their duties. Zhu doubted any of them cared what they were up to. The few who noticed shot them contemptuous glares and gave them a wide berth. They reached the guardhouse and huddled around the entrance.

"How do we get the keys from the húndàn twin?" asked Bo. They exchanged glances.

"Well, *I'm* certainly out of the question, unless you want to use me as bait," said Zhu.

"I can tell him this is my new assignment and relieve him," said Bo.

Zhu shook his head. "He'll never buy it."

"I can just stand outside and scream for help," Elena suggested.

"He'd probably just stay inside and listen to you scream," said Zhu. "Then someone else will come and make things worse."

In the end, they kept it simple. Elena rushed through the guardhouse door, sounding panicked but not loud enough to attract too much attention. "Help, there are four jiāngshī just outside." They had agreed on four, which was enough for it to be dangerous for one person but easy to handle with two.

When the húndàn twin followed her outside—no one could remember his name—Zhu and Bo were waiting on both sides of the doorway. Zhu's punch to the jaw should have dropped him, but he was tougher than he looked. The man staggered and blindly lashed out, clipping Zhu across the side of the head. Fortunately, Bo was there, wrapping him into a choke hold and squeezing with his big beefy arms until the húndàn went limp. They dragged him back into the guardhouse and trussed him up. Elena patted him down and produced a ring of keys.

They hurried to the container, where all the villagers were crammed into three cells. They appeared to be expecting to be saved and cheered when Zhu appeared. He was relieved to see Meili standing near the center gate waiting, and he was shocked—and a little disturbed and anxious—when Elena walked straight up to her. Several of the villagers were openly glaring at her.

"Is this everyone?" asked Elena, fumbling for the right key. "Did you find your people?"

Meili shook her head. "There's still twelve out there. I couldn't find them. We can't leave until we do."

"There's no time," said Elena. "I'm sorry."

"Wait, how do you two know each other?" Zhu asked Meili.

"She was the one who told me to gather everyone and prepare to leave."

As soon as the gate opened, the villagers streamed out. Guan, a middle-aged man, grabbed Elena and pinned her against the wall. "You killed my son, you white devil."

Before Zhu could jump in and prevent the situation from escalating, Bo intervened and escalated the situation even more. He roared, his voice carrying loudly inside the container, and charged the man, knocking half a dozen people over before getting between Elena and Guan.

"Don't you dare touch my xiǎomèi," he snarled.

Guan did not appear to be intimidated by Bo and punched him in the stomach. If Bo felt anything, he didn't show it. Everyone around went in for Bo, and he shoved back.

"Stop!" cried Zhu, frantically trying to separate them. No one listened.

The middle-aged Guan was nearly berserk with grief, punching and kicking, trying to lunge past Bo to get to Elena. Bo defended her with ferocity, throwing wide ham-fisted punches at anyone who got too close. Elena made no move to defend herself. She just stood behind her friend, her eyes downcast. One of Guan's wild punches clipped her in the shoulder, causing her to stumble.

Zhu didn't know he still felt this way, but the moment he saw Guan strike her, he went blind with rage and plowed into the fracas. Fortunately, one calmer head with an extra loud pair of pipes prevailed.

"Stop it!" Meili screamed. Her voice echoed across the container. Everyone froze. One by one, they all turned to face her. "Do you all want to die here, or be slaves to the Beacon?" When no one answered, she continued. "Now, Guan, we all love Jincai and miss him terribly, but he wouldn't want you to die. He definitely wouldn't want you to endanger the rest of the village."

Tears rolled down Guan's face. He shook his head, deflated, the fight leaving him as quickly as it had come.

"We have a plan to get all of you out," said Elena quickly. "It'll be dark soon. Most of the guards are busy trying to plug the hole in the collapsed wall. I can lead you to the cable transport around the back way. If we hurry, we can overwhelm the guards and sneak everyone out before they realize we're gone."

Meili stepped up next to Elena and took charge, ordering the rest of the village to stay quiet and follow Elena closely. The pair exuded firm authority. Everyone immediately complied. Zhu found himself following their orders automatically.

He joined Bo to check if the coast was clear, and then they moved, quickly making their way around the back of the container to a narrow alley between the north wall and the purification plant. Zhu stopped at the doorway to the adjacent container. The Smokers were being held there, and the Heaven Monks in the one next to it. He took several steps toward it when Elena grabbed him by the collar.

"We can't rescue everyone. If you try, chances are no one will make it out alive."

Zhu cursed again, but stopped. The group of fifty or so continued, moving in twos and threes through the narrow gaps between shipping containers, cutting through the area the Beacon used as a landfill and then creeping through a narrow stretch of cornfields that bordered the west wall. They had just left the field and were making their way through the final stretch behind a row of tents that led to a rarely used catwalk when someone, hidden in the shadows, coughed.

Zhu looked off to the side and blanched. Wangfa was sitting on a broken bench smoking a cigar. The defensemaster gave the group of villagers a bemused look, his gaze briefly locking on Zhu before settling on Elena. He took another puff and then carefully removed a box from his lap and placed it to the side.

He stood up, brushing his hands off and taking the cigar out of his mouth. "I've been saving those cigars. Pilfered them from the governor's office when that dog tried to run away. Thought I'd put them to good use and smoke them when the time is right." He shrugged and tried to pronounce the cigar's name. "Art-too-ros . . . Foon . . . fun . . . tes. They look expensive. The way I see it, now is as good a time to smoke it as any."

"Defensemaster—" said Elena.

Wangfa held up a hand. "Shut up. All of you return to your cells right now. You better get some rest because I'm putting you all on the front line for a double shift."

She tried again. "Please, let these people—"

"If I have to repeat myself, all of you will stay at the front line tomorrow until you're all dead."

"Staying here is a death sentence, Defensemaster," Bo pleaded.

"I'm the most disappointed in you, Ming Haobo, taking the side of these vultures. You were always a stupid fool." Wangfa shook his head. "Frankly, I don't blame any of you for trying to leave. I'd like to escape this death trap as well but that bastard Hengyen has the entire place locked down. Not even I can leave, so as long as I'm here, you are all staying as well. All of you return to your cells. Now!"

"No." Zhu picked up a sawed-off piece of lumber lying nearby. "Elena, get them out of here. I'll take care of Wangfa."

"Zhu, you can't," she said.

"Go, I'll catch up."

Bo moved next to him and drew his sledgehammer. "Don't worry, xiăoméi. I'll make sure Zhu is all right."

Elena hesitated, and then threw her arms around him, kissing him on the cheek. A moment later, the sounds of movement and fifty pairs of footsteps faded into the distance. Zhu didn't take his eyes off Wangfa as he hefted the lumber in his hand. It was shorter and heavier than his machete, but it would have to do.

He took a deep breath and glanced over at Bo. "In case something happens, you'll always be my brother, my friend."

Bo grinned and raised his sledgehammer. "And you'll always be my best friend, xiăodì."

They confronted the defensemaster together.

Wangfa looked amused as he casually took another puff of his cigar. He made a show of cracking his neck and loosening his shoulders as they approached. He didn't even bother reaching for the knives at his belt. "Are you fools actually going to test me?"

Zhu reached him first, waving his lumber over his head like a sword. He aimed for Wangfa's head, and was surprised when the defensemaster, instead of dodging the attack, stepped into the swing. The lower third of the lumber bounced ineffectually off Wangfa's shoulder. He retaliated with an uppercut that lifted Zhu's feet off the ground. His head snapped back and the world spun as he crashed into the mud.

He must have also dropped his lumber because Wangfa plucked it out of the air just in time to block Bo's attack. The big man brought the sledgehammer down, pushing the defensemaster back and banging away at the piece of lumber until it cracked. Then, Wangfa kicked his foot out as Bo pressed his attack, sending him sprawling flat on his stomach.

Wangfa took another puff of his cigar. "You idiots think you can take me on? You may be an above-average windrunner, Zhu, and your mother may have mated with an ox, Bo, but I'm career military. I've been fighting since before your balls dropped."

Zhu scrambled back to his feet. The world was still wobbly. He probably should have taken more time to recover. He tried to surprise Wangfa while the guy was still monologuing with the cigar in his mouth. All four of his punches fell woefully short. His efforts were rewarded with a punch to his gut that doubled him over. A whoosh left his lips as Zhu fell onto all fours. A nudge from the defensemaster's boot put him back on the ground.

Wangfa shook his head mockingly. "Your problem, Wenzhu, is that you only learned how to fight jiāngshī. You haven't had to deal with an opponent who thinks. You just fight decomposing punching bags that occasionally bite back. You never had to worry about telegraphing your movements or feinting or watching for counters." Wangfa was so busy bragging that he nearly missed Bo's attack from behind. He noticed at the very last second and tried to jump out of the way. Bo's long, looping punch found Wangfa's jaw with an audible crack, sending the cigar flying from his mouth. The defensemaster staggered as Bo pulled his arm back for another swing. Unfortunately, it was a long windup, and Wangfa managed to recover quickly enough to duck. The punch flew harmlessly over his head. Wangfa spun low and shot his foot out, sweeping Bo's leg from under him.

The defensemaster stood up, rubbing his jaw. "And you, Bo, you might be strong but you're as slow as a jiāngshī." He walked over to his dropped cigar and scowled at it sitting extinguished in a muddy puddle.

Zhu and Bo took this opportunity to scramble back to their feet. Bo picked up his sledgehammer, and offered Zhu his dagger. Both men brandished their weapons and circled the defensemaster on opposite sides.

Wangfa finally drew his long knife and flicked it casually at his waist. "You're finally using your heads. Next time—" he hesitated. "Well, there won't be a next time."

"You talk too much," Zhu growled.

They came at him again. The sledgehammer just missed his head and then he was within range of Zhu's dagger. Wangfa parried Zhu's thrust and then dabbed the tip of his blade into Zhu's shoulder as he spun away, causing Zhu to stumble as his shoulder gave way.

"You exposed your neck just now," Wangfa quipped. "I could have ended you right—"

His chatter was cut off as Bo roared and charged him like a rampaging bull. Wangfa barely avoided the first two swings. It looked as if he wouldn't be able to dodge the third when he suddenly changed directions and pounced, slicing Bo's side open just as the shaft of the sledgehammer struck him in the ribs. Both men bounced off each other and fell to the ground.

Wangfa grimaced as he rolled to his feet, holding his ribs and sucking in shallow breaths. At least they managed to hurt him. Zhu tried to take advantage, getting into Wangfa's face and drawing blood with a slash just below his eye. Another slash nearly sliced his belly open, but the defensemaster turned away in time.

He retaliated with a cut to Zhu's thigh that buckled his legs. Zhu shot back with a clumsy punch that clipped Wangfa's shoulder, but these were desperate strikes. He had already spent most of his energy.

Wangfa pulled Zhu's arm away from his body and torqued his elbow in an unnatural angle. Fresh waves of pain crawled up Zhu's arm as he screamed, the dagger slipping from his grasp. Another blow to his eye sent him back to the ground. Wangfa towered over him, his knife dripping with blood. He pressed a blade down on Zhu's neck.

"You two actually hurt me. I'm impressed. Bo did all the work. You were just a distraction." He pressed the tip of his blade to the soft part of Zhu's neck. "As a reward for your efforts, I'll make your death quick."

"No!" The roar was earth-shattering.

Wangfa moved instinctually, flinging his knife at the source of the sound. The shout was cut short, replaced by a grunt and labored wheezing. Zhu looked to the side and saw the sledgehammer slip from Bo's hands as he gripped the hilt of the knife embedded in his chest. He staggered a few steps and then collapsed onto his side.

A sigh escaped Wangfa's lips as he walked over and studied his handiwork. Bo spasmed as blood spilled from his mouth in spurts. His eyes were alert. He looked worried.

"Defensemaster," he pleaded in between short breaths. "Please spare Wenzhu."

Wangfa tsked. "You're too good for this world, Bo." He pulled the knife from Bo's chest and plunged it into his head. "You deserve to rest in peace, you dumb ox."

The shine in Ming Haobo's eyes dimmed. His eyes lost focus and stared off into nothing. A moan escaped Zhu's lips as his heart ached for his friend. "No, you bastard."

Wangfa turned to him. "You're the one responsible for Bo's death. You killed him."

"You're the one who stuck a knife in his chest. I'm going to offer you the same send-off." Zhu pawed the ground for his dropped dagger.

The defensemaster stomped over and kicked the blade spinning out of reach. When Zhu tried to stand, he smashed Zhu in the nose with a knee. Fresh blood sprayed everywhere. Wangfa wrapped his fingers around his neck and began to squeeze. Zhu tried to beat him back, but he had nothing left. His struggles weakened as everything slowly grew dark.

A part of him desperately hoped to see a vision of his family as he died, inviting him to join them in the afterlife. Instead, all he saw was Wangfa's cruel curling lips scowling as he squeezed his neck tighter.

Just as his consciousness was fading, a strident voice rang through the air. "What is the meaning of this!"

26

FOR THE LIVING REVOLUTION

Hengyen walked over to Wangfa choking a seemingly already unconscious Wenzhu. He grabbed a fistful of the defensemaster's collar and yanked him off, sending the him tumbling to the ground. Hengyen surveyed the carnage: a bloodied head of defense; a traitorous, possibly dead windrunner; and poor old Haobo lying off to the side. A curse escaped his lips. Haobo was a good man.

He rounded on Wangfa. "You're the defensemaster of the Beacon of Light. You are supposed to be leading the fight against the jiāngshī, not rolling in the mud while the settlement is under siege. Act your rank."

"These traitors were trying to escape," Wangfa said, pointing at Wenzhu, who was just starting to come around.

"Who cares! The Beacon is under attack and her leader is nowhere to be found. Didn't you hear the alert?" Hengyen pointed up toward the sky at the panicked loudspeaker. It had been blaring for several minutes already: "Emergency warning. The jiāngshī have broken through the walls. They are swarming the inner court. All guards and windrunners are required at the front. Repeat. The jiāngshī have broken through . . ."

Out of the corner of his eye, Hengyen noticed Wenzhu get to his feet and stagger away. Wangfa noticed too and moved as if to chase him down. Hengyen pushed him away. "Forget the traitor. We have to save the settlement."

He dragged the head of defense of the Beacon of Light with him toward the south wall.

Along the way, they passed hundreds of people fleeing in the other direction. Hengyen tried to rally those close to him, but it was a losing effort. The settlement was in full panic. Fear was contagious. He tried to stop a group from passing, but the cowards just ran around him.

Hengyen refused to join them. He gritted his teeth and continued toward the battle. Running away did little except delay the inevitable. There was nowhere safe to go, no place to retreat. There was only one thing to do if any of them were to survive.

Hengyen grabbed Lin as the man tried to flee. "Wrong way, windrunner."

Lin tried to break free. "They're pouring through by the hundreds. We're all going to die!"

Hengyen held on tightly. "Then die like a patriot. Fight alongside your brothers and sisters. Make your death count."

Lin looked indecisive to the point of being frozen. He looked back the way he had come before finally taking a deep gulp and nodding. "I'm with you, dàgē."

"Good man." Hengyen turned to his other side. "Defensemaster Wangfa, head to the southwestern . . ." He was speaking to air. Hengyen cursed. Wangfa was no longer there. He must have slipped away while Hengyen was busy marshaling their people for the counterattack. "Coward," he muttered. Just as quickly, the former defensemaster of the Beacon of Light was forgotten. They had a settlement to protect.

Hengyen hurried to a loudspeaker station and projected his voice across the entire settlement. "This is Windmaster Ying Hengyen. This will be my final broadcast. To my people of the Living Revolution, now is the time to stand with your brothers and sisters. This is the moment where you choose if you wish to succumb and walk with the dead, or stand against them. This is not only for yourself or your family or your countrymen. This is for every living soul in this Land Under Heaven.

"The time to run has long passed. I regret to tell you that escape is no longer an option. All we can do now is fight and resist death's onslaught. Be strong. Stand shoulder to shoulder with your fellow patriots. Show the dead that we intend to carve a future not only for our sons and daughters but for their children as well. That stand must begin here, now, or else there will be no tomorrows for which to fight. Who will stand by my side?"

The crowd close to him roared. It was a rousing speech. Whether it inspired the rest of the Beacon remained to be seen. Hengyen drew his blades and continued walking with his head high toward the front line with the crowd growing behind him. They picked their way against the current, calling out and grabbing any brave soul and challenging them to stand with the Living Revolution to their dying breaths. Most continued to flee, but there were still a few courageous souls left. Within a minute, a dozen brave people were standing with him. Within five, a hundred.

More and more joined them every second. Some must have realized there was no place they could go. Others wanted to die fighting. Most, however, had just been missing leadership and direction. Hengyen called several orders: five people here to defend the alley, three at the intersection to erect a barricade, six more to plug the entrance of a container leading to the wall. He took his place at the front of the line. To both sides, the defenders stood grim-faced as the jiāngshī's buzzing filled the air. The sounds were soon joined by the echoes of footsteps on metal as the shipping containers in front rattled.

"Stay close! Shoulder-to-shoulder. Watch your footing. Close that door. Flip that wagon and block the alley. Lace barbed wire over the fencing. Do not fail your brothers and sisters!" Hengyen stayed at the center, shouting orders and trying to rally the people around him. "The living will stand against the darkness. We will keep the Land Under Heaven alive." He finally realized he was shouting to himself. The battle was a frenzied melee.

A jiāngshī appeared out of a tent to their left. It was felled by an old woman holding an ax. Three more appeared in front, squeezing through the narrow gap between two containers. They were met by two guards. More came from all sides, from behind buildings, from inside containers and over barricades. The noise was coming from every direction. Someone in the back shouted a warning as five jiāng-shī appeared from behind. Another warning as a dozen fell from the wall. The dead came at the living from every side.

Hengyen encountered a group of three jiāngshī, his knives flashing in the fading light. One blade punctured an eye socket, another entered the soft flesh under a jaw. He yanked knives back and kicked the third in the chest, sending it tumbling backward and knocking over two more jiāngshī in the process. He hurdled over their bodies to take on another group of enemies. At the same time, the people behind him pounced on the fallen jiāngshī, stabbing them with whatever weapons they had on hand.

A jiāngshī nearly ended his battle when it stepped off the roof of a shipping container and almost fell on top of him. He was saved, however, by the guard and windrunner fighting alongside him. One pulled him away to safety while the other plunged a sword into the creature's skull.

"Thank you, Fang, Shanshan," he said in between deep breaths

"It is the greatest honor of my life to fight by your side, dàgē," Fang declared.

Shanshan nodded, holding up her spear. "For the Living Revolution."

Hengyen nodded and took the opportunity to reassess the situation. It looked grim.

A seemingly endless number of jiāngshī continued to encroach on the living. They were an unstoppable force of nature. Waves of the dead swept over the walls and buildings like an ocean storm over the shores, washing over the containers and barricades and people, knocking over tents and fortifications with equal ease. Soon the entire area was a boil of close combat, the last of the Beacon of Light's defenders fighting against the inevitable. More of his people fell. No matter how much and how hard they fought, the jiāngshī continued to advance.

Hengyen was still trying to devise a plan when the inevitable finally dawned on him. It was over. This was the end. It didn't matter anymore. There was only one thing left to do. Only one thing left they *could* do.

Ying Hengyen, captain of the Falcon commando unit of the Armed Police Force of the People's Liberation Army, Windmaster of the Beacon of Light, gripped his knives and raised his arms in the air. With a loud battle cry, he charged into the heart of the typhoon.

27

THE ESCAPE

Zhu hobbled toward the cable transport as fast as his busted-up body could move. He hoped he wasn't too late. Still, he had accomplished what he had set out to do, which was delay Defense-master Wangfa and give the villagers and Elena time to escape. He was surprised he had survived the fight. Wangfa had thrashed him thoroughly.

His thoughts flashed to Bo. His knees weakened and he was tem-porarily overwhelmed with a deep sense of loss. Bo had been his good friend long before any of this horror had been inflicted upon them. Through it all, the big man had been a steadfast friend: loyal to a fault, kind beyond all others, and beloved by everyone who knew him. He was among the people who had suffered the deepest losses, yet somehow found a way to never lose his hope and happiness.

The only thing that prevented Zhu from falling to his knees and weeping was the immense pain cutting into seemingly every part of his body. It reminded him that he was still alive and in danger. That although Bo was gone, there were still Meili and the villagers. And Elena. Bo's spirit would never forgive him if Zhu wasted this opportunity to save these people because he was too preoccupied with self-pity. If Zhu could have taken Bo's place, he would have gladly. But since he couldn't, the only thing he could do now was honor his friend's sacrifice.

He continued along the settlement's outer wall, occasionally leaning on it for support. His leg wasn't doing well. It's a miracle the defensemaster hadn't slashed a major artery. The world was swaying, making walking in a straight line surprisingly difficult. Zhu was pretty sure both his jaw and nose were broken, and one of his eardrums ruptured. His entire face was numb with pain, and the blood congealing in his throat made it difficult to breathe. If he survived today, he foresaw drinking his meals for the next few weeks.

Several guards rushed past him. Zhu stepped to the side and bowed his head, but it didn't appear necessary. They were in an awful hurry, and none gave him a second glance. One looked familiar, and Zhu expected that the woman would have recognized him if it were not for his freshly rearranged face. That was a positive spin on the beating Wangfa had given him.

Zhu continued to hug the wall and move through cover, doing his best to stay unobtrusive, but it appeared unnecessary. Something bad was happening to the south, but his vision was so blurry he could barely see more than a few meters ahead. He reached the catwalk to the cable transport and found it abandoned. Where were the guards? If Elena and the villagers had gotten here first, where were the signs of struggle? Where were the bodies?

He climbed the stairs, fearful of what he'd see at the top. It had been heavily fortified when they came in. Maybe the villagers were battling guards. Perhaps they had already escaped. Maybe they were already torn to pieces, and all he would encounter once he reached the parapet were their jiāngshī. Every subsequent thought was worse than the one before.

He hurried up the stairs as fast as he could, doing away with his usual caution. No sooner had he reached the top than someone tackled him, which wasn't so hard, considering. Rough hands pawed at his shoulder and waist and dragged him to the ground. A blurry figure appeared and kicked him in the stomach, doubling him over.

"Take that, you ugly húndàn." Another blow to the face nearly loosened his consciousness from his body. That voice sounded familiar, though.

"Huangyi, it's me, Zhu." Talking hurt like hell. Each word shot pain up his skull, jabbing mercilessly into his brain.

"Chen-shūshu, is that you? What happened to your face?"

Zhu grunted as the teenager helped him to his feet. "That's twice you've kicked me in the stomach."

"Sorry," said Huangyi, actually sounding sincere. "Hey, Meili, it's Zhu."

That caused a small commotion, and Meili flew into his arms. "We thought you were dead."

He held her tightly for a few seconds, and then leaned on her for support. He looked over her shoulder, scanning the faces present. He frowned. "Where is everyone? Why are there so few people here?"

Meili pulled away and pointed at the horizon past the Charred Fields. "Most have already crossed. We've been going in small groups."

"Everyone made it?"

"We're still missing the twelve people I never found." She turned her gaze toward the settlement as if desperately hoping to catch sight of their missing people at that moment.

He squeezed her shoulders. "Don't think about them. Think about the people you've saved. These people owe you their lives."

That was when Zhu's eyes finally landed on who he was really looking for. Elena was standing by the platform's controls. Her eyes were locked on him, her face a mix of relief and continuing worry. Zhu let go of Meili, and they walked toward Elena through the remaining villagers.

She met them halfway and threw her arms around him. "Thank the Lord you're all right, Wenzhu. I was afraid you weren't going to get here in time."

"I'm here now." He scanned the familiar faces. Most of his students were gone. "How much longer?"

"We've made four trips so far," she replied. "Three more to go. The seniors insisted we send the younger ones first."

Shenyang ran up to them and spoke with Meili. The girl visibly flinched when Elena looked her way. Her hands moved up to cover the long red gashes on her cheeks. "The next group is ready."

Meili moved to the cable transport as it docked. She slid the door open and herded ten villagers inside. Once they had all shuffled in, she checked the space and sent in three more. It made for a tight fit, but no one complained. "Squeeze in," she ordered. "Hug your neighbors."

Zhu watched the cable car lurch from the platform and struggle on the wires. He counted the villagers still waiting. One more trip, and they would be free of the Beacon forever. He turned his attention away from the platform. His vision was still hazy, but he could just make out silhouettes running along the top of the southern parapet. The loudspeakers were continually blaring, and there were screams in the air, a chorus of a thousand people yelling out of tune. There was now a steady stream of people on the ground fleeing north. Things were getting really bad.

Huangyi shouted a warning, and several villagers moved to confront a small group coming up the catwalk. The windrunners stopped at the top of the stairs and drew their weapons as they eyed the villagers.

"Get out of our way," shouted a familiar voice. Its owner had just killed his best friend.

"We were here first," Meili retorted. "You can use this once we are through."

"You're just a bunch of vultures. We're getting on next." The group pressed forward.

The villagers closed ranks, their clubs, staves, and knives drawn. "When we're through." Meili was unwavering, her voice cold.

Burning rage filled Zhu's soul. It was all he could do to stay in control and not to attack Wangfa and push him off the parapet. At that moment, he wouldn't even mind if they both went over the side. Every nerve of his being begged for him to avenge Bo. He nearly succumbed to his instincts, but the sight of Huangyi standing next to him tempered his anger. The boy was terrified but still defiant, ready to help and fight for his sister and his village. Zhu closed his eyes. As much as he hungered for revenge, his priority should be to the living, his village and his people and his loved ones, not to the dead.

Zhu pushed himself in between the groups. "Listen, murderer, enough bloodshed. If we fight, we're as good as dead. There's only six of you. Just let us go first, and then you can follow. Would you rather wait a few minutes or die on these steps?"

Wangfa spat. "I should have known you were behind this, traitor. Get out of the way. We have guns." The guard standing at his flank aimed a hunting rifle at him.

"You have *a* gun," said Zhu, softly. "We outnumber you two to one."

He stepped forward until the muzzle of the gun touched his chest. He'd much prefer to take the bullet than let it hit any of the villagers. No one moved. The guard's fingers twitched. For a second, it looked as if Wangfa and his people were going to call his bluff.

"Stop it, all of you!" shouted Elena, getting between them and pushing the barrel up. She shoved Zhu back. "You don't get to survive this far only to die like an idiot." She turned to Wangfa. "You six can cram in with the next group. We'll just do two trips." She shook her head, disgusted.

The cable car was returning. Zhu reluctantly stepped aside as

Wangfa sneered and led his people past the villagers. They insisted on going inside first and were soon joined by seven villagers.

Zhu scowled as the cable car pulled away, slowly shrinking in size as it crossed the Charred Fields. There were only a few people left on the platform. If more trouble came, he doubted they would be able to do anything about it. The round trip was only about ten minutes, but the wait was excruciating.

Meili was scolding Huangyi for not being part of the group, but the boy crossed his arms stubbornly. "You're my sister. I won't leave you behind."

She poked him hard on the head. "You have to live to take care of Huangmang if something happens to me."

"You take care of Huangmang yourself," he shot back. His face fell. "Besides, we've already been gone for so long. A lot can happen in so little time in this world. I have to stay close to the only family I have who is still alive." Meili looked as if she were about to scold him again, and then threw her arms around him and buried his face in her chest.

"Zhu, where's Bo?" Elena asked.

He squeezed his eyes shut and shook his head.

"No." A choked sob escaped her lips.

A commotion erupted near the center of the Beacon. There would be time to grieve later. Zhu scanned the platform and held her arm. To his horror, he saw a wave of jiāngshī, hundreds of them, washing over the ground. The few people down there who were still trying to flee were quickly engulfed by the dead pouncing on their bodies. Within seconds, the typhoon had flooded into the entire settlement.

Zhu stared at the approaching cable transport with renewed urgency, willing it to move faster. It was still halfway, rolling at a slow, meandering pace. The seconds ticked by as the number of jiāngshī on the ground continued to increase. A few—as in several dozen—saw the humans on top of the parapet and began to stumble up the catwalk. While the dead weren't great with stairs, they were slowly making their way up.

Elena cried out in alarm and pointed further down the parapet. Another stream of jiāngshī was approaching them from that direction as well. She drew her short spear while Zhu picked up a discarded metal pipe. He pointed at the console. "Meili, as soon as the car gets here, slide the door open, then hit the yellow button. The car won't start moving until the door is closed. We'll buy everyone time."

The first jiāngshī reached them a few seconds later. It was a boy, probably no older than ten. He was still wearing his pajamas. Zhu swung his pipe, connecting solidly with the skinny boy's chest and sending him flying over the side. The next jiāngshī was a soldier wearing riot gear. His first two blows bounced ineffectually off its head. His next one went low, cracking its kneecap. As soon as he jabbed with the pipe, the jiāngshī topped over.

Elena was a one-woman killing machine, impaling the dead left and right with her spear. She stabbed one in the chest and pushed, forcing it back until it fell into the Charred Fields. There was a heightened desperation to this melee. Zhu snuck a peek at the catwalk; the jiāngshī climbing up were turning the last corner. Once they reached the top of the parapet, there was little he and Elena could do to stop the platform from being overwhelmed.

The momentary distraction proved costly. A jiāngshī lunged for him. Zhu swung his pipe blindly but missed, and a jiāngshī in scrubs tripped over the soldier and plowed into his legs. Zhu's balance was already precarious. He fell over easily, and it crawled on top of him. Zhu flailed his arms, but could not fight it off. Huangyi charged in, kicking the jiāngshī in the head. It bought Zhu enough time to scramble back to his feet while Huangyi stomped on it.

Before he got too carried away, Zhu grabbed the boy and pushed him back toward the platform. "Stay with Meili."

"But I want to help!"

"Help by staying with your sister and getting that door open." Zhu snuck another look at the cable car and was relieved to find it finally pulling into the platform. He grabbed Elena by the collar and shoved her toward the car. "Everyone get in. Go."

She shook her head. "I'm not leaving your side."

Instead of wasting what little energy he had left arguing, Zhu charged the first jiāngshī who reached the top of the catwalk, putting the sole of his foot on its chest and giving it a hard kick. It toppled back down the stairs, arms flailing, bowling over several of its fellow deceased. The screech of the cable car's metal door opening was a welcome relief as Zhu continued swinging his bat in wide arcs, knocking two more jiāngshī over the side.

"Hurry, Zhu!"

By now, everyone else had moved inside the cable car. They were frantically waving for him. There was not a second to spare. The jiāngshī on the stairs had picked themselves up while the main body on the parapet were almost within arm's reach. Fingers grasped at him. Zhu dropped his pipe and noted with satisfaction one of the jiāngshī stepping on it and taking a tumble. He sprinted to the cable car, hurdling over the soldier on his way up the platform, just staying out of reach of the half-dozen jiāngshī grasping at him.

Zhu should have paid more attention. He landed awkwardly, and his already poor balance did him no favors as he found himself losing control. He gasped, pushing himself up and struggling to get to his feet. A shadow passed over him, followed by a groan. Before he could turn around, Elena was there, her spear thrusting into the dead man's stomach. Meili appeared an instant later, helping him to his feet. Together the three scrambled into the car and slid the door closed behind them. The jiāngshī surrounded the car and began to pound on the metal grating. More appeared, crawling over each other, desperate to claw or gnaw their way through to the living. Then, just when he thought nothing was happening, the cable car shuddered and lifted off the platform.

Several jiāngshī continued after them, pitching forward into the Charred Fields. The ground beneath the cable car was a sea of claws and groans, but for the first time, they finally felt safe. Zhu didn't take his eyes off the parapet. He subconsciously reached for Elena and found her waiting hand. They laced fingers and watched together as the Beacon of Light was snuffed out.

Elena squeezed his hand. "We did it. We made it out."

"What did we do exactly?" he said, bitterly. "What have we accomplished? Thousands of people died today."

"You survived. Your village survived. I call that a victory."

Zhu looked unconvinced as he continued to stare hauntedly back toward the Beacon. He turned toward her. "The villagers found a safe place up near the Precipitous Pillars. I'm going with them. Will you come with us?"

She hesitated. "I don't know. After what I did, I don't think I can. Your people hate me."

"Yes, well, you have to earn their trust."

"What about you?" she asked. "Do you trust me?"

He squeezed her hand back. "No, but, to be honest, I think we both have some work to do. I'm sorry I lied about the hidden village. I just wanted to keep them safe from the Beacon."

She pursed her lips and nodded. "It's okay. I understand. The one thing I have wanted more than anything else is to see my family and friends again. You want the exact same; how can I find fault with that?" She swallowed, and continued, "I think the least I can do is prove—"

The cable car squealed, and then shook to a violent stop. Meili pointed back to the platform. The mass of jiāngshī had now covered it, like ants on a mound. One of the jiāngshī had gotten caught in the chains, and its body was slowly getting torn in two as the gears ground its bones.

The car shook again. Metal tore and screamed. One of the chains holding the cable car snapped, and it tilted sharply toward one side. Zhu managed to hold on to Elena while Meili and her brother did the same, all four of them sliding across the carriage, bouncing off the walls and seats until they smacked against the far end. They were fortunate the grating held and they didn't plummet through and down to the seemingly endless number of jiāngshī below.

"Zhu, what do we do now?" asked Elena, digging her nails into his flesh.

He looked up. "Maybe we can get out and move along the line."

A moment later, a solution was forced upon them. Another harsh squeal of metal pierced the air, and then they were falling. They became weightless as gravity momentarily abandoned them. It returned with a vengeance a moment later as they crashed down onto the Charred Fields.

Zhu's head smashed into the metal roof, and stars flashed across his field of vision, followed by a deep darkness. When he came to again, a bloodied Elena was hovering over him. Next to her, Meili was cradling her brother's head, but the boy's eyes stared off, lifeless. The other two villagers with them weren't moving. One was lying facedown and the other was sitting against the wall with her neck turned unnaturally. All around, the jiāngshī just outside in the field were hammering at the gates and the door.

A roar filled his ears. Elena was mouthing silently to him. When he tried to sit up, he felt a sharp pain at his side, and his left arm gave out. He grimaced as she helped him up. Meili finally accepted that her brother was dead and broke down. Elena hesitated and moved to comfort her, wrapping her arms around her shoulders. Meili sobbed in her embrace.

Zhu struggled to his feet and stared out at their new dilemma. The cable car had fallen onto its side in the middle of the Charred Fields, crushing several jiāngshī. As far as he knew, their bodies had cushioned the car's fall and saved them. Just outside the car on all sides were snarling faces and hands pressed against the metal, a wallpaper of horrors. The hatred on their faces was palpable. There was no escape. Perhaps it would have been better if they had all died from the fall.

"You have to stay strong," Elena was saying to Meili. "The rest of your family needs you. What's your brother's name?"

"Huangmang," sobbed Meili, after some gentle urging.

"You need to stay alive for him," Elena continued. "My brother's name is Robbie. Every day I fight with the hope of seeing my family again."

"There's no use. We're trapped here," Meili sobbed. "Promise me you won't let me turn into one of them." She stared at her brother and pulled out her knife.

Elena, who was staring at him, grabbed her wrist. "Wait. Let him turn."

Meili's mouth fell. "What? What sort of monster are you?"

"I have an idea," said Elena. "You're going to have to trust me. Zhu, remember how I escaped from that garage?"

He pointed at the sliding door above their heads. "Escaping this cage isn't the problem. It's what we to do after we get out."

"No, I mean how I was able to hide from the jiāngshī."

He brightened. "Do you think that will work again?"

"Only one way to find out," she shrugged. "What do we have to lose?"

It took some convincing before Meili signed on to their plan. The three waited until Huangyi and the other two bodies in the car began to stir, then put the three new jiāngshī out of their misery.

Then the butchering started.

Meili couldn't do it, so Zhu urged her to close her eyes as he and Elena cut open the three corpses and smeared the blood and entrails over their faces, arms, and bodies. They looked like a horror show.

Elena even had intestines wrapped around her neck, which was a step too far for Zhu. Meili was still sitting off to the side balled up with her arms wrapped around her knees, her eyes squeezed shut tightly. Zhu stripped the clothes off one of the other dead and laid them over Huangyi's body.

He touched Meili's hand and helped her to her feet. "Keep your eyes closed. Follow me." He led her to the bodies and sat her back down. Elena got to work, smearing thick, red blood on her face.

"It's just like putting on makeup," she said soothingly. "Keep your eyes closed."

After a few minutes, Wenzhu, Elena, and Meili emerged from the cable car covered in the blood, guts and entrails of their fellow villagers. Zhu slid the door open on the now roof of the car and pushed Elena up, followed by Meili. They pulled him up together. He grimaced as pain rippled all over his body, and scowled with each step as he limped to the edge of the car.

To his relief, the camouflage appeared to be working. The jiāngshī surrounding the car paid them no attention. One jiāngshī stared at Meili curiously, but then ambled off in search of a meal. Zhu climbed down first, half expecting the mob around him to pounce. He exhaled in relief when he realized he was still alive a few seconds later, then helped the other two down. The three held hands and slowly threaded their way through the sea of jiāngshī. Zhu's hands were slippery with blood, but he held onto Elena in front and Meili behind him.

They kept their heads low. Everywhere he looked, the dead's faces stared back: old, young, strong, weak. There was a businessman, a nurse, a student. He passed by a woman with an infant still strapped to her back. A hunched-over grandfather still holding a cane. A woman in a traditional red wedding dress. A convict with his wrists shackled. Everywhere he looked, he saw people, people who once had had families and loved ones. Many lives now twisted into this ugly tableau of who they had once been.

A precious life once lived within each of these rotting and decaying bodies, one filled with laughter, love, and angst. Whatever this twisted visage, this shadow of the beauty that once lived was trapped inside. The curse of being undead, and unable to pass through death's final door. As their countrymen, as their fellow human, it should be their noble calling to help shepherd them through to heaven. For the first time, he understood what drove the Heaven Monks' crusade.

It took longer than he would have liked for them to finally climb up the small ridge that marked the end of the Charred Fields. The jiāngshī here were sparser, scattered. They were able to weave through them to the platform.

There was no one there.

"How could they not wait for us?" said Meili.

"It took us a long time to get here," replied Zhu. "They probably thought we were dead."

"We know where they're going," Elena added. "It shouldn't be hard to catch up."

"Wait, over there." Meili pointed up the ridge. Several small silhouettes were waving their hands, jumping up and down, trying to get their attention. All three broke into grins as they hurried off the platform. It was a straight shot up the path to the rest of the villagers.

Meili began to sprint up the hill toward the rest of their people. Elena was following close behind, and Zhu was doing his best at the rear. His leg was dragging, and he could feel the numbness radiating up from it. Finally, the pain became too much. He fell to a knee and grasped his foot.

"Elena!" he nearly shrieked.

She turned and grabbed his other hand to pull him in close. "Are you hurt?"

Zhu shook his head, and then hissed when a fresh surge of pain shot up his thigh. He glanced down and clutched his leg, wiping away the dried mud and blood smeared all over his skin.

There, on the side of his ankle, was a deep, angry bite mark.

28

THE STORM PASSES

Wangfa wiped the sweat off his face with a dirty cloth as he split cords of wood at the small clearing in front of the grain silo. He had always thought the settlement a disgusting dump, but he never realized how good he had had it until it was gone. He swung the ax again, chopping another log down the middle. He missed being someone important, or at least having someone else do all these menial chores. He was the defensemaster of the Beacon of Light, after all.

At least he used to be. Wangfa had returned to the Beacon three weeks after he fled, roughly a week or so after the typhoon had passed. Everything was as he had expected. There was nothing left but the

bare ruins of what had once been a large settlement. Most of the perimeter walls were intact, but little else. There were jiāngshī everywhere, more than he had ever seen in his life, save for when they had
first discovered the typhoon from Hengyen's lookout. It appeared
many of the jiāngshī who had broken through the Beacon's defenses
had decided to stay, or more likely hadn't known how to get out. Many
of those who were still behind the walls were the settlement's previous
residents.

In any case, Wangfa didn't bother trying to get any closer than the
outer edge of the Charred Fields. That, and he didn't really care. What
mattered to him was that he had gotten out, and now he had enough
supplies and food to last several years if not the rest of his life. All he
had to do was keep his head low and wait things out. He doubted
things would ever get back to the way they had been, but he hadn't
been doing all that well before the world fell apart anyway. When the
outbreak began, he had been waiting in a cell for his court-martial
date.

The silo door banged open and Guo walked out, wearing a
button-down shirt over dress pants held up by leather suspenders. At
least he had finally stopped wearing suits, that pretentious prick. The
man, smoking a pipe, scanned the area and pointed at the pile of
cords Wangfa had spent most of the morning building.

"Look at this mess," he grumbled. The least you can do is stack it
neatly."

Wangfa let it slide. Guo's usefulness would soon run out. The old
man still believed all this foolishness about the Living Revolution
even as he willingly abandoned the Beacon of Light. All his long-

winded speeches about retreating to rebuild and how this was the new Long March before taking back the land were just the delusions of an old man clinging to power.

Unfortunately, at least half of the people who had fled with them here to the Smoker's silo still believed in the secretary. His support was eroding by the day, however. It would only be a matter of time before Wangfa disposed of the useless fool.

But not yet. "Yes, Secretary," he replied, splitting another cord. He finished his work and brought the pile inside, nodding to a few guards busy with their assorted chores. There were twenty of them total, approximately half administrators and half guards. Five to ten too many in his opinion. They had needed the manpower at the time to transport all the supplies. Soon it would be time to whittle down the excess.

They were still trying to get settled. Who knew smoking food was so difficult and time-consuming? In any case, after nearly a month, Wangfa was beginning to get antsy from being cooped up here. They had cleared nearly a third of the Beacon's armory and had more guns and ammunition than they could use in a lifetime. Guo had initially planned to use it for barter if the need arose, but Wangfa had other ideas. As soon as he took over, he planned to round up some of the stronger guards and raid their surroundings. Maybe now was the time to bring back the age of warlords. He was still stacking the cords of wood—neatly—when Guo shouted for him.

"Wangfa, there's a jiāngshī out here! It's coming for me!"

Wangfa rolled his eyes and exchanged knowing looks with Lubin, or the húndàn twin as they called him behind his back, as he took his time putting the last few cords onto the pile. This happened every few days. A jiāngshī would wander near the silo, and Guo would lose his mind. It baffled him how it was even possible that Guo had yet to kill one. He headed back outside. The silo was far enough away from the main roads that they weren't in any real danger. The building was also near-impregnable, and with several years' supply of food on hand, they could wait anything out.

Wangfa stood next to the cringing Guo. Just as he suspected: a lone jiāngshī was plodding slowly toward them. It was a big boy, well-fed in his previous life, wearing what looked like workman's trousers. Wangfa was about to pick up his rifle when he yanked the ax out of the wood stump instead. Why waste a bullet? He hefted it over his shoulder and strolled forward.

He was about to shear the thing's head off when something familiar about it stopped him. Wangfa squinted, and then he laughed. "Hey, it's Ming. He finally found us."

It was Ming's job to cook the books so no one would know that the secretary was moving the supplies from the settlement to the silo. Because of that, he had to flee the Beacon right after people started having problems trying to locate nonexistent pallets of foodstuffs while at the same time opening empty crates that were supposed to contain weapons and ammunition. Guo had sent the quotamaster to the horse ranch to hide. Nobody had faith that Ming would hold up under interrogation.

Wangfa had journeyed to the horse ranch a few weeks ago to check up on Ming. He and his small group of collaborators weren't there. Wangfa hadn't shed any tears.

Guo must have thought the same thing. "At least we know now."

One hard swipe with the ax cleaved Ming's head clean off, sending it bouncing on the ground. Wangfa gave himself a running start and kicked it, sending the head flying off into the bushes.

"Hey," yelled Guo. "What did I tell you about leaving body parts scattered about? I don't want this place to smell. Go pick it up and dump the body down the hill."

Wangfa bit back his sharp retort. "Yes, Secretary."

He bent down to pick up the decapitated body.

Guo continued to bark. "Next time kill it farther away from where we eat and sleep, so it doesn't make a mess all over—"

Wangfa grunted as he wrapped his hands around the body and lifted it up. Guo did have a point. Still, what was he saying before he got cut off? Wangfa had dragged the body only a few meters before he turned and saw another jiāngshī. This one was in military fatigues and looked familiar too, except there was so much crud on his face Wangfa couldn't make out who he could have been. He must have been a guard or a windrunner. Maybe he was one of Ming's men.

In any case, it was just one more slow, stupid jiāngshī to kill. He needed the exercise after being cooped up in the silo. Wangfa dropped Ming's headless body unceremoniously to the ground and hefted the ax again. Interestingly, the jiāngshī wasn't coming at him. It was just standing there. Well, maybe this thing had been supremely lazy in life, which somehow carried over to unlife. Wangfa aimed for the crown of its head and swung his ax.

The jiāngshī stepped aside and the ax sunk harmlessly into the ground. Stunned, Wangfa scrambled backward. The thing just stood there, looking at him with a strange intensity.

Wangfa squinted again, throwing a thumb at it as he turned toward Guo. "Did you just see . . ."

There were two more standing next to the secretary. One had a hand covering Guo's neck and a knife pressed into the soft flesh of his throat. Like the one standing in front of him, they were wearing some sort of military or police fatigues, like what windrunners wore . . .

That's when Wangfa realized why the first looked familiar. He began his next ax swing without even looking, hoping to catch the one standing close to him off guard. As his ax whistled through the air, he turned to face his foe; a hard blow to his gut knocked the wind out of him and doubled him over, gasping.

A pair of intense, yellow-tinted eyes stared into his. "You look well, Wangfa."

"Hengyen . . . I thought you were dead." The blade twisted in his stomach. Wangfa's body gave, and he fell onto his knees.

"Unfortunately for you, no. The typhoon tried, but as you can see, the true Living Revolution does not die so easily. It took me a while to track Ming down. He gave you away so quickly."

"That bastard," hissed Wangfa. "That's what we get for trusting an accountant . . ."

The blade twisted once more, and then Hengyen let him crumple to the ground. The world went sideways as Hengyen left him where he lay and walked toward Guo. Several more figures appeared from the woods. He recognized several familiar faces: Fang, Shanshan, Lin . . . windrunners and guards who had stayed at the Beacon and fought with Hengyen until the very end. How did they survive the typhoon?

"Windmaster," Guo quivered. "I'm so glad to see you're alive. You were right all along. A tactical retreat was the right decision. That's what I'm trying to do. We needed a contingency plan to safeguard our supplies. I'm ensuring the survival of the Living Revolution."

"You are correct, Secretary," Hengyen said. "The Living Revolution is indeed alive and well. Its true nature, however, is not to simply stand against the dead. The dead are not our only enemy. Like the Civil War and the Cultural Revolution before, the Living Revolution must not only defeat enemies from the outside, we must also cleanse ourselves from the inside. Only when the tainted and corrupted are gone will the survivors be pure and golden."

Hengyen flicked his hand, and Guo fell to the ground, his head separated from his body. Wangfa tried to crawl away, but the debilitating agony was too intense, and his legs refused to do as they were told. Hengyen looked at him one last time dismissively before heading into the silo.

Screams began to fill the air.

EPILOGUE

Elena's breath caught as the shadow of the impossibly tall, alien, and utterly beautiful column stretched along the ground, creeping toward the mouth of their caravan. Several other huge stone columns jutted into the sky, red stone layers framed by vegetation that somehow managed to grow on the near-vertical buttes. This magical moment was the only reason she volunteered for predawn watch duty. It gave her a small reminder that not all was ugly in the world, that there was still beauty if you had the patience and the perspective to look for it.

She shifted on top of the hood of the hollowed-out utility van holding their dried fruits and grain, her bow resting in her lap. The caravan had arrived at Zhangjiajie National Park near Yuanjiajie, or Hallelujah Mountain, as it was known in English, three days ago. Though the trek was only slightly over two hundred kilometers, it had taken them over a month to negotiate the long, winding, difficult landscape, fighting jiāngshī every step of the way. They were forced to circle around to the western side of the park to avoid several impassable villages.

But they had made it. The caravan had cleared a stone square in what was once a tourist area. They set up a temporary camp and circled the wagons like in those old American Westerns, and for the past three days, they had sent out scouting parties to search for Ahui's team. The park was huge, and their best guess was they were somewhere on the northwestern side, which was honestly a lot of ground to cover. It could take weeks if not longer, Xupin had said. He was the scout who had returned to gather the village. That was fine with Elena. It wasn't like she was in a hurry, at least not anymore.

A rustling from the trees caught her attention. Her hand drifted to her bow, and she loosely nocked an arrow. A few seconds later, the jiāngshī of a young man wearing a Houston Rockets cap appeared. He ambled up to the paved stone and made a few more steps before an arrow through the throat sent him flying back into the grass. Elena grimaced at the errant shot. She had missed his eye because she was trying to avoid hitting the cap.

Elena slid off the hood of the van and walked over to the jiāngshī, casually drawing her knife from her hip. The jiāngshī, an American by the looks of it, was still writhing on the ground, wiggling side-to-side like a turtle on its back. Elena had seen more foreigners at the park in three days than she had seen since the outbreak. In fact, probably half of the jiāngshī she had put down since she arrived had been Caucasian.

She sank the blade into the thing's eye, then picked up the dirty cap. It smelled like rot and stale water, but not anything she wasn't used to. A good cleaning should do the trick. This cap was probably the closest thing to home she was ever going to get. Since she had agreed to accompany Zhu to the Pillars, she had essentially accepted the fact that her chances of ever seeing home and her family again were zero.

Elena would never know what had happened to her family. She would never come home, never hug her mom, laugh with her dad, poke fun at her little brother. She would never get to tell them how much she loved them, never get to apologize for not being there when they needed her. As far as Elena was concerned, she did not deserve to have closure. This was her penance for her sins.

Elena scanned the brush for any more movement. Finding none, her eyes drifted to the canopies of trees growing outward from the sides of the pillars in the distance. This place sure was beautiful. She rinsed the cap in a nearby puddle to get any traces of jiāngshī off it, then hung it off her duffel to dry.

As she returned to the caravan, Shenyang walked out from the circle to take the next shift. The girl's face tightened when she noticed Elena, and a hand unwittingly rose to her scarred cheek. The gash on her face had healed, but other scars would stay with her for the rest of her life. Shenyang wasn't scared of Elena anymore. The girl had had plenty of time to wean herself of the terror during their long trip to the Precipitous Pillars. Now that fear had been replaced with pure hatred, and, like the jiāngshī infection, hatred was contagious.

Never underestimate the rage of a teenage girl, not that Elena blamed Shenyang after what she had done. The girl had told the entire village multiple times in gruesome detail about her torture. Everyone had already hated Elena; they despised her even more after. Not even the fact that she was the one who had rescued them and kept them alive during the journey. As far as the villagers were concerned, the white devil was the one who had singlehandedly put every villager in chains. Never mind that she had just been a peon following the orders of others . . .

Elena was the only one here for them to focus their rage on, so they did. She didn't blame them. Their anger wasn't misplaced. Their family and friends had died. She deserved every ounce of enmity thrown her way. Elena stayed humble and tried her best to fit in. She shot Shenyang a smile and waved. "Good morning."

"*Yángguǐzi*," the girl spat, turning her back to Elena.

That meant "foreign devil," which might as well be Elena's new name, since many of the villagers now called her that. If Zhu and Meili hadn't pleaded for them to allow Elena to join the moving village, they probably would have killed her. They may still have done it, but they all quickly realized that she was far and away their best fighter, forager, survivor—everything, really. They knew that the village would not have made it to the Precipitous Pillars without her. It didn't make them like her any more; it just forced them to tolerate her.

Elena brushed it off and was about to head inside the circle to find some breakfast when Shenyang whistled a warning. Both women raced to the edge of the northern clearing, bow and crossbow at the ready. Within a few seconds, a half dozen villagers appeared at the perimeter. Thirty more joined them ten seconds after that. Elena took a quick check of who was there, and who was supposed to be there. As the unofficial—but de facto—head of security, it was her job to keep the village's defenses sharp. They were still a far cry from the windrunners back at the Beacon, but they were getting there.

Something substantial was emerging from behind a small pillar. By the sounds of it, a large group. Whatever it was could be big enough to give the village trouble. Elena made a series of hand signals: no shot until her first, no chasing, no guns unless humans. The village had managed to scrounge up two pistols and three rifles during their journey, along with exactly 142 rounds among all the guns. Her brother had had more than that in his gun locker at home.

A few moments later, several figures appeared out in the open. Elena counted twenty. The moment she recognized a friendly face, she raised her bow so it pointed straight up. The rest of the village immediately lowered their weapons.

"It's Xupin," someone called out. "He's found Ahui!"

Elena had tried to instill some discipline during their journey. The village had chafed at first, but they came around to her rules quickly once they began encountering gusts of jiāngshī daily. Right now, however, all her training fell to the wayside. The villagers rushed their kin like students rushing the court at a basketball game.

A smile broke on her face at the revelry. There was much hugging and pats on the back and laughter. Lots of laughter. These were not only old friends reuniting: the village finding the group here meant they were one step closer to settling down and starting over. It meant their long journey was finally coming to an end. Elena was all right letting discipline slide for this. She made it her business to keep watch while the rest of the village celebrated. This wasn't her party, anyway.

It wasn't until the merriment subsided that a face caught her attention. Meili was embracing one particular woman for so long that they could have been mistaken for lovers. That wasn't what caught Elena's eye, however.

That woman could have been his twin. They had the same face; both were thin and lanky. Zhu's younger sister, interestingly, looked more assured and seasoned than Zhu ever had. Elena kept her distance, watching as the young woman worked her way through the crowd. She was popular; everyone wanted to talk to her. Elena could tell that when she spoke, people listened. People looked up to her. She might not yet, but Chen Ahui was going to run this village one day.

Eventually, Meili pulled Ahui away from her adoring fans and dragged her over. Elena couldn't help but feel nervous. Had they already poisoned her opinion of Elena? At least Meili was making the introduction. Elena counted Meili as her only friend at the village. She was the only one who voluntarily spoke with Elena and ate with her.

The women met between the bicycle wagon and the hollowed-out minivan. They had already heard much about each other, had already sized each other up. They were connected, in a way, through Zhu. Elena didn't know how much that meant to Ahui. Her love for the man did not justify her crimes to these people.

Elena wasn't surprised when Ahui took the initiative. No sooner were they within arm's length than Ahui reached out and embraced Elena. "Meili told me you were the most important person in Wen-zhu's life. That makes you one of the most important people in mine as well."

That came as a shock. Out of all the ways for Zhu's sister to greet her, warmth was the last thing Elena expected. A little sliver of her soul, a taut hanging thread, snapped. Elena wept as she held on to this stranger. She squeezed Ahui close and buried her head in the woman's shoulder. There were so many things she wanted to tell her, to explain, to apologize for. So many emotions she needed to let out. It was all Elena could do not to let it tumble out at that very moment. She had to remind herself to keep it in for just a while longer.

To her credit, Ahui was patient. She stood there and held Elena, letting her work through all of it. Finally, Elena managed to speak. "Do you want to see Zhu now?"

Ahui nodded. The two left the main group and made their way across the circle toward a horse trailer at the rear of the caravan. Elena turned the large bolt and slid it down. She glanced at Ahui hesitantly, then went inside.

It was dark here except for the thin beams of light slanting down from the windows near the ceiling. The trailer was cluttered with boxes of clothing, Buddhist shrines and other nonessentials like paper, pencils, and books. It held basically everything they did not need on their journey to survive, but would need to build a new society.

Something shifted in the darkness. Elena could make out a silhouette in the corner, leaning against the wall. A man, rail thin and stooped. He made a coughing sound and turned awkwardly. Ahui gently pushed Elena aside and stepped deeper into the trailer. "Wenzhu, is that you? It's Ahui."

Elena sucked in a deep breath as Zhu, head still leaning against the wall, lurched forward until the chains binding his neck stopped him. His mouth was covered with a leather mask and his hand was bound behind his back, but otherwise Wenzhu looked very much like he did before he had died.

"Oh, gē. You look terrible." Ahui turned to Elena. "How did it happen?"

"We were fleeing the Beacon of Light. A jiāngshī bit his ankle," Elena explained. "We immediately amputated his leg above his knee and cauterized the wound, hoping it would stave off the infection. At first we thought it had worked. We made it back to the village. The morning we set out to leave for the Precipitous Pillars, Zhu took ill again. We amputated the rest of his infected leg, but by then it was too late."

Ahui looked away, her eyes wet. "You should have just killed him."

Elena blinked back her own tears. "I wanted to, but Zhu made me promise. Before the life left his eyes, he asked for three things: to protect the village and help them reach you, to give him the chance to be buried by your side, and to make sure he sees you one last time. I didn't want you to see him like this"—she shook her head—"but I couldn't deny him his dying wish."

A long silence passed between them. It was finally broken by the sound of a blade hissing from its sheath. "I understand. I'd like to spend some time alone with my brother now. Consider your promise to Wenzhu fulfilled."

Elena nodded. She forced herself to look at Zhu one last time, mouthing a final "I love you" before turning away. She pushed that image out of her head and replaced it with the one of them having dinner that night she was supposed to return to the United States. Back when he was so innocent and vibrant, and they were in love.

GLOSSARY

bà: dad

dàgē: big brother

dì: little brother (abbreviated)

gē: big brother (abbreviated)

gǔzhēng: also known as a Chinese zither; a plucked string instrument with a history that stretches back more than 2,500 years

Hànzì: Chinese characters

húndàn: asshole, bastard

jiāngshī: literally, "hopping vampire"; an animated corpse from Chinese myth that feeds on the life force of the living, and the closest thing culturally to a walker in China

jiě: big sister (abbreviated)

Lān! Ná! Zhà!: Left block! Right block! Thrust!—fundamental spear technique

mā: mother

nǎinai: grandmother

pǔdāo: long-bladed weapon with a lengthy handle, sometimes called a horse-killer

shīfù: master

shūshu: uncle, mister (unrelated)

wǔxiá: Chinese martial arts genre

xiàngqí: also called Chinese chess; a strategy board game for two players.

xiànshēn: mister

xiǎodì: little brother

xiǎomèi: little sister

yángguǐzi: foreign devil

yéye: grandfather

ACKNOWLEDGMENTS

When I got the phone call from my editor at Skybound, Mike Braff, asking me if I was interested in writing a "Walking Dead book set in Asia. Anything you want," I initially thought I couldn't do it because I didn't have the bandwidth.

However, over the next few days, I began to think about all the possibilities with this project, and quickly zeroed in on China as an incredible setting. How would a country of one billion people with barely any firearms deal with a zombie infestation? How would their government and people survive in that very unique part of the world? My imagination ran wild. Eventually, I knew I couldn't say no: I had to do this book! I called up my agent and asked him to work with the editor to make it happen.

You're holding the result of those conversations in your hands right now.

Publishing is not unlike a zombie apocalypse: it's terribly slow and messy, filled with terror and angst, and often leads to dead ends. To survive in publishing, you need the right band of people to have your back. If you don't, you just wind up joining the herd. But if you do, you could end up with something special.

There are many people responsible for making *Typhoon* happen. So, here goes.

Thanks to Joe, Madison, LJ, and all the wonderful folks at Simon & Schuster. To all the folks at Skybound: To art director Andres and artist Jasper for creating this amazing cover. To Shauna for helping launch this book into the world. To Kate for helping make things happen. Big thanks to Sean, who gave us the freedom to stretch our minds but also waded into the trenches when necessary.

And a special thanks to Robert, who immediately saw the vision and allowed me to be part of his incredible world full of vivid, iconic characters.

To my editor, Mike: You're the guy who made this happen. From the first phone call when you told me to think big to the very last edits on the smallest changes, you were patient, you were methodical, and you deviled the details.

To my agent, Russ: It's been a long journey. I would have gotten lost a hundred times over and chewed up by some zombie along the way if it hadn't been for your guidance, gentle (and otherwise) correction, and constant support.

Finally, to all you readers: Thank you for picking up the book and experiencing this journey alongside me. We make a fine team.